On the run from beings that can't possibly exist...

Grace Harper has spent her life on the run, ever since her mother's unnatural death at the hands of creatures that shouldn't be real. It's hard to believe in vampires, but the things chasing her fit every legend she's ever heard. She dubs them "Pretty Boys," though their beautiful faces hide ugly appetites.

For twenty years, she and her father have stayed ahead of them, but for the last five years, their lives have been quiet. Grace has found a home, a life, and people she could even care about. She thinks the nightmare is finally over, but then a man shows up asking questions about a missing woman who's somehow connected to her and her mother. He might also have answers about her mother's death, if she's willing to take a risk.

Before she can decide, she's attacked by a Pretty Boy and barely escapes. If the Pretty Boys have found her, it's time to run. Reluctantly, she prepares to abandon her life, possible answers, and the only friend she's ever had.

Until they take her father.

Fleeing is no longer an option. To find him, she must face ancient secrets, creatures from legend, and an unbelievable truth that will shatter her world. But to *save* him, Grace has to do the hardest thing of all: stop running and start fighting.

Novels by J.T. Hardy

The Grace Harper Series
Blood Ties

Novels as Janice Hardy

The Healing Wars Trilogy
The Shifter
Blue Fire
Darkfall

BLOOD TIES

A Grace Harper Novel

J.T. Hardy

*For everyone who's ever asked
"What if?"*

Acknowledgments

This book was born on a long car trip, when my husband asked a "What if?" question that made me want to pull over and start writing. It's easy to say, "Without him, this book wouldn't have been possible," but it's true. He had the idea that sparked this series, and we worked together to develop the world, characters, and story. He earned his "T" in the byline.

I'm also eternally grateful to my critique partners and beta readers who read the various drafts of this tale. Some of you (such as Ann), read this back when I foolishly thought it would be a YA novel, and nearly every draft since.

Big hugs and thanks go out to Ann Meier, Bonnie Randall, Alex Hughes, Juliette Wade, Dario Ciriello, Cathy Hall, Claudia Pearson, Ginger Garrett, Carol Malcolm, and Ian Blew, for their sharp eyes and insightful feedback. I've said it before, and I'll say it again—you guys rock.

Thanks also go out to my agent, Kristin Nelson, and the gal who catches my typos, Dori. It's a great comfort knowing you two have my back.

And finally, thanks to my brother-in-law Charles, who keeps me motivating by asking "Where's the next one?" every time I see him.

CHAPTER ONE

The child was pure evil, no doubt about it. The bane of the entire prosthetics ward, so naturally they'd dumped her on me. Being the new gal anywhere had its share of drawbacks, and Andrews Medical Center was no different from any other hospital I'd worked at, hence the Saturday shift, and the problem-patient hazing. For five days I'd put up with Daisy's faux woe-is-me show, even though I'd stopped falling for that trembling lip and tear-soaked-eyes act on day two.

"I know it hurts, Daisy, but you can do it," I said, voice level. One did not cajole the Devil Child lightly.

"You don't know anything, Miss Legs."

Not her best rejoinder, but I admired her skill at avoiding repetition. I knelt beside her and placed a hand on her shoulder. "I know if you don't do your therapy you'll be stuck in that wheelchair." I tipped my head at the chair, crammed into the corner next to therapy stairs like it had pissed off its father. "Put your other leg on and let's get to work."

"I hate these things more than I hate you." She glared at the prosthetic she hadn't yet put on as if she could make it burst into flames by sheer will.

"So don't let them win."

Her glare shifted to the floor in front of her and I mentally crossed my fingers. One, two, if she made it to five—

"They're not alive! They can't win *anything*!" she screeched, swinging her leg at me. I braced for impact. "You're so stupid! Go away."

I granted her two hits, then caught the leg in both hands and jerked it away from her. I was all for catharsis, but those things were expensive.

"Daisy, put your leg on."

"No! I hate it."

The newer patients shot her sympathetic glances while the regulars rolled their eyes and shook their heads. Many a physical therapist had fallen to Daisy's mighty tantrums, and she'd gone through every assistant on the floor. I was a little surprised they hadn't saddled me with her sooner, to be honest. It would be quite the coup if I managed to get her walking again.

To do that, though, I'd have to stay. The travel aspect was a big part of being a traveling physical therapy assistant. Thirteen weeks, then it was off to a new town, new hospital, new set of faces, and all the security life on the move brought me. Even if it *did* seem safe here.

Besides, nice as Ft. Lauderdale was, it was half a country away from Dad and the call I'd been dreading for far too long.

Still. I liked it here. Enough that I was on my third temp rotation, and actually knew most of my coworkers' names. For the first time in my life I actually *had* a life.

And Mrs. Johnson had even asked me about staying on permanently. A permanent home, a permanent life, no more running—was that even possible?

Dad would say no. I wished I could say yes.

Sighing, I dropped the prosthesis in Daisy's lap and a hint of sweaty neglect wafted up from it. *Some*one wasn't keeping it clean, but that was an argument for another day. "Okay, if that's what you want."

"Seriously?" She peeked up at me through her protective shield of blond hair.

"It's your life. I'll get your chair and you can go." I turned my back and headed for the wheelchair. Yesterday, tissue-paper flowers had been taped to the handles, but only a few bits of torn paper remained. They shone bright against the hospital-beige walls and the poster for the weekly amputee support group.

She let me reach the chair this time. That was new. She'd never struck me as a quitter, despite the tantrums and the attitude. I flipped the chair around and wheeled it back, locking it down in front of her. "All yours."

Summoning the melodrama only a twelve-year-old could muster, she dropped her leg to the floor, ripped off the second one in record time, and flung herself into the chair. "I hate you."

Maybe she meant me, maybe the chair; with Daisy it was hard to tell. "Take care of yourself, kid." I ruffled her hair for good measure.

"Stupid physical therapy," she muttered, rolling away. She slapped the wheels with every push. Determination, thy name was Daisy. If only she'd channel that into learning to walk again.

One of the other PTAs, Libby Torres, caught my attention from across the room and raised an eyebrow at me. I could almost hear the supportive, "*You good?*" that had started plenty of conversations my first week here. Her friendly tenacity had led to a bunch of dinners and a lot of laughter—and shockingly enough—an actual, honest-to-goodness friendship.

It had been years since anyone had been that nice to me at work. I wasn't sure *anyone* had ever put effort into being my friend. I'd never lived anywhere long enough to *make* friends.

I smiled and waved her off, a silent thanks for the backup. *It's fine*, my casual head toss said, but Daisy had never gone this far before. I'd only been working with her a short time, but I knew the type.

Hell, I'd *been* the type.

Come on, Devil Child, turn around. The "pity me" routine was a load of crap and we both knew it.

On our first session, she'd dug her fingers into her chair arms every time her mom fussed over her as if she were a delicate little flower no stronger than the ones taped to her chair—Mom's idea of course. The third time her dad had "atta girled" her she'd flipped him off when his back was turned. She'd made gagging motions through their entire "she's such a brave, brave girl" speech.

I didn't know about brave, but she was pissed, and it wasn't over losing her legs. First person to figure out why might be able to help her.

She rolled on, still no signs of stopping.

I couldn't have read her wrong. She was a fighter for sure. She needed an enemy to fight, and it couldn't be her legs. She'd never accept them if they took the brunt of all that anger.

Five feet from the elevators she stopped. Her head cocked to the right the tiniest bit, and I caught a flick of her eye checking up on me. *Atta girl.* I walked into her field of view and picked up her legs, then turned toward the trash bin on the far wall next to the nurse's station.

A cute guy in a cheap suit glanced our way while Nurse Williams eyed me over her bright pink glasses with all the disapproval of a foreman behind schedule. Please. As if I'd throw away perfectly good prosthetics.

The frown reminded me of Dad, though, and the worry I'd been fighting all year chipped at my tough-love facade. *Not here, not now. Focus on Daisy's pain, not yours.*

I reached the trash bin, pushed open the lid, and wrinkled my nose. Someone had had fish tacos again for lunch. I made a show of trying to find the right angle to shove the legs in. *Come on, cry uncle, kiddo.*

"Ms. Harper, wait," Daisy said softly.

Yes! I heaved a sigh as dramatic as hers and turned around. "Need something?"

Daisy scowled at me, her shoulders stiff, pouting like a pro and clearly wanting to tell me to go to Hell. But I *had* her. I'd passed whatever test her parents kept failing. She rolled over to me and held out her hands. "Fine, I'll do the stupid exercises."

"Suit yourself. You paid for the full hour." I wiggled one of her legs. "You ordered the extra crispy two piece, right?"

I damn near got a smile.

"Just give 'em to me," she muttered. She shoved herself past the guy in the cheap suit and nearly ran over his toes. He didn't even glance at her, just kept his gaze on me.

"Grace Harper," he said. Short, clipped, not a question.

I froze for a second longer than I should have. Daisy had already identified me, so it wasn't as if I could say no. "Yes?"

"May I ask you a few questions?"

I gestured at Daisy, glowering at us from a minimal safe distance. If this guy screwed this up… "Sorry, I'm with a patient right now."

"It'll only take a minute." He reached into his jacket and pulled out a yellowed piece of paper. Nurse Williams shot me a look that said, "Keep it short." I planned on it.

"And you are?" No badge, but he acted like a cop. Hopeful, yet wary blue eyes hinted that he'd seen things he wished he hadn't. His black hair had a distracted scruffiness to it—neat on the back and sides, a tad long on the top. Almost a professor vibe, though he couldn't be older than thirty.

"Nate Cavanaugh. Are any of these names familiar to you?"

"I don't have time for—"

"Please, Ms. Harper, a woman's life is at stake." He held the paper closer.

I took it. Not paper, something thicker and glossier, even though it was yellowed and old. It reminded me of the scrolls I saw at a museum Dad took me to once. Eight names were listed in delicate script, four names crossed off. The ink looked just as old, faded and dark red.

Except for the name on the bottom. That looked brand new in bright blue ink.

"Why is my name on this list?" I asked, chest tight.

"That's what I'd like to know."

The first two names on the list were so faded it was tough to read them—the top name was crossed off, but the second one wasn't. I squinted closer. Rebekah Antonelli and Hannah Antonelli.

All the air vanished from the room.

"Ms. Harper?" Cavanaugh said. "Do you recognize another name?"

"Where did you get this?"

"It was found in the apartment of a woman who disappeared two days ago." He pointed to a crossed-off name third up from the bottom—Anita Rosenberg. Her ink also looked fresh. "Does that name sound familiar to you?"

"Are all these people missing?"

"Have you given blood recently?"

"Have I what?"

"Bloodmobile, office blood drive, that sort of thing?"

"What does that have to do with this list?"

He frowned, his brow furrowed. "Did you have *any* blood drawn recently? For a procedure perhaps? Routine physical?"

An awfully personal question for a total stranger. "Are you sure it's me? Grace Harper's a common—"

Daisy's exasperated sigh cut through the room, louder than the grunts of the patients and the clank of the machines. "C'mon Grace-face. You're eating up my minutes here."

I jumped, shaking off the urge to get the hell out of there. Running only drew attention. "Be right there," I called to her, then handed him back the paper. "Sorry Mr. Cavanaugh, I need to get back to my patient. I'm afraid I can't help you, but I hope you find Ms. Rosenberg safe and sound."

His shoulders slumped a little, and he offered me his card. "I understand. If you think of anything that could help find her, please give me a call. Her family is devastated."

"Of course."

I tucked the card into the pocket of my scrubs, mentally repeating the names until Cavanaugh was gone and it was safe to write them down.

"Sorry about that," I said, walking beside Daisy's chair. I didn't turn around, didn't give any indication that all I wanted to do was grab my phone and call Dad.

Cavanaugh left, but there were four people I didn't recognize still on the floor. Any one of them could be his backup, waiting and watching to see what I'd do after he'd gone. I couldn't afford to be anything but normal until I was sure I was alone.

"What are you looking at, butt-head?" Daisy snapped at Libby's patient as we passed her and a muscled guy about twenty with high-and-tight hair and a *Semper Fi* tattoo. He did not seem amused. Neither did Libby, but I spotted concern for me under her irritation.

I cleared my throat.

Daisy stopped rolling. "Sorry," she tossed back. "Legs made me do it." Then she was off again, headed for the parallel bars.

Libby gasped and put a hand on her chest, her dark eyes wide. "She *apologized*? Where did you learn to do exorcisms?"

"My dad. Old family tradition." The familiar pang tightened my chest, worsened by Cavanaugh's visit. Dad *had* to be safe—the schedule he'd e-mailed me said he'd have chemo all morning, surrounded by nurses and doctors. No one was heartless enough to go after a man in the cancer ward—not even out there in Vegas.

Libby grinned, but still looked worried. We'd gotten close enough over the last few months that she'd probably figured out all was not well in Graceland. "That's it, you have to stay now. You've made progress with the Devil Child."

If only I could. Grace Harper's life was a lot better than any of the half dozen others I'd had before this.

I smiled back. "We'll see."

She glanced at her patient, then leaned in closer to me, her black braid sliding forward over her shoulder. "You good?"

Until today, everything had been great, which was the problem. I nodded, but couldn't fake the smile to back it up. "Yeah, it's nothing."

"If that changes, you can call me next week if you need to."

Libby was on vacation as of 4 p.m. today. I hadn't even asked her where she was going, and she hadn't wanted to talk about it, so I hadn't pushed. It was one of Dad's many rules—don't get involved. I suddenly wanted to know her plans. I wanted to make plans, do the best friend stuff we'd joked about, but hadn't quite gotten to yet. "I'll call if I need you," I said instead.

I trotted after Daisy, hope and dread fighting for control of my heart. Cavanaugh's list of names might finally give me answers, and those answers could give me my life back.

Maybe even let me keep the one I'd grown *really* fond of.

AFTER DAISY HAD finished her therapy and I was sure Cavanaugh had truly gone, I slipped outside and headed for a picnic area that was always deserted this time of day. By the time I arrived, sweat dampened the hair along my neck, despite it being February. Florida had its sunshine and beaches, but it was like living in a sauna with giant flying cockroaches and lizards the size of toddlers. The flowers smelled nice, though. Sweet and citrusy.

Weird as it was, I'd miss it if I left. Not a lot of places had it rain in the front yard and not in the back. The state had character.

I sat on a nearly concrete bench and pulled out my phone. The list of Cavanaugh's names I'd jotted down earlier was still on the notes screen, but I swiped over to the phone and tapped Dad's name. I'd research the names as soon as I knew he was okay.

The phone rang a few times before Dad's voice broke in. "Stella's House of Massage, we never rub you the wrong way."

His bad joke code phrase told me everything was fine, though he'd obviously gotten a new nurse. I relaxed against the picnic table. "Stella? What happened to Tracy?"

"They moved her to cardiology." He paused, and I caught the distinct tone of scolding nurse in the background. I grinned. I guess Stella didn't appreciate Dad's sense of humor. "I miss Tracy," he mock whispered into the phone.

"You miss the sponge baths."

"And the drugs."

I laughed, my heart lighter at how good he sounded, even if it wouldn't last long. "She's glad to be done with you."

"Stella has a better use for my bed is all. Has her eye on a cute dentist with stage two non-Hodgkin lymphoma."

More grumbling in the background. I smiled. "Be nice to people with access to defibrillators."

"Oh, all right. How's it going, Butternut?"

Question of the day. I hesitated, sliding my Star of David charm along the necklace Dad had given me when I was ten. "A man came to see me today, asking questions about a missing woman. He showed me a list of names." I rattled them off.

Pained silence. "Haven't heard some of those in a while."

"Why is her name there? Why is *my* name there? Who are those other people?"

"Cops asking?"

"No ID, but he acted like one."

Dad paused. A siren wailed and faded as an ambulance pulled into emergency. Finally, he spoke again. "Pretty Boy?"

"Didn't feel that way. He gave up too easily." Plus, I was still alive.

"You sure? Was it the same one we saw the other day outside that ice cream store you like so much?"

I bit my lip and squeezed my eyes shut. "That was in Birmingham, Dad."

"Oh yeah, yeah. You're in Florida now," he said, voice rock steady, even if his mind mixed up dates and places at an increasing rate. I imagined the father from my childhood—his smile, his bright eyes, the dark curly hair the chemo had stolen from him.

A year ago, his oncologist had told him, "You have six months tops. Get your affairs in order." Some docs called him a medical miracle for lasting so long, but dying was still dying, even if you did it in slow motion. He'd had three close calls, and every one had torn out my heart.

There were only so many times I could say goodbye.

"Has anyone come to see you, Dad?"

"How's school going?"

"I graduated three years ago, remember?"

Silence for a few heartbeats, then the muttered litany of details and places we'd lived.

"Dad, look around. Do you know where you are?"

"Hospital."

"Do you remember why?"

He was quiet again, but then he groaned like he did when he rubbed his eyes in frustration. I'd been hearing that groan a lot the last few months. "'Cause there's a tumor named Glioblastoma Multiforme trying to kill me."

"Right. It also lies, Dad. Focus, *think*. Has anyone come to see you recently?"

"Just the nurses."

"Do you know why someone would have a list with Mom's name on it?"

"I don't know. He never told me why they came after her."

After *us*. My name was on that list, too. Twice. Plus all those other people I'd never heard of. But not his. Did that mean he was safe?

"Dad, is there someplace you can stay besides your apartment or the hospital for a few days? You have enough cash for a motel?"

"Always do."

I'd stopped asking him to come live with me months ago. He always said no and swore we were safer apart, but the urge to start that argument again was strong. If he had one more bad memory lapse, I'd drag him here whether he liked it or not.

"Time to go, Grace."

I'd heard those words all my life, right before we'd pack everything we owned into the car and vanish. It wasn't real this time, only his faulty memory, but the familiar fear crackled through me same as it had six months ago when I'd fled Santa Fe for Ft. Lauderdale. Except then, he hadn't even *remembered* he'd told me to run.

Stay or go? I knew which one Dad would insist on.

I sighed and gave him the expected coded response. "Gotta run, Dad, talk to you soon." *Love you, Dad.*

"Stay safe, my radish. We'll chat soon."

Heart pounding, I stared at my phone. It had been five years since we'd had a legitimate Pretty Boy sighting. I'd started to think maybe it *was* over, that we were finally safe, until Cavanaugh showed up with that damn list.

But was he a threat? He didn't fit anything Dad had trained me to watch for. Cavanaugh knew *something*, but it couldn't have been about me specifically or he'd have known who I was. Maybe I was part of something else? *That* opened up a whole list of new and unsettling questions. I'd always thought the Pretty Boys were only after our family, but that list suggested otherwise.

Was it a clue about what happened to Mom, and why we'd been running ever since? If Cavanaugh *wasn't* a threat, he might be an opportunity for answers. Though he could be both.

I pulled up the list and a browser and typed in the third name from the top—I already knew what had happened to the Antonellis.

Number three—name crossed off. The woman was fifteen years dead, with a straightforward and detail-free obituary.

Number four followed the trend with a line through it and a twelve-year-old obituary, plus a news article. Girl's body found. Exsanguination. Police baffled.

I huffed. Join the club. But it was another indication that *this* was connected to Mom.

Number five—also crossed off. No search results, but my money said she was dead as well.

Number six was a college student who'd been in an accident six months ago and was still in a coma.

Number seven was Anita Rosenberg, also missing.

And then me.

No, that didn't bode well for my future at all.

I rubbed my temples. Running sucked, and Dad couldn't do it anymore. Another few weeks and he'd need supervision, maybe even constant care. Living with me near Andrews Medical was better for him than living alone in Boulder City, Nevada. We'd have backup here.

Unless the Pretty Boys *had* found us.

I pulled out Cavanaugh's card. Threat or opportunity? Unsure, but worth the risk. I typed in the number. I needed answers before I threw my life away again.

"Yes?"

"Hi, it's Grace Harper. I think I might have remembered a name on that list. Someone I might have gone to school with as a kid."

"Which name?"

"Can we meet around, say five, at Frisco's? Sports bar down the street from the hospital."

No answer right away, then a sigh so soft I barely caught it. "Sure, I'll meet you there. Five at Frisco's."

"See you then."

I tucked the card away. If he gave me any hints he wasn't alone, he wouldn't see me at all.

CHAPTER TWO

Frisco's smelled of cheap beer and suntan oil, but the tables were clean and the bartenders the right level of sexy. I headed for a small corner booth under the head of a stuffed moose with rhinestone sunglasses and a nose ring, right across from a giant mirror that showed most of the bar and its inhabitants.

I checked the mirror first. The patrons' reflections all looked solid and normal—no hazy ghost images—then I settled in facing the door and scanned the room. The place had a slew of weekend regulars, with plenty of groups talking and hanging out, a few singles, a handful of pairs. Local bar, local clientele. No one skulking in the shadows or staring too long from behind a menu.

I set the alarm on my phone for twenty minutes anyway.

I made note of the exits while I twisted up my hair and clipped it. If the heat was this brutal in winter, summer would be apocalyptic.

An uncomfortable shiver ran along my skin and the hair on my arms stood straight. Someone was watching me. Inside I tensed, but outside I forced calm, faked unaware. I fiddled with my hair again and re-scanned the room for whatever I'd missed.

There.

Guy by the bar, major eye candy with the perfect chest for a T-shirt, though his dusky looks were a little too male model for comfort. He ignored everyone around him—including the brunette practically stripping in front of him, vying for his attention.

I wasn't the Cuban beauty Libby was, but I held my own. It wasn't inconceivable that a hot guy would be scope locked on me. In my experience, though, anything that sexy meant trouble—one way or another.

Like Dad always said, ignore coincidences at your own peril.

I moved the drink ads and condiments around, angling for a view of the mirror with him reflected in it. *Please be normal.* I found the brunette, shifted my gaze right and—

He moved, zipping out the door like he'd spotted someone breaking into his car. The brunette tried to stop him, but the eye candy was *fast.* Maybe *too* fast.

Don't be paranoid. What if Cavanaugh knows what happened to Mom?

The eye candy could be nothing, or Cavanaugh could have set me up for the Pretty Boys. Maybe they realized they'd been made and were switching to Plan B. Or this was me being ridiculous and the eye candy was some gay guy who forgot to put money in the meter and had no interest in a flirty brunette.

It was more likely a lifetime of Dad's safety tips had made me as paranoid as a junkie.

Cavanaugh wouldn't have tipped his hand and questioned me if he'd planned to set me up. Pretty Boys didn't work that way. They'd have jumped me as I left the hospital.

Okay, so reconnaissance first, then plan accordingly.

I left the booth and headed for the brunette and her friends by the bar. She shot me a double take as I walked up.

"Hi," I said, smiling. "This is going to sound strange, but that guy you were talking to, did he say where he was going?"

"Why do you want to know?"

I held up both hands. "I'm not poaching, I swear. He was a real jerk to a friend of mine and I want to make sure he's not coming back anytime soon before she gets here."

She glanced at her friends and frowned. They shrugged. Finally, the brunette crossed her arms, only a little less wary. "Said he was late meeting a friend."

Believable. Also plausible if he wanted to get away from her. "Thanks." I turned, but she grabbed my arm.

"Hey wait. What did he do to your friend?"

"Charmed the pants off her, never called."

The brunette nodded slowly with a knowing frown. "One of those."

"Proceed with caution if that's not what you're after." I grinned. "If it is, then have fun."

They laughed and asked me to offer condolences, then turned their attentions to the rest of the guys in the bar. If the eye candy was on the level, he might find a few cold shoulders for a week or two, but no lasting damage to his reputation.

The door opened and I tensed, but it was only two women dressed in adorable flouncy sundresses. The dresses didn't match exactly, but they'd clearly shopped together.

Shopping with a bunch of girlfriends sounded nice. Libby had talked about a pair of boots she'd seen just yesterday, and I'd held back suggesting we hit the store at lunch. I should have asked her; that's what friends did. It's also what following Dad's rules earned me—a life of solitude.

And safety?

I was still alive, so, yes. That, too.

I glanced at my watch. Cavanaugh was officially ten minutes late. Possible answers weren't worth the risk anymore.

The eye candy hadn't come back inside either, and for all I knew he was lurking outside, waiting for me. This could be nothing—probably *was* nothing—but I didn't like the way he'd been watching me.

A group of tourists seated at a hightop table stood and started their goodbyes. I slipped in behind them, searching my bag for my keys and a little protection.

The door opened ahead of us.

"Ah, Ms. Harper," Cavanaugh said, dodging the tourists. "I'm sorry, I had the worst luck finding a parking space. Quite the crowd." He smiled, seeming as non-threatening as the brunette, but looks were deceiving.

"Shall we grab a seat?" He gestured toward the table the trio had vacated.

Bolting would tip him off if he *was* working with the eye candy who *might* be a Pretty Boy. I glanced at the mirror behind him. His image reflected the A-OK that he was human.

"Sure. Thanks for meeting me."

We sat, awkward as two people on a blind date neither wanted to be on.

"So," he began, "you were saying you remembered one of those names?"

For a moment the words froze on my tongue, but I forced them out. "Rebekah and Hannah Antonelli sounded familiar. Are they sisters?"

"Mother and daughter."

I barely remembered her, but it still hurt to hear us described that way. I cleared my throat. "I'm sorry, what precinct did you say you were from? Maybe that'll help jog my memory."

"I work out of Pensacola."

Where Mom was buried. "It's possible I went to school with the daughter. Are they missing, too?"

"The daughter is, but it's a very old, very cold case. Do you remember any classmates disappearing?"

I mimicked careful consideration. "Been a long time. I remember someone dying. A traffic accident? That sound familiar to you?"

"It tracks with what I know."

I shook my head. "That was ages ago. You think it's the same person who took your missing woman? Like a serial killer?"

"I'm still trying to put the pieces together, and most of them don't fit. How long did you live in Pensacola?"

"Couple of years. Am I in any danger?"

He paused and glanced away for an instant. "If you *are* the Grace Harper on the list, I'm afraid you might be."

Damn. Dumb me just confirmed I *was* the right Grace.

"Do you have any leads on who's behind this?" I asked, playing into his whole "I'm a cop" expectation.

Another shift of his gaze. Cavanaugh could use a few lessons on lying. "I'm still exploring how the list is connected to Ms. Rosenberg. I'd hoped you could shed some light on that."

I doubted that "we're all being hunted by the same monster" was the kind of help he wanted. "I don't know why I'm on that list."

And clearly, neither did he. I was risking my life for nothing. This was a fishing expedition, nothing more, and he was here because his only clue was my name. He still had a cop feel, even without flashing a badge, so this could be a case he was working off the books. Maybe it was personal. Maybe this woman had been a lover, or a close family friend and he was going behind his captain's back to find her. He might not even be an actual detective, but some lab tech playing cop.

You should stop watching so many police dramas on TV.

"Have you noticed anything strange recently?" he said. "Unfamiliar people, unusual questions, anything feel...off?"

I flashed him a sheepish grin. "Aside from you?"

He smiled back. A nice smile, trustworthy, though he might be anything but. "Aside from me."

"No, not really. A few weird street people, but that's normal around here." My alarm chimed from my pocket. *Finally.* I jumped and pulled it out, pretending to read a text, and frowned. "I'm so sorry, but I have to go."

Cavanaugh gaped at me a moment, disappointment in his eyes, but he recovered. "It's nothing serious, is it?"

"Are you in town long? I'll let you know if I think of anything else."

"I'm here all weekend."

Acting preoccupied with my phone, I nodded absently and hurried out the door.

The sun had set and traffic crept along the street, but only half the cars had their lights on in the shadowy twilight. A muggy breeze swept away some of the bar stench and lifted my hair off my neck. People walked past in both directions, a normal street on a normal Saturday.

No signs of an ambush, but then, there never were.

Except it was a *terrible* spot for an ambush. Too many people and no good cover.

My car felt a million miles away, backed into a space in the small parking lot next to the bar, directly under a hazy orange street lamp. I reached into my bag and put on the silver-plated brass knuckles Dad had given me for my bat mitzvah. The engraving on the knuckledusters winked at me—*May the three enfold you, hold you safe, and keep you strong.*

I checked the area again. Clear.

Gravel crunched under my feet as I made my way toward my car, keys in one hand, thick bands of silver-coated steel wrapped around the knuckles of my other. A second breeze brushed me, this time unnaturally cold and scented with ozone and woodfire smoke. Gooseflesh peppered my skin.

I slowed my steps. Cool breezes and ozone often preceded thunderstorms, but the sky was clear, no sign of lightning at all. Ten feet from the car, I hit the unlock button and peeked into the back seat. No one there.

The traffic sounds cut out. No horns, no rush of passing vehicles, no boom of radios spewing too much bass.

I checked the street over the roof of my Honda. No one moved. People stood on the sidewalk like mannequins, and even the cars sat motionless.

Shit, shit, shit.

I lunged for the door handle.

"My, aren't you a curious thing, walking when you should be still," a man said, and arms solid as cables grabbed me from behind. The smell of old things burning stung my nose; the ancient stench like a shield around him. I swallowed my panic. The eye candy from the bar had been a Pretty Boy. I leaned into his chest, placed both feet against my car door, and shoved with all my strength.

He staggered and cried out, knocked off balance. His hold on me loosened, and I wriggled my arms free. We fell to the gravel, him on his back and me flailing on his chest. I elbowed him hard in the ribs with both elbows. And gasped.

Damn, that hurt!

Arms stinging, I rolled off the Pretty Boy and onto my knees, my fists up, moving at the speed the world *ought* to be moving at. But it was still… *still.*

Familiar model-quality good looks stared up from the ground. He was indeed the eye candy from the bar. Okay, good. Odds are it was just the one Pretty Boy, then.

He moved within a blink, on his feet in a blur.

I jabbed with the knuckledusters—hard.

Metal met groin and the Pretty Boy gasped. He stepped away, but didn't go down in a pile of screaming sleazeball like a human guy would have. *Balls of steel or no balls at all?*

I jumped to my feet and threw an uppercut at his chiseled jaw—a solid impact we *both* felt this time. Jarring pain shot up my arm and rattled my teeth. The Pretty Boy's head snapped around and yellow-green spittle flew from his lips in sparkling chartreuse drops.

City noise flooded my ears, breaking the eerie silence.

Gotcha.

Not for long, though.

He glared at me, something dark and predatory in his wide eyes, but a bit of shock, too. I'd bet not many of his victims got a shot in. He shook it off and smiled.

"I *hate* when he's right," he said an instant before he blurred toward me. A breath later he seized me by the upper arm and hauled me toward an alley at the edge of the parking lot. I struggled, but we marched deeper into the shadows cast by the surrounding buildings.

They were stronger in the shadows.

I punched, writhed, flailed at him, but he still wouldn't let go.

"Be still, you," he said, as if I were a wriggling puppy.

My wriggling earned me a bit of leeway as my sleeve tore and his grip slid down to my forearm. I couldn't hit him with my knuckledusters from this angle, but if I hung back a little...

He kept moving forward, dragging me along. The seam of my sleeve cut into my skin under his grip, but his back was to me now. An opportunity at last. We were less than ten feet to the alley and the death I'd had nightmares about all my life...

This didn't make sense. Why hadn't he *already* killed me?

I slipped the dusters off the arm he had a hold of and onto my free hand. I wasn't much of a lefty, but it would have to do.

At the edge of the shadows I pressed the silver dusters deep into the crook of his elbow. Flesh sizzled and blue and white sparks danced like the Fourth of July. He shrieked and yanked away.

I staggered and fell into the gravel. He snarled, a sound as unnatural as his speed. A second voice shouted from the alley in a language I didn't recognize. Deep, angry, yet beautiful at the same time, like a piano melody under a thrash metal guitar riff.

The Pretty Boy glared at the alley and growled. A second man stepped out of the shadows, equally hot, equally dangerous. Bad. Very bad. This was not the Pretty Boy behavior I'd known all my life.

Grace, time to go.

Time froze again as I scrambled to my feet and raced for my car, my shaking legs hobbling me.

The Pretty Boys crashed together like sumo wrestlers and a crack echoed in the still air. One of the Pretty Boys grunted, the other roared, and they both hit the ground and rolled my way. I dived out of their path and fell hard onto chunks of gravel and rock. Pain shot through my thigh and down my calf. I officially hated gravel.

Another smack, another grunt as they wrestled, and a curved knife skittered across the stones and halted by my foot. It had a bone handle, wrapped in leather, its blade black as a beetle shell.

I snatched it from the gravel and scooted away. The tussling Pretty Boys blocked my escape to the car, intent on pummeling each other into goo. I scrambled to my feet and circled around toward the passenger side.

The Pretty Boy from the bar snarled and threw a swift punch to the other one's gut. He clutched his stomach and staggered to one knee, an easy target. The Pretty Boy kicked him in the head and knocked him to the pavement. Then he turned to me.

"Stay the hell away from me!" I thrust the knife forward as he shot toward me. Little good it would do.

The blade sank into his chest up to the hilt. Chartreuse light burst from the wound, not viscous like blood or even the green liqueur it resembled—just light. The Pretty Boy gaped at the widening hole.

"How?" he said, more wonder than fear in his voice.

More light burst from his chest and he shattered to pieces.

That was new.

Chapter Three

Green fire whirled around me and knocked me flat. My ears rang, my skin stung, and something was wrong.

Screaming.

People were screaming.

Run—run—run—

I pushed myself up and squinted past a too-thin haze of gritty smoke that didn't smell like smoke, but also didn't stink like the Pretty Boys always did. This scene was spicy, woodsy even. The edges of the nearby cars glowed with a chartreuse luminescence, like—

Images of Mom flashed across my mind. Darkness, the car swerving, crumpling. Chartreuse-green fire. A handsome man with kind eyes leaning over me.

"What did you *do*?" he asked, voice muffled.

Wait...the man was *here*, it wasn't my nightmare, wasn't my memory. Past and present slammed into focus, and I was no longer five, no longer crying on the side of a dark road. A dusky man had kneeled in front of me then, too, with chartreuse dust smudged across his face and clothes.

My mind buzzed louder than the throbbing in my ears. I shook my head hard, and the fuzz finally cleared. My memories fell back into place, sorting themselves, filing the past and returning to the here and now. A man *was* kneeling in front of me, his hair dark and shining, his skin brown and dusty. He smelled like exotic food simmering over a campfire.

A Pretty Boy. Right here, right now.

"Stay back!" I ordered, brandishing the surprisingly effective knife. Chartreuse goo coated the black blade. Pretty Boy blood? I hadn't even known they *could* bleed.

He held up his hands, his dark eyes a mix of fear and wonder. His shirt was torn, and a hint of yellow coated the ragged edges. More blood? How many colors did these guys bleed in?

"I won't hurt you," he said softly. Anyone else would have believed him. A whisper in the back of my brain told me I was nuts for even suspecting him, but that's how Pretty Boys worked. Lured you close with their charm and then ripped out your throat.

"Stay *back*!" I staggered to my feet and the world tipped sideways. He caught my knife hand gently, his fingers cool on my skin.

"I would, but you—" His words died as his eyes widened, staring over my shoulder. Awe. Longing. Gold dusted the edges of his brown irises.

What the?

I craned my head around. No one was behind me but shocked pedestrians and indifferent traffic. The parking lot tilted sideways again and—

—*Soaring. I'm drifting on air currents shimmering silver and bronze, watching an emerald field below. A woman walks, her hair long and dark, her skin the color of strong tea. She glances up, smiles, waves—*

I gasped and yanked my arm out of his hand. The dream-like vision vanished. What the *hell*?

"Impossible," he whispered, his gaze glued to the car window behind me.

I looked behind me. Nothing in the glass but the ghostly half-reflection of a Pretty Boy—pale and insubstantial, proof they didn't fully belong in our world.

"What *was* that?" I asked. "What did you put in my head?"

"Ms. Harper!" Cavanaugh's voice rose above the din and he pushed his way through a growing crowd of onlookers.

The Pretty Boy who'd helped me jerked his gaze toward Cavanaugh and frowned. "You're not safe here. Leave before he sends another. I'll find you later."

"You'll what? He who?" Yet the warning and the voice were familiar, another déjà vu memory from that night on the road. "Who are—"

My helpful hottie blurred to a sprint and was gone.

"Wait! Oh come on!" I took a deep breath and centered myself. My hands hung empty and shaking at my side—damn it! He'd taken the knife.

Cavanaugh caught up to me, genuine concern on his face. "Ms. Harper, are you all right?"

Stupid question. No, I was not all right. I'd been attacked by a Pretty Boy. I ought to be dead. "Did anyone call 911?"

"Half the block I'm sure. What happened? Was that an explosion? Is there fire?"

The *only* other time a Pretty Boy had helped me had been the night Mom had died. There'd been that weird green light then, too, but it hadn't been like this. There'd been more mist than fire, and nothing so explosive.

That Pretty Boy had also smelled like woodfire smoke.

Get real, Grace-face, that was twenty years ago. It couldn't be the same one.

"Ms. Harper?"

I pushed my hands through my hair, pulling myself together before I said anything stupid. "Must have been a gas leak." Did they even use gas in Florida? Maybe that was a northern thing.

He gently took my chin and turned my face toward him. "You're bleeding. Did you hit your head?"

I jerked away. "I'm fine."

"You're not fine. You need a doctor."

"I'm...a little dazed is all. Ears are still ringing." And bruises aching, but a hot bath and some aspirin would help that. My helpful hottie had vanished, but my skin crawled as if more Pretty Boys were watching, a distinctive itch, like ants across my skin, and the burning smell still lingered in the air.

Sirens wailed in the distance, getting louder. I swiped a hand across my temple—a little blood, but not too terrible. I wiped off what I could and rearranged my hair to hide the rest.

"I gotta go."

Cavanaugh gaped at me as if I'd grown another head. "You might have a concussion."

"I'm fine." I had to get out of there before whatever emergency vehicles were on the way blocked me in. "Where's my bag?" My knuckledusters had fallen off somewhere, and they weren't exactly legal in the Sunshine State.

"Ms. Harper, please sit down. You're acting irrationally."

I caught a flash of silver buried in the gravel. Yes! I scooped it up and grabbed my backpack a few feet away.

"I'm just a little shaken." Memory lapse or not, Dad was right—it was time to go.

Cavanaugh frowned, but his eyes were soft. "You seem more scared than shaken. Let me help you."

I opened my car door, avoiding the chartreuse grit best I could. "Thanks for the brotherly concern, but I don't need anyone's help."

He was still gaping at me as I sped out of the parking lot.

A FEW BLOCKS away, I pulled into a gas station and called Dad, tensing tighter and tighter as it rang and rang. "Answer, dammit."

Dad always answered.

I hung up and dialed another number. It clicked immediately to voice mail.

"*I'm being followed, my squashling,*" Dad's message began. "*At least two. I'm headed for the safe house. You know the drill. I'll contact you on the alternate line. Stay safe.*"

My shoulders dropped. He was okay. I had no clue how they'd found us, but clearly this was a synchronized attack if they came for both of us at once. Maybe they hadn't wanted to kill him until they knew they had me—

I stiffened.

A Pretty Boy had tried to *kidnap* me, not kill me. He could have snapped my neck instead of grabbing me, ripped out my throat like—I closed my eyes. *Focus on the present. Not the past.*

The Pretty Boys wanted us dead. That's what Dad always told me. If they caught us they'd kill us.

We don't kill *them.* It wasn't possible.

Guess again, Grace-face.

I rubbed my arm, sore where the Pretty Boy from the bar had gripped me. He'd had time to kill me before, during, *and* after our scuffle, even before the other one had appeared. Yet he hadn't.

Something had changed.

Was it connected to Cavanaugh or his list of names? That couldn't be a coincidence. Years without a sighting, then two in one day? And I was still breathing?

Apparently, they had a new plan. Well, screw that. Whatever it was, I wasn't about to make it easy for them. Time for me and my go-bag to—

I stopped. "Crap."

Fingers uselessly crossed, I jumped out of the car and opened the trunk. A dank odor wafted out—the mildew from a leak I hadn't known

I'd had until I took the job in rainy Florida. Instead of a duffel bag filled with supplies, a damp, empty spot where my go-bag usually sat stared back at me. It stank—on multiple levels.

The package of weather stripping was on the table in my apartment. I'd planned to fix the leak this weekend.

So stupid. I slammed the trunk shut and dropped into the car. My go-bag was in the hall closet by the door of my apartment, utterly useless for a gal on the run, but I couldn't leave without it.

I put the knuckledusters back on my hand and gave myself even odds the Pretty Boys knew where I lived.

I sat outside my apartment building, casing my own joint for fifteen minutes—watching the windows and doors, the easy-to-see-the-entrance spots where I'd lurk if I were waiting for someone who lived here to come home. So far no one had shown up, but that didn't mean they hadn't gotten here before I had. For all I knew, they'd been waiting here all day for me.

Well, they could wait a little longer while I sorted this crap out. The Pretty Boy from the bar must have followed me from the hospital to the bar. No way he could have known where I'd be, unless Cavanaugh had told him, which felt unlikely. They guy was lying through his cute smile, but it didn't feel malicious, and I doubted he worked for the Pretty Boys. Unless they were following him, too?

I shook my head. I was turning into a conspiracy theorist.

Fine. Ditch the paranoia, focus on the facts and logical connections. I didn't know enough about Cavanaugh to classify him as friend or foe yet, and until I did, I had to assume he was what he claimed—a man looking for a missing woman for reasons he felt he had to lie about. If the Pretty Boys had also taken her, lying made sense. Caution was smart, but assigning ulterior motives to his questions was jumping to reckless conclusions that could get me killed.

Less shaky, I climbed the stairs to my third-floor apartment. The hall was clear, no sounds but the faint whoosh of traffic and the squawks of one of the small green parrots that nested in the courtyard palm tree. I pressed my ear against the door and listened. No subtle taps or rustles came from inside. I unlocked it and slowly turned the knob. The door tended to squeak, but pulling up hard on the knob as I opened it usually kept it quiet. It creaked softly, but just once. I let it swing wide enough to peek inside.

Nothing out of the ordinary. Thrift-store-grade furniture sat in the kitchen and living room, with hotel carpet built for durability, not for comfort, and surely not for style. It wasn't as bad as my place in Memphis, which must have hired the designers of the local no-tell motel to decorate it, but it was no Rockport Apartments either.

I sniffed. Nothing but the overpowering smell of brand-new vanilla plug-ins.

Yeah, okay, buying those had been a bad idea. I crept forward a step at a time. No one jumped out, no soft thuds of hidden lurkers echoed. No creepy sensation of anyone but me being there. I kept walking, but froze two steps into the living room.

The coffee table sat an equal distance between the couch and the two chairs, not pressed close to the couch as a makeshift ottoman like I'd left it. Yesterday's mail suffered from the same precision on the old desk, stacked largest envelope to smallest. And the throw pillows I'd bought in a moment of weakness were missing.

A burglar with OCD? Except the radio was still there, as was the change from last night's pizza delivery—stacked by size, same as the mail.

It could have been maintenance, prepping the "fully furnished" apartment for the next occupant. A kind old man who took a few minutes to spruce up the place for a new tenant—that wasn't too far out of the realm of possibility.

Yes it is. No one's that nice.

I eased a few steps sideways and peeked down the hall. The bedroom door that refused to stay closed—no matter how hard I yanked it shut— was closed.

Cold sweat broke out above my lip. Last time someone had been waiting for me at home, I'd suffered a bad night in the emergency room.

Moving slowly, I retreated toward the hall closet. My go-bag was exactly where I'd left it in all its pink-and-blue-striped glory. I picked it up carefully, not shifting the contents or rattling the zipper, and backed away. This time, the front door closed silently.

My hands shook as I locked it.

Walk away like nothing is wrong.

If anyone *had* followed me, they knew which way I'd come in. If they were watching the back stairs, they'd spot me on the way to my car.

What makes you think your car is safe?

Right. If they were in my apartment, they could have my car surrounded by now. I couldn't assume anything was the same as it had always been, not if they had indeed changed tactics or goals.

I'd never bought a car that wasn't disposable, but I'd never had to abandon one before. I'd miss the old clunker, mildewed trunk and all.

Heart racing, I headed for the elevator on the opposite end of the third floor—the reason I'd rented this place. It opened up out of sight of the stairwells and near the lot where the delivery trucks parked. It was also my best option back to street level unless I suddenly manifested parkour skills.

The moment the elevator doors closed, I pulled a pink sunhat and flowered beach cover-up out of the go-bag and put them on. I rolled up my pants legs as far as they would go. Tight on my thighs, but high enough to hide under the hem of the cover-up. The lock picks went into my back pocket for now. The knuckledusters stayed put on my clenched hand.

One more floor.

I moved against the front wall of the elevator, putting my back to the buttons. The door chimed and slid open. No one entered. I wrapped my fingers around the door edge and peeked out.

The parking lot sat on the right. Safety beckoned on the left; a path leading through a peaceful courtyard filled with palm trees and hibiscus bushes off the pool area, sparse enough to make lousy cover, but enough to shield me from anyone watching the building. To them, I was just someone heading down to the pool. A side path cut through the bushes and emptied out on the street by a juice bar with a back door I'd scouted my first day here.

Here goes nothing.

I sauntered out. No quick movements, no nervous actions, nothing that would draw the eye of anyone on a stakeout. Just a gal going for an evening swim—who was ready to kick ass if someone got in her way.

THREE BLOCKS AWAY, I darted into a convenience store across from a Fast Auto Fix and bought two bottles of water, a packet of tissues, a bottle of aspirin, and a bar of chocolate. The chocolate I ate in the bathroom, letting the sweetness soothe my frazzled nerves. One bottle and the tissues went to cleaning up the scrapes and cuts Frisco's parking lot had gifted me with, though my jeans had taken the brunt of most of it. I'd have bruises tomorrow for sure.

I opened the other bottle of water, swallowed some aspirin, and tossed the trash away. Okay, so they had finally found me. They usually didn't get this close, but it wasn't unheard of. It had been super close in Atlantic City, too, but Dad had been prepared and sneaked us out of town safely.

I could do the same now. I didn't *have* to go back to my apartment. Everything of value was in my go-bag, my emergency stash was still safe, and it wouldn't be the first time I'd replaced my ridiculously limited wardrobe. I loved those lacy tank tops, though. And the leather jacket I'd gotten in Baltimore.

I gulped the water dry.

Dammit, I'd never find that jacket again. There's was a lot here I'd never find again.

The cab company's number was already saved on my phone, but I scrolled right past it and stared at another name and number I'd also saved.

I hesitated. Debated more chocolate. Then tapped it anyway. The phone rang twice.

Libby answered. "*Hola*, Grace, what's up?"

"Hey. Sorry to bug you, I know you're getting ready to take off," I said in a rush while I still had the nerve, "but my car died and I could use a ride. Possible to pick me up? Pretty please?"

A short pause, but not long enough to suggest fetching me was the last thing she wanted to do this evening. "Sure, I'm not leaving until tomorrow morning. Where are you?"

I gave her the address of the auto place across the street. "Thanks, you're a life saver."

This was the best and worst idea I'd ever had. You didn't stay around when the Pretty Boys found you—that rule had kept Dad and me alive. But Cavanaugh's list might hold answers about Mom, and more than that, it might hold a clue to why things had changed and *that* might keep them off my back once and for all.

No more running. No more hiding. A real life with real friends like Libby.

Dad wanted me to run, but Libby's apartment was as good as a safe house for now, probably better with someone to watch my back. If the Pretty Boys could change tactics, so could I.

Chapter Four

The hat and cover-up were back in my go-bag by the time Libby's car pulled up outside the Fast Auto Fix. I slipped out of the waiting room and into her car, checking the street as I moved.

Nothing out of the ordinary but me.

"Thanks for the ride," I said, setting the go-bag by my feet. Libby had changed into a dark gray T-shirt and white shorts that looked tough and summery at the same time.

"No problem, but don't you live around here?"

"Don't go to my place," I blurted.

She shot me a wary glance. "Oh-kay, why not?"

Dialing Libby's number had felt right at the time, but this was above and beyond the friendship we'd started. Sure, she'd stood up for me when that X-ray tech was convinced I'd taken her yogurt, and she'd had my back when some of the other PTAs started hazing me, but could I honestly expect her to...*ugh, this sucks.*

"Have you eaten yet?" I must have hit my head harder than I'd thought not to have an excuse ready.

She kept looking at me, but her expression was more puzzled than worried she was riding with a crazy woman. "Not yet."

"Want to grab a bite?"

"Grace, what's going on?"

"What do you mean?"

She scoffed and flicked a hand at me. "Please, you have suspicious written all over you. What is it, guy trouble? Dodging creditors? An awkward pass in my direction?"

"No, nothing like that."

"Enlighten me."

That was a peek into the mystical she *really* didn't want. "It's stupid."

"You think I've never been stupid before?"

From what I'd seen? Probably not.

I sighed and fished out a pinch of truth. "I was at Frisco's earlier. A gas leak exploded in the building next door while I was in the parking lot. It was small, no big deal—" I hastily added as her questions started. "But I guess it wigged me out more than I'd thought. I didn't want to go home."

"Are you okay? Was anyone hurt?"

"I'm fine, a small bump on the old noodle is all." I smiled and lightly rapped my knuckles against my head.

"Paramedics said you could go home?"

A simple *yes* would get me off the hook, but the lie didn't want to pop free this time. "I barely bumped it."

She rolled her eyes and muttered something in Spanish. "You're coming home with me."

"I don't want to spoil your vacation." But a weight lifted off me.

She waved a hand as if brushing away my hesitation. "It's not a real vacation. Makes no difference when I get there."

A dark sedan slid out of a side street two cars behind us. I kept one eye on it. If it didn't turn, I wasn't leading it back to Libby's.

"I don't want to be a burden."

She grinned. "Sure you do."

"What?"

Laughter this time. "You got spooked and wanted some company. Who else would you call? Daisy the devil child? You don't know anybody." She made a left. The sedan rolled past us on its original course.

"I suppose not." I smiled back, and actually meant it. Dad would scold me for a week when he heard about this, but some things *were* worth the risk. "I know it's silly."

"It's fine. We've all had those nights. Besides, my family would tear me a new one if I ignored a friend in need."

My throat tightened. I'd met people I'd liked before, but friendships were too painful when you knew you'd have to vanish with no notice or explanation. Libby had made it easier to try. We'd just clicked, right from the start.

"Thanks," I finally answered. "I appreciate it."

I leaned back against the seat and felt, well, not safe exactly, but not in any immediate danger. One night at Libby's would give me time to think and figure out what to do.

"You look pensive," Libby said.

"Hmm? Sorry. You might have been right about that guy trouble thing."

"Boyfriend or ex?"

I winced. Me and my big mouth. "Neither. It's nothing."

Her eyes narrowed. "Stalker?" Her tight grip on the steering wheel hinted she knew something about that. The coldness in her tone said she wasn't going to let this drop, either.

"Yes and no. It's complicated."

"Ay, *mamita*, it always is."

LIBBY UNLOCKED THE door and led me into her apartment. I'd been there a few times, but had never stayed long. The place was homey. Photos of handsome, smiling guys—most of them in fatigues—hung on the walls. She'd decorated with stylish furniture in muted colors, soft, yet not overly feminine. A bookcase filled with novels in English and Spanish sat behind an overstuffed chair with a matching ottoman. I kept meaning to ask her to explain the custom-painted three-foot model of an Imperial AT-AT Walker standing next to a piano.

I took a deep breath. No spicy woodfire scent, and everything smelled fresh and clean.

"I don't mean to pry," Libby began, "but what are you hiding from?"

"Hiding?"

She tossed her purse onto a writing table by the door that gave the room a finished look. "You're jumpy, and you checked the mirrors all the way over."

"I *was* almost blown up. It unsettles the nerves." And batters the body, which I was definitely starting to feel despite the aspirin.

"Plus, you know how to evade a question. What is it? Witness protection?"

"They told us not to talk about it. People might die."

Libby snorted.

"Have I mentioned how much I like your place?" I said, envious.

She rolled her eyes. "Is this a temporary wig out or do you need a night to regroup?"

"Uh..."

"Answers that. There's a fold-out couch in the room down the hall. You'll find a spare toothbrush in the drawer under the mirror in the bathroom, and some hotel soaps and shampoos are in the basket on the vanity. Help yourself."

"Thank you." Unexpected tears welled. I'd gone to a sleepover once when I was twelve with the daughter of one of the guys Dad worked with one summer. Seemed dumb to me, sleeping on the floor, telling scary stories, though it might have been more fun if I'd participated. I had the scariest stories of all.

She hesitated, staring at me again like she was waiting for me to come clean. "Feels like a hot chocolate night," she said when I stayed silent.

"It's eighty degrees out."

"You're turning down chocolate?"

"I didn't say that."

"Didn't think so." She shot me a "whenever you're ready to talk" look as she bustled about the kitchen. The two cabinets on either side of the sink had glass doors, and all of the glasses inside matched. Mugs on one side, wine on the other. More photos of soldiers on the refrigerator. Somebody had a fetish.

Libby heated the milk without a word, staring out the window over her sink at an actual view to a park across the street. No sounds broke the quiet but the clink of spoon on metal. She used real milk and squares of chocolate melted in a real pot. She even added cinnamon and what I'd swear was chili powder, though I had to have misread that.

Once it was melted, she pulled out a gizmo and whipped it into something frothy. It smelled amazing. Exotic and sweet. Gooseflesh rippled down my arm. *It's just chocolate, relax.*

She slid the mug to me, still quiet.

Maddening.

Libby reminded me of one of my fourth-grade teachers. Whenever anyone screwed up, he'd stare them down until they confessed. Took him fifteen minutes to crack me when I broke the projector once. Probably still a record.

I blew on the frothy goodness and sipped cautiously, mind whirling, sorting through lies and half-truths. The real truth kept knocking them aside, demanding to be heard.

I wish.

The hot chocolate was amazing. Rich and creamy, with a hint of heat.

Libby grabbed a box of Girl Scout cookies from the cabinet and rolled a tube of Thin Mints toward me. She hadn't blinked since I sat down.

Damn, the girl was good.

Nine cookies in, I caved. "Fine, someone broke into my apartment."

"Did you call the police?"

I shook my head. "Nothing was stolen. I had this weird vibe I wasn't alone, so I left."

She slid her phone across the counter this time. "Call the police."

"And say what? The heebie jeebies spooked me after a bang on the head? No. Waste of their time."

"They can send someone to check it out. Trust your gut."

"Yeah, well, my gut is calling me a wussy girl."

Her huff said she didn't buy that either. "I'll go over with you in the morning and we'll make sure everything is secure."

"You don't have to do that."

"I know, but I'm super nice that way." She sipped her drink. "Any news on your dad?"

My whole body jerked. "Excuse me?"

"I overheard you a few times on the phone. I wasn't trying to eavesdrop, but you hear "chemo," you notice, even in a hospital." She shrugged. "I figured you'd talk about it eventually, but I've known chattier SEALs"

"Everything's fine." I gestured at her fridge with the mug. "You date a lot of soldiers?"

"Not especially. How's he doing?"

"Staying positive. Brothers?"

"Four of them are. You heading home to see him between assignments?"

I sighed. "Why do you care?"

She took another cookie and pointed it at me. "Because you're my friend."

"You've known me six months." But it felt like I'd known her forever.

"So? My parents fell in love and got married in that amount of time. There's no minimum on friendship."

"You're going to make me cry."

"Grace, cut the crap. The loner act is getting old."

I gripped my mug. "Who says it's an act?"

"I do, and I know it well. I also know that look."

"What look?"

She took another cookie. "The same one I had right before I bought that damn piano."

"I've no intention of buying a piano." I'd asked for lessons once. Dad bought me a harmonica and a teach-yourself-to-play book. *Dad, please call back.*

"Neither did I, but I was a girl who lived out of a duffel most of her life. Then I was struck with this irrational urge to own something I couldn't shove into a suitcase." She popped the cookie into her mouth and crunched.

I pictured my impulse-buy throw pillows, which I might not see again. They were just *pillows*, but it hurt.

"You're tired of temporary, you're tired of being alone all the time, and you're tired of lying to everyone that you actually *prefer* it that way." She cocked her head and studied me through squinted eyes. "Unless I read you wrong."

I doubted Libby had ever read anyone wrong in her life.

"It's a brain tumor," I said, my throat catching. "Grade four."

"Damn, that sucks." Sympathy softened her face, but no pity ruined it. "How long does he have?"

"Should have died a year ago."

Her eyebrows raised. "Tough bastard. I know the type—my dad was career military."

"You were an Army brat?"

"Marines. You name a country with a base in it, and I've probably lived there."

"I've lived in thirty-seven states."

"Seriously?"

I nodded. "Six were on assignment, but the rest were regular moves. My dad's in construction, so we changed cities a lot." Usually unexpectedly.

"Sounds like the military. What about your mom?"

I twitched, but she didn't seem to notice. "Died when I was five. Yours?"

"Was the terror of whatever base she was on. I've seen four-star generals cringe in her presence."

I chuckled, but the coiled knot in my chest wouldn't loosen. Dad had had plenty of time to get to the safe house by now. Unless he didn't remember where the safe house *was*. If he'd had an episode, he might forget he was running at all.

Worrying is pointless until you know something.

I held up my mug, nerves—and muscles—screaming so loudly Libby was bound to notice. "Have anything stronger to mix with this?"

"I do indeed."

She opened one of the cabinets by the sink and pulled out a bottle. Fruity sweetness filled the kitchen as she poured what smelled like cherry liquor into my mug.

I sipped. It burned smooth and silky down my throat. "Mmm."

"Bought it in Paris from a little old Italian guy. Didn't speak a word of English, but what a riot he was."

"That was pre-piano I take it?"

She nodded. "My brothers took me there for my twenty-first birthday."

Libby seemed a little older than me, so maybe twenty-seven, twenty-eight now. "How long have you lived in Lauderdale?"

"Two years. Did the traveling PTA gig for a while, too."

"And then you bought a piano."

She chuckled and licked some spilled liquor off her finger. "Craziest urge I ever had, but it's my anchor now. I figured I'd give the whole roots concept a chance. Gave it six months. Plan was, if it didn't take, I'd sell the thing and take off."

"Do you miss it?"

"Sometimes. Still get restless though. I indulge in a lot of road trips. Good for the soul." She sipped her chocolate and fixed her gaze on me. "You could try it."

"The piano? I don't play."

She shot me an "oh please" look.

I hunched over my mug. "I'd have to learn everybody's names."

"That's what I said, and before long, I *knew* everybody's names."

"Some of us aren't meant to put down roots."

"Some of us topple over if we don't." She tipped her mug toward me. "You look like you're looking for a solid patch of dirt, is all."

A default ring tone burst from my pocket. I grabbed the alternative phone, my stomach twisting.

"Dad? Are you okay?"

"I'm fine, Apple-cheeks, are *you* all right?"

"Yes." I glanced at Libby, who turned away and started cleaning up the kitchen as if she wasn't listening to every word. "There was an explosion, sort of, but I'm fine."

"Leave right now if you can. Go to your mother's."

Code for dump your ID, grab one from your safety stash, and go someplace you've never been to before. Icy cold shot through me. "What about you?"

"My running days are over, Butternut. If they find me, they find me. Maybe that'll be enough to keep them away from you."

"No, you need to—"

"I love you, Grace."

Those words were off limits, had been for months. Saying I love you was too much like saying goodbye.

"I love you, too, Dad."

"Now run." The phone went dead.

Chapter Five

"Problems?" Libby asked the moment I set down the phone. I struggled not to hurl it across the room and scream.

What did he mean he wasn't running? He couldn't order me to uproot my life and do nothing to protect himself. That was insanity!

"No, just Dad being Dad."

"The answer is yes."

"To what?"

"Would you flat out lie to me."

I winced. "It's complicated."

"I'm sure it is," she said, checking the window again, "but I need to know what's up, because that overly clichéd black van pulled up when I started the hot chocolate, and it's still idling out there."

"What van?" I jumped to the window and looked down. Crap. The damn Pretty Boys weren't even being subtle about it.

"My next question—do I call the police now?"

"I'd prefer you didn't."

"Give me a compelling reason not to."

"Libby, you—"

"Stop." She held up her hand, palm out. "I have a cousin who's in perpetual trouble, so I know the signs when someone is after you. I've hidden him from lowlifes many a time. Who'd *you* piss off?"

"I should go." But I didn't *want* to leave. Not the apartment or the city. Certainly not my whole life.

"Bad idea with that van out there."

"I've put you in enough danger already."

"The building has a doorman who did three tours in the Gulf. Besides—" She reached under the sink, coming out with a gun that looked military. "I can take care of myself, which is more than I can say for you."

I scoffed and put my knuckledusters on the table. Not as flashy as her military hardware, but *they* hurt what was after me. I *really* should have held onto that black knife tighter. "I do all right."

"Pretty." She set the gun down next to it. "Fine, so we've established we're both armed and dangerous. Now tell me what's going on or I'm calling the cops."

Either she was an exceptional liar or she wasn't bluffing. My money was on both.

"I'm not a hundred percent sure—honestly," I added quickly when she gave me a dubious glare. "Unpleasant people are after us. Dad always called them the Pretty Boys."

"They're pretty?"

"Drool worthy. I know it sounds crazy, but remember I told you my dad worked construction? He saw somebody killed when I was a kid and we had to go on the run. The Pretty Boys have been after us ever since." True, more or less.

Libby narrowed her eyes and stared me down. "I can't tell if you're lying or not."

"It's safer if you don't know all the details." For both of us.

She gazed out the window for a few seconds, then blew out a breath. "I guess I was right about the witness protection."

I smiled tight.

"Did he witness a hit?"

I stayed silent. I'd tell fewer lies if I let her fill in the blanks.

"This is unreal," she said.

And how. "We're not safe here. They're only watching now, but it won't last." Soon as they figured out which apartment we were in, they'd come through the door like it wasn't even there. I'd no idea what they'd do to Libby, but odds were they'd tear through her just as easily. I was *not* going to let that happen.

"If your dad was the witness, why do they want you?"

Question of my life. "I don't know. I have to go, but you should head for the Keys as soon as we get out of here."

She frowned. "You're going to take off?"

"It works."

"How much cash you have on you?"

"Enough. I'll have more once I pick up a few things."

"I thought your apartment wasn't safe?"

I hesitated. "They're not at my apartment. I rented a storage locker near the interstate."

Libby's eyes widened, and then she shook her head slowly. "Look at you and your be preparedness."

"This isn't the first time I've had to run."

She paused, and for a moment I feared she might throw me out after all. Then she squared her shoulders. "Well, we have options."

"There's no *we* here. I'm not dragging you any further into this mess."

She held up a finger. "Non-negotiable. Unless you want to revisit the police thing?"

"Cops and my life don't go well together."

"Then you're stuck with me a little longer, because I'm not letting you run off after hearing a story like that. You're the only PTA at work I actually like. Give me a sec." She drummed her fingers on the counter a few times. I waited. I had no good ideas at the moment, so why not?

"All right," she said. "You're coming with me to Key Largo. No one would search for you there."

No way was the proper response. I liked Libby. I didn't want to see her get hurt. But she was nice to have around—hell, *helpful* to have around.

"That's not going to solve anything." Though a condo on the ocean with backup sounded better than staying alone at the cheap motel I'd targeted as my safe house.

"It'll get you out of town for a few days, and give me time to talk some sense into you about calling the cops."

The out-of-town part wasn't a bad idea, but even Libby couldn't convince me to call the police.

"I guess that would be okay. Thank you."

"Good." She took out her phone. "Don't freak out."

"Who are you calling?"

"Yes, I'd like to report a suspicious van in my neighborhood. Yes, I'll hold."

"What are you *doing*?"

She pressed the phone to her chest. "I said, don't freak out," she whispered fast, then put the phone back to her ear. "Hi, yes, there's a van that's been lurking outside the building for the last fifteen minutes. Black, tinted windows. I've *never* seen this van before and there's a playground down the block."

"This is a bad idea," I whispered back. I didn't want innocent cops hurt. "These guys are dangerous."

Libby shushed me with another flick of her hand. "Hang on, someone's getting out of the car. Older guy, creepy. I think he has a weapon."

I raised my eyebrows. The girl was good.

"Thank you so much." She hung up and gave me a wry grin. "Now we wait."

THE COPS ARRIVED faster than I'd have thought possible. Libby had grabbed her overnight bag and we were waiting in the lobby, watching. The second the van was rousted, we moved.

"We'll get your things," she said on the way to her car, "and then we'll head south."

She took an intricate route to the storage unit, filled with random turns and a few double backs. I kept an eye out for a tail—paying a *lot* more attention this time. I was still kicking myself for missing the van earlier.

The moon wasn't up yet and darkness covered us nicely as we put distance between us and the building. Libby took enough turns to expose—and then shake off—anyone following.

Either her dad was special forces, or she'd had to evade a few tails herself. I guess I wasn't the only one with secrets.

"Think we're clear," I said, hoping I was right. "But I'll keep watching."

"Good idea."

More than one Pretty Boy had been watching me and I'd had no clue they were there until I'd spied the hottie at Frisco's. They knew where I lived, where I worked, and had even followed me from my place to Libby's. More evidence that killing me was no longer the plan.

She glanced over. "That man from this morning—is he part of this? You seemed freaked out after he left."

"I'm not sure." Cavanaugh bugged me, but I couldn't say why exactly. A man with secrets who knew my real name—even if he didn't know he knew it—gave me the jitters. "He had a cop vibe, but no badge."

"Fed? Maybe someone from organized crime?"

"He was asking about a missing woman, so probably not."

She paused. "Private investigator, then?"

"Maybe. He *did* ask a lot of questions. He could have been hired by the woman's family." That would explain a lot. During those first few years after Mom died, Dad had tried to find out what had killed her—who they were, what they wanted. He'd found nothing but dead ends, but then, we'd never had enough extra cash to hire an investigator. Cavanaugh could be working for someone like Dad, trying to find out what had happened to his wife.

"How is she connected to the hit your dad saw?"

"I have no idea."

"Maybe she witnessed another hit by the same people?"

"It's possible."

We exited the interstate and pulled into the storage lot. Nothing fancy, but it had small units for cheap, and I could access it at any time. I entered my gate code and we drove in.

"It's over there."

The locker could hold far more than I'd ever used, and my worn duffel bag felt tiny sitting there by itself. Dad had given it to me for my sweet sixteen, filled with everything a girl needed to vanish without a trace neatly tucked away inside. We'd used it the first time three weeks later.

I unzipped the bag. Five thousand in emergency cash lay in plastic bags next to a folder with an ID for Grace Kaufmann—who lived in St. Louis—plus a Social Security card and two credit cards. I'd had a fake ID claiming I was eighteen before I'd had a real driver's license. I'd never been able to afford a fake passport. It hadn't been worth wiping out my life's savings to get one.

"Good to go." I shut and locked the locker. Also inside the duffel was a letter canceling my service, and I'd drop that in the mail when I wasn't running for my life.

Libby gave me sidelong glances on the way to the car.

"What?" I asked.

"I'm not sure if I should be impressed or concerned. Did I see fake IDs and a wad of cash?"

"Better if you don't think about it."

"Hard *not* to."

I stopped. "Listen, Libby, I understand this is freaky shit. I know how it looks, and I don't blame you if you want to walk away now and forget you ever met me."

She considered it. "Are you doing anything illegal?"

No laws existed for pretending to be someone else as long as I didn't defraud anyone. Though the fake IDs crossed a line.

I held my thumb and finger an inch apart. "A *teeny* bit. But nothing that hurts anyone."

"Such as?"

"I pay my bills no matter what name I use. Changing names is how we stay alive." I just hadn't had to do it since college. Damn it, my PTA license was in this name. Changing that would be way too expensive for my budget.

I tossed the duffel onto the back seat. "How far is it to the Keys?"

"Couple of hours."

"I'll stay a day or two, then I'll be out of your hair."

"You don't have to run. You can call witness protection and tell them what you saw. They'll be able to do something to help."

"I'm sure my dad would have done that had it been an option."

Cool as WITSEC looked on TV, they couldn't do anything to help us hide from what was after us any better than we could do for ourselves. At least we *knew* how bizarre our story sounded and how dangerous the Pretty Boys were. If I didn't have a bump on my head and green grit in my hair to prove it, *I'd* think this was all in my mind.

Like I'd once thought it had all been in *Dad's* mind.

Guilt poked me. When I was fifteen, I'd wondered if the Pretty Boys and the danger were a delusion. I'd been so young when Mom died—my memories of green fire and men with superhuman strength couldn't have been real. Trauma, nothing more. I'd wondered if Dad had been crazy. That made more sense than monsters trying to kill us for unknown reasons. After all, *he'd* always spotted the Pretty Boys first, and then we'd run. A strange, good-looking man pointed out from a distance wasn't the same as seeing a Pretty Boy up close.

I'd changed my mind when one came for us and I discovered my knuckledusters were damn effective against men who showed no weakness.

And who froze time.

I had Libby watching my back, but Dad had no one watching his, and a memory currently leaking like a sieve.

"Change of plans," I said. "Take me to the airport. I need to find my father." And I needed to find answers to a lifetime-long question. He remembered the past more often than the present these days, so maybe something in one of those memories would tell me why I'd spent my life running from monsters.

"You think they went after him, too?"

I nodded. "He said he went to his safe house, but with the tumor..." Too hard to finish that sentence. "I'll feel better when I know he's okay."

"Are you sure about this? You'll be alone."

I shrugged. "Nothing new there."

She headed for the airport while my worry ate at me. Libby sneaked me equally worried looks. Something on her mind, but she was already a good enough friend to keep her mouth shut when I clearly didn't want to talk. Damn, I'd miss this.

"Where's your dad live?"

"Outside Vegas."

She nodded slowly, drove fast. The minutes clicked by in silence.

"What if I come with you?" she said at last.

"No way. Too dangerous."

"It's more dangerous if you go alone." She drummed her fingers on the wheel a few times. "I could use a Vegas trip."

"You've done enough. I can do this on my own."

"I'm sure you can, but you don't know what you're up against, and you're too emotionally distracted to watch your own back."

"Lib, no sane person would offer to come with me. Just asking proves you can't be trusted to make major life decisions."

She glanced in the rearview and shifted lanes. "I'd rather face your demons than mine, okay?"

"What are you talking about?"

"I'm not going on vacation to the Keys. I'm going to clean out my father's fishing cabin. I'm closest, none of my brothers are man enough to do it, and my mom can't walk in the place without crying, so it's on me." She took a deep breath. The kind I took whenever I thought of my father and that last goodbye. "I don't want to do it either."

"Why didn't you tell me?" I asked softly.

She shrugged. "Because he was killed two years ago and you're dealing with death right now."

I wanted to ask how he died, but Libby's stiff shoulders and set jaw kept me quiet. Maybe that's why we got along so well. Sisters in silent denial.

"You'll still have to clean out the cabin. Going with me won't change that."

"No, but you'll owe me. You'll *have* to do it with me or you'll be the worst friend in the entire world. You'll never live that rep down."

I hesitated. She'd been pretty sly calling the cops, and she evaded a tail better than I ever had. And knowing Dad, it would take two of us to convince him to come with me for his own protection.

Libby lifted her chin and huffed like it was all settled. "Accept it, I'm going. Plus, I've got an uncle who runs an exotic gun range off the Vegas strip. He's been hassling me to visit since the funeral, but—" She squeezed the steering wheel and took another breath. "It's hard seeing him. He looks too much like...all I'm saying is, you be my backup, I'll be yours. Deal?"

Staying with her wasn't only better, it was safer.

"Okay. Girls' trip to Vegas, then."

Chapter Six

Even at three in the morning, Vegas sparkled. From the air it was all strings of diamonds in perfect grids, brightest where the strands overlapped. On the ground, the lights blinked and twinkled in every direction and every color—even a sickly neon green that looked way too familiar for my comfort. Flashy as they were, none of the arrows pointing toward riches would show me where my father was.

Hello, Sin City.

If I were a Pretty Boy, this is where I'd live. Everything open all the time, strangers by the thousands arriving every day, distractions galore to keep prying eyes turned away. You could even travel from hotel to hotel and never step out into the light. Fake some "Free Weekend in Vegas" passes and you could lure anyone you wanted here and no one would be the wiser.

I put the rental car on my shiny new credit card since the Pretty Boys had seen Libby and me together. If they figured out who Libby was, they'd eventually pick up her trail on the flight, but using a clean card would buy us some time.

Following the signs, we headed out of the rental lot and tuned onto the 215, headed south, past perfectly squared blocks of houses in desert styles.

Dad lived in Boulder City, about twenty-five miles southeast of Vegas, smack dab between his two favorite things—or so he claimed—Paigow poker and the Hoover Dam. I had my doubts about the poker, but the dam I believed. He had a fascination with construction marvels. We'd stopped at practically every dam, mine, and oil rig we'd passed on our way from town to town.

I called again, but Dad still wasn't answering his phone, nor did he pick up on the alternate burner phone in my go-bag.

"Stop calling," Libby said, yawning, so it sounded more like "cawlig." We'd gotten a little sleep on the plane, but not nearly enough. "If he's safe, he'll call you. If he's not, you might give away his position."

"Right." I stared at my phone. No photos of Dad on it—or of anyone. Blank and empty as the rest of my life.

"We'll find him," she assured me yet again. "But if we don't, we call the police, got it?"

"Got it."

This time, the lie came easy.

DAD'S SAFE HOUSE motel was across the street from the Hoover Dam Museum, and walking distance to every Dam-related business in town. An excuse to say, "I had lunch at the Dam diner, then headed over to the Dam store to grab some Dam gear."

Always cracked him up.

"Wow," Libby said as we pulled into the parking lot. "I was expecting something more...sleazy."

"Same here."

The hotel was charming. A cross between a southern plantation and the Alamo, it looked like the quaint vacation spot for newlyweds or couples off for a romantic weekend. I'd never have thought to look for Dad there—aside from the Dam name of course—and I doubted the Pretty Boys knew of his dam fixation.

We walked into a floral-scented lobby decorated in rich woods and thick, elegant moldings. The furniture looked new, but the styles were as classic as the rest of it, with deep browns, grays, and the right amount of maroon accents.

I particularly liked the maroon-and-gray-striped throw pillows.

One sleepy-eyed guy stood behind the registration counter. He perked up a little as we approached.

"Good morning," he said. "Checking in?"

"Meeting my Dad. He should have checked in earlier today. Our reservation is under Henry Kaufmann."

He shifted to the computer and asked for my ID. I handed him the new one. "I don't see him, and there's no reservation for Kaufmann."

"Maybe it's under his girlfriend's name. Harper?"

He checked. "No, no Harpers either. Are you sure it was this hotel?"

"That's what he said."

"We're not the only Dam hotel in town, you know." He grinned.

Definitely this hotel.

I grinned back, though my heart felt shredded. "That must be it. I'll check one of the others. Thanks."

Libby followed me out of the hotel. "Right hotel?"

"Right hotel."

"Grace, it doesn't mean anything."

"It means he never made it here."

She pulled open the car door. "But it doesn't mean he isn't home fast asleep."

"Let's find out."

WE PULLED UP to the Spanish-style apartment complex Dad had lived in for the past year. I'd forgotten how orange the stucco walls were, even in the lights from the parking lot. The terra cotta tile roofs all matched, as did the transplanted trees that didn't belong in a Nevada desert.

I parked at the far end of the building, lights off. "See anything weird?"

She shook her head.

We exited the car and quietly shut the doors. Libby dug around in the trunk and found a tire iron while I pulled out my knuckledusters. TSA tended to frown on those in carry-on luggage, but I'd checked my duffel. Worth the extra time at baggage claim to bring them along.

I put them on. "Ready?"

"Affirmative."

Dad never lived anywhere that didn't have multiple exits, and Vista Canyon Villas was no exception. Each building stood two stories, with heavily walled balconies instead of rails out front. We'd climbed down an emergency fire ladder more than once in the middle of the night.

We took the stairs. Sin City might be going strong at—I glanced at my watch—five-thirty a.m., but it was quiet in the suburbs. One soft radio played soft music from the only apartment with the hall light on, two units down from Dad's.

Along the breezeway, an actual breeze chilled my skin and I smelled bacon. Somebody worked the early shift. We sidestepped a scattering of red pebbles outside Dad's door and braced ourselves.

Libby pantomimed knocking on the door.

I shook my head and showed her the key. I pressed my ear to the door and the door opened a crack. My breath stopped. Dad would *never* leave his door unlocked, let alone open.

I glanced at Libby and she hefted the tire iron. I pushed the door. It swung slowly inward.

Nothing. Quiet as any apartment at five in the morning.

We entered, eyes and ears alert for trouble. Streetlight streamed in through the window and cast shadows on what little furniture he had.

"Was he robbed?" she whispered.

"No, it's always like this." But the worn easy chair was angled away from the couch, and one of the dining room chairs was on its side. "Except for the knocked-over furniture."

I pushed down my dread. A break-in only suggested they'd come here looking for him. Maybe they'd kicked the chair over in frustration when they'd found the place empty.

Libby held out a hand. "Stay back." She crept past me, leading with the tire iron. I stayed against the wall and scanned the room.

Dad's place was sterile. No pictures hung on the walls. No photos on the shelves. No TV or stereo. Aside from the bottle of bourbon on the kitchen counter, nothing of *him* existed in this place. So different from Libby's apartment, filled with images of love and laughter and family.

My reflection stared at me from a mirror over the desk that had to have come with the place. If I had to run again, *this* was my future—me standing in a generic apartment in a random town, nothing to show for my life but some clothes and whatever mementos fit in a single go-bag.

More than anything in the whole world I wished I could call Dad and hear him say he was okay, not to worry, that life was about more than trinkets collected and items possessed. It was about...about...

He'd never told me what it was about, only what it wasn't.

We'd spent too much time running and not enough talking. When we *did* talk, it was about rules and how to spot a tail, and how to walk the fine line between nondescript and noticeable loner.

And what to do if the Pretty Boys ever found us.

Libby moved through the emptiness, her shoulders squared, arms locked, turning at the waist as she checked the rooms. Not many of those. Living room, kitchen and dining area, one bedroom in the back, bath on the side. She swept back into the living room like GI Jane. "Clear."

"That was kind of badass," I said. Easier to focus on her than what the room represented.

"Please don't ever say that around my brothers."

"They don't think you're badass?"

"Oh they know I am, but if you sound the least bit impressed, they'll be all over you."

I reached over and clicked on the light. The easy chair wasn't just out of place—it had been shoved aside. A tear ripped through the upholstery in the back, and a few coins and a half-melted mint lay scattered on the floor beside it. Even the coffee table was pushed back, with a long scuff across the top, and two gouges. I kneeled by the table and ran a finger along one of the gouges. Red grit stained my fingers. More red pebbles lay tangled in the carpet.

"Grace." Libby said, her tone wary. She stood in the foyer. "Look at this."

I returned to the door. A doorknob-sized hole had punctured the wall and snapped the doorstop right off the trim. "It took a lot of force to do that."

Libby nodded. "Frame's not broken though. He opened the door first."

In unison, we looked from the doorway to the living room. I didn't know what her GI Jane senses were telling her, but I saw someone knock on the door and Dad answering. Not a Pretty Boy, because he would have spotted one through the peephole, so it had to have been a minion or lackey. Someone who looked innocent and safe. Whoever they were, Dad opened the door, and the Pretty Boy burst in and slammed Dad against the table. Maybe he tried to scramble over the chair and get away. He was too sick to have done that. He could have broken something, or fallen and done real damage.

My throat tightened. With Pretty Boys in the room, he'd never have made it out.

Libby put a hand on my arm. "It doesn't mean they—"

I darted to the closet by the door and yanked it open. The last of my hope faded. "His go-bag is still here." But no body. If they were going to kill him, they'd have done it here and left. There was no reason not to unless... "They took him." Just like they'd tried to take me.

Why hadn't they killed us?

I ran through Cavanaugh's list of crossed-off names and obituaries. Dad wasn't on that list. He shouldn't be missing. Cavanaugh's list suggested it had actually been me they were after, though I still had no idea why.

"All right," Libby began, pulling out her phone. "A deal's a deal. We call the police."

"Don't."

"Grace, this is serious now."

"The cops can't do anything to help us."

"Of course they can."

I grabbed her phone. "They *can't*. You don't know these people—they're not your...typical mobsters. The cops will only make it worse, and they'll get themselves killed."

She waited, her expression stuck somewhere between pissed off and worried. Then she crossed her arms and pinned me with a military stare. "What aren't you telling me?"

"Only the crazy crap that might get you killed. Trust me or go home."

Her eyes narrowed. "Answers. Now. What the hell is really going on?"

She meant it. She was absolutely prepared to turn and walk right out the door if I didn't level with her. Safer for her, but my stomach churned just thinking about looking for Dad on my own. The Pretty Boys had changed their playbook and I had no idea what threats I might face next, and no idea where to start searching for Dad.

"I honestly don't know anymore." Not that she'd accept that answer. I could hardly blame her, but it was inconvenient.

"You told me people wanted to kill you and your father."

"That's what Dad always said."

She huffed. "You're saying he lied."

"I'm saying that's what he told me," I snapped. Unless he'd known all along? "It's not like we had time to ask the thing that murdered my mother *why* it did it."

"Your mother was killed?" Libby had the good sense to wince. "I'm sorry. I didn't know. But this is all a little—" she waved a hand about "—hard to take in."

"I know."

She hesitated, her head cocked. "Wait, what do you mean by 'The thing'?"

"Hmmm?"

"You said 'the thing that murdered my mother.' Not who."

Think before you speak, girl. "I'm tired is all."

"Bullshit. Either trust me or I go home."

"You won't believe me."

"I might. You don't know how open-minded I am."

I hesitated. She had gone along with everything so far. Maybe she *could* buy into the truth. I debated stalling her until we got someplace safer, but if the Pretty Boys were still watching the apartment, I'd be eligible for a milk carton by now.

"Okay, the truth. But when you think I'm a nut job, remember you asked for this."

Chapter Seven

"Do you believe THERE's evil in the world?" I said, taking a seat on the couch. Libby took the other side.

She frowned. "Oh, this is not starting out well at all."

"Answer the question."

She glared at me, her expression poised to blow me off, but then her eyes darkened and she was suddenly a million miles away. Finally, she nodded. "Yes."

"So do I, but my definition of that has changed over the years." I paused. This wasn't something you blurted out.

"When I was five," I began, "my parents and I were driving home from dinner. It was in Pensacola where Dad was working for a group building a new hotel. We were singing. Dumb kid songs that made me laugh.

"We were the only car on a side road when Mom screamed. Someone was in the middle of the road, and we hit him."

"You *hit* someone?"

"More like we hit some*thing*. He barely moved, but our car crumpled and spun out, round and round until it slid over the embankment."

"That's impossible."

Until then, I'd thought so, too. "My head was still spinning when he ripped Mom's door off the car and yanked her out." I closed my eyes, the shriek of metal mixing with the screams of my mother echoing in my memory. "Then he bit her in the neck."

"Grace—"

I opened my eyes again and held up a hand. "Let me finish. This is hard enough."

"All right."

It rolled through my mind for the second time in two days. "Mom fought whatever he was, but he wouldn't let her go. He...licked her blood off her neck. Dad leapt from the car and ran to her, but before he could reach her, the thing roared like it was pissed as hell, and tore out her throat."

So much blood, dark like shadows running down her chest. It hadn't seemed real. I'd had no words to understand it then.

Libby gasped and pressed a hand over her mouth.

"Dad reached Mom in time to catch her body, but he couldn't stop the bleeding." I gripped myself tight with both hands. "He couldn't save her. He tried but it was—" I stopped and sucked in a breath. I'd never told anyone this before. Dad and I had lived it. We'd had no reason to talk through it again.

I blew out the breath. "That *thing* walked away from her and came toward me, blood all over his face, and I swear to God he *smiled* at me and said, 'Maybe you'll be the one.'"

"You're making this up."

"I wish I were."

"How did you *survive* that?"

The dusky man with the knife. Although it wasn't real, I smelled his woodfire smoke and spice scent as clearly as I had that night. "Someone saved us. He was like the other one, but, I don't know, *good* versus evil. He came out of nowhere and tackled the thing. They fought. There was a flash, then the thing...disintegrated...into glowing chartreuse mist. All that was left was the dusky man who saved us. He told us we were in danger, that we had to run and keep moving or they'd find us."

"Damn." She pulled her knees up to her chest.

My own chest burned as if I was still running for my life along a dark road. Dad had gone to the police, but no one had believed his story.

"Last night, a Pretty Boy attacked me in the parking lot outside Frisco's." I managed to keep my voice calm and steady. "But he didn't kill me. He grabbed me and tried to drag me into an alley. I don't know, maybe he planned to kill me there, but he had no reason to take that extra step. These things are *fast*—he could have killed me before I'd known he was there. And just like before, a dusky man showed up and saved me. He dropped a knife during the fight, and I grabbed it."

I paused, my hands shaking. Libby was still as stone, her eyes wide, her arms wrapped around her knees.

"I stabbed the Pretty Boy who'd attacked me and he exploded into green grit and dust, just like the one on the road that night."

Libby jerked. "Biting necks, drinking blood, death by dust," she whispered. "That sounds like…"

I met her frightened gaze. "I know what it sounds like. It looked like it, too."

Libby unfolded and walked to the kitchen. She grabbed the bottle of bourbon off the counter and fetched two glasses. I said nothing as she poured us both generous shots.

"Still think helping me is the right call?" I asked.

"I should have you committed." She gulped her drink. "But…I had a cousin who was a priest. Couple of years ago everyone was over for Thanksgiving, and the nieces were watching TV—some old rerun—and they were going on and on about the sexy vampire with a soul, and how cool it would be to live forever. My cousin lost it and turned off the TV. He yelled at them for ten minutes about romanticizing evil.

"They blew him off, and even I laughed a little. He was upset about something ridiculous. I asked him, 'Who cares if they watch? It's a show.' He told me, 'If they fantasize about evil, how could they avoid the real thing?'"

"He said vampires were real?"

"Not in so many words, but he said he'd seen things that couldn't be explained, and that evil shouldn't be glorified." She swigged the last of her bourbon, then laughed wryly. "Yes, I still think helping you is the right thing to do."

"Think your cousin would know something about all this?"

She shook her head. "He died last year. An animal attack while camping."

I chugged my drink, but the burn didn't chase away my chill. "Are you sure?"

"Until now I was."

We sat in silence for a while, letting my story—and the bourbon—sink in. Libby believed me, or at least, enough to give me the benefit of the doubt.

"Pretty Boys," Libby said softly. "Let's stick to calling them that."

"Agreed."

"Why would Pretty Boys kidnap your father?"

"I have no idea; but according to that guy who came to the hospital, others are also missing. The kidnappings are new—they always killed before. It makes no sense."

She groaned and rubbed her eyes. "I can't even parse this. It's too much."

"I know, believe me. I go through it every few years myself, doubt what I saw happened, think I'm losing my mind, the whole works. But it *did* happen. It's all real."

"How do we fight...*Pretty Boys*?"

"Silver hurts them. That knife killed one."

She paused. "Have you tried shooting them?"

"No, but if a car doing forty didn't splatter them, I have my doubts about bullets."

"Holy water?"

"Never tried it. We focused on protecting ourselves and running. They're just too strong, and they move too fast. The only way to survive is to run when you get even an inkling that they're nearby." I gave a tight laugh. "Killing one was a fluke, and I don't have that knife anymore. The guy who saved me took it."

She rubbed her face with both hands and paced the room. "Isn't there someone you can go to? What about a church?"

"Dad tried that. They told him he was crazy. The second one he went to for help sent social services after me. We barely got out of town in time."

"So you kept running?"

I nodded. "We kept running. And lying. And pretending everything was normal in the world when it certainly was *not*."

"You have vampires chasing you."

I nodded again. "I have vampires chasing me."

She paced some more, then stopped. "Organized vampires."

"They seem to be, yes."

"List-carrying, people-abducting, organized vampires."

I rubbed my eyes. "What's your point?"

"I have none. I hope saying it out loud helps my brain accept it."

I almost smiled. Breaking the rules had been a good idea. I couldn't imagine doing this without Libby. Trusting one person wasn't so bad. It felt...good. Safe even.

"What do we do now?" I asked. It was also nice not to have to think up everything on my own.

"Improvise, adapt, and overcome." She shrugged. "I'm still working out the details."

I looked around the room. "This is the crime scene, so I guess we start with a thorough search." The apartment *was* pretty bare, but we might find something besides rocks and old mints that could give us a lead. Besides, it was a lot safer if we kept our names off the hotel registers for a while.

"I'll get the door and foyer," Libby said. "You'll know the personal space better than I will."

"Got it." I checked the couch and chair area again, moving the furniture aside and rooting through the shag carpet. A few more coins, but nothing we hadn't already found. The rip in the chair didn't hide any clues either. No torn off pieces of matchbook covers with a hotel logo, no rare seeds found only in the Vegas Botanical Gardens. "The cops on TV make this look easier."

"They have forensic consultants."

We searched in silence for a while.

"Anything?" I asked.

"Just dirt. There's no doormat." She paused. "Did he have a doormat? Is it significant that it's missing?"

"No to both."

I moved to the closet again and pulled out Dad's go-bag. A glint in the mashed carpet underneath caught my eye, square and shiny.

I crouched and picked it up. An amethyst as big as my thumbnail sat in the middle of dark wood shaped like a plus sign. Gold wire wrapped the wood and the filigree setting, a little tarnished like the jewelry in the estate sale counters. Grandma jewelry. A pendant?

Libby came over. "Find something?"

"Maybe." I showed it to her.

"Looks like a cross."

"It's square."

"Not all crosses are T-shaped. My Great Aunt Rosa wore something like this on a chain thick as my pinky. Used to kiss it and wave it at us when we were acting up. One of my cousins always thought she was cursing us."

"Dad only curses the old-fashioned way, but it was under his bag." It wouldn't be the first religious trinket of his I'd found. Growing up, our car's glove box had always been stuffed with them. He'd even engraved that bit of scripture on my knuckledusters. We'd never let a Pretty Boy get close enough to test the vampires-and-crosses theory, but he'd kept some around just in case.

"Is it a clue?" Libby said.

"No." I tucked it in my pocket anyway. It was still Dad's.

We combed through the rest of the apartment but found nothing. The other rooms showed no signs of a struggle and hadn't been disturbed.

"I'll check the hallway," Libby said. "It's a longshot, but there's nothing in here."

I nodded and set the go-bag down on the coffee table. Although it held lots of useful items, none of them helped me find Dad. The extra cash would be nice if I had to run, but I didn't want to run again. I liked being Grace Harper, and I liked her life. I even enjoyed working with Daisy the Devil Child. All that would vanish once I became Grace Kaufmann.

The door opened and Libby came back inside, shaking her head. "Nothing weird outside."

I blew out a breath and dropped onto the couch. "I'm running out of ideas."

"I think we should call my Uncle Roberto."

"It's six in the morning on a Sunday."

"He's been up for an hour already."

"It's bad enough I dragged you into this, now you want to put your uncle at risk?"

"We don't have to tell him the specifics. He'll understand need-to-know."

Sitting around here wasn't getting us anywhere. I was almost desperate enough to use my credit card or do something to draw the Pretty Boys to me just for a lead.

"Grace, you know sooner or later you're going to have to deal with them." She crossed her arms. "Would you rather face them with serious firepower that gives us a fighting chance or unarmed?"

That was a no-brainer. "Bring on the big guns. I'm done running."

THE BIG BRASS Commando Experience was an unapologetically squat, bunker-inspired building off the Vegas strip, not far from a pair of hotels that cost hundreds of millions to build. Camo-colored Jeeps and military vehicles were parked outside next to a lone truck. In a few hours the parking lot would be full, but at 7 a.m., it was just us.

Libby hesitated by the car. "Silver hurts them, right?" she asked.

"Hurts who?"

"The Pretty Boys. In the myths, they can't stand silver."

"My dusters hurt the one the other night. Why?"

"Thinking about what to ask Uncle Roberto for." She looked at the gun range again. I'd say she was stalling.

"Getting cold feet?" I asked.

"No." But she still didn't move. "Maybe."

"We can leave if you want."

She shook her head. "We need supplies. No, I can do this." She took a deep breath and marched up to the door. I followed, less certain about this whole idea.

Inside, cream cinderblock walls gave off a high-school-hallway vibe, if you ignored the rifles and machine guns hanging on racks behind the counters. Dad had owned a small revolver, and he'd taught me how to shoot, but we never spent much time at a range beyond a monthly skill brush up.

I admired the cases full of survival gear, an impressive assortment of knives, guns in all shapes and sizes, and everything a gal needed to carry them. In the event of a zombie apocalypse, I knew where my first stop would be.

"Liberty!" bellowed a solid chunk of man across the shop.

Libby held firm, and even smiled. "Uncle Roberto."

He moved from behind the counter like a ship smashing through ice, stopping when he reached her. After a barely perceptible awkwardness, he scooped her up in a hug that would have snapped a weaker woman. "I've missed you, *chula*."

Libby hesitated for a heartbeat, but hugged him back. "Me too." They stared at each other for a moment, and then she turned to me and made the introductions.

"Grace, Roberto Torres, Uncle Roberto, Grace."

"Nice to meet you," I said.

"Same. My girl said you're in some trouble."

Libby told me to be straight, yet vague, with the guy. "I am. Missing father. Bad people looking for us both. I'm all kinds of screwed."

"It happens to the best of us. Tell me."

Libby jumped in, summarizing my messed-up life with military precision. I wasn't sure if it sounded better or worse that way.

Roberto didn't hesitate. "Come with me."

We followed him into a back office. Photos of a much younger Libby and a bunch of guys in fatigues hung along one wall. Four of them had "Torres" stitched on their pockets, and looked like the guys in the photos in her apartment. An older shot had a young Roberto and another guy who looked a lot like him sitting on the hood of a Jeep.

Roberto shut the door and crossed his arms. He gave Libby a look I was happy not to be on the receiving end of. This time she did flinch.

"Liberty, does Jacqui know you're here?"

Her mother, I assumed.

She raised her chin. "I don't need her permission to help a friend."

"Did I say permission, *chula*? Something happens to you on my watch, it's my ass."

"It did not occur to me to tell her."

He harrumphed. "I don't see you for two years, then you call with a crazy story and request an arsenal."

"If you don't want to help—"

"Did you hear the word no? I was worried about you."

"I'm okay."

He frowned. "You haven't been okay since Luis—"

"*Tio*," she barked, glancing at me. "*No saques los trapos sucios.*"

He shifted to Spanish, and while I could only pick out a few words here and there, I didn't need a translator to know Libby was getting the old, "I'm concerned about your behavior and you're denying there's a problem which will only make it worse" speech. I'd heard that one many a time, from teachers, guidance counselors, and even a few times from Dad.

I edged away as much as I could in the small office and focused on anything but them. Lots of photos of soldiers on Roberto's desk, though I doubted they were all family members. I checked the names, noting at least three non-Torres, then froze. Libby wore a uniform in one of the photos. She stood between two other women in tan fatigues with her own name stitched on the pocket. *Well I'll be dammed. That explains a lot.* She looked good with short hair.

I guess she really could take care of herself.

"Fine, I will," Libby said, throwing her hands up. "*Dejalo ya?*"

Roberto considered it, lips pursed, then nodded. "*Si.*" He sighed, and I got the feeling neither of them had won this fight.

She put a hand on his impressive arm. "Can we help Grace, now, please?"

"What do you need?"

"A pair of self-defense packages if you could spare them. Do you have any stun gun brass knuckles? Grace is partial to the knuckledusters. And anything coated in silver that packs a punch."

"Silver?"

"Special circumstances."

Roberto hesitated, but nodded slowly. "Let me see what I have in stock." He left the office.

I turned to Libby. "He's going to just hand over weapons?"

"He's family."

"He doesn't even know me."

"I vouched for you." She poked me in the chest with one finger. "Don't make me regret it."

Aside from Dad, no one had ever given me weapons before. "I'm kinda choked up over here."

"It's non-lethal, no need for tears."

"Still, I'm touched."

Roberto returned with two backpacks and set them on the desk. He opened one and rooted around inside. "Nothing silver, but we have your standard pepper spray—" he pulled it out and set it on the desk "—stun gun, personal alarm—" these also went on the desk "—an expandable steel baton." He flicked it open, then slid it closed again. "And finally, your Zappers."

"Sweet." I picked one up. Similar in shape to my knuckledusters, but with sleek black rubber, raised sections on the middle knuckles, and metal stunner pieces. Plus a safety switch button by the thumb. A good left-handed weapon for the next time a Pretty Boy got handsy. Provided, of course, that forty thousand volts worked as well as silver.

Roberto turned to Libby and pulled something out from behind his back. "For you—Lola."

Libby pressed a hand to her mouth. "You're lending me *Lola*? I'd be fine with a loaner SIG, maybe a Glock, but *her*?"

Lola was a gun, and despite Libby's enthusiasm over it, it didn't look any different from the one she'd had at her apartment.

"Thank you," she said breathlessly.

"There's ammo and a vest in each of your packs."

I put the Zappers and the rest of the gear back into the open backpack. I'd move the rest of my stuff into it later. "I appreciate this, Mr. Torres. I feel safer already."

"Roberto, please."

"Roberto."

"Liberty, you need me to watch your six?"

She tossed the pack over her shoulder as natural as could be. "Not yet. If I do, I'll call you."

"I expect regular sitreps or I'll send in the Marines." He smiled, but based on the amount of fatigues in the photos, he probably meant that literally.

"Daily sitreps then."

"Oh eight hundred hours."

"Roger that."

Roberto hugged her, then nodded at me. "Be careful. Tell me all about it when it's done and over."

I nodded. "I'll buy the beers."

We stopped at a diner a few blocks down the road for a quick breakfast, our stomachs rumbling almost as loudly as the highly unusual thunder. Vegas didn't get a whole lot of rain.

"That wasn't so bad," Libby said. We slid into a booth, setting our backpacks down beside us in sync.

"He seemed nice."

"He is. He held back on the lectures with you there, so, thanks for that."

I paused. "Lectures?"

"It's—" She waved a hand like I shouldn't worry about it.

The waitress arrived and took our order, delaying my questions. Libby got the eggs, I got pancakes, and we both got the biggest coffee they served. Adrenaline was the only thing keeping either of us standing.

Libby was as unreadable as a rock, except for the "don't ask" vibe. I had so many questions, but I'd be quite the hypocrite if I asked them.

She leaned back and closed her eyes. I'd have been wise to follow her lead, but catching a catnap in public wasn't part of my skill set. Too many people in the diner, even though none of them looked like a threat. Just tourists beginning their days with full bellies of cheap food before trying their luck at the casinos.

I could use a little luck myself.

My phone vibrated in my pocket. I snatched it, heart racing, but it was just the reminder about Dad's chemo. He had a treatment today. What happened if he didn't get it? He had medications to take, too. Did he have enough? Would the Pretty Boys let him take them? If they wanted him alive, they'd have to.

Dad had never been a quitter, but a year was a long time to fight dying, especially when it was inevitable.

The waitress returned with breakfast and set the plates down. Libby opened her eyes with a small shake of her head and grabbed the salt. I poured syrup over my short stack and sighed.

"It'll be okay," she said.

"Sure, now that I've got military protection."

"You saw the photo."

"You were a Marine."

She nodded, grabbing a bite of her eggs and chewing slowly. "Family tradition. Did my three years, got out."

"Didn't like it?"

Her shoulders tensed. "Some of it. Not all of it." She gestured at the bagel on my plate. "You eating that?"

I slid the plate over to her. She spent too much time spreading the cream cheese and not looking at me. I could take a hint, and I owed her the discretion.

I nibbled on my pancakes. Not enough butter, but it wasn't worth asking for more. I barely tasted it anyway. I set my fork down and sighed. "This sucks."

"Told you to get the eggs."

"That's not what I meant."

"I know. We'll figure something out."

"How?"

She opened her mouth, then closed it and shrugged. "I've no idea."

"We could set a trap." It was crazy, but a thrilling thought all the same. Turn the tables on *them.* "They want me, so we set up an ambush and use me as bait."

"You've lost your mind."

"Have you got any better ideas?"

"*Not* being the bait?"

"Might need to work on the specifics on that one."

She huffed, but didn't suggest any safer options. "Fine, I'm not saying it's a good idea or that we should do it, but how would your trap work?"

"We'd, uh, build something Pretty Boy proof and lure them into it."

Libby rolled her eyes and threw some cash down on the table. "Might need to work on the specifics on that one."

"What if I swallow a tracker and let them kidnap me?"

"I think we'd better keep thinking." She slid out of the booth. "Be right back," she said, heading for the restroom.

I grabbed my wallet and paused, fingers hovering over a ten. My Grace Harper credit card was right there, snug in its pocket. I've always assumed they could only track us by name, since leaving town and changing our IDs shook them off our trail, but I've never put it to the test before. One tiny charge could bring a Pretty Boy right to us, and through him, we could find Dad.

How? Think about how stupid this sounds.

I didn't have any more time to think. It wasn't much, but what evidence we'd found strongly suggested that Dad was in Pretty Boy custody, probably without his meds. He was sick, and I'd be damned if I'd let him die surrounded by monsters.

But he is *dying, and he told you to run...*

I winced. The cold, calculating part of me he'd trained to be rational heard the truth in it. A brain tumor was killing him already, so why was I risking my life to get him back? We'd have mere months, maybe, and it would be just as painful to watch him wither away and die. He wouldn't want me to risk myself for that. He'd certainly not want me to risk my life on the chance that he was still alive.

And all my instincts said he *was* alive.

He's my father. My family.

I had my silver knuckledusters, and we had the zappers and all the weapons. Libby even had a pair of handcuffs. I bet the first place they'd look would be Dad's apartment, and we'd have time to get ready for them. No way would they find us before tomorrow.

The waitress appeared. "All set?"

I threw down the card. "Absolutely."

Chapter Eight

Halfway back to Dad's place, I got the shakes.

I was an idiot. A sleep-deprived, impulsively reckless idiot. What was I *thinking*? Even with days to prepare, we weren't ready for an up close and personal Pretty Boy encounter.

"If I tell you something," I said, "will you promise not to be mad?"

Libby glanced sideways at me. "That question alone has me on edge. What did you do?"

"Paid for breakfast with my credit card."

Silence for a heartbeat, though she gripped the wheel so tight the veins in her hands stood out. "Why?"

"Moment of weakness."

She took a slow breath. "That was..."

"Moronic. Idiotic. Ridiculously stupid."

"Yet you did it anyway."

I nodded. I wouldn't have blamed her if she'd thrown me out of the car right then and gone home.

"How soon until they find us?" she asked instead.

"I don't know."

"Dammit, Grace!" She slammed her palm against the wheel. "You're smarter than this."

"I just..." had no good excuse.

"Well, we can't stay at your dad's apartment anymore."

"But it's the perfect spot for a trap."

An angry string of Spanish poured from Libby and she pulled over into the closest parking lot. "You want to launch an attack against an enemy you don't know the full capabilities of."

"I want to catch one of those things and force him to tell me where my father is."

"How?"

I hesitated. "Um, what if we collect some holy water and a few stakes, gather as much silver as we can buy. We hit a few pawn shops and I bet we can buy enough silver necklaces to make a net."

"So your plan is to rely on every vampire cliché in the book and hope one of them actually works?"

"Silver *does* work."

She rubbed her eyes and groaned. "Grace—"

"What stupid thing would you have done to save *your* father?"

"He was killed by an IED some asshole buried in the road," she yelled. "I could have been sitting next to him and it wouldn't have made a damn bit of difference."

I flinched. "I'm sorry."

"You should be."

We sat there without looking at each other. I hadn't had enough friends to know how to apologize to one.

"Maybe this wasn't such a good idea," I muttered.

She scoffed. "You think?"

"Let's just go."

"Fine."

NEITHER OF US said a word the rest of the drive. We climbed the stairs in silence and walked down the hall just as quietly. I'd blown it. I had lost not only my friend, but the best backup I'd ever get. She'd probably even take back the backpack of goodies Roberto had given us.

The worst part? I couldn't even be mad. I deserved it.

I opened the door and pushed inside. Someone spun around and gasped.

My heart stopped for a beat, but whoever this was, it wasn't a Pretty Boy. Too small, too nervous, too sneaky. All the Pretty Boys I'd seen were tall, dark, and dangerous.

"Down!" Libby shoved me aside and drew Lola. Metal cocked. "Show me your hands!"

Skinny arms flew straight up. "Don't shoot me," said a Latino boy about sixteen or so. Scruffy enough not to be noticeable, but not so much he gave off homeless vibes. I knew the "don't notice me" look well.

"Don't give me a reason to," Libby said as I put on my dusters. He might not be a Pretty Boy, but no way was he some random burglar. "You have a name?"

"Eddie."

"We're off to a good start. Sit." She indicated the couch. "Keep your hands up."

He sat. She moved and faced him, keeping Lola out.

"What are you doing in here?"

He licked his lips. "I wanted a place to crash is all. Storm's coming."

"On a Sunday morning? Try again, Eddie."

"It's true! I saw the bald dude who lives here leave. Figured it was empty for a few days, you know?"

I stepped forward, my heart pounding. "When did he leave?"

"Last night."

"Time?"

He shrugged. "Dunno. After dark."

"Was he alone?"

"No, he had some buds with him. Two big guys." His gaze slid down to my dusters. His eyes widened and he jerked away.

"You don't like my jewelry?" I held the dusters under his nose.

"They silver?"

"Why would you ask that?"

He licked his lips. Swallowed. Stalled. "Cause they're shiny."

Libby raised her eyebrows at me and I nodded. Oh yeah, he knew something. I ran a finger along the edge of the dusters as if I threatened teenagers all the time.

"Why were you watching the bald dude?"

He kept stalling, trying to fidget without moving enough to piss Libby off. "I dunno."

"Yes you do, Eddie. Did someone ask you to watch him?" Libby had said earlier that Dad had opened the door, and he wouldn't have done that unless he'd thought it was safe. A scrawny kid standing in the hall looked safe. "Did you help them?"

"What? Nah, man, I happened to be in the area, it's no—"

"I'm gonna shoot him," Libby said. She sounded bored.

Eddie's hands rose even higher. "Wait, wait! Zack. It was Zack."

My ears perked up. We'd never learned any of the Pretty Boys' names before.

"Zack have a last name?" Libby asked.

"Not that he told me."

I sat on the coffee table in front of him, but not so close he could grab me if he lunged. "Did Zack take him?"

His eyes widened. "The bald dude? No way. He's not like that."

Not evil? Or not a Pretty Boy? "But he had you watching him?"

"No law against that."

Probably several, but not the point. "Why did Zack ask you to watch the bald dude?"

"He pays me to check on some people sometimes, give him a heads up if they act all weird. Dude acted weird."

"Did you see where he went?"

"No."

"Did you see the car he and his buds got into?"

"Was a white van."

"Did he go willingly?"

"No." He glanced at my dusters again. "You ask a lotta questions."

I had the feeling he wanted to ask me a few himself. "You should ask more before you start working for someone."

He snorted and tossed his head. "He's aiight."

Like hell he was. Pretty Boys were dangerous and this poor kid had no idea what he'd gotten involved with. I tightened my grip on my dusters. Or maybe he did know.

"We can help you get away from him," I said.

"If I wanted that, I just walk off."

"Like he'd let you? He's dangerous."

Eddie scoffed. "I've seen 'em worse. Zack's a good guy."

Not if he was a Pretty Boy. Except, I'd met one who was a good guy. My helpful hottie. "What does Zack look like?"

"Like the guy from the food shows who does the road trips. Crazy white hair."

Not the man who'd saved me. I'd never seen a Pretty Boy with that description. Hard to imagine one bleaching his hair, but everything about the Pretty Boys was crazy. "White guy?"

"Nah, man, brown dude, but he's not from around here, ya know what I mean."

At least that fit the Pretty Boys. "What if I wanted to meet Zack?"

"Not gonna happen, *chica*."

"Why not? He talks to you."

"I'm special." He looked at me, something in his eyes that felt a lot older than sixteen. My guess was his life hadn't been any easier than mine, though I didn't think it was for the same reasons. But maybe they were similar. Maybe he had his own dusky hottie watching over him.

I nodded slowly. "So am I, and I need some answers or both me and the bald dude are dead."

Eddie's gaze darted everywhere but at me, then finally stopped. "Give me your number and I'll ask him, but don't get your hopes up, aiight?"

"You have Zack's number? I'll call him myself."

"I don't have a phone."

Libby huffed. "Everybody has a phone."

"Not me. Those things give off radiation that rot your brain, you know?"

She gestured the gun at him. "Stand up." Then to me, "Search him."

I did, patting him down and trying not to feel weird about practically feeling up a teen-aged boy. If he stashed his phone in or near his undies, I'd never find it.

"Nothing."

"Told you." He huffed. "You guys cops?"

"Do we look like cops?"

He shrugged. "You gonna call the cops?"

"Not if you give me the names and addresses of the other people Zack has you checking up on," I said. One of them might know more about this Zack.

"He won't like that," Eddie grumbled.

"I don't care."

Eddie grudgingly recited the names and addresses. "What are you gonna do with me?"

Unless we tied him up in the closet, we couldn't exactly hold him. Even I recognized kidnapping a minor was a no-no, though the thought had lingered longer than it should have. Eddie could lead us to the Pretty Boys. He knew one, worked for him even. If we kept him here, Zack might get worried and come looking for him. *Are you honestly considering using this kid as bait?*

"Ask Zack to call me," I said, tearing off a corner of a takeout menu. I wrote down my number and handed it to Eddie.

"Can I go now?"

"Go."

Libby stepped back, but the gun never wavered. Eddie rose slowly, hands still out, and backed toward the door. He gave me one last glance, his mouth open as if he was about to speak, then shook his head and darted into the hall.

"He could have led us right to them," I said.

"He still might. He'll tell this Zack guy you want to talk."

"And if he doesn't call?"

"We'll find another way."

I blew out a frustrated breath. It didn't matter whose side Zack might be on—Dad's apartment was no longer safe.

WE FOUND A nearby hotel that took cash and asked no questions, and must have been decorated by the same people who'd designed my apartment in Lauderdale. I'd recognize those ugly drapes anywhere.

"Could Zack be the one who saved you when you were a kid?" Libby asked. She tossed her duffel on the foot of the bed closest to the door.

"Description didn't fit."

"How many Pretty Boys *are* there? Are we talking a few evil SOBs or a whole murder of them?"

"Murder?"

"Like crows." She shrugged. "Flock? Herd? What do you call a group of vampires?"

"Terrifying."

She snapped a finger and pointed at me. "That's it. A terror of vampires."

"Delightful." I rubbed my eyes, dry as grit from lack of sleep. "Okay, so we need a timeline. Dad called me last night—" I checked the log on my phone "—at six-forty-three. Eddie said it was dark when he saw him being kidnapped. It gets dark here around what? Seven? Eight?"

"Full dark, by eight probably."

"Unless Eddie was out there all night, odds are Dad was grabbed between eight and midnight."

"By two Pretty Boys in a white van." She made a face. "That sounds mundane. Any weird freak could use a van. I'd expect something more exotic from a terror of vampires."

"You sound crazier than me."

Libby shrugged. "It's the sleep deprivation. We've been awake almost thirty hours. I say we grab two hours of rack time and see if Zack calls. If not, we track down that van, or the people on Eddie's list."

"Rack time?"

"Sleep."

I hated losing the time, but I was so tired I could barely think. I'd be no good to Dad if I missed the very clue that would lead me to him. "I'll set a wake-up call."

Zack didn't call, but I felt worlds better after a nap and a shower. We had no way to chase down the white van, so we turned to the only lead we had—Eddie's list. Maybe someone on it could point us in the right direction.

Maybe this was how my name got on Cavanaugh's list. One of the Pretty Boys gave it to a human minion to keep track of people they wanted to eat, kidnap, or protect. Or one gave it to another Pretty Boy so he'd know who to go after. I had clearly been on the kill or kidnap list, not the watch and wait list.

"We should reconsider calling the police," Libby said. "They can't do anything about the Pretty Boys, but they could put out an alert for a missing person."

I sighed. "We can't. They'll do a background check and discover Grace and Anthony Harper didn't exist prior to five years ago. We've been *running*, Libby. We had to break a few laws to stay alive, and the cops won't care why we did it."

She didn't say anything for a minute, just stared at the floor. "I didn't realize it was that bad. I'm sorry, Grace."

If Eddie's names didn't pan out, I might never know what happened to my father. What they wanted us for was a mystery. How either of us was connected to the people on Cavanaugh's list was also a mystery.

"Cavanaugh," I said, jerking straight.

"Who?"

"The guy from the hospital. He had a list of names, too." I grabbed my phone—the Harper one, not the burner—and told her about Cavanaugh's list of dead and missing people.

She frowned at me. "You have to stop keeping things from me."

"Sorry, I didn't think about it til just now. Eddie had a list with Dad's name on it. Cavanaugh had one with mine, my mother's and a recently missing woman's. It's too much of a coincidence not to be connected, and Cavanaugh might have better leads. He found *me*, so he's got skills." I hit Cavanaugh's number.

"Hello?" he answered after the second ring.

"I'm sorry to bother you, but it's Grace Harper. I have questions about that list of yours."

"Ms. Harper? Are you all right?" he asked, rushing the words out. "You weren't at the hospital or your apartment. I was worried."

He went to my apartment? The hairs on the back of my neck twitched, but he was probably only doing his job. "I'm fine. Your missing woman. Do you think she's been kidnapped and is being held somewhere, or was she killed?"

"What? Why are you—no, wait, tell me where you are first. You're in a *lot* of danger."

"Kidnapped or killed? I need to know."

Something rustled on the other end of the line. "Looks like a kidnapping. There were no signs of struggle or violence. She simply vanished."

"But not the old cases?"

"The old—? The names on the list? No, the older ones are all dead as far as I could tell."

"How far back?"

"Six years is the oldest I think. Ms. Harper, what aren't you telling me?"

Six years. For some reason, the Pretty Boys had changed tactics within the last five or six years. "So you believe she's still alive?"

"That's my hope. You *need* to tell me where you are."

"Do you have any idea where she's being held?"

He said nothing for a few seconds. "None. The only clue I've found so far is a list with your name on it. There's compelling evidence that someone is stalking you. Let me help you."

He sounded so sincere, but clueless. He was unprepared for what took Anita Rosenberg.

"Where did you find the list?"

Silence for several heartbeats, then a heavy sigh. "A student at Florida State was mugged outside her apartment. She's been in a coma the last two months. The list was found at the scene. Her name was on it, along with yours and Anita Rosenberg's. A contact of mine at the police department slipped me the list when he heard I was looking for her."

"Where did Rosenberg disappear?"

"She was on vacation in New Mexico."

Close enough to Vegas to possibly connect with Dad. "Did she live in Florida as well?"

"Yes, Jacksonville." Another connection, though a loose one.

"Did everyone on that list live in Florida at the time of their disappearance?"

Cavanaugh groaned. "I'm not saying anything until you tell me what you've found."

It didn't matter. I could find that out on my own. Safe bet said they were, though. Not that it helped any. So we were all from Florida, so what? Dad had lived there at that time, too, and he wasn't on the damn list, he was on Eddie's.

"Ms. Harper?"

To get more, I'd have to share, and I'd broken too many of Dad's rules already. Besides, it didn't sound like Cavanaugh knew that much anyway. The Florida list was twenty years old, but the New Mexico angle was newer, and at least put it in Dad's neck of the woods. Had the Pretty Boys traded lists? Did they have hunting grounds or territories?

"Thank you for the info, Mr. Cavanaugh. I appreciate your help, but for your own safety, you might want to drop this case." I hung up the phone and updated Libby.

"Not enough yet to go on," she said, "but anyone on Eddie's list who has been running like you and your father might know something."

I nodded. "If we can figure out why they want us, maybe we can figure out where they took him."

Chapter Nine

Three names besides Dad's graced Eddie's list—one man and two women, all in the Vegas area. If Eddie was covering all four of them, he'd done a lot of commuting between Boulder City and the Strip.

Address number one was a run-down house near Winchester, south of Vegas and not far from the community college. Caleb Marlowe held no job I could find online, but there had been several articles about his arrests. B&Es, a few assaults, a person of interest in a shooting—just about what you'd expect to find for a garden-variety criminal. His mug shot looked like a side of beef with bushy blond hair and very nasty eyes.

I parked in the strip mall lot across the street.

"You might want to keep the weapons handy," said Libby, scanning the neighborhood and the bar behind us. "I'd say keep the engine running, but that might bring more attention than we want."

Still might be worth the risk. The area had "we rent to criminals" written all over it.

I watched the house through a pair of exceptional binoculars. Roberto had the best toys. Some of the houses had yards, but Marlowe's was just dirt, some reedy weeds, and an assortment of cars in progressive stages of repair.

I tensed every time a car rolled past or someone exited a house. If I didn't know better, I'd think the street was a set for some gritty cable channel crime drama.

"Have you ever been attacked in the daylight?" Libby asked. Took me a second to figure out she was back on her Pretty Boy research. I could hardly blame her.

"Not in full sun." Despite all the stories I'd read and seen growing up, I *had* encountered them in the daylight—but only on cloudy days, at twilight, or in the early morning. "They seem to do okay as long as it isn't shining on them."

"Can we assume the sun hurts them?"

"Maybe."

She nodded slowly.

At first, it had been a little annoying. She'd dredged up every vampire cliché, movie trait, and TV trope she could think of to compare against my experiences. There was a *lot* of vampire lore in the world, and some of it *had* gotten it right, or close enough.

Sunlight, for example. They didn't like it, but they didn't burst into flames. Silver also put the hurt on them. The turning to dust thing when they got staked was pretty close to reality, though wooden stakes didn't appear to be required. Not appearing in mirrors was also close enough to fit the myths. They were blood drinkers, no question. They had super speed and strength. They absolutely had that whole "sexy beyond compare" thing going for them.

I'd never seen them turn into bats or rats, and I doubted they slept in coffins—if they even slept at all. No fangs. Garlic was an unknown, as was holy water.

"I wonder how long they've been around?" Libby said. "*Dracula* was written in the late 1800s. And Vlad the Impaler was what, fifteenth century?"

"Sounds about right."

She pulled off her jacket and tossed it into the back seat. "They must be older than that, though."

"Depends on which legend you prefer. The stories go back about four thousand years. Ancient Greek tablets, Sumerian poems, memos from the Inquisition."

Libby whistled. "You've done your homework."

"I was motivated." I shrugged. "None of it helped."

Once upon a time, I'd hoped to find something in the books and legends that would save us. A special trick or long-lost secret that would render us invisible to the Pretty Boys, or a weapon to make us invulnerable. Later, I'd just wanted to find some way to defend ourselves when they got too close.

I knew a lot, but little of it was useful.

And now I knew they used innocent kids to help them hunt.

The Pretty Boys rarely attacked in public, so clearly, they didn't want anyone to know about them. They'd kept chasing Dad and me, so they didn't hunt randomly and chose their victims for a reason. Me being on Cavanaugh's list twice confirmed that. No matter what I'd called myself, I still matched whatever their hunting criteria was.

They kept lists, so they had to have records somewhere. If they kept records, they had something that needed recording, and everyone on the lists most likely had whatever that something was in common.

What did my family have in common with Caleb Marlowe? Or Anita Rosenberg? Or any of the other people on either list? The only thing we shared was a stalker.

Libby nudged me and pointed at the trash can by the street. "That's a lot of beer cans. Caleb would be a terrible food source. He's practically pickled."

"Could we not talk about *that* aspect of the Pretty Boys, please?"

"Sorry, it's hard not to think about it." She hesitated, shooting me a sidelong glance.

"What?" I asked.

"I'm not sure how to discuss this without sounding insensitive."

"Dad and I found that the more ridiculous it sounded, the easier it was to talk about it."

"Fair enough. They might be stocking the pantry."

She couldn't mean..."The names are a shopping list?"

"A Pretty Boy's gotta eat. Can't be easy finding food nowadays, not with security cameras all over and people with cell phones recording everything. Could be why they're stalking thugs and...people with no family."

I blanched. "That's a horrifying thought."

"If it's true, then your dad's probably alive, being held somewhere to um..."

"Tap like a keg when they get thirsty?"

"Not the image I was going for, but yes. It takes six to twelve weeks for hemoglobin levels to replenish. Depending on what they need in the blood to survive, that's up to three months before they can tap that person again."

Morbid, but true, and a best-case scenario. "If it's plasma, that's only forty-eight hours."

"Then they'd need fewer people for the pantry."

I groaned, really not wanting to do the math on how many people a single Pretty Boy would need to feed himself. "Still doesn't explain why they've switched to kidnapping specific people."

"Blood and vampires go together, so it's a reasonable guess it's about the blood. Think it's a taste preference? They all have the same blood type or something?"

"Millions of people have the same blood type. What the Pretty Boys are doing is deliberate and well-researched. They found Dad and me even though we'd changed our names several times, and I have no idea how."

She reached into the cooler behind her seat and opened a bottle of water, passed it to me, then dug out one for herself. "Then it's your blood specifically."

"Us and the people on those lists."

Remembered words clicked in my mind. "When Cavanaugh questioned me at the hospital, he asked if I'd donated blood recently."

"Had you?"

I shook my head. "But Dad did all the time. They took it from him for testing." My heart raced. "If Cavanaugh was asking about it, he must have seen a pattern. I bet more than one person on that list had given blood before they disappeared."

"Vampires and blood banks also go together."

"There must be dozens in Vegas alone." Not as bad as a needle in a haystack, more like a needle in a ball pit, but it would take time we didn't have.

Libby wiggled her fingers. "Hold that thought—we've got movement."

I lifted the binoculars. Marlowe had left the house and was walking to a red pickup truck. His plaid shirt strained at the buttons and fit close around his sizable biceps. The guy moved like a boulder rolling downhill.

"Even if I were a Pretty Boy, I wouldn't want to mess with him."

Libby frowned and moved a hand to her stun gun. "Talk to him or try the next name?"

"I seriously doubt he's going to talk to us, though he might murder us and bury our bodies in the back yard. After he's gone, we'll search the place. If he donated blood, he might have a receipt or a sticker in the trash that says where."

"Did he *look* like the kind of person who would donate blood?"

"No. I won't think less of you if you wait in the car."

"Now that's just insulting." But she didn't look any happier about the idea. "People will notice us kicking in the door."

I rolled up my pants leg and pulled a thin, nylon case out of my sock. "Do you always go right to violence?" I waved the case. "I have lock picks."

"You have *lock picks?*"

"A gift from Dad when I was twelve. I had a bag of locks to practice on in the car during long trips."

"And here I'd thought *I* had an unconventional upbringing."

"Pull into his drive. It'll look less suspicious than if we walk over."

She huffed as she turned on the car. "It'll also keep the car close if we have to run for our lives when the neighbors call the cops."

"I doubt they have a neighborhood watch."

"I bet they're people who shoot first and refuse to answer questions later."

We drove across the street and pulled in where the pickup had been. Libby tucked the stun gun into its holster and I double-checked that both sets of my dusters were on me—the silver ones in case we ran into Pretty Boys, the zappers if something human jumped us. I wasn't sure if Libby had Lola on her or not, but odds were good she wouldn't leave it behind.

It wasn't far from the car to Marlowe's door. We passed several beer bottles that had presumably fallen out of the trash, and an empty bottle of Jack. Libby blocked the view while I knelt and worked on the lock.

"Are you any good at—"

I opened the door. "Yes. We made *a lot* of long car trips."

"Color me impressed."

I paused, listening. No beeps warned of an alarm, no scratch of canine toenails suggested a guard dog. Just silence. "Looks clear."

We slipped inside and closed the door behind us. Libby locked it. "Feels weird doing this without an M16."

"At least no one is shooting at us."

"Yet. Try not to touch anything."

Marlowe spent just as much time on housekeeping inside as he had outside. Dishes in the sink, mail piled on the table, giant-sized jeans and T-shirts hanging over the backs of three chairs. An oh-so-pleasant scent of *eau de* body odor mixed with pine.

No stickers or Band-Aids in the kitchen or living room bins. I stopped outside the bathroom. Several handfuls of dried, bloody gauze and tape filled the upper half of the trash bin. More tissues and an empty aspirin bottle sat on top. "This could be something." Not something I wanted to touch, but something.

Libby came in and leaned over my shoulder. "I'd hate to see the other guy."

"Remind me to buy latex gloves on the way home," I said, picking up an empty toilet paper roll with two fingers. I pushed it around the gauze and other garbage, thankfully mostly paper products. A familiar strip caught my eye, but there was no way to pick up the ER ID band without touching it. I gritted my teeth and gingerly lifted it from the trash. "Score."

"Marlowe visited the ER."

"No hospital listed though." I dropped it back and wiped my fingers on the back of my pants. "Probably local."

"Question is, was he injured enough to need blood?"

"And if so, did they test his?"

Libby stepped out of the doorway. "And the million-dollar question— who's checking the blood and what are they checking it for?"

There was no way to know. "It supports the 'finding the victims through their blood' theory. Maybe we'll narrow down the hospital at the next house."

"That would be Ivy Helgarson," Libby said. "Fingers crossed for the suburbs."

LIBBY GOT HER wish. Ivy Helgarson lived in the suburbs, in a tightly packed and carefully designed development in Summerlin. Cream-colored houses with terra-cotta tiled roofs lined the streets, the only differences between them the shapes and layouts of the homes.

Early afternoon on a Sunday, people were out and about and kids played in the yards and on the cul-de-sacs. Looked nice, if a bit cramped.

"I take it back," she said, frowning as we passed happy-looking families. "I don't want anyone here to be a potential Pretty Boy snack."

I pulled up outside a house for sale two doors down from the Helgarson's.

"This doesn't look like the neighborhood of people on the run," Libby said.

"Not all potential victims know they're in danger."

"True."

I dug out the binoculars again. Ivy's front door opened and a dark-haired boy about eight ran out. A woman followed, matching the photo of the Ivy Helgarson we'd found online. Short, easy-to-care-for brown hair, tan and athletic enough to suggest she played a sport or two. Just a normal, suburban mom dressed in blue slacks and a cute floral top trimmed in lace.

"There she is."

Ivy walked to the mailbox and pulled out yesterday's mail, idly sorting through it. The boy leaned against the car door, peeling a sticker on and off his chest and sticking it to random parts of his body. Cute kid.

"I want to talk to her," I said.

"You can't walk up to a total stranger and ask questions."

"You can if you do it right." I jumped out of the car and hurried over.

Ivy looked up from her mail as I approached, curious, but not scared. I smiled and she smiled back. This was not a woman who feared for her safety, or had ever had any reason to be wary of strangers.

"Hi," I called. "I'm sorry to bother you, but my husband and I are thinking about buying the house across the street, and I was curious about the neighborhood. Can I ask you a few questions?"

"The Glick place? Sure."

"You like it here?" I glanced around. Basic middle-class security, so nothing that would keep out a Pretty Boy. "It seems nice."

"Oh, we love it. There's a real sense of community and we all look out for one another."

"How long have you lived here?"

"About nine years. We moved in when I was pregnant with Jared." She gestured at the boy and I spotted a small, yellow bruise in the crook of her arm. The boy's sticker was red with "I donated!" on it. Bingo. "Do you have any children?" Ivy asked.

"Not yet, but fingers crossed." I held them up and grinned. She chuckled, and I joined her. "Any safety issues? My last place had a problem with a stalker lurking around outside." I glanced around and leaned a little closer. "You ever see anyone watching the houses?"

"Well, no. It's pretty safe here."

"That's good to know. Do you work at home?"

Her smile grew wary. "I'm sorry," she said, "but I need to get going. I've a lot to do today and my husband is waiting inside for me." She laughed nervously. "I'm surprised he hasn't come out looking for me already."

Damn, sloppy. "No problem at all, thanks so much for the information. I can't wait to show Robert the house."

She ushered Jared inside, casting glances over her shoulder the entire time. I walked back to the car, looking around as if I was getting a feel for the neighborhood like a normal potential buyer.

"Pushed it too far?" Libby said. "She looked a little freaked out there at the end."

"A little, but she's normal. Lived here for years and I'd guess nothing's tried to kidnap or kill her. She gave blood recently, and not more than a week ago from the look of the bruise on her arm. The kid was also playing with what looked like a sticker from the blood bank, though I didn't get a close look."

Libby raised her eyebrows. "That's confirmation—there is a blood donation-victim connection."

"I couldn't figure out a graceful way to ask about the bruise in time though."

"Should we warn the Helgarson family they're in danger?"

"I would, but they won't believe us. Hopefully I creeped her out enough to put her on guard for a while."

Of course, if the Pretty Boys *were* finding their victims through blood donors, then Ivy was my best lead to finding the ones who'd taken Dad. If we knew where she'd donated blood, we might be able to find whoever had tipped off the Pretty Boys.

And dumb me had spooked her, so she'd never tell me where she'd given blood. We'd have to figure that out another way.

The final address on Eddie's list was in Vegas proper, one half of a duplex with a Catholic church practically in the back yard. An interesting place to hole up if you were being hunted by the undead.

"Does Kurt Smith sound especially Catholic to you?" I asked Libby.

"Sounds more like an alias."

To me, too. "I have a good feeling about Kurt."

I could have chosen this apartment. Good exits, plenty of routes to the highway, clear fields of view. Sticking close to a church was genius.

Libby checked the place out through the binoculars. "Taking the sneaky route or the direct approach?"

"Not sure. If he sees us lurking it might spook him, but he might not be too keen on talking, either."

"Undo a few buttons. He'll answer the door."

I did as instructed, tucked my dusters into their leather sheath in the small of my back, and climbed out of the car. "Stay put and keep your eyes out for anything weird."

"I'll honk if things go sideways." She slid over into the driver's seat.

I knocked on Kurt's door and stood as non-threateningly as possible. Faint sounds emanated from behind the door—someone moving carefully and trying not to be heard. If I hadn't been listening for exactly that, I'd have missed it.

The door opened a crack and Kurt peeked out from behind the chain, bright, wary eyes in a dark face. A giant crucifix around his neck glinted at me from the dim light.

Oh yeah, I had the right guy.

"What?"

Bullshitting him would only get the door slammed in my face. Of course, being honest would, too. I wouldn't talk to *me* in this situation if I were him, but he was a few steps ahead of me in the protection department. Staying alive meant staying informed.

"I'm not trying to scare you, and I know this is going to sound weird, but I'm pretty sure we're both being watched by the same people."

His eye twitched just a little. "What the hell are you talking about?"

"Weird guys who stop time, move super fast, and are a little obsessed with blood. Ring any bells?"

He stared long after I would have slammed the door. A normal person would have called the cops by now.

"Did you give blood recently?" I asked.

The door banged shut. Strike one for the direct and honest approach.

I knocked on the door again. "Kurt, they took my father. Anything you can tell me might help me get him back. Please."

No sounds at all from inside.

"I need your help."

"Get out of here you crazy bitch!" he yelled through the door. "I can't help you."

"Please, I—"

"Go or I'll shoot you where you stand!"

"Sorry, I'm going." I backed away, hands out so he could see them, all the way to the car. Libby slid back into the passenger seat and I got in.

"How's Kurt?"

"High strung."

"I take it he wasn't forthcoming in the details department?"

I shook my head. "He knows *something* though." Aside from Eddie, I'd never met anyone besides Dad and me who'd encountered a Pretty Boy before. "There must be a way to convince him to talk to me."

"Um, Grace?" Libby nudged me and tipped her head at Kurt's place. "We've got a runner."

Kurt was hurrying down his front walk, a worn backpack slung over his shoulder and a duffel in one hand. His stance was one I knew well—forced casualness, yet the shoulders rounded just a little with the need to hide without drawing attention. He'd been running a long time, I'd say.

"Oh no you don't, Kurt." I started the car. "You're not getting away."

Kurt's pace picked up.

"Crap, he's made us. Do I block him in?"

"Not unless you want to get shot."

Kurt dived into his car and peeled out, tires smoking as he raced away. I pulled after him anyway, but he knew the streets and left us behind after only three turns.

"Dammit." I smacked the steering wheel.

"It's not your fault."

"Yes, it is."

I'd been followed my whole life, but being on the other side was a lot harder than expected.

"Maybe he'll come back," Libby said.

"He won't. He's gone for good." That didn't mean the trail was cold. I turned the car around. "Let's search Kurt's place and see if we get lucky."

"Another break in?" Libby frowned and tucked her hair behind an ear. "We're on a regular crime spree."

"Technically, it's trespassing since he likely just abandoned the place."

"Remind me to get you a legal dictionary for Christmas."

"Chanukah, my Mom was Jewish. Make it pocket-sized, please."

She chuckled, but her apprehension hadn't gone away. I passed Kurt's place and took a right at the corner.

"Change your mind?" she asked.

"Taking a loop around the block in case nosy neighbors are watching after his hasty exit."

She gave me a look. "You have an odd set of skills."

"A gal picks up what she needs to get by."

I gave the neighbors another loop to get bored, then pulled into Kurt's driveway. We grabbed our gear and exited the car, strolling up the walk like two friends visiting. Libby once again kept me covered while I checked the door.

"It's open."

We walked inside, cautious, but odds were the place was empty. As I'd thought, Kurt had no intention of ever coming back here. Everything he knew ran with him.

"Not much here," Libby said, closing the door behind us.

"Probably came with the apartment."

Worn carpet that had once been brown, a tan and green striped couch with a green chair, builder-beige paint on the wall. Not a single photo or personal item in sight.

"Try the drawers. I'll check the bedroom," I said, following the only hallway.

"Roger that."

A cheap nightstand and a bed with no headboard greeted me in the back. The sheets looked stolen from a local motel, but everything was clean.

I searched the drawers in both the nightstand and the chipped dresser, but found nothing inside but thrift-store quality clothes and three copies of *Saucy Babe* magazine. I elected *not* to touch them or the bottle of lube beside them.

The bathroom held even less. Aside from a few curls of hair and some fuzz on the soap, it contained nothing to suggest anyone lived there.

I walked back into the living room. "Any luck?"

Libby shook her head. "I've seen more personable hotel rooms."

I turned away, throat tight. "Check the kitchen yet?"

"Nothing there but four boxes of pasta. You think Kurt lives like this all the time?"

"Yes." No reason to stock a fridge when you might have to leave if a stranger bangs on your door and starts asking questions.

"Must be lonely."

"It is."

She sucked in a breath. "Shit, Grace, I'm sorry. I didn't mean—"

"There's nothing here that connects to my dad." Only the same lack of everything found at my apartment. At least I had those throw pillows. That was something, right?

She paused, her expression dangerously close to pity, then glanced away. "Would he have had any hidden compartments or secret stashes?"

"We can check, but it's safer to hide gear outside where you can get to it if your place is compromised."

I checked the floorboards, closets, searched for false bottoms in drawers and loose trim along the floors. Pointless, all of it. The only clues were halfway to who-knew-where by now.

"Grace!" Libby whisper-yelled from the other room. She sounded scared.

I let the mattress fall and hurried into the living room, the hairs along my arms standing at attention.

Libby stood by the front window, off to the side and peeking out between a sliver of curtain and the wall.

"What is it?"

"Company."

Chapter Ten

"Eddie is outside." Libby glanced at me. "Think he's following us or doing his job by watching Kurt?"

"A little of both?" I nudged her aside and took a peek. Eddie wasn't standing out in the open, but he wasn't trying hard to keep out of sight, either. Just sitting there with his back against a parked car at the curb, under a giant tree. No hat either, or any attempt to disguise his identity.

"He doesn't act like he cares if we see him. He might not be worried about Kurt spotting him."

"*Would* he spot him?"

"In a heartbeat."

"Would that have made him run?"

"In a heartbeat." I groaned. "He's got to be here for us."

"Maybe he has news from the mysterious Zack."

Hope fluttered in my chest, but this all felt wrong. "Then why didn't he call? You know he had a phone somewhere."

"He might not be on our side."

Eddie turned and leaned into the side window of the parked car. "Hang on. Someone's in that car." I pulled out the binoculars. I could see the driver, but the angle on the passenger was wrong to see more than a shirt. "Two men, driver has wild white hair."

"Zack?"

"Has to be. I can't see the other, but he's talking to Eddie now."

"Both Pretty Boys?"

The windows were heavily tinted, but the windshield gave a decent enough peek. Zack had dusky skin even with that white hair. The passenger leaned over and spoke to Zack, gesturing with a hand the same color. Every Pretty Boy I'd ever seen had that sexy Mediterranean tint.

"I'd say yes."

"Setup?"

"I don't know."

Libby stepped away from the window and scanned the apartment. "No back door in this place?"

"No, or Kurt would have used it." The only mistake he'd made, but it was hard to find apartments with back doors.

I'd trusted the kid and he'd brought the Pretty Boys right to us.

I put away the binoculars. "Let's test the size of those back windows."

WE LEFT OUR rental car in front of Kurt's duplex and grabbed a cab two streets over, directing it to a random block on the Strip. There'd been no sign of anyone following us from Kurt's.

Libby's stomach growled and we dodged into a nearby burger place to kill time until it was safe enough to go back for the rental car. Besides, food sounded good. We hadn't eaten since breakfast.

We ordered a pair of burgers, fries, and chocolate shakes, and then grabbed a table in the back, facing the doors. TVs showed various games and an assortment of news on screens lining the walls.

"Think Eddie's a ghoul?" Libby asked.

"A *what?*"

"Like Renfield. Minions of the Dark Lord. They do a Pretty Boy's bidding in exchange for special powers and the chance to become a Pretty Boy themselves one day."

"I had no idea you were such a Pretty Boy aficionado."

"I read *Dracula*. I know stuff."

I took a bite of my burger. Swiss cheese oozed out, and I swiped it with a finger. "Eddie didn't strike me as a Child of the Night looking for immortality."

"Could just be a job. They don't come easy these days. A guy's gotta take what he can get."

"Even if it's with a blood-sucking fiend?"

"Hey, they'll have a dental plan."

I chuckled, though none of this was funny. Two Pretty Boys with their own minion were following us now, and doing a damn fine job of it.

"What now?" Libby asked.

"If Zack's not talking, Ivy Helgarson's blood donation is our only lead," I said, wishing it wasn't. "After we get the rental car back, let's figure out a way to ask her where she gave blood that won't have her calling the cops."

Libby scoffed. "Good luck with that."

"No kidding. Backup plan, we watch her and see who *else* shows up to watch her, then follow *them*—hopefully back to where they're keeping Dad."

"I've *seen* you follow someone. If you want to tail this guy, we'll need something a little more reliable."

WE MADE ONE stop on the way to Ivy Helgarson's—the local Smart Buy to pick up a nifty little GPS spy tracker. Libby set it up without even looking at the directions.

"Cheating boyfriend?" I asked.

She laughed. "Brothers and I played a gag on our little brother last summer. We tracked him for two weeks and one of us showed up wherever he was like it was a huge coincidence. Sometimes we even figured out where he was going and got there ahead of him."

"Glad I'm an only child."

"It's linked, so walk away and let's test it." She tossed the little black rectangle to me and I caught it. Small, an inch-and-a-half long and about a half-inch wide.

I walked down the block until she waved her arm and gave me a thumbs up.

"It works," she said when I returned. "Five-day battery life, sends messages with locations to an app on my phone. If the target leaves the neighborhood, we'll know."

WE PARKED A few doors down and watched Ivy's house. It was the same as we'd left it earlier. Ivy's car sat in the driveway, no sign of kids playing or people putzing around in the yard. Everyone had gone inside, probably to get ready for dinner. We still hadn't come up with a plausible reason to ask her about the blood. Our best plan so far was to hope she set out trash we could search.

I pulled out the binoculars.

"See anyone suspicious?" Libby asked.

"Just us. No shadowy figures lurking in the bushes." I swept the area, the binoculars bringing everything close enough to touch. "FYI, I'm keeping these. Think Roberto will give me a discount?"

"He can be sweet talked."

I refocused on the house. "The mailbox is open. She was getting mail when I spoke to her. I'm sure she closed it."

"Mailboxes fall open sometimes."

"I suppose." I turned around and scanned the other side of the street. A man exited a house a few doors down, his face tight in a classic worried frown. He left one house and marched right up the drive of the next one and knocked on the door.

"That's odd."

"More open mailboxes?"

"No." The man spoke with whoever answered the door, then turned around and headed for the next house. "That man's going door to door questioning the neighbors."

"Pretty Boy?"

"No. Fortyish, looks like a banker." After each house, his frown deepened.

"It *is* Sunday. Maybe he's a door-to-door preacher."

"Still doesn't feel right."

Libby sighed and leaned toward me, peering over my shoulder. "Lost dog?"

"He *did* have a 'searching for something' vibe."

After three more houses, the man reached Ivy's drive. He shuffled up the walk, head low, unlocked the door and entered the house.

"It's Ivy's husband."

"Oh no."

I slid out of the car and Libby followed. "We need to talk to him."

"And say what?"

"Just play along."

We walked up the front walk and knocked on the door. The man answered immediately.

"Ivy?" he said breathlessly.

My heart broke for him. "Excuse me, Mr. Helgarson?"

He stepped back half a pace and looked at us as if unsure who or what we were. "Yes?"

"I'm sorry to bother you, but we were speaking with your wife earlier—"

"When? Was she acting strange to you?"

I paused. He was near panic, and my "we're looking to buy the house down the street" lie wasn't going to fly again. "Is your wife missing, Mr. Helgarson?"

He sagged against the doorframe. "She went to get Jared's backpack from the car and never came back."

"When was this?"

"Around three o'clock."

Not long after we'd been there. Damn. I should have warned her. We should have waited.

"Have you notified the police?" Libby said.

"They said sometimes people just leave and there's no law against it." He wiped his eyes. "She wouldn't *do* that. I asked the neighbors if they'd seen her, but no one has."

If a Pretty Boy took her, they wouldn't have.

"I'm sorry," he said, wary at last. "Who are you?"

Cavanaugh flashed through my mind. "We're private investigators on another missing persons case, and it looks like it's related to your wife's disappearance. May we speak inside?"

"Missing persons? Uh, of course, please come in."

He led us to a lovingly decorated living room of creams and teals. Most of the *tchotchkes* and pictures were bird related, with marshland landscapes in needlepoint on the throw pillows. No sign of little Jared.

"Is your son at home?"

"In his room." He sat down and ran a hand through his hair. "I don't want to worry him. You said someone else is missing?"

Libby and I sat as well. She pulled out her phone and sat poised to take notes.

"Yes," I said, "a man named Anthony Harper. Does the name sound familiar?"

"No."

"How about Anita Rosenberg?"

He shook his head.

"Do you know a boy named Eddie? Sixteenish, brown hair, Latino, sometimes hangs out with a man named Zack. Spiky white hair, olive skin?"

Ivy's husband shook his head harder. "I don't know any of them. Are they missing, too?"

"Your wife gave blood recently, is that correct?"

He nodded.

"Do you remember where?"

"Um, a bloodmobile came to her office I think. They were there Monday."

A bloodmobile sounded like a safe way for Pretty Boys to get blood samples. "Where does she work?"

"She's an accountant at Meier and Randall."

Libby broke in. "Do you have the address?"

He gave it to us and she jotted it down.

"What does this have to do with Ivy's disappearance?" he asked.

"Our client's father also gave blood the week he disappeared. We believe there's a connection. Was your wife acting unusual in any way? Afraid or concerned about anyone?"

"No, she was normal. All she did was go to the mailbox." His voice cracked.

I glanced around the room, but everything seemed in place. "Did you notice any signs of a struggle inside the house?"

"No."

"May we look around?"

He nodded, but made no move off the couch. I tipped my head at Libby and we rose as one, then headed for the front door.

"We know they have a van," I said. "Easy enough to drive up and yank her inside when she took out the mail."

Even if someone *had* been watching, to them, Ivy would have just vanished into thin air between blinks.

I started my investigation at the door. No scuff marks or scrapes on the walk, no broken plants along the drive. The open mailbox.

My foot slipped on some gravel by the mailbox. Just a few red stones and bits of red sand that didn't match the rest of the dirt or gravel in the yard. I kneeled and picked up a pebble. Not just red, but striped like the cliffs of the Grand Canyon and perfectly round.

"I've seen these rocks," I said, mind racing.

Libby kneeled as well. "Your dad's apartment."

"What are the odds of finding red pebbles at two Pretty Boy kidnapping sites?"

"Pretty high if they came from the Pretty Boys."

"Get me something to put these in, would you? If it matches the rocks at Dad's, we might have found our first tangible clue."

AFTER WE'D FINISHED at the Helgarsons', we went back to Dad's place. The sand and pebbles in the hall were still there, though they'd been knocked around and spread out along the floorboards. I picked up the pebbles while Libby brushed up the sand into her palm, and then we poured both into a baggie and sealed it. We did the same with the rocks inside the house.

I held up the three baggies side by side.

"They look identical." Same stripes, same deep red color that almost looked dyed, same perfect round shape. The sand around Vegas had an orange tint, but not like this. This was more canyon-colored, less desert dirt. Arizona or Utah maybe. Someplace with big, red rocks.

"We need a geologist," Libby said.

"UNLV probably has a geology department."

"Not one that's open on a Saturday. We might be able to persuade one to meet us, though. We'll say it's a geological emergency."

I sighed.

"Cheer up, Grace, we're getting closer. We have real evidence now."

"It might not lead anywhere."

"Or it could be one-of-a-kind graveyard dirt."

I doubted that, but red rocks narrowed it down to a few states at least. "We can hope."

We left and headed back to our hotel—though I hoped Libby remembered where it was. I couldn't have found it if my life depended on it.

"Red sand and bloodmobiles," I said as she pulled onto the 515 back to Boulder City. "Not much to go on."

"I'll call the accounting office Ivy works at in the morning and see who they used for their blood drive."

"Sounds good." But I had another, more mundane problem to deal with. "I'm supposed to be at work tomorrow."

Libby made a face. "Ouch. What are you going to do?"

"Mrs. Johnson knows Dad isn't well. I hate to use that as an excuse, but she'd buy it."

"It's a *little* true. You had to leave town unexpectedly because of your father's health. His life being in danger does affect his health."

"It does."

My phone rang as I pulled it out to call work—an unknown number. "Yes?"

"Nate Cavanaugh."

"Mr. Cavanaugh," I said, giving Libby a look. She mouthed *talk to him* as she changed lanes, zipping around a beat-up convertible. "What can I do for you?"

"Talking to me would be a terrific start." His voice had a teasing undertone, but it wasn't a joke. "I'm worried about you, Ms. Harper. You're in more danger than you realize and you seem determined to ignore it."

"I'm better off than most."

Libby rolled her eyes at me. "Let him help," she whispered.

I hesitated. Cavanaugh was pushing *awfully* hard to warn me—harder than I'd pushed to warn Ivy Helgarson. Maybe this was more than just a PI doing his job, and his blood-drive clue *had* already helped us. "Another woman is missing."

"Where?" he asked.

"Summerlin, outside Vegas. Ivy Helgarson. I think she's connected to your missing woman, and the Tallahassee girl in the coma."

"What are you doing in Nevada?"

"My father is also missing. I'm trying to find him."

Cavanaugh groaned and sputtered and made a lot of noises without swearing. I covered the phone again. "He sounds pissed."

"Can't blame him."

I returned to the call. "Since you're so concerned about my well being, maybe it's time you told me why."

"Your name is on a list of people who have been killed or kidnapped. I'd think that would make anyone nervous."

"Oh it does, but it doesn't explain why you, specifically, care."

Silence.

"Mr. Cavanaugh, if you know something that can help me find my father, tell me now. Otherwise, stop giving me cryptic warnings we both know I'm going to ignore."

"You don't understand who's pursuing you."

I paused again. Don't get involved, that's what Dad always said. Keep everyone at a distance. But trusting Libby had been the smartest move I'd made in years.

Could I trust Cavanaugh?

As the reckless said, go big or go home. Playing it safe had kept us safe, but it also kept us afraid, and that was no way to live. "I understand exactly what's after me. What I want to know is, do *you*?"

Chapter Eleven

Cavanaugh maintained his silence, but I swear I heard him squirming on the other end of the line. A good sign. A clueless man would have called me crazy by now. I watched the Nevada landscape swoosh by outside and waited.

"We should talk," he said softly.

"I'm listening."

"Not over the phone."

"Our swarthy buddies might be scary, but they're not the NSA."

"I'll call you when I get to Vegas."

"When you—" And then he was gone. "Sonuvabitch hung up on me!"

Libby huffed. "You were rude. Sounds like you rattled him."

"I did. He's flying to Vegas so we can talk face to face."

She chuckled wryly. "Good, then. He wouldn't come out here just to bullshit you."

"He would if he thinks I'm way too close and wants to mislead me."

"You have trust issues."

"I have vampires trying to eat me."

"Point taken." She took the offramp and we coasted to a stoplight. The neon lights of the city were just starting to flicker on. "A face-to-face isn't a bad idea. He obviously knows something."

"And he's being a dick about sharing." I dialed work without interruption this time.

"Maybe if you show him yours he'll show you his."

I scoffed. "What are the odds his is worth seeing?"

Libby managed to find a geologist willing to help us. We drove up to University of Nevada-Las Vegas first thing in the morning, right after Libby made her 8 a.m. check-in with Uncle Roberto. They kept the geologists in the Lily Fong Geoscience building, so we parked outside the boxy white structure and headed inside. Dr. Aidan Bloom was waiting for us when we arrived, focusing on what I assumed were students' papers.

I'd been expecting a gray-haired man with a jacket, but Dr. Bloom was a dark-skinned man is his mid-forties, with the trim yet muscular build of someone who spent a lot of time climbing around on rocks. I imagined he had more than a few students with major crushes on him.

"Thank for seeing us on such short notice," I said. I withdrew the baggies and handed them to him. "Any chance you could identify these?"

"Looks like sandstone." He pulled one of the red pebbles out and rolled it around in his palm. "Ah yes, I know these little guys. Perfectly round. And see this red color? It's found exclusively in Sedona. I go hiking there a few times a year. Color like this means it's part of the Schnebly Hill Formation and a member of the Supai Group."

"There's no way these could exist naturally in Boulder City or near Vegas?"

Dr. Bloom paused and looked at the stones again. "No. You won't find stones like this in Nevada. Look." He rose and walked over to a case filled with rocks in all shapes and colors. "This is a beauty I picked up a few weeks ago." He held the rock up against our pebble. It matched perfectly. "Gorgeous, aren't they?"

"Pretty. Where did you find yours?"

"Bell Rock." He ducked his head a little and gave us a sheepish grin. "I'm dating a woman who wanted to visit the vortexes."

"You lost me."

He laughed. "Vortexes. You know, those spots in the earth that spiral spiritual energy? Some people believe Sedona is a spiritual power center. The Native Americans consider the area a sacred place."

"I see." If this New Age-y stuff was for real, I could see the Pretty Boys being drawn to power centers. "Do a lot of people visit these vortexes?"

"Thousands a year I think. They're very popular."

Which meant they'd be unpopular to a Pretty Boy. "We'll have to check them out. Thank you so much for helping us."

"No problem. Sedona's only a five-hour drive from here. You should head out there one weekend. Fantastic hiking—" he grinned "—even without the hocus pocus."

"Magic vortexes?" Libby asked on the way to the rental car. "He must *really* like that woman."

"It's no stranger than what we're dealing with."

She shrugged.

"What *is* weird, though," I said, "are rocks from Sedona."

"If watching *CSI* has taught me anything, it's that dirt gets tracked to places it shouldn't be."

I guessed. Dirt got stuck to the bottom of the Pretty Boys' boots and was knocked loose in a super-fast blur move to grab Ivy and Dad. Especially if they tracked it into a van. They had to be using a big enough vehicle to grab a person off the street and keep them out of sight.

Two victims, two sets of Sedona pebbles. The Pretty Boys who took Dad and Ivy likely came from there. Did they take them back though, or were they still in Vegas?

"Road trip to Sedona?" I said.

"Road trip. Bloodmobile first though. We need a place to start looking or we'll be just as lost in Sedona as we are here."

Libby had charmed the receptionist at Meier and Randall and gotten the name of the company who'd sent the bloodmobile to the office. Just a half hour from UNLV, and the traffic was light this time of the morning.

I walked into Universal Blood Centers half expecting a staff full of Pretty Boys, but they were the normal med folk types I'd worked with for years, dressed in the obligatory red scrubs. Past the waiting area—also decorated with lots of red and gray—rows of chairs lined either side of the room, and technicians were drawing blood from a number of donors. Happy, smiling cartoon blood drops informed everyone of the upcoming blood drive.

I frowned. That was an image I didn't need.

Three people sat in their chairs, quietly reading or playing on their phones, with two technicians tending them, and a receptionist with a tight afro cut up front, watching us with a cautious eye.

"You're on," I told Libby softly, letting her take the lead.

She walked up to the receptionist and smiled, and the woman's wariness disappeared. "Good morning! I'm a writer, and I'm researching a book where the main character works at a blood bank. Could I ask you a few questions, maybe get a tour so I can be accurate?" She laughed. "I don't want to get my facts wrong and have people send me angry e-mails."

The receptionist glanced at the waiting room, but no one was waiting. "What did you need to know?"

"Awesome! What's your name?"

"Selene."

"Thank you so much, Selene." She wiggled her fingers at me and I pulled out my phone and brought up a note app like a good little assistant. "Okay," Libby continued, "so in my story, it's a mystery by the way, the main character is framed for murder. Her blood is found at the scene of the crime. She's sure her boyfriend's ex put it there—she works at a blood bank you see—so I need to know how hard it would be for someone who works at a place like this to steal someone's blood."

"Uh…"

"I imagine you have security?"

"We do. The donations are kept secure."

Libby nodded and I made notes.

"How tight?" I asked as if it mattered to our story. "Just a regular lock or like PIN numbers and tracking software?"

Selene laughed. "That's a little extreme. It's blood, not gold."

Libby rubbed her hands together. "Good, that makes it easier for my bad girl then. What about before you lock it up? Like, could a tech sneak an extra vial of blood?"

"Maybe. We collect a pint-sized bag, plus a few vials for testing."

"Perfect! She could steal one of those."

"Wouldn't your character recognize her boyfriend's ex taking her blood?"

"No, she's never met her. She finds out about her later."

Selene nodded slowly. "Oh. She could do it, then. People might not notice an extra vial."

Libby nodded excitedly and I took fake notes like a madwoman. Even I was buying her cover story. "This is fantastic, really. What about bloodmobiles? Same procedures?"

"Yes, though the blood is brought back here for testing."

"What happens then? Do you test all the blood here or do they do it at the branches?"

"This is the main branch for the area, so we do the bulk of the testing here. The lab screens all donations for HIV, hepatitis, and whatnot." She pulled out a pamphlet and slid it over to Libby. "It's all here."

"Perfect." Libby scooped up the pamphlet. "It is possible to see the lab?"

Selene hesitated. "We're not supposed to let anyone back there."

"We won't touch anything, I swear. Just a quick peek to get a feel for the place so I can describe it later. Please?"

Libby's eager smile won her over. "I guess that would be okay. Alice?" she called to a woman setting out supplies. "Could you watch the front for me for a few minutes?"

"Sure."

We followed Selene back, Libby chatting the whole time, *oohing* and *ahhing* and asking questions, me taking discreet videos as we moved.

The lab looked like most labs I'd worked in. Basic Formica counters, refrigeration units for the blood, a sink reminiscent of high-school chemistry class. Rows of plastic vial holders lined a counter next to a centrifuge.

"This is the lab," Selene said, waving at the two techs working there, both middle-aged women, one Latina, one redhead. The Latina was fiddling with the vials and a giant needle-looking thing while the redhead did paperwork at a desk up front. A small pink Jeep sat next to a vase with fake flowers. Selene grinned. "It's not fancy, so feel free to spruce it up in your book."

The vial tech looked up questioningly.

Selene jerked a thumb at Libby. "She's a writer working on a book."

"Ay," the tech said, smiling. The other didn't bother to glance up from her papers. No sign of any Pretty Boys, and neither of these women looked like Mediterranean models or minions of the undead.

Neither acted suspiciously either. No furtive glances, no sudden interest in who we were or what we were doing. No behavioral traits of anyone who regularly stole blood and helped bad people target good people.

"Do you keep track of whose blood is whose?" Libby asked. She studied the lab like she planned to rob it later. No one batted an eye. The woman could have a future as a criminal mastermind if she wanted one. What had she done in the Marines—black ops?

Selene picked up a blood bag and showed it to Libby. "The bags have a collection ID number, but no, we don't track names on the individual bags. Just basic patient records."

Most likely stored on the computer in the corner, where the paperwork woman was working. Ivy's name was in there. Maybe the other names of the people Eddie was watching as well.

"Where does the blood go from here?" I asked. The lab didn't appear to have advanced testing equipment, and I doubted the basic tests revealed enough specific information to track someone like the Pretty Boys were doing.

"Hospitals mostly."

"Any hospital, or specific ones?"

"We usually work with hospitals in our area." Selene gave me a funny look. So did the paperwork woman, but hers was just an annoyed glance. "Is that important to the book?"

Libby laughed and waved a hand at me. "Oh, she's already thinking about book two. Totally different plot. The ex's revenge might be connected to a much larger crime. We're still working out the details."

I grinned. "Sorry, didn't mean to confuse you."

"Yeah." Selene looked at her watch. "Listen, I need to get back. You got everything you needed?"

"I did, thank you *so* much. This was a huge help. I might even name a character after you." She winked.

"Oh, that would be cool."

LIBBY DROPPED THE act on the way to the car.

"You were amazing," I said.

She fanned herself with a hand. "Oh *stop* you're gonna make me blush."

"Are you sure you're not an undercover spy?"

"Like I could tell you if I were." She rolled her eyes.

The video was a little choppy, but it was good enough to peek into all the nooks and crannies we hadn't been able to poke around in.

"I knew I liked you for a reason," I said.

"Yes, but did we learn anything?"

"Ivy gave blood here and then she disappeared. Either someone is a great actor, the minion wasn't at work today, or the victim's blood is getting identified at one of the hospitals this center uses."

"Is your dad's hospital near here? Do they use the same blood center?"

"It's in Boulder City, but Universal Blood Centers is a chain, so it could be the same. I'd have to ask, or maybe get a look at some labels or records."

I unlocked the doors and Libby and I got back into the car. She pulled her seatbelt on. "If whoever is supplying the Pretty Boys names is at one of the hospitals, they'll be a lot harder to find."

"Much." Practically anyone on staff had access to the blood bank. "And unless the Boulder City hospital gets its blood from just *this* branch, that rules out the Pretty Boy spy being here in Summerlin."

"I wouldn't take the odds on that."

"Me either. I think it's more likely the spy works in a hospital or testing facility with access to multiple blood banks and branches."

Libby frowned. "Unless it's a lot bigger than we think and the Pretty Boys have people everywhere."

"That's a depressing thought." I reached for my phone. "I wonder if Universal Blood has a headquarters or testing lab in Sedona. Something that fits all our pieces of the puzzle."

There had to be a link between the blood bank, the red pebbles, and the missing people. Ivy Helgarson had no connection to Kurt Smith or Caleb Marlowe, aside from being people Eddie was ordered to watch. It was possible both Ivy and Marlowe donated to or received blood from UBC. Marlowe *had* been to an ER recently, and that ER could have been served by UBC. Dad also had his blood taken and tested, though I'd need to check on who handled the blood at Thompson General. Kurt Smith had no connections to blood at all, but if he was already on the run, his connection could be as old as mine was.

My web search came up empty. "No Sedona branch of Universal Blood Centers."

"That doesn't mean there's not a hospital or lab there they use."

The engine idled, the AC slowly cooling.

"Go or no go?" Libby asked.

We just didn't have enough to link Sedona and the blood bank yet, and I didn't want to leave the area if Dad was potentially still here. "Let's watch the blood bank a while, see if Eddie or Zack show up. Maybe Eddie's mom works there and she doesn't even know he's using her to find people with the right blood."

"Worth a shot." Libby picked up her backpack and left the car. "I'll cover the back. Keep your phone handy."

"Will do."

I watched the blood bank, taking advantage of the downtime to reexamine my puzzle pieces. Libby's stocking-the-pantry theory made sense if the Pretty Boys were creating some kind of people herd, but snatching homeless people off the street was a much easier way to do it. These victims were being *selected*, but why?

With the exception of Kurt Smith, Eddie's list had confirmed the blood link, so it was reasonable that the Pretty Boy victims on Cavanaugh's list were also connected by blood. It couldn't be through blood banks, though. I was five when someone had written my name down on vellum.

Cavanaugh's list was from the Florida and Southeast region, but Eddie was watching people in *this* area, so the Pretty Boys were what? Regionalized? Or were we dealing with two different groups?

I'd seen my share of cop shows. Zack displayed stalker behavior, but it was *also* protective detail behavior. Eddie had seemed convinced that Zack was a good guy. What if Zack *wasn't* looking for victims to kidnap, but to protect? Just like the Pretty Boy who'd saved Dad and me twenty years ago, and the one who'd shown up in the nick of time at the bar. How had he even *known* I needed help? Did he have his own Eddie keeping an eye on *me*?

That was a little disconcerting. I'd never spotted anyone watching me like that, but there had to have been someone or I'd be discovering first-hand what the Pretty Boys wanted with me.

Two groups, two different methods of finding them. That would explain why Eddie's list had the clearer connection and Cavanaugh's went back twenty years. It would also explain why the people on Cavanaugh's list were all dead, and the ones on Eddie's were still breathing.

If Eddie had been following us for nefarious purposes, and he had known we were in Kurt's apartment, he'd have told Zack and his buddy and they would have come in after us. Yet they didn't; they just sat outside and watched.

It didn't feel like these two Pretty Boys meant me harm.

I dialed Libby. "Cancel the stakeout," I said. "I think we're chasing the wrong Pretty Boy."

A GOOD DINER menu ought to mimic a small novel, and the Sunset Diner didn't disappoint. Page after page of heavy laminated paper offered breakfast in every shape and size, lunch favorites from around the globe, and good old-fashioned dinners from the 1950s. It was a time machine of yumminess.

"I don't think Zack took Ivy Helgarson or my dad," I told Libby after we ordered. A gyro for her and an open-faced turkey sandwich for me. I outlined my two types of Pretty Boys theory.

Libby didn't look convinced. "It fits what we've observed, but if he's protecting people on the list, wouldn't he have rescued them by now?"

"Not if he's outnumbered. There might be two or three good ones versus six or seven bad ones."

"Where do you get that number?"

"That's how many we've seen over the years."

"We need to talk to Zack."

"He's not being cooperative in that regard." My phone rang and I snatched it up. Cavanaugh.

"I just landed. Where are you?" he said, sounding winded. I pictured him hurrying down the concourse, lugging his bags.

"Sunset Diner off the 515."

"On my way. Don't go anywhere."

I hung up. "Cavanaugh's inbound."

"How much are you going to tell him?"

"Depends on what he tells us." I twisted my hair back into a knot. Our waitress was also inbound with our food, and I'd gotten enough gravy in my hair during my lifetime. She set the food down on the table. It looked and smelled divine. Dad and I had never done the whole Thanksgiving turkey and all the trimmings thing, but open-faced sandwiches we could manage.

"Crazy idea, but what if you *are* honest with him?" Libby said, popping an olive into her mouth as the waitress greeted another table.

"He'll have me committed."

"I didn't."

I sighed and mopped up some gravy with my bread. "Fine, if he's honest with me, I'll be honest with him. But if he gives us attitude, he gets that thrown back in his face instead."

"Only fair."

We'd finished our meals by the time Cavanaugh strolled in the door.

"Ms. Harper."

"Mr. Cavanaugh."

I gestured at the empty chair and he took a seat. He looked at Libby questioningly, but he didn't need to know her name.

"We're face to face. Let's talk." No sense dragging our feet on this.

"I had a good flight, thanks for asking."

I opened my mouth, but Libby kicked me under the table. She shot me a glare. *Be nice.*

"Sorry," I said. "It's been a long day. Thanks for coming all this way on short notice to meet with us." Though it had been *his* idea to drop everything and come running.

He paused, glancing at both of us as if questioning my sincerity. "Thank you. It looks like the Helgarson case *is* connected to Anita Rosenberg's," he said. "I'm not sure about your father's case, however," he continued.

"Oh, they're connected all right."

He paused, giving me a look that should have been done over the top of glasses. You got the most bang for your condescending buck that way. "What makes you say that?" he asked.

"I followed the blood trail."

Cavanaugh sighed. For a guy so insistent on seeing me, he wasn't very forthcoming. "Ms. Harper, a dangerous killer is kidnapping people and you're on his list."

"You've told me. *Three times.*"

"I'd like to take you into protective custody until this is resolved."

Like hell. That explained the "I'm in charge here" attitude.

The waitress returned and handled Cavanaugh a menu. He shook his head. "Anybody up for dessert?" she asked instead. "We've got the best pie in town."

"Apple," Libby said. "Three slices."

"You got it." The waitress headed back to the kitchen.

"Whose custody?" I continued.

Cavanaugh seemed confused. "Excuse me?"

"You're not a cop, or a fed, and you haven't once shown me a badge—even though you've done your best to make me think you're law enforcement. I ask again—whose custody would I be in?" Not that I had any intention of going with him. No way was I sitting locked in a windowless room somewhere waiting for scraps of vague information.

"I'm not at liberty to say—"

"Wrong answer," I said, slapping the table. He jumped, and several heads turned our way. I smiled until they turned back around. "I'm not going anywhere with you unless I know who you work for and why you're trying to find these people."

"I work for concerned parties—"

Libby snorted. "Knock it off. You asked for this meeting, so say what you wanted to say."

His face reddened and he moved his hands under the table. I tensed, but if he'd had a weapon he would have pulled it by now. I fought the urge to check.

"Ms. Torres, I'm trying to protect your friend."

Libby's eyebrows rose. "You know who I am?"

"I'm doing my job."

I leaned forward and placed my palms flat against the table. "What job is that exactly?"

"Protecting innocent people from dangerous men."

"They're not men and we all know it. Isn't that why we're here? Quit stalling and talk."

He paled, all the anger and frustration draining out of him like we'd pulled a plug. Ah, *finally*, we were getting somewhere. "Then let us protect you, Ms. Harper."

"I've been protecting myself against blood-sucking fiends my whole life, so excuse me if I don't jump into your arms and cower."

Cavanaugh blinked. For a moment he sat staring, his jaw clenched, his breathing shallow. He licked his lips, sweat beading up along his hairline.

I'd freaked him out for sure, but I couldn't tell if he was scared for me or because of me.

"You think you know what you're running from, but trust me, you don't. Let us protect you. *Please.*"

His desperate tone made it past my defenses. That didn't sound like a tough guy act, or a fake cop act, or a hard-ass trying to make you do what he wanted act. It sounded real. I just didn't get this guy.

"I don't care about me," I said softly. "I'm trying to find my father. Talk to us and we can share information and find our missing people. If not—" I held my hands up, palms facing him "—then we're done here and you're wasting time my father doesn't have."

His shoulders sagged and he leaned back. "I'll need to speak to someone first."

"We can wait."

He glanced at Libby, way too many conflicting emotions rippling across his face, then rose. Without a word, he turned and headed into the parking lot. Once outside, he made a call.

Libby leaned over and watched. "Secret government organization?"

"I'm thinking shady pharmaceutical company that hopes Pretty Boys are the key to immortality drugs."

"Nice. All kidding aside, who *do* you think he's working with?"

I sipped my iced tea. "Not sure. Partner or organization? If he's offering protection, he might actually have some muscle backing him. Secret organizations don't like to share, though."

Cavanaugh's request didn't appear to be going well. He raked a hand through his hair, arguing and looking more frustrated by the second.

And also more human.

"I must be tired," I said. "I'm feeling sorry for him. He *wants* to talk to us, but it looks like someone else is running the show."

"Also my take," said Libby. She signaled the waitress for the check. "Vampire hunters? Watchers' Council? Protectors of the Innocent Masses?"

"D. All of the above."

Cavanaugh banged his fist against the roof of his car.

"If he'd just tell us who he's working for, we might all get the answers we want."

"He didn't blink when you mentioned blood-sucking fiends."

"I noticed that."

Cavanaugh started shouting, gesturing like he was fighting off giant insects. After a few more shouts, he shoved the phone in his pocket and stormed back into the diner.

"I'll have to get back to you," he said through clenched teeth. "My colleague isn't open to sharing information at this time, and I'm not permitted to reveal anything without approval."

"I'm sorry to hear that."

"I'm not giving up. He'll come around, but until then, will you *please* consider protective custody?"

He stared at me so hopefully, his eyes pleading for me to say yes, to trust him even though he'd told me squat.

"I'll call you if I change my mind."

Not the answer he wanted, but he nodded as if it was the one he expected. "I'll be in touch." Dejected, he shuffled out of the diner and into his car.

"He seems intent on saving my ass," I said.

"Well, it's a nice ass."

"That it is." I tossed some cash down on the table. "Road trip time or wait on the menfolk for answers?"

"Screw the menfolk. Let's see what magical wonders await us in Sedona."

Chapter Twelve

Yellow scrub and khaki cacti turned to rich green and deep red as we drove from Arizona desert into the mountains of Sedona. The streets rose and narrowed, and signs along the side of the road informed us we had crested the mile-high mark. The buttes kept going though, topping out as high as nine thousand feet—or so the signs claimed.

For a popular vacation spot, there wasn't much to it. Route 89 took you from end to end—with way too many roundabouts—and everything in town seemed to be huddled up against it. Sedona was cut right out of the red rocks, and some of the shopping plazas and hotels required hiking-level fitness just to reach them.

But the views. Damn.

The town was tight, but the countryside went on for miles—up *and* out.

"We fell into a postcard."

Libby chuckled, but even she couldn't stop staring. Despite our impressive combined list of previously lived places, neither of us had ever been to Sedona.

Everywhere we looked, spectacular views of majestic red rocks and buttes against perfect blue skies greeted us. Mixed in with the red were waves of green trees and white flowers. I'd been all over the country in my life, but nothing had ever compared to this. Dad and I had passed close by a number of times, and he used to take me camping to see the old mining towns all across the Southwest, but Sedona had always given him a weird vibe. I guessed he hadn't liked the "magic vortexes."

Plenty of others did, though. I could easily see why so many people retired here—and retired they did en masse. White hair was as prevalent as the white flowers, sprinkled in between the families and couples ready for outdoor adventures.

Not that we planned to linger in town or do any sightseeing. Dr. Bloom said the pebbles had come from the Bell Rock area, so a-hiking we were going.

We found a hotel in our price range along the main road through town, within walking distance of a pizza joint, a damn fine-smelling bakery, and a church. If we were in the heart of Pretty Boy country, we'd need every advantage and protection. Dad and I had never tested the "Pretty Boys can't step on holy ground" theory, but maybe Kurt Smith had.

The Winchester Arms Hotel sat behind a row of shops and restaurants, offering multiple exits and escape routes should the need arise, plus a constant crowd outside to mask our comings and goings. On the downside, the rooms were decorated in 1970 Western Motor Lodge, complete with a fake cow skull over each bed.

I looked for outdoor gear shops while Libby checked in with Roberto. She neglected to tell him we'd left the state, which I wholeheartedly agreed with. He seemed like the kind of guy who would either lecture us, or drive right over to help us—neither of which we needed at the moment.

"There's an outfitters a few blocks down the road." We both had decent shoes and backpacks already, but we'd need canteens, sunscreen, and something warmer to wear besides jeans and our snazzy T-shirts. The temps wouldn't even hit 60 in the day, and unlike Lauderdale, it got downright cold in February at night, especially in the canyons.

The Pretty Boys who took both Dad and Ivy had dropped red Sedona rock. Unless Zack or Cavanaugh called with better information, red rock was all we had, even if there *was* way too much of it to search.

Libby looked over the map we'd picked up on the way in. "There's a lot of ground to cover if we don't know what we're looking for. Hire a guide?"

"Do you want to bring some poor stranger to a Pretty Boy barbecue?"

"Isn't that the first rule of hiking? Bring someone you can outrun?"

"I'm not sure The Flash could outrun the Pretty Boys."

It wasn't a terrible idea, though. You couldn't walk past a row of stores without seeing a tour or guide to all the "magical places." Someone like that had probably heard rumors about strange Pretty Boy-possible sightings.

Or they might know where near Bell Rock someone might be able to hide. Caves, mines, old homesteads. The Pretty Boys went *somewhere* in those rocks, and we just needed to find it.

"Think there's a guide with supernatural knowledge?" I said.

"In a city with 'magic vortexes'—" she made air quotes "—there must be at least one person who fits that description."

Libby checked online as we walked the few blocks to the outfitters, finding a slew of tours to the vortexes, but no one who fit our specific, if weird, requirements.

"Let's ask inside," I said, climbing the stairs from sidewalk to doorway. I doubted anything in this town was level.

Built in the classic adobe style, Rock Rollers had wooden beams, a trellis, and even a bell. Inside, it smelled like new leather and citronella candles. It also had everything a gal could ask for when going on a search through the wilderness for an evil lair—including wooden stakes.

"It's like they knew we were coming." I wiggled the package.

"Toss 'em in the basket."

A girl in a red polo shirt with "Harmony" on her name tag appeared. "Can I help you find anything?"

"Hiking gear."

"What do you need?"

Libby gave her the list. Harmony was around nineteen, with multiple piercings and impressive ink—all nature themed. A free spirit with an open mind? Worth a shot.

"We're also looking for a guide to the more, shall we say, mystical trails," I began. "Would you happen to know anyone?"

"There are brochures for vortex tours by the register."

"We were looking for something *other* than the vortexes." Anything that touristy would be a lousy place to hide a secret evil lair.

"You'd have to ask the individual guides. I don't get into all that. Ben might be able to help you. He's in the back. Did you need jackets?"

Libby nodded, and I made my way into the back.

A guy a little older than Harmony was stocking an end cap of Sterno stoves. Same red polo shirt, with "Ben" on the name tag. Looked like he walked right off a college admissions brochure.

"Excuse me?" I asked.

"Yes?"

"Harmony said you might be able to help us find a guide to the weirder side of Sedona."

He looked me over as if gauging my kink factor. "How weird?"

"Weirder than magical vortexes."

Another pause, then he nodded. "I know a guy who does monster tours. Louis Rafael, works over at CPYou Tech Help off Oak Creek."

"He's a guide?"

"Not officially, but he knows where all the weird shit goes down around here. It's a hobby for him and his girlfriend. If you're looking for non-vortex voodoo, he's your guy."

"Thanks." I hurried back to Libby. She and Harmony had our basket filled with enough supplies to last a week, so either she was one hell of a salesgirl, or Be Prepared worked as well for the Marines as it did for the Boy Scouts.

"We have everything?" she asked me, her gaze flicking toward Ben's shelf-stocking back.

"And then some."

CPYou Tech Help didn't cater to the Sedona tourist crowd, but they still welcomed walk-ins for anyone on vacation who ran into computer trouble. They had a brightly colored statue of a giant pig and her baby out front and a cactus in the reception area. I suspected "desert decor" was some kind of Sedona law. We'd seen the same pig and baby statue all over town, painted in a variety of crazy colors and patterns.

Louis was a beefy guy, more muscle than fat. Dark hair, dark beard, pushing thirty. He had kind eyes in a startling blue that matched his thin, out-of-style tie.

He scanned us both and gave us a puzzled look. "Picking up?"

"Other business." I smiled and rested my arms on the counter. "Ben over at Rock Rollers said you might be able to help us. We're looking for a guide to the 'weird shit' of Sedona."

Louis glanced over his shoulder at his fellow tech guy, busily at work on a system that looked older than Louis's tie.

"What kind of weird do you want? I can take you to El Chupacabra, the Mongollon Monster, La Llorona, skinwalkers, the underground Lemurian base—you name it."

"How about fast, swarthy, perpetually anemic. Rumor has it they hang out near Bell Rock."

He nodded slowly and leaned closer over the counter. "Ah, the new weird. I hear ya."

"New weird?"

"Oh yeah. Stuff has always been weird around there, but it's been getting *weird* up in those rocks lately. Hardly anybody's talking about it, and trust me—people here, they *love* their monster legends and alien conspiracies."

"That could be the place."

"Bell's all wrong, though. You want the Boynton Canyon area. *Way* past the regular trails and Jeep paths. It has the largest concentration of misplaced hikers in the past four or five years. They get lost out there, but wind up a hundred miles away with no memory of how they got there. The tin hat crazies blame the aliens."

They were half-right. "How much to take us there?"

"Three grand."

I rolled my eyes. "I'll give you two hundred bucks."

"Tourists pay more than that for a few hours' drive and a couple of chants."

"We don't need the full mojo show, just a guide."

"It's a lot of guiding, my friend. It takes half a day to get there, easy, plus the rental gear, not to mention the risk involved. This kind of service doesn't come cheap. Two grand is the lowest I'll go." He pointed a finger at me. "But you'll have to cover the rental gear."

Still felt like we were being mugged. "Which is?"

"You know how to ride a dirt bike? Where we're going, we won't *use* roads."

He expected me to laugh, but this wasn't funny. I didn't have that kind of money—not without wiping out most of what I had. Saving Dad was worth it, but only if I knew for sure this guy could help us find the Pretty Boys' evil lair.

"If I decide to this, how soon can you be ready?"

"A day."

"A whole day?"

"Unless you call me before it gets light out. To make it there and back before nightfall, we'd have to hit the trail at dawn. Otherwise we'd get stuck out there at night, and you *don't* want to be in those buttes when the sun goes down, even if you don't believe in monsters."

"I'll let you know."

"I'll be here."

We needed another guide. Or enough evidence that his prices were worth the risk to my savings.

By the time dinner rolled around, we were well-stocked on gear, fresh out of ideas on where to look for additional clues, and craving burgers. We stopped at the place across the street from the hotel—a cute two-story outdoor plaza around a courtyard, nestled below street level. According to the locals, their burgers brought in more tourists than the landscape.

We ordered a plate of spicy poppers and a couple of prickly pear margaritas.

"Like the sign says, you really can't beat the views in this town." Libby leaned back in her chair and gestured at nature's majesty spread out before us. The sun was low on the horizon, casting gold shadows across the rocks. Pink and orange smeared the sky like a chalk painting, setting everything around us aglow.

"We don't see those babies in Lauderdale. Less work to look at them over a margarita than hike them, though." Nothing that rose up that high and straight was meant to be scaled.

"The bikes should help."

"Not very stealthy."

"Are you going to hire him?" She refilled her drink from the pitcher.

"Not unless I have no other options." This sucked. "We could rent some bikes ourselves. People hike up there, so how dangerous can a peek around be? We'll look for another clue, maybe find some hint about Pretty Boys in the desert, and then we'll concentrate our search with more firepower."

"We'll call Uncle Roberto."

"Works for me."

Our burgers arrived on glazed terra cotta plates with blue and yellow piping. Swiss cheese oozed over the side and I caught a whiff of something sweet, yet spicy in the sauce. I took a bite. Oh yeah. They earned their "best burgers in town" slogan.

We ate in silence, too busy enjoying the sunset and the food to worry about it possibly being our last meal. Dessert was a given. Lava cake with vanilla ice cream. You can never go wrong with the classics.

I paid the check and we left the restaurant, heading down the stairs to the courtyard. Night had come and tiny white lights along the shop awnings twinkled on one right after the other, almost as bright as the stars in the sky. A cold breeze blew, but not quite enough for a full shiver.

Nothing about Sedona suggested vampires lived in its hills. Tourists strolled along the busy street laughing and pointing, or bobbing their heads to the band playing on the deck of a nearby restaurant proclaiming the best wood-grilled pizza in town—and smelling yummy enough to back it up.

"We should crash early," I said, heading for the crosswalk to the hotel. Even the sidewalk was decorated with inlaid stones and patterned brick. And the ever-present pig statues, which the waitress had informed us was a javelina.

"Not a problem. I apologize in advance for how hard I'll be to wake up tomorrow. Consider yourself warned."

I tossed her a jaunty salute. "Roger that."

In the street ahead of us, a string of pink Jeeps with "Pink Jeep Tours" rolled past. They turned down a side street behind the restaurant and into a rear parking lot.

"Wait, I know that Jeep." I'd seen it before, but where wouldn't come to me. Parking lot of the hotel? Back in Vegas? "Lib, do you remember seeing a pink Jeep recently?"

No answer. Not even the snappy tunes from the band broke the all-too-familiar silence.

I turned. Libby stood a few paces behind me. She stared into nothing, not moving, not talking. Just like everyone else on the street.

"Aw hell, not again."

Chapter Thirteen

Two Pretty Boys stood on the sidewalk. Behind them, a white van idled at the curb, its side door open and dripping with cliché. Unless another Pretty Boy was dyeing his hair, the redhead at the wheel had to be human.

Which just pissed me off.

The Pretty Boy on the left was as handsome as they always were, clearly getting his fashion sense from the covers of romance novels. The other was so unbelievably beautiful he damn near stopped my heart. Unlike every other Pretty Boy I'd seen, this one was pale as marble, with delicate features and white-blond hair flowing across his shoulders in waves. His eyes swirled with color like opals in the light. *I dub ye Fabio and Handsome Vlad.*

"Grace," Handsome Vlad said, his voice like sunlight on wind chimes. "Come to me."

I wanted to. My feet moved forward, dragging the rest of me with them. He was just so *beautiful.*

Handsome Vlad gestured for me to come closer, his long, pale fingers elegant and dancing in the night air. I took another step.

He smiled. So did Fabio, but his was the grin of a predator, romance cliché or not.

I stopped, part of my brain screaming at me from deep down and far away. This was wrong. I didn't want to be anywhere near those things, no matter how yummy they looked on the outside.

"No." All I could manage, but saying it gave me the strength to shake my head.

The air pressure around me changed and both Handsome Vlad and Fabio glared, their gazes sliding slightly past me.

"Be a good girl and run," a man said softly on my right.

I jerked and turned, certain no one had been there an instant ago. A man stood beside me, tall, dark, and sexy like all the others, only this one was familiar. My helpful hottie from Frisco's.

"No need since you keep saving me," I told my rescuer, prince of the good Pretty Boys. How had he even *found* me? Whoever his minions were, they deserved a raise. I wasn't that easy to track.

Which was creepy, sure, but at least it worked in my favor.

"Stop chasing monsters and I won't have to."

"But I don't see you in between rescues," I said, reaching for the dusters at the small of my back. "You don't call, you don't write—"

"Run!" he said. An instant later he blurred and vanished.

Like hell.

A wall of char-scented air hit me from the side. Pain exploded from shoulder to hip. I curled sideways, the air rushing from my lungs as the world swooshed past. I flew into the air and my backpack shot from my shoulder. It fell to the sidewalk a few feet from Libby, still frozen in time.

I braced for impact, and—

No ground rushed painfully toward me. The sidewalk flowed below me like a river, punctuated by the *slap-slap-slap* of quickly running feet. Stores jiggled past, staying even with my sight line.

One of those pretty sons of bitches was *carrying* me. He'd snatched me off the street like some cheap smash and grab!

This is not how *I go out.*

I yanked my arms tight against my sides and hung limp, willing myself to turn slippery as an eel. The Pretty Boy stumbled and I broke free of his grasp, sliding down his body, and hitting the sidewalk at an ill-advised speed. I bounced and skidded, cursing every decorative bump and red rock I hit.

Stonework was only pretty from a distance.

I looked up. A third Pretty Boy glared down at me. Not nearly as pretty as his buddies, and twice as rude.

He blurred and grabbed my ankle, cold fingers against my skin.

"Hey!" I glared at Rude Dude, but he—

—I stand in a dirt street lined with wooden huts. Sunset glows on the horizon, the same orange as a fire consuming the village. Women in heavy-

weave tunics run screaming as giants chase them, snatching them into the air with massive hands. Behind them, a wall of water rushes forward, churning with trees and debris and the bodies of those unable to flee its path. In seconds it washes over us, slamming me into the earth. I scream, choking as water fills my lungs. Anger fills my soul. We were betrayed, betrayed!

—I was dry and breathing, the village and the women shifting back to the star-speckled sky and the bright lights of the shops.

What. The. Hell?

Rude Dude gaped, his mouth slightly open, his expression awed and befuddled. It took me longer than it should have to realize he'd let go.

Something whooshed past, immediately followed by a crack sharp as shattering rock. Rude Dude vanished in a blur.

I groaned. How many freaking Pretty Boys were we facing?

I scrambled to my feet, no desire to look a gift rescue in the mouth no matter how weird the situation was. Rule one: Survive the weird shit first, then figure out what it all meant later.

Time rebooted and music filled the air.

Movement flickered in my peripheral vision, and I dived sideways a heartbeat before Fabio blew by. His coal-black hair swirled behind him like a cape as he skidded to a stop. His moves were pure action flick.

If this fight hadn't appeared—to everyone else's perspective—out of thin air, people would think we were filming a movie.

"Feel free to yell 'cut' anytime," I muttered.

Fabio turned and tossed his locks off his impressive shoulders with a shake of his head. Either my adrenaline was going full tilt, or he'd done it in slow motion.

"Grace?" Libby called, sounding bewildered. I couldn't imagine how this pause-and-play reality must look to her.

"Battle stations!"

She stared for half a second, then dug into her backpack. I hoped she grabbed anything but Lola. Guns brought cops even faster than supernatural kidnapping attempts.

She pulled out her taser.

Good girl.

The happy tourists sitting at the courtyard tables had figured out something uncool was unfolding and the screams began. Libby fired the taser at Fabio, but the electrodes bounced off his back.

"We're screwed," she said.

"Six ways from Sunday." I dropped into fighting stance, fists up and ready. Fabio laughed. I sneered. "Oh, that's just mean."

A growl split the air—deep, guttural, angry—but it hadn't come from Fabio. Air whooshed again and a streak of spiky white zipped in front of me.

"Didn't Daniel tell you to run?" said a white-haired Pretty Boy who had to be Zack. He launched himself at Fabio and fists flew.

Okay, fine, maybe running wasn't such a bad idea after all.

People were freaking out all around us, pouring up the plaza steps and racing down the sidewalk. Even traffic had stopped. The cars that hadn't turned and taken off had been abandoned, engines still running, in the street.

An angry shout just shy of a roar shook the ground as a *fourth* Pretty Boy stepped from the van.

"Oh come on!" Like we weren't already outnumbered.

He was, however, the first one I'd ever seen who wasn't pretty. Practically a walking rock, his skin rough and gravelly, a body almost as wide as it was tall, and all of it hard muscle. He lumbered into the fight like an avalanche.

"Nice to meet you, Rocky."

"Quip later." Libby grabbed my hand and dragged me away from the battling Pretty Boys. "Tactical retreat, now."

"But—"

"Move your ass!"

I tugged back. "Four against two are lousy odds. What if they kill them?"

"They're not easy to kill, but we *are*."

I ran with her, approving her tactical retreat as soon as I figured out where we were headed. Morning Light Community Church, just a few hundred feet away.

We stopped on the other side of the sign. It didn't feel any different from the street, but then we weren't undead spawn on holy ground.

"What the hell is going on?" Libby asked, breathless even though the run wasn't that far.

"Pretty Boy attack."

"Where did—how—I don't...?"

"It's okay, just breathe."

She wiped the sweat off her upper lip.

"This is going to make the news," I said, my heart still racing. Rude Dude had mad kung fu skills and Zack wasn't doing so well. I looked past them toward the van with the traitorous redhead. Handsome Vlad circled my helpful hottie—no, *Daniel*—and Fabio like a white panther. Even his stalking was gorgeous.

Fabio didn't look so handsome anymore, his hair mussed and matted. Daniel wasn't moving so fast and he favored a leg.

Fabio blurred and a fleshy *thwack* echoed. He flung Daniel to the ground near a javelina statue painted bright blue, pouncing on him a heartbeat later. Daniel shoved him off and drew the small, curved knife I'd grabbed days ago. He staggered to one knee, hiding the dark blade behind his leg.

Fabio fell for it. He pounced and Daniel struck. Fabio staggered back, glowing from within, and then his muscle-bound body dissolved into a misty haze of chartreuse spray. No boom this time, no explosion of grit and green grime.

That wasn't right. Why hadn't he exploded?

Daniel crashed against the van and rolled into the street. Handsome Vlad was on him in seconds, fists blurring, feet kicking. Daniel balled up and defended himself, but tough as he was, even he couldn't take such punishment much longer.

Zack cried out and collapsed. Rude Dude slung him over his shoulder in a fireman's carry and trotted toward the van.

"They need help," Libby said.

"I know." But I had no idea how to give it. Silver worked on them, but electricity did not. Nor did hitting them with a car. Church bells rang and I snapped around. Libby and I started running at the same time.

Great minds think alike.

We burst through the door of the church. She dodged right, I dodged left. I snatched a vase of flowers off a table and flung the contents away. *Sorry, God.* People sitting in the pews turned, their shocked faces gaping, thankfully too surprised to tell me I couldn't do that in a church, young lady.

Libby had found a decorative bowl, and was already heading for a birdbath-looking basin just past the lobby. A good thing, as I'd have taken forever to figure out where they kept the holy water. She dunked the bowl.

One of the priests glanced over, did a double take, and started toward us.

"Hurry, we're about to be busted."

I dunked the vase the instant she was done.

The angry shouts of both priests and parishioners chased us out the door. We outran the priests, but I had mixed feelings about them following us into potential danger. Bringing a priest to a vamp fight wasn't a bad idea, though.

Libby and I raced as one, in sync with the craziest plan of all time.

Daniel had managed to get back on his feet. As we closed on them, Rocky kicked him in the stomach. Handsome Vlad followed up with an elbow between the shoulder blades and knocked him back down.

Almost in range.

"Left!" I yelled.

"Right," she answered.

We flung a respectable amount of holy water on the Pretty Boys. I doused Handsome Vlad while she soaked Rocky. Blue sparks sizzled and smoke hissed. Their shrieks split the night like metal tearing.

I darted forward and grabbed Daniel's arm. "Come—"

Something hard and fast crashed into us and we both went flying.

I hit the street beside Daniel. Handsome Vlad yanked him up, then tossed him away. He turned on me, his opal eyes wide and hungry. Tendrils of pale smoke curled off his still-wet skin.

Libby drew her gun and fired three times in quick succession.

Handsome Vlad jerked back and dropped to his knees, lightning arcing off him in ozone-scented tendrils. Chartreuse light seeped through three tightly grouped holes in his shirt and spread quickly across his chest. He pressed a hand against it and stared as if he'd never seen his own blood before.

Maybe he hadn't.

I rolled to the side and scrambled to my feet. Daniel hadn't moved, looking dazed and barely conscious.

"Grab him," I said, ducking a flailing and sizzling Rocky and taking hold of Daniel's slightly damp and smoking arm. Libby grabbed the other and we hauled him off the sidewalk and toward the church. Music reverberated through the stone.

"What if he self-combusts?" Libby asked, her face flushed.

"If he sparks we leave him at the border."

Handsome Vlad's and Rocky's shrieks faded to screams, and then snarls. A wall of wind closed down on us from behind, pressure thick as a wave.

"Move move move!"

We passed the Morning Light's sign, dragging a stumbling Daniel between us. He didn't burst into flames or show any signs of instant, divine death.

"Is this good or bad?" Libby asked.

"No clue." If being on church grounds didn't bother him, it wouldn't affect them either. "Maybe we need to be inside the church?"

Another shriek, much closer now. The hair on the back of my neck quivered from the expelled breath.

I tripped and we fell in a tangle of arms and legs.

Handsome Vlad stopped at the edge of the grass. Pale green light leaked from the bullet holes in his chest, but he didn't act hurt in any way.

"You must help me," he said, but it didn't sound like a request. I felt the urge to obey tug at me again.

"Are you high? I'm not helping you with anything, you moron."

He took another step and crossed the church's property line. Blue fire sparked and smoked around him. He shrieked again and jumped back.

Holy ground. Check.

No sparks on my guy.

"I *must* have your blood," Handsome Vlad called.

I dug my fingers into the ground under the church sign and flung a handful of pebbly dirt at him. It splattered across his face and he let out another shriek. He rubbed frantically at his freaky eyes and backed away, his green-shot gaze boring into mine.

Shouts cut off whatever he was about to say next. Rocky frowned and tugged at Handsome Vlad's arm. I glanced over my shoulder. Four priests in robes were running toward us.

"Here comes the cavalry."

With a final, I-will-make-you-pay-for-this glare, the Pretty Boy twins blurred back to the van. Tires squealed a moment later and they were gone.

Chapter Fourteen

I'd seen a lot of weird in my life, but even I had no words for what had just happened. I sat on the gravel, clinging to Daniel's hand, and shared bewildered looks with Libby.

"What the fuck?" she whispered. Her face was pale and sweaty, and a bit of red dirt smudged one cheek. I'm sure I looked no better.

"New to me, too."

That attack hadn't been a lone Pretty Boy ambushing a family on a dark road. That had been a coordinated attack by four Pretty Boys to grab me off the street.

Four Pretty Boys, for little old me.

If the good Pretty Boys hadn't been there… I shuddered.

The priests were almost upon us, but I didn't spot a single worried expression or first aid kit on any of them.

"They look pissed," Libby said softly. "Angry priests are bad."

"It was just holy water. Can't they make more?" I let go of Daniel and rose. We could discuss this like—

Blue sparks sizzled across his skin. He whimpered, his unfocused eyes flying open. We gasped. The priests jerked back as if they'd hit a wall.

"Demon!" the oldest priest cried out, pointing a finger at us.

I grabbed Daniel's hand again. The sparks vanished and he moaned.

"Um, Grace?" Libby began.

"Still no clue." Maybe it was like inviting a vampire into your home. Bringing him onto church grounds was okay as long as he had, oh, I don't know, permission or a divine day pass.

The old priest yelled at us in a weird mix of what sounded like Spanish and Latin. Two of the others turned and ran back toward the church, while the last one rummaged through his robes and thrust a crucifix at us.

"Must...go." Daniel struggled to speak. He kept his eyes and head down, avoiding the glare of the priests and the crucifix.

"We need to get him out of here," I said, pulling him up. People were staring, and this many panicked priests couldn't be good for anyone. Libby helped me get him to his feet.

"Monster!" the old priest shouted. "Defiler!"

"He just saved our lives, you old coot."

Libby cleared her throat. "Please don't yell at the priests. It's disrespectful."

"Fine."

We half-dragged Daniel down the block toward the hotel. People pointed and stared, and way too many cell phones swung in our direction.

And froze.

Libby's eyes widened as the world stopped around her. "How did—"

"Can't hold...long," Daniel said, straining.

I picked up the pace. "Move faster, Torres."

We lugged Daniel to a sofa in the hotel lobby before his legs gave out and the world started moving again. People were still running all over and chattering like crazy, but no one looked at three tired people taking a breather on a plaid couch.

"Are you all right?" I asked him. He was pale and bruised, his face sweaty. The fight and hitting the pause button on time must have taken a lot out of him. He'd fought for us like a badass out there, but he'd taken his own share of hits. Bad ones.

"I'll heal. You?"

"I'm fine."

"I'm Daniel."

"I know. Zack told me." I would have guessed something exotic and Goth, maybe Lucien or Erebos—a name befitting a vampire who'd turned to the side of Light. Though I supposed I could be overthinking it. For all I knew, he'd gone vamp in the 50s. He did have a James Dean bad boy thing going on. Throw a leather jacket on him and he'd be set.

"Where's...Zack?" he asked, struggling to get the words out.

"Rude Dude took him. He threw him in the van before they took off. I'm sorry we couldn't save him, too."

Daniel's brow furrowed. "Who?"

"Big guy with an attitude."

He sighed and closed his eyes, sinking back onto the couch. His breathing sounded ragged, a little labored, though I wasn't about to put an ear to his chest to find out for sure. My throat didn't need to be that close.

I glanced at Libby. She shook her head, still looking confused and worried. We were way out of our depth here, but wasn't this what I'd wanted my whole life? To find someone who could give me answers?

Was it tacky to question a beat-up immortal being who just saved your life?

"What do you need?" I was raised on the run, not in a barn.

"Water."

A glass water cooler sat on a table by the wall, next to the coffee Thermoses and tea bags. I filled a cup and brought it back. He nodded thanks and drank every drop.

"Another?"

I filled the cup twice more before he stopped looking like he was going to drop dead on us any second. He still looked wrung out, though.

"Better?"

"Yes, thank you."

A complete sentence, no weak or breathy pauses. Standing and walking might still be a pipe dream, but talking didn't seem to tire him out anymore. A good thing for us, but if his speedy recovery was common to all Pretty Boys, we were in deeper trouble.

Daniel glanced around the lobby as if just realizing where he was. "How did you evade...the others?"

"Inspired creativity. Who is after me and why are they so obsessed with my blood?"

His eyes widened the teeniest bit. That surprised him. Good to know. "How...?"

"I pay attention. Are they drinking it?"

"I have to go after Zack." He leaned forward, winced, and fell back down, pressing a hand to his ribs.

"You can barely move, and your buddies could still be out there looking for us. The safest thing right now is to stick together."

Daniel shook his head, but he didn't try to move more than that. "You're not safe if he knows where you are."

"Who is he? What does he want with my blood?"

"You need to run," he said. "How do you feel about The Bahamas? Or Scandinavia?"

Libby huffed and rolled her eyes. Not her usual level of sass, but getting there. "He's as bad as Cavanaugh."

"Who's Cavanaugh?" Daniel asked.

I crossed my arms. "Someone who sucks even worse than you do at giving straight answers. Come on," I cajoled. "We saved your life, you owe us."

Daniel shook his head.

I looked at Libby. "I was wrong. He's *worse* than Cavanaugh."

Karma was real. Perfect. "Talk or we're out of here. I need to know where my father is. How I get him back. Why you're protecting me. I'll settle for just answers to the first two, but I'm running out of time to save him."

He took my hand and covered it with both of his. His fingers trembled softly, almost a vibration under my skin. I should have felt the same itch of spiders, but I didn't. Maybe my warning signal didn't work with the Pretty Boys trying to help me. "Grace, you can't save him."

I snatched my hand away. If only I could take back his words as easily. "You don't know that."

"I don't know where he is."

"I'm working on that."

"I've been chasing them for decades and I still don't know where they are."

"Bullshit. You found me, you can find him. We're close. I know we are or there wouldn't be so many of them."

"Perhaps." He hesitated and looked away. "Kokabiel *was* here," he mumbled.

"Koka-who?" I leaned forward. "Is he the one who took my father?"

"Why won't you listen? Your father did, and it kept you safe for years."

The truth of it stung. Dad wanted me to stay safe, to change my name and run, to live and let him go.

*Hang on a sec...*I rewound the conversation. Chilled. Burned as Daniel's words sunk in. He *knew* Dad. Knew me.

"You're the one who saved me and my father when I was little." Just like he'd come for me in the parking lot outside a dive bar in Florida. And come for me here in the desert when he had no idea I'd even *be* here.

"Yes."

"Why?"

"You were in danger."

Thank you, Mr. Obvious. "Why was I in danger in the first place?"

He shook his head. "Safer if you don't know."

"Screw that. Four of your buddies just tried to snatch me off the street. If I hadn't been a *little* prepared for that, I'd be lunch right now."

"They're not my buddies."

"You're missing the point. Tell me about this Koka-cola guy?"

"No."

"We can get more holy water you know," I said, narrowing my eyes and putting my bad girl face on. "I'm not above holy waterboarding you."

Daniel smiled, just a little. Slapping him was probably a bad idea. "Yes, you are."

Cocky little... "You—"

"Grace," Libby said, thumping my shoulder. "Police."

I followed her gaze. The cops had finally arrived and were swarming over the shopping plaza. Bright lights swept the sidewalk as reporters set up shop. Only local channels so far, but if the story developed into something interesting—say about a vampire attack on a crowded street in Arizona—we'd be all over the media.

"Let's continue this argument in the room."

"I need to leave," said Daniel, but he struggled just to sit up. He hadn't sparked, but maybe being on holy ground had done internal damage, or drained him in a way we couldn't see. It had been quite the knock-down out there and he was in no shape for a round two.

"You need to stay with us. If they come after you now, you're dead."

"They can't—"

"Shut up and let us help you."

He grumbled, but stopped pulling away. Libby and I each took an arm and helped him to the elevator and up to our floor. Night had fallen and the A/C air felt good against my flushed skin. I had way too much adrenaline in my system still.

Libby unlocked the door while I scanned for any uninvited guests hanging around the halls. Everything looked and felt clear, though

Daniel's woodfire scent gave me the willies—even as it made me think of campfires and s'mores. We entered and made our way toward the double beds with wagon wheel headboards. Yeehaw.

Daniel stumbled. I lunged for him, but only managed to grab his wrist. He landed hard on the foot of the bed.

"You okay?" I asked, steadying him.

"I'm fine—" His gaze shifted over my shoulder and he froze, eyes wide, incredible sadness and joy in his expression. "It *was* real," he whispered. His other hand reached toward the mirror.

Shivers tickled down my back. *Don't look, don't look, don't look.* I didn't need one more freakishly unreal aspect in my life.

Libby gasped, pointing at the mirror over the desk. "What the—those are—?"

I don't want to know. I really don't. Bracing myself, I turned, Daniel's hands still tight around my wrist.

His hazy reflection greeted me, same as every other Pretty Boy I'd seen. Pale and translucent, like a memory of what he once was. Nothing new there, but behind him, barely more solid than his reflection, golden wings shimmered. They arced from his shoulders and poured down his back. A mere suggestion of delicate feathers traced in sunlight rippled as he moved.

Tears welled in my eyes. Beautiful. Like an—

I sucked in a breath.

Daniel wasn't a vampire. He was a God-damned *angel*.

Chapter Fifteen

Impossible. He'd smoked and sparked on church grounds. The priests had called him a demon. He didn't show up in mirrors. Holy water *hurt* him. His not-buddies were after my blood.

That meant *vampire*.

Libby ran both hands through her hair. "Those are—"

"They are," I said.

"That's not—"

"Guess it is."

"This is *real*?" she said.

"Yes."

"If this is all real, I'm so going to Hell."

"Not necessarily," I said.

She snorted. "I've broken *commandments*, woman. Don't tell me where I'm spending eternity. I'm gonna need a minute here." She flopped back on the bed, arms extended, eyes closed, and took several deep breaths.

Daniel still gripped my wrist, his expression joyful and sad and confused. He clearly didn't believe what we were seeing either. His gaze darted between me and the mirror.

With the wings.

The damn angel wings.

"What *are* you?" I said, awed, terrified, confused out of my mind.

No answer, just his intense gaze at the mirror. He wasn't even looking at me anymore.

I smacked the back of his hand. "Focus, Daniel-san."

His gaze jerked back to me.

"Vampires don't have golden wings!"

"You thought I was a vampire?" Daniel had paled to the color of old parchment, but the corners of his mouth twitched.

"Best guess based on the evidence."

"I'm not."

He had to be. The alternative fell well beyond even *my* crazy-world comfort zone. Pretty Boys were evil, blood-obsessed fiends. They murdered innocent people and ruined families, and in the dictionary under "scourge of society" there was a group photo with a Pretty Boy in the middle. They were bad news, they weren't...

"You're an *angel*?" I forced the word out, but it didn't feel any less impossible.

He shook his head. "Not anymore."

"But the other ones...this Koka-dude, and the guy who attacked me at Frisco's—*those* are all vampires, right?"

"No, we're all the same. Mostly."

I jumped to my feet, the urge to run racing through me. The feet had the right idea—turn and flee right out this door and never look back, but Daniel still had a death grip on my wrist and a summer camp love affair going on with his wings in the mirror.

"How are you doing this?" he asked in a strange, dreamy way. "How did you give me back my wings?"

"I'm not doing anything!"

"Is Kokabiel right?" He stared at me like *I* was the myth in the room. "*Can* you get us home?"

Vertigo sent the room sideways and—

—Streets of light shimmer below towers of glass and silver. Laughter plays sweetly as music across the square, and winged beings dance. They welcome me, call to me, and I want to go to them so badly it—

"Stop doing that!" I yanked my hand away, back in myself again, but part of me ached for the light and sun. I knew that lonely feeling, that longing for home. But that wasn't *my* home. It was...*no, no, no.* I was not going to think about *his* home.

Without my touch on his skin, the wings in the mirror had vanished, though Daniel's ghostly, hazy image remained. The same Pretty Boy image I'd always seen from them.

"Bring them back, please!" He reached for me like I reached for brownies after a lousy day.

I shied away. "Down, boy."

He waited, trembling ever so slightly, looking a little like a puppy who just wants a treat. Angel puppies. *Pull it together, Grace-face.*

Curiosity overcame my leeriness. "I'm going to test this, okay?" I said, hands up. "Just stay quiet until I'm done."

Daniel nodded, practically vibrating in his eagerness. I'd had some hot dates before, but no man had ever literally quivered awaiting my touch. *Stop stalling.*

I reached out and placed my fingers against his arm. The wings in the mirror shimmered into view. I lifted my hand and they vanished once more. Down—wings. Up—no wings.

It *was* me. Funny, I didn't remember being bitten by a radioactive angel.

Daniel sighed, but the hunger in his eyes remained. "You're miraculous."

Libby half whimpered, half laughed. "Coming from him that means something."

"Libby—"

"Still processing!"

I backed up and sat down on the chair by the desk. I'd always known the Pretty Boys weren't human, so their true nature ought to be only a surprise, not earth-shattering. If I could believe in vampires, why not angels, right? Supernatural was supernatural.

So why is this harder to believe?

"Are you my *guardian* angel?"

Daniel chuckled wistfully, but shook his head. "Not a real thing."

"Oh, I think it is. You randomly pick people to protect and save from the…what did you call him again? Koka-cola?"

Daniel cringed, but he'd already let the angel out of the bag. "Kokabiel."

"He sounds like a perfume," Libby muttered.

"The blond guy?" I gathered Kokabiel was the pale arrogant one I'd dubbed Handsome Vlad. He'd acted like the one in charge. Looked like it, too.

"Yes."

"The others?"

"Unimportant. They'll do what Kokabiel tells them, but they don't care about you on their own."

"Minions."

"You could say that."

Who knew angels had minions? "Is that why you could kill Fabio?" I asked. "He was a minion?"

Daniel gave me a funny look. "Do you give everything strange names?"

I scowled at him. "Answer the question." *Helpful Hottie.* Not that I'd say *that* out loud.

"He's not dead, I only…reset him, you might say." He paused and looked at me through narrowed eyes. The hairs on my neck tingled. "You're the only one I know who's killed one of us."

"Me?"

"You killed Baraqijal in Florida. I didn't know we *could* be killed."

The eye candy from the bar. "That wasn't me, it was your magic knife."

"It's not magic. It's a claw from an extinct animal."

"Damn big claw."

"Damn big animal."

Libby held up a finger. "If he says velociraptor I'm walking right out that door."

"Not a velociraptor." He pulled out the knife. "It's from a Ziz. Similar beast, but the Ziz is more birdlike. Very rare, very special."

Yeah, *that* I didn't need to know.

Daniel put the knife away and turned back to me. His color was improving by the minute.

"You can't stay here," he said. "Kokabiel will heal and he'll come after you again."

"Because he wants my blood."

"Yes."

"Why?"

He paused, cheek twitching.

"You gotta work with me here, dude."

"Another peek?" He held out his hand, a coy glint in his eyes that would have been hard to resist on a normal human guy.

"I'll make you a deal," I said, clenching my hands behind my back. "Facts for…wings. As long as you answer my questions, you can hold my hand."

"I accept your terms."

I wrapped my fingers around his and gave him and his wings a second alone. His hand felt…normal. No tingle, no jolt, nothing that said "supernatural phenomenon in progress." Cool and dry, despite how nervous he'd acted.

"I'd thought I'd lost them forever," he said, and my heart pinched with longing for a shining city I'd never seen.

I didn't look at the wings, but I could feel the damn things flickering behind me in the mirror. "Start talking or I let go. Why does Kokabiel want my blood?"

"I don't know."

"Liar." I tugged back my hand, but he held firm.

"Stop! The deal was for facts, and I don't know for sure."

If only I had a stake handy. "Stick to the spirit of the deal, then."

He dipped his head at me. "He wants to go home, him and the others. Kokabiel claims he's found a way, but he's been saying that for centuries. I *think* he wants your blood for a ritual, but that's a *guess*, and I don't know what type of ritual even if I guessed right. Few still believe he can do it. He's tried and failed many times before. But if he's right, then the others will come for you as well."

My stomach flipped. Just what I needed—more Pretty Boys. "How many are there?"

"Now that Baraqijal's dead? One hundred-ninety-nine."

Two hundred Pretty Boys. I couldn't fight that many. Hell, I couldn't even run from that many.

"Who were the angels with him in the van?" Another phrase that sounded bizarre coming out of my mouth.

"Kokabiel's dominions. Servants you could say, but their names won't mean anything to you. Your colorful monikers are good enough."

"How many does *he* have with him?"

"Three dominions serve him. Kokabiel has allied himself with another, and he also has three dominions." He paused. "Two now. Baraqijal was his."

I did the math. We were missing one. "What about Fabio? Who did he belong to?"

"He was Kokabiel's, but he'll be back eventually."

The reset thing. "If you didn't kill that angel, what did you do to him?"

"I...separated him from his physical shell." He shifted in what could have been a shrug or a tell. He was too hard to read. "It's difficult to explain, but as I said, he'll reconstitute in time."

"And rise from the dead?"

"He was never dead, so no. He'll be back."

"How long?"

"Depends on his strength. I've never banished him before, so I don't know for sure. Some are gone months, but others return in a week."

That I could handle. I planned to find Dad and be done with all this mystical mojo before "eventually." "What's his name? The ally?"

Daniel hesitated and I loosened my grip on his hand. "Suriel," he said grudgingly.

Finally, we were getting somewhere. Kokabiel and Suriel and their four little minions. Six angels. Swell.

"Did Kokabiel or one of his dominions kidnap my father?"

"I assume so, but I didn't *see* him do it, as I was protecting *you*. Anthony's always run before. Are you sure he didn't this time?"

My anger simmered. Not at the question—that was valid—but at how casually he spoke of what Dad did or did not do. A reminder that he'd been part of our lives for years, directing our fate, ruining my childhood, and all from the shadows.

"I'm sure. Did Kokabiel kill my mother?"

Another telling pause. "No."

"Did his partner, Suriel?"

Daniel's gaze slid sideways, away from me. "One of his dominions did, yes."

"Why?"

"For her blood."

The images of that night flooded my mind again. Mom in the clutches of a beautiful man, his mouth on her throat, the blood soaking through her clothes and running down her chest.

Daniel winced. "I was too late to stop that," he whispered. Then he twitched, jerking his gaze up to me. "That was not my memory. What did you do? How did you show me that?"

"I didn't do anything!" But our hands were still connected. Maybe the visions worked both ways. "The shimmering city with the towers? Is it real?"

He drew back a few inches, sucking in a slow breath. "Yes. Our home long ago." He shifted uncomfortably, and a hint of fear crept into his dark eyes. "You shouldn't be able to do that either. I don't know what you are."

Aside from confused, offended, and scared? I had no idea either. Granted, freaking out the freaky should have been a rush, but not if it put a divine crosshair on my family.

"Is this why Kokabiel wants my blood? My family's blood? Because we can show you your long-lost wings in the mirror and share home movies in our heads?"

"No. Memories aren't enough for Kokabiel or his followers. They want the real city. But if you can do such things...perhaps he's right about you. Maybe you *could* send them home." That sounded like a good thing to me, but he swallowed and looked nervous.

"Why is that bad?"

Daniel's jaw clenched. "He was obsessed before, but now he's unsettled, behaving erratically. The more you reveal your...uniqueness, the more he'll pursue you."

"If all he wants is some blood, what if I just give him a pint of it?" I asked. "How much could he possibly need for a ritual?"

Daniel blurred to his feet and grabbed my shoulders with both hands. "You *can't* help him." Nervousness had turned into full-on panic.

"Whoa, back off, dude!" He released me, but kept his hands hovering above my shoulders. "Who cares if he goes home?"

"Kokabiel *can't* return to Heaven on his own. We *have* to serve our punishment. If he forces a judgment now, he might bring judgment on all of us—humanity included."

"Judgment." He'd lost his mind. "As in Judgment Day?"

"It's had many names over the millennia, but yes."

I gasped. "Helping Kokabiel could destroy the *world*?"

"Yes."

"That's insane. Why would anybody risk that?"

"Desperation."

"What did you people *do* that going home would end the world?"

Daniel pushed both hands though his hair and paced the small space between the door and the A/C unit under the window. "It was our task to watch over humanity. To protect you. But we did more than watch— we guided. We gave you knowledge, and tools, and broke our vows." He stopped and a palpable wave of sadness rolled off him and through the room. "We were punished for our arrogance. All of us."

"You and the other angels?"

"Us and the world we'd created. It was washed away."

I blinked. "Uh..."

"The flood," Libby squeaked from the bed. "He's talking about Noah's God-dammed *flood*."

"Wait." I needed a second to get my heart started again. "That shit can't be real."

"The destruction was real," Daniel said, shrugging. "But stories evolve over time."

"Oh really? How *much* time? Because my science teacher, Dr. Skorzeny, had some pretty solid evidence about that and—"

Daniel chuckled as if he thought my entire frame of existence was *cute*. "He's not wrong. The universe is very, very old. Older than us."

It was too much to take in. There was weird, and then there was *holy-crap-I've-lost-my-freaking-mind-weird*. Mind-bending as all this was, it was doing nothing to help me find my father. The nature of life, the universe, and everything wasn't going to draw me a map to where Kokabiel was keeping him.

Taking a deep breath, I shoved everything but the here and now out of my brain. Dad. Focus on Dad.

"My father—"

"Who art in Heaven," Libby mumbled, followed by a disturbing giggle. She raised one finger. "Sorry."

I refocused and turned back to Daniel. "I want to find my father."

"I told you, I don't know where he is."

"You found me, and I was well-hidden. Why can't you find him?"

Daniel dropped back onto the bed, his fingers interlocked and hanging between his knees. Hesitant hands, a hesitant stance. I'd spent a lifetime with a man who'd held himself that same way, trying hard not to lie to me.

"I've said too much. You *know* too much. I can't commit the same sin again."

"This isn't the mob, Pretty Boy."

He gave me a puzzled look, head tilted to the right.

He's cute like that. I twitched. *Stay out of my head, horrifically inappropriate thoughts.*

I had liked it better when Pretty Boys were just vampires. A lifetime of books and movies told me how to *kill* a vampire. I had no idea what to do to fight an angel—no one had written a TV series about *that*. I sneaked a peek at Daniel's waist, but the blade wasn't there. He had to have it on him, though.

"I have a question." Libby held up one finger. "Are there any female angels?"

"Yes, but none of them sinned." He took a deep breath and turned back to me. "Kokabiel knows you're here. He won't leave until he has you."

"Does he expect trouble from us?"

He snorted, but there was no anger in it. "No. He doesn't view you as a threat, but a prize."

"What about you?"

"I view you as a gift."

Uh, not what I was asking. "I meant, does he consider *you* a threat."

"Ah. I'm an inconvenience, though I may be verging on irksome."

"Banish a few more of his buddies and he might change his mind about you, too."

"A worthy endeavor."

Libby sat up and walked over, then perched on the edge of the desk. She looked a hundred times better, more sure of herself and like the Libby who'd backed me up when she had no good reason to do so.

I smiled. "Welcome back."

"Thank you." She crossed her arms and fixed her gaze on Daniel. "These servants and allies—they're angels like you?"

"More or less."

Libby looked him over with a critical eye. "You seem on the *more* side of angel than less."

He said nothing, but I could sense the imperceptible squirm. If angels had minions and leaders, it made sense that some would be stronger than others.

She elbowed me gently. "Sister Mary Margaret was one tough nun, but she was a good teacher, and some of those Old Testament stories were better than what's on the bestseller lists. And from what she taught us, priests don't call *angels* demons and wave crosses in their faces."

Daniel scowled at her. "I'm *not* a vampire. Not every fanciful story you've heard is true."

"You're no angel either," she said, head cocked to one side.

He glowered, and the temperature in the room dropped at least ten degrees. I tensed. "Um, Libby?"

"Grace, he's a *fallen* angel. The ones kicked out of Heaven."

Daniel growled and the walls rippled. I scooted closer to Libby. "I can't yell at priests but you can disrespect an angel?" I whispered.

She turned to Daniel, some healthy fear finally sinking into her brain. "Oh, sorry about that. Still processing. This is weird."

Tell me about it. The only fallen angel I knew was bright red and carried a pitchfork.

"Daniel," I said, drawing his attention back to me. I really didn't like the way he was scowling at Libby. "You got kicked out of Heaven for helping humanity?"

"More or less." He crossed his arms, and the room flickered again. Maybe it wasn't wise to push the angry fallen angel.

"Then why are you helping me now?"

His tough-guy facade crumbled a bit, and his hand dropped to his lap. "Penance." Despair darkened his features, but he glanced at the empty mirror and a flicker of hope brightened it.

"Protecting me is penance?" Not sure how I felt about being someone's punishment.

"It's just."

"Just what?"

He stared at me. Libby clucked her tongue.

"Oh. Right."

Nothing Rabbi Cohen taught me for my bat mitzvah had prepared me for this. I had a million questions, and nearly every single one of them didn't matter. I had to stick with the questions that did.

"This is insane," Libby cried, hands in the air. "*Angels.*"

"I know."

"*Angels* killing people and draining their blood for a ritual? It's fucked up."

I nodded. "Fucked up angels with fangs."

"Fangels?"

Daniel scowled at us both. "You're not taking the threat seriously," he said.

"Yes I am."

Libby nodded, but she still looked pale and shaken. "That's true. She's utterly ignoring the larger ramifications of this conversation, but we were ready for that fight and we saved your ass."

"He also kinda saved ours," I whispered to her.

"Shh."

"Getting lucky doesn't mean you're prepared," he said. "Or capable of fighting what we are. Kokabiel will tear the world apart to find Grace. She must be protected at all costs."

"I'm tired of living in a box."

"Please trust me. It's best for everyone if you *stay here* and let me protect you."

"No, not when we're this close. I don't know where *you've* been looking, but that haughty marble-assed freak has *got* to be a local boy, and I *really* think his evil lair is nearby."

"He's not—"

"I found red sandstone pebbles unique to Sedona outside my father's door, and more of them at the home of another victim—one of the women Eddie and Zack were watching." I smirked. Gotcha. "The minions work for you, I take it."

"I don't have minions."

"No, you're just *allied* with others." Two sides, one trying to find people with the right blood for a ritual, the other, trying to save the people from—no, not save. *Protect.* Once Kokabiel snatched them they were on their own. Stupid if one of them might actually end the world. "Are you going to help me or not?"

His threw his hands in the air just as Libby had done. "I'm *trying* to help you, but you won't listen."

"If it won't help me find my father it's the wrong kind of help."

I turned and marched toward the door. The crime scene was still fresh, so there might be more clues in the plaza to Kokabiel's whereabouts. If not, we'd head into the canyons where all the hikers had gone missing, and we'd turn over every red rock until we found something creepy underneath.

Daniel blurred to my side and grabbed my wrist, firm, but more gently than his zip across the room implied. "Grace, please."

"Let go." I tucked my hand behind my back and slipped on my knuckledusters.

"If you pursue him, he'll—"

I swung, cracking him right across the jaw. He flew back with an *ooof* and landed on the bed.

"How did...?" Daniel rubbed his jaw, eyes and mouth wide. The fact that he'd stayed down proved he was weaker than he'd let on, despite the showy zipping about. No wonder he didn't want me leaving.

"You should see her left hook," Libby called back, and we stormed out of the room.

Chapter Sixteen

⟆⟅

As we rode the elevator down, Libby and I just stared at each other. Eyes locked, a kind of shared insanity that transcended society, family, even friendship. A new reality clicked into place around us.

"Holy crap, what did we fall into?" I asked.

"Looks like holy crap to me."

The doors opened into the lobby. The chaos outside had calmed down a little. News crews were still wandering around, but the police presence was small considering what had just happened. It was odd, but maybe without evidence that anything *had* gone down, there wasn't much they could do.

I cut through the lobby and went out the door. The valet handed us both bottles of water and we took them. Dehydration was just as dangerous as Pretty Boys in the desert. We cautiously made our way back to the plaza. The big clock above the courtyard read eight twenty-five, and it seemed busy for a Tuesday night that had just experienced a supernatural event.

"What do we do about Daniel?" Libby ducked around a trio of elderly women in straw hats. "I admire a good storming off, but he does make strong backup."

"I know, my temper got away from me. Don't worry, I'm sure he'll be lurking around before long." Lurking was unfair. He was *protecting* me. I should be grateful someone was watching over us, but it ticked me off anyway. "I'll apologize later."

Dad must have known all these years who Daniel was. Maybe he didn't know he was a freaking *angel,* but he'd considered himself a good Catholic and rarely missed a Sunday at church, even when I'd stopped going to temple. His old Bible showed up at every apartment we stayed at, same as his crucifix and rosary beads, plus all those trinkets in the glove box. Oh sure, he downplayed it all and claimed they were weapons against the Pretty Boys, but obviously that had been bullshit.

Libby trotted along beside me. "Where are we going?"

"Scene of the crime to look for clues." A mundane task after revelations of, well, Revelations, but hitting the pavement and following the evidence had gotten us here.

I stopped where time had frozen and scanned the area, then gave it a good sniff. Nothing smelled burnt, but Southwestern spiciness drifted through the air. Libby stood back-to-back with me and we rotated slowly as one.

It looked normal, which was weird all on its own. People ought to be scared, freaked out, hiding in their rooms and terrified to come out, but everyone shopped and walked and talked like there hadn't been a huge angel throw-down right here less than half an hour ago.

How powerful *were* those time stops?

"Is it me," Libby said, "or is it too calm out here?"

"I was just thinking the same thing. Maybe it was the time stop."

"Come again?"

"You didn't notice that before? Kokabiel froze the whole plaza right before he jumped us."

She turned back around and faced me. "I don't remember that."

"You remember a bunch of Pretty Boys appearing out of nowhere and starting a fight, right?"

Her face wrinkled, eyes troubled. "Yes, but it's fuzzy. I remember you were in trouble, and we got the holy water, and I shot that guy. I don't remember them showing up."

This was new. I'd never spoken with anyone who'd witnessed a time stop before. I had theories, of course, but they were just that. What else could the Pretty Boys do?

"The legends say Pretty Boys can cloud men's minds." That would explain why no one was running around crying the apocalypse was upon us. And why so few people throughout history had ever seen a vampire or an angel.

"I think that's The Shadow."

I huffed. "Same principle. They put the whammy on everyone so people forget they were here and what they did."

It didn't, however, explain why it hadn't affected *me*. I'd *never* been frozen, not even when it had been one on one. I didn't think Dad had either, otherwise I'd have noticed it long before this. And Mom? Had she been "special" like us, too?

"Well that's disturbing," Libby muttered. "I don't like having my mind messed with."

Very disturbing. I'd never felt normal in my life, but I never suspected I had a legitimate reason for it. "Uh, I don't think they did anything to your mind, it's more like your perception they screwed with."

"Just as bad. I see a few security cameras," she said, pointing them out to me. "Maybe they didn't affect digital perceptions. We might get a license plate number off the van." She brightened a little. "Though if no one remembers the fight, then the police have no reason to check the security footage, so we won't show up on the news."

"Maybe we can get a peek at those recordings." The right sad story could get us access. We could claim a missing sister. The truth might even work if a missing father tugged at the heartstrings.

Not that getting a license plate number would help. I didn't know a single person who could run it for us.

Libby walked to the edge of the street and stared out toward the mountains. "Do you remember which way they went?"

I pointed. "Only one way to go, really."

"There was a van?"

Oh boy. "A white one."

"I hate this. I can't trust my own brain."

"Maybe it'll come back to you."

I didn't know how many traffic cameras covered the streets between here and Boynton Canyon, but someone with connections to law enforcement could access them and see how far the van drove, and maybe pinpoint where they'd turned. That could help narrow our search area.

If we were incredibly lucky—and Kokabiel was incredibly stupid—there might even be an address on file at the DMV. The van had to come from somewhere.

Of course, the odds of that were the same as the odds of me gaining access to such records, so it was a moot point. We needed resources we didn't have.

"Damn," I said.

Libby tensed, eyebrows raised. "Problems?"

"If Cavanaugh really *is* an investigator working for a larger organization, he might have law enforcement connections who could get us that footage, *and* find out who owns the van—maybe even track it if it passed enough traffic cameras. He did say he knew a cop in Florida who'd helped him."

"You may have burned that bridge."

"I don't know. He wants to find his missing woman—I want to find my dad. He has to be as frustrated as we are." He'd followed me to another state, so clearly he wasn't giving up yet.

"What do you have against him?" Libby asked.

"He's arrogant. Doesn't like to share."

She chuckled and held up her hands. "And you do? He's chasing monsters. I had to threaten *you* to get any information and I'm your friend. You've disliked the poor guy since you met him."

"He asks too many questions."

"He's looking for a missing person, same as you."

I bristled, turning away and taking refuge on a nearby bench. I had no answer for her. At least none that made any sense. Cavanaugh set off every one of my warning flags, made me want to sneak out the back door and disappear, put me on my guard the moment I heard his name let alone his voice.

"I don't trust him," I said at last, weak as the answer was.

Libby wrapped an arm around my shoulders and gave me a squeeze. "You don't have to trust him to work with him. You need his intel, and the woman he's looking for needs your help same as your father does."

No way I could argue with that without looking like a heartless witch. Anita Rosenberg was in trouble, and as much as I pretended I didn't remember her name or that she wasn't important, painful questions had been slithering into my mind for days now. Did she have a family? A daughter who missed her and wondered what had happened to her? I knew Ivy Helgarson's family was out of their minds with worry.

Besides, Cavanaugh *had* found me in Lauderdale, and made the blood connection, so he was a decent investigator. I supposed I did owe him the benefit of the doubt.

"Okay, fine, you win," I mumbled. His phone rang four times before he answered.

"Good evening, Ms. Harper. Apologies for not getting back to you yet. My colleague is still being difficult, so I thought it best if we had a face-to-face conversation. It's taking longer than anticipated."

"That's fine. Listen, I could use a little help getting some security footage from local street cams. Could your contact at the Tallahassee police department help us out?"

"I could ask, though I don't know how much pull she has with the Vegas police."

"It's not Vegas. I'm in Sedona now."

Dead silence for far too long. "Sedona."

Not a question, and he sounded as wary as I now felt. "Yes. That mean something to you?"

"I had no idea you'd left Nevada."

And that wasn't an answer. "The blood trail led to Sedona, so we followed it. I think our missing people are here or close by."

More uncomfortable silence. "I see."

I covered the mic on the phone with my hand. "Something's off," I whispered. "He's quietly wigging out about us being here."

Libby's eyes widened. "He knows something, then."

I agreed. I hesitated a breath longer. Maybe I *was* going about this the wrong way. "You know what? Why don't we work together on this. Compare notes, consolidate clues. We're basically on the same case, so we might as well share." Especially any clues he was holding back about Sedona.

"I think that's a very good idea," he said without pause. "Meet you in the morning?"

"*Meet* me?" I'd expected to share info over the phone. This was starting to feel a little stalker-y. First, he tracked me down in Lauderdale, then he followed me to Vegas, and now this?

"If Anita Rosenberg is being held in Sedona, I should be there to help find her, don't you agree? After all, we *are* on the same case."

"Yes, that does make sense." So why didn't I like it? My natural distrust of everyone, or a lifetime of sniffing out danger? I could make this work, though.

I glanced around. A café sign on the tour shop on the corner said they served breakfast and opened at seven. "Is seven-thirty too early for you? We have another lead to chase down and need to get moving at first light."

"Tell me where to be."

I gave him the address and hung up. "He's meeting us in the morning."

"He's coming here?"

"I know, it's weird, right? He says it's to help find the Rosenberg woman."

"Could be true. He acts like he cares." Libby scanned the street like a pro. "We really ought to continue this in private though. We're too exposed out here."

"You're right." I really needed to get more sleep. "But there's one stop I'd like to make first."

"For?"

"If we're going after big game, we'll need bigger guns."

She grinned. "I'll call Uncle Roberto."

"I have a better idea."

Chapter Seventeen

Morning dawned gray and pale. The temp had plummeted overnight, and a bite in the air promised either icy rain or a light snow before the day was over. The bright red rocks of Sedona stood dusky and dark, foreboding more than majestic. Even the birds sang softly under their little bird breaths.

I still hadn't seen Daniel, but I caught a hint of spice and smoke when the wind blew strong. I couldn't tell if after all these years of watching me he knew well enough to stay out of sight, or if he just didn't want to argue with me anymore.

Libby and I waited for Cavanaugh at the barely-more-than-a-coffee-shop café I'd seen last night, right next to a small public parking lot. Our breakfast had come and gone before the sky changed colors. I hadn't spotted anyone suspicious so far, and neither had Libby.

We were fairly certain we didn't look suspicious either.

No sign of Pretty Boy activity, but then, there never was until the world froze around you.

The café might have been tiny, but the coffee was top-notch. I'd only had generic coffee before, but this was silky and smooth and everything you want when you need a moment of caffeinated bliss before the day starts kicking your ass.

"I'm so buying better coffee when we get home," I said.

"Damn straight we are."

We enjoyed the brew and the quiet until Libby shifted in her chair. "There he is."

Cavanaugh pulled into the parking lot. If he'd looked up and over he would have seen us, but his focus seemed elsewhere.

He parked and eventually walked into the café and toward our table, a thin leather computer case slung over one shoulder. His button-down was clean and pressed, but his hair barely looked combed. Shadows under his eyes and on his jaw suggested he hadn't gotten much sleep. Mussed and rumpled worked for him. It softened some of his hard edges.

"Good morning," I said, pushing a chair out for him with my foot. He hung the case on the chair and sat down.

"Is that for me?" He indicated the cup on the table.

"They just brought it."

He wrapped his hands around it. No cream or sugar. "You look more awake. Why don't you tell me what you need."

I glanced at Libby and she gave me an encouraging go-ahead nod.

"Last night's security footage from the Yavapai Plaza." Risky, as the footage would also show Daniel and Zack, but they were big boys. They could take care of themselves. "We're looking for a white van parked out front between eight and eight-thirty. I need to know where it went, track it as far as you can."

A bird chirped high and sharp as Cavanaugh considered it and my unease grew. "Do you know which cameras?" he said at last.

I slid a piece of paper with a list of store names, addresses, and times to him. "It's all here."

"I'll see what my contact can do." He tucked the paper into his front pocket. "Why is this van important?"

"The people in it tried to kidnap me last night."

He straightened, concern pushing past his weariness. "Are you all right?"

"We're fine. We fought them off, and they escaped in that white van. We hope the security footage caught a plate, or at least where they left the main roads."

"You fought them off?" he asked slowly, a hint of disbelief in his tone. "Just the two of you?"

I glanced at Libby. She'd heard it, too. It wasn't a sexist, "Aw shucks, two purty gals can't defend themselves," kind of surprise, but a shock that we'd survived at all.

"Sure. I doused them in holy water while Libby shot them." Let's see how much he really knew.

Cavanaugh's eyes widened. "That worked?"

"Well enough." I picked up my cup and took a sip. He watched as if unsure what to make of me or Libby.

"So tell me," I began, "how long have you known about the existence of vampires?" I liked the way it sounded, all official and in the know. We were serious people who knew serious things.

Cavanaugh twitched, but didn't look at me like I was nuts. He swallowed his mouthful of coffee and gently set the cup back down. He stared at it a moment longer, but then something in his demeanor shifted. Looser shoulders, a lower wariness level, and a glimmer of hope now shone in his eyes.

"A little over a year," he said. "My colleague has known much longer. I discovered them when he asked me to look into a missing boy from Mobile. He knew the grandmother."

"You found vampires?"

He cringed. "I found something. I smelled the garlic before I got to the front door. The entrance reeked of it. Crosses hung on the door, the walls, even the doormat had a cross on it. The mother refused to talk to me. Only screamed, 'Vampires took my son,' every time I asked a question."

"You believed her?"

Cavanaugh shook his head. "I thought someone ought to call the FBI. The father had also gone missing and no one was doing anything to find him. Grandma swore the crazy wife was to blame, but my colleague thought there was more to it. He neglected to mention what took them when I agreed to speak to the boy's mother."

"What changed your mind?"

He shifted in his chair, looking anywhere but at us. The bravado was gone, as was the law enforcement vibe. This felt like the real Cavanaugh—a man in over his head who was more worried about me and a woman I didn't even know than his own skin.

"I was approached at my car." He took another sip and another deep breath, paying way more attention to his cup than it deserved. "I never heard a thing until it spoke, and when I looked up, I saw...something... reflected in the window."

"Blurry, distorted, like looking at a movie projected on wrinkled plastic wrap?"

Relief flashed in his eyes and he nodded. "It gave me chills. It looked like a man but everything about it was *wrong*. It asked me who I was. I said a friend from work, checking on a woman who'd just lost her son in an accident." He paused and shook himself. "I've no idea what possessed me to lie to it."

I placed a hand on his arm. "It probably saved your life."

"Maybe, but two days later the mother took hers. Her suicide haunts me as much as the monster."

How awful. The poor woman had lost her husband *and* her son, and I'd bet no one believed her when she explained what had happened to them.

"How did you find out about them?" Cavanaugh asked softly.

Dad's voice whispered in my ears to cut this guy loose, walk away and start my life over again. It was risky enough Libby knew the truth, but at least she was an asset. Cavanaugh was...

I looked at those hopeful, grateful brown eyes.

I sighed. He was my father twenty years ago, asking questions about a dead wife and finding no answers. Dad would have given everything he'd had to have found someone like me, who had answers to those impossible questions. Cavanaugh was *definitely* hiding things, but I believed he wanted to help me and the Rosenberg woman. Maybe even help my father.

Alone and on the run had gotten me no peace and no answers. I'd learned more in days with Libby at my side than I had in years on my own. I didn't have to trust him completely, just open the door a little.

"One of them killed my mother. They've been hunting my family and I want to know why."

"I'm so sorry. When did she die?"

"Twenty years ago." I bit my lip, debated how open I wanted to be. Rolled the dice. "Her name is on your list, right at the top, right above mine."

He blinked, confusion wrinkling his brow. "I don't..." His eyes widened and he sat straighter. "You asked me about Rebekah and Hannah Antonelli."

"I did."

"You and your mother."

"Yes."

Sadness filled his eyes, but he didn't let it tip over into pity. "Rebekah was killed on a road in Pensacola under unusual circumstances. Police thought the husband might have done it, but the evidence made no sense and scared them half to death. Nobody who worked that case would talk to me."

"And now you know why."

Blowing out a breath, he leaned back in his chair, his hands loosely around the cup. "These things have been doing this a long time, then."

"Yes and no," Libby said, glancing at me. My throat was too tight to speak, but I nodded for her to continue. "They used to kill, but now they've switched to kidnapping. The evidence we've found suggests that change happened within the last five years. We still don't know why, but it's related to the blood."

"That's why they're using the blood banks?"

"We think so. Best guess on what we've gathered so far, they're somehow identifying and tracking their victims through their blood."

He placed a hand over his mouth and stared off into the street. After a moment, he shook himself and looked back at us. "From what I've been able to uncover, these, uh, vampires, are getting bolder. They're escalating the kidnappings and people are disappearing after smaller and smaller intervals. It's terrifying."

"Any leads on your missing person?" I asked.

His face clouded and he shook his head. "All I have is the blood connection you also found."

"The most recent victim, Ivy Helgarson, gave blood at a Universal Blood Center the week she was taken," Libby said.

He nodded. "That fits the pattern. Every victim I've found also gave blood or had blood taken within two to six weeks of disappearing. It's how I was able to find other possible victims of, uh..."

"Vampire kidnappings," I said, even though it wasn't technically true. "It helps to say it out loud. Is the blood bank a vampire front?"

"I don't know. It seems legitimate, but I don't think everyone who works there is. I suspect the Ascendant Health Hospital Network is also connected. Universal Blood works with Ascendant, and several of the victims gave blood or had procedures at an Ascendant hospital shortly before they were taken. And Ascendant's headquarters is in Phoenix."

Only two hours away, and central to the kidnappings in this region. Impressive detective work. "Do you know if Thompson General is part of that network?" Dad received his treatment there. I'd bet a week's pay they belonged to the same group.

"Yes, they joined a few months ago. Anita Rosenberg also had her gall bladder taken out at an Ascendant hospital three weeks before she disappeared."

Which explained why they hadn't found Dad earlier. "They have people working inside the hospitals and blood banks. Any theories on why they need the blood?"

"Could it be a ritual of some type?" Libby added. Daniel had thought so.

Cavanaugh shook his head. "I doubt it. Rituals are traditionally performed at precise dates and times, and these kidnappings are erratic. I've found no patterns that suggest victims are taken at predictable intervals or at a specific pace." He reached behind him into the case and pulled out a small, silver laptop. "However, I did find this."

He brought up a file and showed us a map of the country. Red dots filled multiple areas of the map like a grid, most heavily concentrated in South Florida, New York and the Tri-State area, and California, with smaller areas in Georgia and Arizona, and bits around the Midwest and the Northeast.

Libby made a surprised noise. "That looks like a search pattern."

"That's what I thought, too." He tabbed over to another image, this time of Europe. Same dots, same grid. "It's not only in the U.S. I've found this same pattern internationally."

The sheer scope of it was chilling. This wasn't some crazy Pretty Boy with a wild idea—this was a systematic search of the entire human population. "How long have they been searching for people?"

"It's harder to uncover records the farther back you go, and in some of these regions it's impossible to find any records at all, but—" He paused and took a breath. "Thirty, forty years at least."

Kokabiel's interest in blood predated that by centuries if you factored in the vampire myths. Impossible to map those numbers out on a grid, but surely you could still track deaths and missing persons beyond the 1980s. I didn't want to think about how they tested the blood before science.

Images of Mom's ripped out throat kept popping into my mind. The Pretty Boy who'd killed her had been furious—yet disappointed—after he'd bitten her. Somehow he'd known from the taste that she didn't have what he wanted. I shuddered. Had he literally *taste-tested* her?

I shook the images away, a tiny voice echoing as they faded, that if she'd been taken later she might still be alive. Foolish thoughts. Pointless thoughts.

Cavanaugh frowned and leaned closer. "My colleague insists these creatures aren't sophisticated enough to organize like this, but I can't ignore the evidence."

"Vampires have always looked for blood," I said as if I was an expert, "but it's been random and disorganized before now. A person snatched here and there, maybe entire small towns back in the Dark Ages and whatnot. What changed? Why use blood techs and hospital labs? What do they hope to find?"

Because *that* was the million-dollar question.

Libby sat straight. "DNA?"

Cavanaugh snapped his fingers. "DNA testing was developed in the mid-80s. My research shows that the search increased exponentially since genetic testing became widespread."

"They're also taking families," I said. "It's genetic." A protein in the blood perhaps? An enzyme, something the fangels need to survive? Kokabiel had figured out how to identify whatever it was he needed. With minions placed in the hospital network testing blood, he only had to grab those with the best odds of being the right match. But why keep them? "How many blood centers and hospitals have facilities capable of testing the blood?"

"Most of them, I'd gather," said Cavanaugh.

Libby waved a hand as if this was inconsequential. "He can buy the equipment. All he needs are people to bring him samples of the blood."

Which he obviously had from the sheer number of missing persons. For all we knew, Kokabiel had been planning this for centuries, building wealth and power and cultivating, seducing, or kidnapping the right people to help him. He could have put minions in every hospital in the country, built or bought blood centers in key areas to collect the samples without anyone being the wiser. Universal Blood Centers might even be Pretty-Boy-owned and internationally operated.

Cavanaugh raised one finger. "Excuse me, *he*?"

I winced. Damn. I'd hoped to keep that little ace up my sleeve for now. "We think there's a ringleader. Someone running the whole operation."

"An organization of this size does suggest someone's directing it. Do you know who?"

I looked at Libby, unsure how much to divulge, but a string of pink Jeeps passing on the empty street behind him caught my eye.

And my memory.

"Pink Jeeps," I said instead. I'd seen those same Jeeps last night, right before Kokabiel had ambushed us. My mind flashed to a much smaller pink Jeep in the blood bank lab.

Cavanaugh's brow furrowed. "I don't understand."

"A woman at a Universal Blood lab had a smaller version of that same Jeep on her desk. She was the one doing all the paperwork." She must have come here at some point, maybe to deliver blood, maybe for some evil minion orientation, maybe even a weekend away with the fam, but she'd *been* here. UBC *was* part of this and they *were* here.

"Kokabiel's mole?" Libby said.

"Did you say *Kokabiel?*" Cavanaugh said, going pale despite the brisk chill in the air.

Damn. "Uh..." I said.

"That's the name of one of the biblical watchers of mankind."

"We were never properly introduced."

"He's mentioned in the *Book of Daniel* and the *Book of Enoch!*"

I paused. Nah. Couldn't be the same guy.

He shoved back his chair and rose, throwing his laptop into its case before he'd even stopped moving. "I need to talk to my colleague."

"Right *now?*" I said.

"I'll call you. Don't do anything until I do." Cavanaugh fled as if his life depended on it. He had his phone out the instant he was far enough away not to be overheard.

"Well," Libby said. "That was suspicious."

"It seems our mild-mannered investigator knows much more than he's letting on after all."

"Follow him?" Libby asked.

I tossed down cash for the coffee. We'd paid for our breakfast already. "Absolutely."

"I'll drive. You suck at spy craft."

Chapter Eighteen

Our rental car had been parked on the street outside, perpendicular to the main road. We got to it and scrunched down in the seats before Cavanaugh's Camry emerged. A few minutes later, he left the lot. Libby pulled out slowly and followed him at a distance. Few cars were on the road, and one glance in the rear view would spot us.

"Maybe you should hang back some?" I said.

"I know what I'm doing."

The sky had grown considerably darker as the sun rose, the storm clouds thickening to a deep blue-gray. If it dumped all that moisture while we were behind him, this would be a short tail.

Libby let what few cars were on the road pull in between us. Cavanaugh didn't act like a man trying to shake a tail. No random turns, no varying his speed. He stayed consistently ahead of us, and after a few blocks, he turned into the parking lot of a large and unmistakable building.

Big, stylish, built from red and white stone that both caught the eye and blended into the landscape. A gardener in a wide-brimmed hat was hard at work trimming the already perfectly formed bushes around a sign that read St. Mary's Catholic Church.

"He hadn't struck me as the religious type," I said. "So I'd guess his colleague is a local boy."

"Wonder if Cavanaugh thinks you followed *him* to Sedona."

Possible. It did explain why our being here had surprised him. "Odd that he didn't mention that, isn't it?"

"Affirmative." Libby idled at the edge of the lot. "Keep following?"

I hesitated. If Hollywood had gotten it right, this could be a Pretty Boy-hunting HQ full of warrior-priests dedicated to the eradication of evil. Cavanaugh might actually work for people with power and influence, who really *could* help me get my father back.

"Yes. We need holy water anyway."

A LONG ENTRY hall opened up to a room full of red cedar pews. Stained glass sat at the far end, with a lone spotlight illuminating a crucifix hanging above the altar. To my immediate right sat a large room with a conference table. On the left, a door led to an area marked "Offices." A school events poster hung next to it, divided into bright, cheerful boxes announcing bake sales and Bible study.

No sign of Cavanaugh or any warrior-priests-in-training.

Libby paused at the marble basin of holy water by the door and dipped in her fingers. She crossed herself and gave a little curtsy, then scanned the foyer and peeked down the halls.

All clear, she signaled.

In unison, we pulled heavy-duty water pistols out of the plastic bags from our shopping excursion last night and sank them into the basin. We'd hit a toy store and purchased the highest-volume Super Soakers they had in both easy-to-hide pistols and larger long-ranged rifles. They hadn't had the kind with water tank backpacks, but Libby had found a vest with ammo packs that held 100 ounces of liquid. We filled as many pistols and ammo packs as we could before the water ran dry, then tucked our gear back into our backpacks, storing what didn't fit back in the bags.

Libby flicked two fingers toward the rows of pews just past the interior doors. I crept forward and peeked inside. No one but a black-haired woman in her forties wiping down the pews with a fruity-scented oil.

White plaster walls gave the room a lighter feel, with soft orange and turquoise patterns painted on the columns and arches. More stained glass windows—these with cheerful blue borders—sat in recessed windows above alcoves displaying brightly colored statues of saints. Wood beams carved in a lacy floral latticework ran across the ceiling, simple, yet elegant. No fuss, no muss, just a quiet serenity.

Pretty.

Still no Cavanaugh.

Libby walked over to a rack filled with candles. About half were flickering, and their golden light danced across the wall and along the floor. She lit one of the candles and mumbled something softly under her breath.

"For the Helgarsons," she said.

"That's nice."

The cleaning woman looked over as if finally noticing us. After a pause, she put down her rag and oil and approached me with a smile. A glint of diamond sparkled in her nose. "Do you need some help?"

"Just looking for someone, but thanks."

"One of the priests? I can find one for you if you need."

I shook my head, keeping my voice low. "That's okay, we—"

"Grace," Libby called softly. "Offices."

"Looks like she found him," I told the woman. "Thank you, though."

"You have a nice day."

I followed Libby back to the foyer and through the inner door, entering a hallway with offices along one side. Tall, narrow glass panels lined the upper half of the doors, just big enough to peek inside the room. At the end of the hall it curved to the right, next to a sign with classroom numbers and an arrow.

Too early for school, but soon these halls would be full of kids. An image flashed through my mind and I grinned. Maybe they were the next generation of hunters, and the school was all a cover. Cavanaugh and his friend found the vampires and a swarm of teen-aged girls slew them.

A soft click broke the stillness and a door opened in front of us. Cavanaugh stepped into the hall holding his open laptop and a thick file folder. He did a double take and gasped.

"What are you doing here?" he said. "Did you *follow* me?"

"I'm told I have trust issues."

His eyes narrowed. "I said I'd call."

"You also know who Kokabiel is."

An uncomfortable pause, then he squared his shoulders. "I know *what* he is. There's a difference. And you lied to me—you know these things aren't vampires."

I pointed two fingers at myself. "Trust. Issues."

His gaze flicked to the folder in his hand. "Fine, let's talk." Stepping aside, he gestured us into the room he'd just left. We entered a small office with an impressive snow globe collection on the bookshelf.

"Those yours?" I asked him.

"No, I don't have an office here." He set down his things and sat at the desk, hands folded neatly in front of him on the deskpad.

"But your colleague does?"

"Yes."

"Is he a priest?"

A slight pause. "Yes."

"Does he lead a vampire-hunting team?"

"He does not." He rolled his eyes, but there was no hesitation this time.

"So there is a vampire-hunting arm of the Catholic Church?"

"The Catholic Church takes your soul very seriously." His lip twitched and a surprising playful side appeared, if only for an instant.

"I can tell by the stories in the stained glass."

Libby cleared her throat. "We were discussing Kokabiel."

"Technically," I said, dropping into a chair, "we were avoiding talking about Kokabiel."

She ignored me and spoke to Cavanaugh. "Does your colleague know there are fallen angels in Sedona?"

He hesitated. "He doesn't know what they are—I haven't had a chance to tell him yet. He was convinced a creature was here, just not where. He suspected Sedona was its hunting ground."

"Did he tell his superiors?"

A longer pause this time. "No."

"Why not?" I asked. "Wouldn't they send reinforcements?"

"He wants to trap it ourselves."

"*Trap* it?" I laughed. It was ridiculous—and dangerous. "*That's* your plan?"

"He feels it's our best option," he said, but the tight white knuckles of his hands said otherwise.

"You honestly think you can grab this guy off the street?"

"He thinks with the right tools, it can be contained—"

I scoffed. "It can't."

"He feels—" Cavanaugh grunted and pushed both hands through his hair. "Fine, you're right, it's foolhardy, especially now, knowing what it *really* is, but Aaron thinks it's barely more than a clever animal."

Clearly he'd never met one face to face. "He's wrong."

"I know, but I've yet to convince him otherwise. He's been chasing them a lot longer and thinks he knows better."

"How much longer?"

"Eight years."

I looked at Libby, who shrugged. "Isn't there someone else you can approach?" she asked. "Who's in charge of this diocese?"

"No one who would believe Aaron. He...has a reputation." He shifted uncomfortably.

"As a crackpot?"

"I wouldn't go that far, but he gets...obsessive...about things."

Crackpot or not, he was here. Coincidence or plan? "Was he assigned to Sedona, or did he come here himself?"

"He's from Phoenix, but he took a sabbatical here, then asked to be assigned to St. Mary's."

"How long ago?"

"Four or five years I think."

The magic number again. "Did he follow Kokabiel here?"

"He followed *something* here. I don't think he knew what he was tracking. He would have told me."

"Like he'd told you about a vampire kidnapping?"

He narrowed his eyes. "He wanted to get my unbiased opinion about the case. He told me afterward."

I glanced at Libby. It was possible Cavanaugh's colleague had followed any one of Kokabiel's minions here. Daniel had been surprised Kokabiel had come after me personally, so it was likely he didn't get out much. This Aaron guy might not have known what he'd been following.

"Let us talk to your friend," I said. "We all have pieces of this puzzle, and the more we fit together, the more of the whole picture we'll see."

He glanced out the window at the ever-darkening sky. After a long pause, he sighed. "Why not? Maybe *you* can get through to him that we need help."

Chapter Nineteen

After a not-so-brief absence to announce us to his colleague and break the news, Cavanaugh led us to a slightly larger office with nicer furniture and a wall-spanning mirror on the front wall, facing the desk. The man sitting behind it checked our reflections as we walked in, but maintained a rigid stance despite our non-Pretty Boy verification. Old books and neat stacks of papers sat in piles around him. A clock behind him read half past eight.

I'd expected a wrinkled, brooding man with bushy eyebrows, but Cavanaugh's colleague was thirtyish, pleasant to look at with sandy-colored hair and bright—if suspicious—blue eyes. The black clerical shirt and white collar seemed out of place on a face that young.

"Father Aaron Dandridge," Cavanaugh said, "this is Grace Harper and Liberty Torres."

"Hey." I gave him a quick wave and a smile he did not return.

"Please sit down," Cavanaugh said softly, stepping into the aisle between us and the desk.

We sat. I waited a moment, but Dandridge stared at us as if he hadn't decided whether we were friend or foe.

"So," I began, breaking the ice, "fallen angels, that's just crazy, am I right?"

"It is." Dandridge glanced at Cavanaugh, his jaw tight. "What makes you think this Kokabiel is real?"

"I've met him."

"You met a man who called himself that." Not a question, a dismissive statement as if I were wrong.

"Excuse me? I know who and what I met. *Not* a man."

"You have no proof—"

"Let's take a step back." Cavanaugh leaned forward, both hands out between us. "Why don't we start with the missing persons cases in the area."

"Fine." I crossed my arms and waited again, but either Dandridge was still reeling from the Kokabiel news or he wasn't happy about meeting with us. Probably both.

"Isn't missing people a bit outside the church's purview?" Libby asked, filling the awkward silence.

Dandridge shrugged. "The Church has been protecting souls from evil for millennia."

I glanced at Cavanaugh, then back to Dandridge. "It's not the souls I'm worried about. People are disappearing. Who knows how many have already been killed."

"The Church has this well in hand Miss Harper. Your assistance isn't needed."

"You get special training to fight supernatural strength and speed at seminary these days?" Libby kicked my ankle and I winced.

"They have no supernatural speed. They're marginally stronger than the physical bodies they inhabit," he said.

I blinked. "The what now?"

Pity flashed across Dandridge's face, and I felt like I'd just given the wrong answer in school. "They're not what you claim they are," he said, just shy of condescending.

"Really?" I shifted my ankles farther away from Libby. "What do *you* think they are?"

Cavanaugh cringed. Dandridge and I stared at each other like gamblers over a bad hand of poker, hoping the other would blink or fold. The awkward silence grew as Dandridge watched us, revealing nothing but an impressive skill at waiting.

Cavanaugh cleared his throat. "Demons," he said. "Aaron believes they're demonic spirits possessing human bodies."

Oh boy.

"Hate to break it to you, but they're *really* fallen angels."

Dandridge's shoulders tensed. "Whoever told you this is lying to you. The archangel Michael bound the fallen in the valleys of the earth. They're trapped."

I shrugged. "Guess they got out."

"Impossible." Dandridge waved a hand. "It's a few demons at most here to wreak havoc and spread evil in our world."

"By kidnapping specific people based on their blood?"

Doubt flickered across his face. "There's no definitive proof of that."

"Have you talked to Cavanaugh?" I pointed at him. "He's pretty convincing. Has a slide show and everything."

He looked *away* from Cavanaugh, who pinched the bridge of his nose with one hand.

"Arguing semantics isn't going to help anyone," Cavanaugh said. "Let's not let it distract us from what's important."

Dandridge nodded.

"We're all on the same side," Cavanaugh continued. "What we know for sure is that *whatever* Kokabiel is, he's taken people we want found. We can help each other if we work together. We *should* help each other."

Damn. Cavanaugh had a few more vertebrae in that backbone than I'd thought.

Dandridge glanced at his desk and shifted slightly in his chair. "Of course. Forgive me." He took a breath and turned to me. "Nate told me a demon's been hunting your family. My condolences."

Wariness still lurked in his tone, but he sounded more like a concerned priest than a defiant demon hunter.

"Since I was five." If Cavanaugh could put up with my crap for the greater good, I could suffer this crackpot.

Dandridge leaned forward, determination in his eyes. "Nate also said you believe that same demon is nesting in Sedona."

I doubted he'd used those words. I pictured feathered demons and nests made of human bones. "That's where the evidence led, yes. Multiple fallen angels working in secret in the Arizona mountains."

His cheek twitched. "You're an imaginative woman, Miss Harper."

"I am, thanks for noticing."

"Why are you *actively* searching for a creature so dangerous?"

"Why are you?"

"It's my job."

"Ah." I nodded slowly. "Saving our souls and all."

"Exactly."

"How's that working out?"

His frown deepened, but sadness lurked behind it. Libby kicked me in the ankle again, harder. I shot her a look. She could scowl all she wanted, but I knew liars. I saw one in the mirror every day.

"I know you don't believe me, Miss Harper, but this *is* a demon and it *is* deadly. If you persist, you're going to get yourself, your friend, and Nate killed," he said.

"I'm willing to take the risk," Cavanaugh said. "These people need our help."

"See?" I gestured toward him, palm up. "He's on our side. You come on board, too, and we have a decent shot at getting the missing people back."

"Not by going after it directly." He rubbed his eyes. "We must draw it out safely on *our* terms, not rush into its den. You claim you've met it, but you have no idea the danger you're both in."

"People keep telling me that, but I've fought them off twice in the last week."

I could practically hear Dandridge's teeth grind. "You can't fight off a demon."

"Done it. Twice." I held up two fingers for emphasis.

After a moment, Libby nodded. "I've seen her do it, Father."

Cavanaugh also nodded. "I was there when she fought off one in Florida."

"Impossible." His eyes narrowed and flicked toward the mirrors again. I'm sure some rather unpriestly thoughts were going through his mind.

I pulled out my knuckledusters and held them up. "Silver hurts them. So does holy water. Sunlight makes them very uncomfortable and they avoid it when possible. They can bleed. They can *die*. If you're the Van Helsing of the Catholic Church, then you should *know* this."

He huffed, eyes wide, and jerked back in his chair. "It's not that simple."

"Demon hunters kill demons. You know where some demons are. What's the problem? Why aren't you guys moving on this?" They were the freaking *Catholic Church*. If anyone had serious fangel-killing gear it was them.

"I told you, it hides among us. I know it's nesting nearby, but I don't know where to start looking to flush it out."

"All our evidence points to *them* being somewhere in the mountains past Boynton Canyon. With a few more bodies to help search, we can find the lair in no time."

"Matthew 24:26," he said. "Wherefore if they shall say unto you, Behold, he is in the desert; go not forth: behold, *he is* in the secret chambers; believe *it* not."

"Which means *what* exactly?"

Libby leaned forward. "That just because you say there are monsters in the desert, that doesn't mean there are monsters in the desert." She shrugged. "Paraphrasing."

"Even if you're right," Dandridge said, "we don't have the resources to search such a large area. It's too dangerous."

I clenched my hands. Cavanaugh's frustration made more sense now. "Fine. I know where one of their human minions works. We watch her, find out who she's giving her information to, follow that person back to his boss, and *then* go stake the whole Salem's lot of them."

"No, it's too dangerous." Dandridge leaned back, but kept his hands on the table. "The safest action is to draw it out so we can capture it on our terms. It'll come for you. It has before."

Hadn't he heard a word I'd said? "*Four* of them tried to snatch me off the street last night. They stop time. They have supernatural speed and strength. You can empty a full magazine of bullets into their chests and they keep on coming. You *can't* capture that."

"And let's all remember," Libby added, expression grim, "capturing one angel isn't the mission. Finding the missing people is. This is a *rescue.*"

"Those people are already lost. We can't help them, much as I wish we could. Our only hope is to capture this demon and prove it exists so we can obtain the necessary resources to fight it properly. Rome will *have* to support my initiative once I have irrefutable *proof.*"

*Sonuva...*I looked at Libby. She rolled her eyes. He wouldn't help us find our way out of the building let alone find Dad and the others.

Cavanaugh closed his eyes and took a deep breath. "Aaron, I know you're struggling with this, but you have to believe them. We were wrong about *so* much."

"How can you take their side? They have no *proof.*"

I shook my head. "You're an idiot."

"We done?" Libby asked, all trace of her priestly reverence gone.

"Hell yeah." This guy was useless. If he wasn't trying to stop the Pretty Boys, then why did he come here? For a snowball's chance to impress the Pope?

I rose, Libby right behind me.

"Wait!" Cavanaugh said.

"Let them go, Nate. They refuse to do what needs to be done for the good of all."

Cavanaugh chased us into the hall. "Ms. Harper, please…"

I'd been lucky to find an ally in Libby, willing to help despite how crazy it was—it was stupid of me to think I'd find another in Cavanaugh. Even stupider to think any of those movies had gotten it right.

"Stop, please! Aaron doesn't see the big picture. He gets caught up in one detail and has trouble letting go," he said, trailing after us. "He's never met one of them, so he doesn't understand."

I scoffed. "He's more interested in proving he's right to his bosses." Annoying as it had been, the morning wasn't a complete loss. We'd gotten some solid intel, filled our pistols with holy water, and soon as we got to the car, we'd fill what was in the trunk.

"He's not like that. He cares about—"

I stopped at the end of the hall, my hand inches from turning the doorknob and leaving. "You really want to help Anita Rosenberg and my father?"

"You know I do."

"All our evidence points to them being held in the Boynton Canyon area. Dandridge admits they're in Sedona, but he's too chicken to do anything about it." Four years of ktracked with what Louis had said about the missing hikers. Dandridge must have somehow figured out the connection. Damn. That was info I'd have liked to know, but that bridge was burning now.

Cavanaugh said nothing, but his left eye twitched.

"He'll come around once he has time to process it." Cavanaugh rubbed the back of his neck, his expression pained. "I've known Aaron for years. He's not going to let innocent people die if he can save them."

"And if he thinks he *can't* save them, then what?"

"I…I don't know."

"He'll do nothing. He's *done* nothing."

Cavanaugh looked at her, then back to me. "I can't believe—"

"We know generally where hikers have disappeared and have seen the unexplainable. If your cop friend in Florida can get me the security footage from last night, we might be able to learn where the fangels who attacked us last night left the main road, and narrow that search area down enough to actually help those people."

"Then we can find Grace's dad and Anita Rosenberg," said Libby. "Ivy Helgarson can go home to her husband and little boy."

Cavanaugh sighed.

"Nate, if you still want to help us, help us," I said softly, putting a hand on his shoulder. "Who do you think has a better chance of saving them, us or Dandridge?"

He glanced down the hall toward Dandridge's office. The door was shut, and I pictured the young coot muttering behind his desk, replaying the argument in his head. He seemed like the type.

"What do you need? Besides the security footage."

"Holy water and lots of it."

He smiled wryly. "That part I can help with."

Libby tipped her head toward the front door. "The big guns are in the trunk."

"Guns?"

"You'll see."

Damp air greeted us as we left the church, chillier than Arizona in February ought to be. Colder than natural weather. The tickle of spiders danced across my skin.

I stopped on the steps and raised a hand. Libby halted, her own hand moving to the small of her back. Cavanaugh took another few steps and stopped.

"What is it?" he said.

"Wood smoke and spiders. They're here."

Libby drew her water pistol. It shouldn't have looked dangerous, but it did. "Where?"

"I don't know, I just feel them."

Cavanaugh gave me a look, but just scanned the parking lot, his gaze darting haphazardly. "What am I looking for?"

"*Him.*"

Kokabiel stood under the overhanging branches of a clump of trees, dressed in a simple button-down and khaki pants. His pale skin glowed, and his white hair flowed around him in the breeze. He really was beautiful to behold, but nothing that strange should dress that ordinary.

Cavanaugh took a step forward as if drawn to him. "That's Kokabiel?" he whispered, voice tight. I grabbed his arm and tugged him back.

"In the flesh."

Libby shifted position and covered our backs. "Think he's alone?"

"No." His minions had to be nearby. Rocky, Rude Dude. Maybe more if he had them. "He's staying off holy ground I see."

"And covering the exits. Smart money says he has someone watching the rear."

"How did he even know I was here?"

She shrugged. "If he has human minions in the blood banks, he could have them anywhere. One could have waited on us at breakfast."

Comforting thought.

"That's an angel?" Cavanaugh ran a hand through his hair, his face pale. "He's so beautiful."

"They're handsome sons of bitches."

"He's smiling at us." Cavanaugh smiled back, an awed light in his eyes.

Which creeped me out. I elbowed him in the side. "Hey! Focus."

I didn't like any of this. Kokabiel hadn't moved, hadn't said a word, hadn't demanded my blood. He stood under the tree, his pale hair blowing around his shoulders like a supermodel on a runway, grinning at me. Daring me to run? Fight?

"Grab the gear and head back inside," I said, stomach twisting. "We're not going anywhere yet."

"IN HERE." CAVANAUGH ducked into the first office and quietly shut the door. Libby took position by the window.

"Rule number one," I began, finger raised. "Don't tell Dandridge Kokabiel's out there." The priest was crazy enough to try to catch him.

Cavanaugh was still gaping, even though he'd known what Kokabiel was and that he was after me. But I guessed knowing and seeing were two different things, and Kokabiel *had* been pouring on the divine charm pretty hard. Maybe we *ought* to drag Dandridge outside and let him see for himself what he was up against.

I opened my pack, pulling out the smaller of the two water pistols I'd bought. One held a lot of water, but it was too cumbersome to use as a concealed weapon. The other looked like a classic squirt gun and snuggled in nicely at the small of my back. My knuckledusters were still in their sheath, the tasers and Zappers in the pack, and our basic survival and/or spy gear strapped down and buttoned up for convenient grabbing when we needed them.

Libby was already loaded and ready to go. "What's our exit strategy?"

"Cavanaugh, is there a secret underground garage to this place?"

He stared at me as if I'd gone mad. "It's a *church*."

"A church that keeps an eye on demons, so I don't think it's that farfetched a question."

"No secret exits."

"Lib, can you think of a way out of here that doesn't involve a fight?"

She considered it. "Surrender and let him take us back to the lab."

"Any *good* ideas?"

"Not at this time."

Cavanaugh stepped between us, his hands outstretched. "Wait, what are you doing?"

"Do we have anything that'll work like grenades?" I asked Libby.

"Water balloons."

"Perfect."

She tossed me a packet of balloons, but Cavanaugh snatched it out of the air before it reached me. "You can't fight something like *that*. You know what he is."

"Pretty tired of waiting for my sorry ass, I'd gather."

"But—"

I took his face in my hands and held his gaze. "Keep it together, Cavanaugh. You know what he is. He's the same evil bastard who kidnapped Anita Rosenberg. Remember her?"

"Yes, of course." He wiped a shaking hand across his face and nodded. "No, you're right. I don't know what I was thinking."

"Wasn't your fault, he worked his mojo on you. He does that." I plucked the bag of balloons out of his hand. "I know we don't have the security footage, but why don't you try to narrow down the search area anyway."

"To find the lair?"

"To find the lair." I guided him to his chair and nudged him down in front of his computer. "Our source said hikers keep going missing around Boynton Canyon, but later they show up miles away with foggy memories."

"If the police were involved, there should be something about it online."

I smiled and patted him on the shoulder. "I was hoping you'd say that. Find out how far back the news articles go."

"I can do that." He shifted his focus to the computer and I went back to Libby.

"That ought to keep him distracted," she whispered.

Hopefully. "You come up with anything brilliant yet?"

"I've had three minutes."

"Slacker." I peeked through the blinds and across the parking lot. Kokabiel hadn't moved, and neither had— "The van."

"What about it?"

"Do we still have the tracker we were going to put on the Helgarson's car?"

"It's in your pack. Front pocket."

"You think you can make it out there unseen if I distract Kokabiel?"

She parted the blinds and studied the street. "If we wait and hope it starts raining or snowing, and there's no one in the front seat looking out the windows, and I can slip out an exit they're not watching...maybe."

"Fifty-fifty chance?"

"Thirty-seventy. Less if he's got decent backup."

Lousy odds. "You'd be on holy ground most of the way." The van was parked right at the edge of the street, with only a strip of sidewalk between it and the church. Could be public ground, could be church property. We wouldn't know for sure unless a Pretty Boy stepped onto it.

She pursed her lips and considered it. "I've got the pistols for the gray areas in between. It's a long shot, but we can't sit here all day."

I didn't know who was crazier, her or me.

"If I get you killed, I'm sorry," I said in all seriousness.

"You'd better be or I'm haunting your ass."

I'd expect nothing less, but if I said that, I'd start crying, then she'd start crying, and that was no way to launch a battle against beings cast out of Heaven.

"Four years," Cavanaugh called out.

We turned, letting the blinds fall back into place. "What?"

"Hikers have been getting lost and confused around that area for the last four years."

That fit the timeline.

"No deaths, though," he said. "Which is odd."

"None?" Common human idiocy should have caused one or two in that many years.

"Nothing but the relocated tourists."

I left the window and joined him behind his desk. "What about the year prior?" Kokabiel had gone from killing to kidnapping in the last five years.

"Give me a moment, please."

He searched, fingers tapping quickly over the keys. "Two people disappeared about five years ago while hiking the Boynton Canyon Trail. Their bodies were found a week later at the edge of the Palatki Heritage Site."

"How close are those two areas?"

"Close enough not to raise eyebrows, but it's unlikely hikers would get lost and wind up there by accident."

Libby tipped her head at me. "What is it?"

"Maybe nothing. Maybe a lead." Two dead hikers was hardly out of the ordinary, unless... "Was there an extensive search for them? Something that brought a lot of unwanted attention to that area?" Something made him change his tactics from kill to brainwash and transport.

"Ah..." His fingers flew across the keys again. "Yes. One of the hikers was a congresswoman's son. He and his girlfriend came here on spring break. They also lost four people during the search, all professional search and rescue."

"Sounds like the S&R teams got too close for Kokabiel's comfort," Libby said.

"He messed up." I grinned. We *had* him. "He saw hikers too close to his lair, so he killed them. But he had no clue they were important and brought down more attention on himself. He must have realized moving trespassers out of the area before anyone noticed they were gone was safer."

Was that what Dandridge had uncovered?

"And if anyone did notice, the facts were too weird to be taken seriously or lead back to him. Anyone who spoke to them would think the hikers were somewhere else, no matter what they said."

Evil and smart was a bad combination. I turned back to Cavanaugh. "What's in that area?"

He shook his head slowly. "Not a lot. Miles of hiking trails, dense forest, mountains. The farther one gets from the trails the wilder it becomes."

I glanced at Libby and she nodded. "That's where I'd hide my secret lair," she said.

Me, too. Hidden in the mountains, shielded by dense forests, *and* a popular tourist vacation spot with a transient population. It was perfect for all manner of unspeakable machinations.

"We need to see what's up there."

"We need to get out of here first."

"Only if we can get the odds up to—" I jumped as a knock rattled the door.

"Dandridge?" Libby crossed the room and opened it, one hand on her pistol.

Something popped, like the muffled sound of a car backfiring. Libby cried out and flew backward, the front of her shirt ripped and frayed. A black-haired woman stood in the doorway, holding a gun.

Chapter Twenty

"Libby!" I dived for her. This wasn't happening. We were in a church! We were supposed to be safe. She stared at nothing, but a single tear slid from the corner of one eye toward her temple.

"No, please no!" I couldn't lose the only friend I'd ever had.

"Grab her," said the woman who'd shot Libby. A diamond in her nose glinted. We'd seen her before, polishing the pews and wishing us a good day.

Fury roared in my ears, sharpened my focus. She'd pay for this. I yanked the steel baton off Libby's belt and flicked it open. "Call 9-1-1," I told Cavanaugh as I lunged.

"Grace, no!"

The woman leveled the gun at me, but she wouldn't dare shoot. *My* blood was too precious to spill.

A man almost as big as the doorway entered and came right at me. I swung the baton at his head with everything I had. He blocked it with an arm the size of my thigh and painful shockwaves raced to my shoulder.

I dropped to the floor and spun, slamming him behind the knees with the baton. The mountain rumbled. He felt *that* hit. His giant body swayed off balance.

Fall, you son of a—

SMACK!

Pain flared across the side of my head and *I* was spinning. A woman's laughter rose and fell as my vision blurred and the corners of my world darkened. Glass shattered, Cavanaugh cried out, but I couldn't focus enough to see.

Hang on, Grace-face, keep it together.

Libby groaned and the world snapped back into place. I crawled toward her. She was strong. Tough. She *had* to be okay.

"Lib! Stay with me!"

Mountain Man yanked me up by my hair and I yelped. Pain burst across my scalp. He dragged me out the door, but it didn't matter. Libby was still alive. Cavanaugh would call an ambulance and get her to a hospital.

The woman stepped in beside me and shoved the gun into my ribs. Her face and skin said mid-forties, but everything else about her fought hard to appear young. Heavy black eyeliner. Lace-trimmed black shirt, combat boots. A little old for the Goth look.

"Not everyone looks good with a nose stud," I said. "No shame in admitting that, especially at your age."

"Shut up."

Our fight hadn't lasted long, but it must have been noisy and the gunshot had to have been heard by—wait, the shot *had* been muffled. I'd hardly heard it myself.

I looked down at the gun in my side, the barrel longer and thicker than it ought to be. A *silencer.* That bitch brought a silencer *and* a throwback to Neanderthal times. Kokabiel outfitted his minions well. Soon as I got my hands on him I'd rip the green stuffing right out of him.

"Hurry," she said, taking the lead. Mountain Man dragged me along beside him, one fist still wrapped in my hair and keeping me bent back and off balance. His other hand crushed my wrist. He hauled me through the door and out into the parking lot.

"You know what you work for, right?" I said over the wind whipping by. The air hung heavy and thick around us, ready to dump the snow it had been hoarding all morning. Dark clouds blocked the sun.

"You know nothing."

"I know your bosses can't walk on holy ground without bursting into flames. Nothing good self-combusts on holy ground."

Aging Goth paused a few paces from our rental car and scanned the lot. "I can overlook a lot for immortality," she said, picking a new direction to drag me.

"You think he can give you that? He's lying."

"You'd say anything to save your own skin."

"I'm telling you the truth. He's not a vampire. If he promised you youth and beauty forever, it's a lie."

"Grace!" Cavanaugh shouted.

Aging Goth spun and fired. Cavanaugh hit the deck in front of the front doors, flinging his arms over his head. I held my breath until I saw him move, scrambling crablike out of the line of fire.

"You missed," I said. Why hadn't he stayed with Libby? Where was the ambulance?

She glared at me. "I *will* shoot you."

"Not if you want to live forever."

"You—"

"She's baiting you," Mountain Man rumbled. "Ignore her and let's get out of here."

I tasted the sweetness of woodfire smoke and burnt marshmallows in the air. "Can I say something first?"

She rolled her black-lined eyes. "What?"

"Daniel!" I screamed, loud as I could. "Help—" Mountain Man cuffed me in the side of the head hard enough to make my ears ring.

Ozone washed over me with the next breeze. I stiffened and braced myself.

A dark shape blurred past. Mountain Man jerked. His fingers spasmed, loosening their grip on my hair. He sank to the ground with a groan.

Aging Goth gasped and swung her gun around. I dived out of the way the instant I'd felt those fingers let go. She fired wildly. Daniel blurred into focus directly in front of the muzzle. The bullets tore his shirt, but dropped harmlessly to the ground.

She whimpered. I rolled to my feet and punched her in the face.

"*That's* for Libby," I said as she crumpled.

Surrounded in a halo of smoke, Daniel hissed in a pained gasp. Sparks raced across his skin, a rough reminder he was standing on holy ground.

I grabbed his hand and the sparks vanished. "They shot Libby! We have to get back inside."

He took a few deep breaths and his face unclenched. "I'll deal with the dominions. You go."

An inhuman roar mingled with the rolling thunder. Kokabiel paced at the edge of the church's parking lot, his hands clenched at his sides, his angry-yet-hungry gaze locked on me.

Images of rushing water and screaming women flooded my mind again—

—Water pours over the houses and the fields as the women run, the giants behind them. One woman stumbles and a giant grabs her and holds her high. She smiles at him, clinging to him as if for protection. The water gets deeper, and he holds her higher and higher as the water swirls around him, engulfs him—

I gasped, desperate for breath, drowning in water that wasn't real. The weight of it pushed me to my knees.

"Grace?" Daniel dropped with me, taking my other hand in his. Kokabiel roared again. "What's wrong?"

"Another memory." I shivered in the rain and waters that were all in my head. "Women running from a flood. Maybe a dozen women and they're terrified, screaming, and giants are chasing them, with floodwaters right behind them. It looks like the giants are after the women, but I think they're trying to save them. They held them above the water."

"They were."

"Were?" I *felt* it, their fear and anger. Someone had betrayed them and that hurt worse than the drowning. They were confused, filled with *so much* regret. But...there was love, too. "Whose memory was that?"

Daniel's gaze shifted over my shoulder to Kokabiel. "Mine. His. Ours. We all remember."

I didn't understand. "Were you the giants?"

"They were our children. They never should have been born, but we loved their mothers and they wanted them."

I shifted, uncomfortable. "Did you...?"

"Break my vow and dishonor my Creator? Yes. I suffered the same punishment as the others." He swallowed, so much pain on his face. "Go to your friend. You shouldn't be out here."

An engine revved and the white van jerked to a stop behind Kokabiel. He smiled at me.

"Grace, come to me."

I gripped Daniel's hand tighter as the traitorous *need* to do as he asked pulled at me. Daniel held tight, my rock against the waves.

Kokabiel's expression changed from persuasion to wonder. He stared at our hands, and Daniel *not* burning to a crisp, and his smile grew wider.

"I've looked for you for centuries," he said. I heard him clear as day, despite the shouts behind me. "You will come to me now."

"Get stuffed."

He gestured and the van door slid open. Rocky appeared in all his craggy glory, yanking someone into view.

My heart stopped. Soared.

"Dad?" It was him. Rumpled and pale, but *him.*

Kokabiel offered me his hand. "Come to me, Grace, or he dies."

"Run, Squashling," Dad said. "Don't look at your mom, just run." He pleaded with me from twenty feet away, but his mind was twenty years in the past, on a deserted road outside Pensacola.

Daniel's grip on my hand tightened, hot against the cool rain. "You can't."

"It's my *father.*"

"He's telling you to run."

"No, he's telling a five-year-old to run. He doesn't know where he is."

"You *cannot* give yourself to Kokabiel."

"I don't care! He's not killing my father!"

"Come to me, Grace," Kokabiel said again. "Or I *will* kill him."

Dad laughed, the hearty and loud chortle that always made me feel safe and loved. He shook his head, rubbed his eyes, came back to me from the past. "Don't y'all know? I'm already dead, jackass."

He looked at me and he was *there*, tired, sad, but in the here and now. "Go with Daniel. I've had longer than I should have. It's time to go."

I shook my head. "I'm *not* running anymore."

"You don't have a choice, and I'm sorry for that."

Kokabiel damn near growled. "Command her to obey or you will die."

"A month to live, big guy." He tapped his temple. "Now's as good a time as any I gather." He looked back at me. My father, my family. The only thing in my life that had ever been constant and sure. "I love you, Hannah Grace, always will."

"I love you—"

Kokabiel blurred and grabbed Dad's head in his hands. I screamed, reaching for the water pistol in my pack that my heart said I'd never get to in time.

Dad sucked in a pained breath and sank to his knees. Rocky let him fall, sliding out of his grip. I flailed against Daniel, screaming, but he refused to let me go.

"No! Dad!"

Dad blinked. Shook his head. One trembling hand rose and he touched his temple, prodding it with his fingers. He looked at me, then back to Kokabiel, uncertainty on his face. "Well, shit."

Kokabiel took two steps closer to me, right to the edge of church grounds. A tiny spark flared by his toes, bright blue and white.

"What did you do to my father?" I screamed.

"I healed him. He'll no longer die unless *I* wish it."

Chapter Twenty-One

Dad's color looked normal and his eyes were clear. Even the harsh pained lines in his face had all but vanished. I'd dreamed of this every night—a healthy father. The cancer gone. But miracles weren't real, not for us. We'd never been that lucky.

It was a trick.

I glared at Kokabiel, my hand so temptingly close to the water pistol. I'd kill him twice for making this hurt so badly.

He smiled as if he'd done me a favor. "He'll live a full life if you do as I ask. Or he can die now and you'll still do what I want."

"Liar." Dad wasn't better, and even if he was, Kokabiel would never let him go.

"I speak truth." He gestured one graceful hand at Daniel. "Ask *him.*"

I backed up, pulling Daniel with me. "Is he for real?"

"Yes."

The world stilled as if he'd stopped time. A brain tumor wasn't going to eat away at my father. He wasn't going to die without remembering who I was. We could have years together, living the life these handsome sons of bitches had stolen from us.

Anger shoved back some of my joy and I glared at Daniel. "Why didn't *you* do that when he got sick?" I gasped. "Libby! You can—"

"I can't! I don't have Kokabiel's skills. I can't heal anyone."

No. The universe had a crappy sense of humor. Who gives life-saving healing abilities to bloodthirsty creeps? It wasn't fair. I winced. I sounded like a child, but I felt like one. I just wanted my father back.

"It changes nothing, Grace," Daniel continued. "You can't give Kokabiel what he wants."

"Stop treating me like I matter more than my father does. Than Libby does." I jerked back, but didn't break free. Damn angel strength. Kokabiel made a noise that sounded far too close to a victory giggle and I screamed, frustrated to my core.

Kokabiel had no reason to let Dad go, even if he had me. He wanted our blood. This was a ruse to get me close enough to grab.

Dad knew that as well as I did. He rose easily to his feet in front of Rocky and gave me a sad smile. "I'm good, Grace," he said. "Don't worry about me. I'll be happy if you're safe. It's all I ever wanted for you."

But I wanted more. I wanted my job and my friend and an apartment with useless things too big to pack in a duffel. I wanted holidays and family, and yes, one day kids running around getting in the way while I tried to do the mundane things like clean toilets or bake cookies.

I wanted my father there to enjoy it all with me.

Kokabiel grew more and more impatient as I stalled. Dad looked annoyed that I hadn't done the most selfish thing imaginable and saved my own skin.

Daniel tugged me back toward the church steps. "Listen to him."

"Will you people quit telling me to abandon my family!"

"It's not just your family, it's *everyone's* family." He licked his lips, such a human gesture and without the awe-inspiring compulsion Kokabiel oozed.

I pushed my hair out of my face and scowled. "I'm not letting my father die because of some crazy end-of-the-world theory with zero evidence to support it."

"Grace, you have no idea what might happen if you go with him."

"Neither do you."

He glanced away. Sure, he'd been around for thousands of years, but he'd been a glorified babysitter. And let's face it, he'd screwed that up.

If the world could end because I saved my father's life, the damn thing was broken beyond repair anyway.

"Can angels lie?" I whispered.

"Yes."

"Is Kokabiel lying? Would he free Dad if I go with him?"

Daniel clenched his lips together and looked away. "Grace, you can't—"

"Answer me!"

"He wants you, not Anthony. If Anthony's blood could get him home, neither of them would be here now."

"Is that a yes?"

Daniel looked back at me, his dark eyes heavy with fear and sadness. "I've never known him to lie, but that doesn't mean he isn't lying now."

I could save Dad's life if I made the trade. If I said no, Kokabiel could kill him and still keep coming after me, same as he always had. He didn't need Dad alive to get to me. This might be Kokabiel changing tactics again, giving me what I wanted to get what he wanted.

This could be a once-in-a-lifetime opportunity.

Or a mistake that could cost me everything.

A life on the run was no life at all. Kokabiel knew I wasn't normal now, and there was no way he'd stop chasing me. Maybe he was lying, but my life was over no matter what he did to Dad. If they killed him, they'd still chase me. If they let him live, he'd always be a carrot to lure me into their trap.

It was just like Libby had told Dandridge—this was a rescue mission.

Movement behind Daniel caught my eye. Cavanaugh was back on his feet, watching us from the church steps, pale and pacing. Distant sirens wailed, growing louder.

"We're going with Libby's plan," I said softly. "I'm going to turn around and speak to Kokabiel in a minute. As sneakily as you can, unzip the front pocket of my backpack and pull out the small black device that looks like a tiny garage door opener. Turn it on, and sneak it into my pants inside my undies." It was small. It ought to wiggle its way low enough not to poke through my jeans.

"This is—"

"Not open to discussion. Libby's pack has the receiver for the tracker." My heart clenched, but the sirens were louder now, closer. "You can follow me with it, you got that?" If the tracker didn't work, or Daniel lost me en route, I was so screwed, but Dad would be okay. Libby would make it. They'd take care of each other.

I turned around and held still, keeping my backpack out of Kokabiel's sightline. "Fine, you win," I called to him. "I'll go with you, but only—" I held up one finger and wagged it, drawing it out as long as possible "—if you let my father go, alive and well, and never bother him again."

"Agreed."

"Whoa, that was, um, super fast."

Kokabiel gestured and Rocky took hold of Dad's arm again. He nudged him forward a step.

"Grace, you can't do this," Dad said, pleading.

"Send him over."

Kokabiel shook his head. "Come to us first."

"What guarantee do I have you won't yank him back?"

Kokabiel's brow furrowed and he seemed puzzled by my question. "Why would I lie?"

I felt something slip into my pants and slide down my skin. Atta boy. "Fine, I'll come forward, but my father needs to be standing well into holy ground before I leave it."

"You are untrusting."

"Keeps me alive."

Dad's eyes pleaded with me to stop this, to run and leave him to die like he would have anyway. Daniel wanted me to think about the world and what might happen. Neither could tell me what Kokabiel had planned or what it meant for anyone. He'd failed for thousands of years to get back to Heaven, so odds were good my blood didn't do a damn thing. Once he figured that out, he might even let *me* go. *Whatever you need to tell yourself, Grace-face.*

I squeezed Daniel's hand. "I need to let go of you. Can you make it to the street before bursting into flames?"

"It'll hurt, but yes."

My heart pounded hard in my chest. "On three—one, two, go." I opened my hand and the sparks danced around him, hissing softly. He grunted, then blurred, scooping up the Aging Goth and Mountain Man and tossing them each over a shoulder like they were nothing. Not part of the plan, but okay. Good cover.

Kokabiel didn't even glance their way or show any indication that he noticed, let alone cared what happened to them. He stood still as marble, smiling, his beautiful eyes locked on me.

This weird fangel glamour aura sucks. So disconcerting to notice the buffness of a guy I wanted to pummel into angel paste. I glanced back at the steps, but Cavanaugh had gone.

Rocky prodded a still-complaining Dad forward until he stood as deep onto holy ground as Rocky's arm would reach. Sparks flared.

"Hi, Dad," I said, walking toward him. "How's it going?"

Dad's eyes glistened with everything neither of us had time to say. "Slow day. Please don't do this."

"I have to. Trust me, okay?"

He hesitated, and a lifetime of unspoken words passed between us. "I'm trying, but this goes against every instinct I have. You sure you'll be all right?"

"I'll be fine. I'm planning a fancy dinner with my guy later, so I have to be back in time. Taking him out for stone crabs."

"My favorite. Hope he knows how lucky he is."

"He does." I threw my arms around him, squeezing him close. His free arm tightened around my waist. Strong, like the father I'd always known. "This is going to work," I whispered.

"It'd better. I can't lose you, too."

I kissed his wet cheek. "You won't."

For an evil bastard, Kokabiel stayed silent and patient as we said goodbye. He kept smiling at me in his weird and dreamy way, hope shining in his shifting opal eyes.

"Hurry up," spit out Rocky, not so patient. But then, he was the one whose arm was frying to a crisp.

I didn't remember much from my early years at temple, but the rabbis talked an awful lot about doing the right thing and taking care of those you loved. Saving Dad was the right thing. Giving Libby a chance to get to a hospital was the right thing. Helping strangers who had been abandoned was the right thing. And like Daniel said, it was just.

"Fine, let's do this."

And if I was wrong, well, there'd be no one left to say I told you so.

Chapter Twenty-Two

Rocky pulled me into the van by his still-smoking arm and yanked my backpack off me with the other, nearly dislocating my shoulder in the process. I braced for a vision, but I guessed he wasn't feeling nostalgic at the moment.

"Sit," he ordered, tossing my mini-arsenal into the back and well out of reach. He searched me with one hand, running it along my back and limbs. My knuckledusters and their sheath flew to the back and landed near my backpack. My water pistol joined it.

I dropped onto a bench running down one side of the van, careful not to crush the tracker nestled just below my left butt check. Rocky sat next to me, close enough to prevent any funny business on my part. The human redhead was at the wheel again, his freckled hands gripping a pink fuzzy cover. He didn't look old enough to drive, let alone carry the gun strapped to his hip. I couldn't imagine how the kid got this job.

The clock on the dashboard read 9:17, but the dark sky looked more like p.m. than a.m.

This is the dumbest thing I've ever done in my entire life.

Kokabiel stepped inside and closed the door, stooping with the grace of a dancer. His butt had barely touched the chair when Red floored it and peeled out. I caught the edge of the seat and steadied myself as the van bounced over the curb and ripped up the grass.

Kokabiel smiled. In the dim light, his eyes were gray and pale, with the occasional orange spark as a lightning flash lit the van. "It's a pleasure to meet you, Hannah Grace."

"Only my father calls me that. You can call me Ms. Harper."

"You're doing a noble thing, helping us."

"This isn't help. It's kidnapping with intent to eat."

The van careened around a corner, but Kokabiel didn't even sway in his seat. "You will be remembered for your sacrifice."

"Swell."

My knuckledusters called from their sheath, so close, yet out of reach. They'd have to wait, same as me. There wasn't nearly enough room to maneuver in the van, and Red would probably start shrieking and drive us right off the road and into a tree if it got hairy back here.

It also wouldn't help the other captives.

As satisfying as pounding Kokabiel into Mushface would be, I couldn't do a damn thing until I got to his lair.

I just hoped there was something I *could* do.

WE HADN'T MADE it out of the city before Kokabiel exhausted his repertoire of small talk, and for the last forty minutes he'd stayed quiet, reading who-knew-what on a pad he'd pulled out of a leather case between the seats. Rocky leaned back, arms crossed, eyes closed, but I was under no illusion that he wasn't poised to smack me down if I so much as breathed wrong.

Orange-red buttes slid by outside, with the occasional burst of juniper and olive-green tufts of grasses, but the trappings of civilization had grown less and less as we drove. Half an hour back, I'd spotted a few tourist signs for the local sites, one billboard for the Gold Spike Mine and Ghost Town, and a cheesy concrete cowboy holding a gold lasso and offering to turn me into a real live cowpoke, but nothing since we turned off SR89 and headed into the Arizona wilderness.

No sign of Daniel, or anyone else, following us.

I hadn't decided if that was good or bad.

We turned onto an even smaller road and Red slowed as it narrowed. It wasn't much more than a dirt path out here, and barely wide enough for the van. Large rocks scraped off the paint, but nobody even winced. Within minutes, we were moving at a crawl, lurching crazily from side to side over the ruts and rocks that passed for a trail.

The van might look like an old clunker, but they'd installed some serious shocks to handle this kind of terrain.

"I'm curious," I said to Kokabiel, gripping the seat with both hands. "What was Noah really like?"

His opal eyes shifted and gazed at me over the top of his e-reader. "Self-righteous."

Rocky grunted without opening his eyes. Even odds it was a laugh.

"Yeah, but I hear he really knew his way around a cubit."

Kokabiel returned to his reading.

"Possible to get some music?" I asked, a hard bump sending me half a foot off the seat. "Unless you've got a paperback tucked in there somewhere, too."

"No signal," Red called from the front seat.

"You must have a CD player. It's a van, it's got to at least have a cassette deck."

"Eight-track." Red snorted. "It's like the stone ages up here."

Rocky grumbled, but no trace of mirth this time. "She talks too much."

"She does," murmured Kokabiel without looking up. "Perhaps you should silence her."

I pantomimed zipping my lips shut. For beings who'd spent thousands of years among humans, they had little patience with one. Maybe we really were just children to them—better seen and not heard.

The Arizona landscape wobbled by, jerking as the van swayed over the rocks. There wasn't much to see at this point, but there might be enough landmarks to find my way back if I escaped. Red rocks. Buttes. Juniper. More red rocks. The occasional half-rotted shed or crumbled old mining camp poked out of the scrub, but they'd long been abandoned.

And ya know...red rocks.

Maybe that's where Kokabiel had holed up—an old mining camp from the good old cowboy days, or an outlaw's hideout deep in the mountains. This whole area had been dotted with mines back in the day, dug by hopeful prospectors searching for gold, silver, and copper. When I was a kid, Dad had taken me all over the Southwest to mining sites off the regular path. There was a lot of wilderness to get lost in out here.

And a lot of places to hide the bodies of those you didn't want found.

RED HIT EVERY bump and hole between us and the lair, but eventually, we bounced to a shaky stop beside a huge chunk of rock the size of a two-story house. Kokabiel yanked open the door and popped out under cover of a camo-colored tent working as a carport. The sides were rolled up and the straps snapped in the cold breeze.

"Out," Rocky said.

I got out, sore and a bit bruised. Nothing but the same walls of red rock and scrub, though the rocks were less red out here and more tan and brown. I'd built a diorama in fifth grade that looked a lot like this, though my scrub had been made of moss I'd found near our apartment. "Where are we?"

"Move." He booted me in the butt and my whole leg spasmed.

"Hey!"

Kokabiel sighed and turned away, heading toward a dark maw in the side of the rocky hill. He stayed under the tent's shade, skirting around what little sun had finally poked out from behind the heavy clouds. "Carry her if she won't walk."

"I'm moving, I'm moving!" Slowly, sure, but it was good enough for Rocky. I stepped out of the van and made a show of stretching, sneaking in a good look around.

Dad and I had spent two weeks at the Grand Canyon during my, as he called it, "difficult tween year," and the sense of being in a red-striped bowl was the same. A gray-blue sky seemed impossibly high overhead, and striated rock carved from glaciers boxed us in. We'd made it here, but there was no sign of an actual road. All I spotted were ruts in the dirt and a lot of flattened weeds.

A wooden shed poked out of a clump of scrub fifty yards away, a few crates and some random tools beside it—hammers, drills, a jackhammer that needed some serious TLC. The shed was old, but the "Caution-No Smoking" sign tacked to the door looked new.

Red lit up a cigarette and put his feet on the dash.

"Stop stalling," Rocky grumbled.

"Fine, fine!"

I walked with him across the boot-flattened path to the hole in the rock Kokabiel had vanished into. Seven, maybe eight feet high, a bit bigger than half as wide, the wall and edges smooth as though bored by water over millennia. It looked like a natural cave or fissure, yet it opened up inside and curved in an S-shape through the rock. Natural faded to man-made, with clear indications of blasting and digging to create the tunnel.

A good entrance for an evil lair. A terrible barrier to my tracker's signal.

The S-curve dumped us out into an entryway about fifteen feet square, directly in front of a set of double doors, ornately carved and polished so smooth they practically glowed. Candles burned in sconces bolted to the walls, marking a wide hallway that led in both directions maybe a hundred feet. Too dark to see the far ends clearly, but they looked like dead ends on both sides.

"Put her with the others," Kokabiel told Rocky. Then he turned to me. "Until later, Ms. Harper." He bowed his head and continued down the right-hand hallway.

"I reserved a private room!"

The smug bastard didn't even turn around.

Rocky pulled me to the left. At the end of the hall stood a door built for security, not beauty. Heavy steel, good lock, solid hinges. He unlocked it and we turned right into another hallway, narrower, but just as long, with electric lights strung on wires and an alcove fifteen feet ahead on the left. Another security door waited at the far end. Two plain wooden doors sat at the midpoint, also on the left, with one more on the right directly across the hall. A lotta space in this lair.

If Dad were here, I'd ask how many holes you could put in a butte before it crumbled down on your head. Kokabiel had to be pushing it.

We continued walking, passing the alcove, which turned out to be a masterfully carved room. *Don't be impressed.* But I was. I'd never seen a mountain with a rec room before. It just needed a pool table and an old refrigerator to complete the image. Three TV screens lined one wall, facing a leather L-shaped pit couch in soft cream with dark green throw pillows. Four café-style tables with chairs sat along the far wall, but still within easy view of the TVs.

Pretty Boys did not seem to me like the hang out type.

Two men somewhere in their forties currently occupied the room, neither handsome enough to be a fangel, so maybe this was a reward for the human minions. They sat at one of the café tables with steaming plates of pasta in front of them, and if fate was on my side even a little, they'd splatter marinara all over their white button-downs. A cute galley kitchen peeked out from off the back left wall. In the middle of the wall across from the entrance was another plain door. Bedrooms? Bathrooms? It was too far for a commute, so they had to live here.

They'd need a serious generator and a lot of fuel to power it all. "What's the rent on a place like this?"

Rocky ignored both me and the men and we continued toward the security door. Another lock, another key, another not-so-gentle shove through.

Beyond the door, recycled air hummed in time with the steady click of keys and the clink of glass. *So this is what an evil lab looks like.* Six faces looked up from their workstations as Rocky kicked the door shut. Hard to tell gender under their lab coats and caps, but Kokabiel looked like an equal opportunity employer as far as diversity went. If you were willing to sacrifice others for a little comfort, you were okay in his book.

"Greetings, evil minions." I waved. No one waved back. No manners at all.

Rocky took me to the closest station and dragged over a stool. "Sit."

I sat.

"Open a new file," he told the tech, a woman pushing sixty if she looked her age. "Preliminary testing."

"Testing for what?" I leaned closer to the screen, but Rocky yanked me back by the shoulder.

The tech slid open a drawer and pulled out a pre-packaged kit for drawing blood. "Hold out your arm."

"I don't think so."

Rocky grabbed my wrist and pinned it to the counter. I struggled until he wrapped the other arm around my neck and shoulders and pinned the rest of me. More effective than a straitjacket.

"That needle better be—"

—a woman holds a newborn babe the size of a toddler. She's pale, but smiling, speaking soft words I don't understand. Her words turn to song, her voice rising and falling with the melody, and I hum along with the notes. The love behind the words is clear, as is the concern. She's scared for the baby, scared for—

"All done," the tech said, snapping the tourniquet off my arm. Three red-black vials sat in a rack with my name on them. "We don't see a lot of fainters here."

Fainting? I didn't faint, but I'd certainly been elsewhere. It had felt like seconds, but it took time to fill three vials of blood. The soft notes of a lullaby still echoed in my head.

"She might need some juice," the tech said respectfully to Rocky. He didn't answer, staring at nothing with a sad expression on his craggy face. A tiny sigh escaped him and he shook himself back to the present and gave me a strange, questioning look.

"Move."

I smiled. "I do enjoy our little talks."

He yanked me up and dragged me around the room to the right, all the way to the far side of the lab, past a row of metal industrial shelves stacked with standard file boxes.

On the other side of the shelves, old-style jail cell bars cut off the entire right side from the rest of the lab. Three cells, and each cell had two cots, one toilet, and no privacy

Ivy Helgarson sat huddled on a cot in the middle cell, wearing the same blue slacks and lace-trimmed top she'd had on when I'd spoken to her. An older woman paced the ten feet allowed them, dressed in khaki pants, a tank top, and a cotton button-down over top of it—hiking attire. Anita Rosenberg? Two men in jeans stood by the bars in the cell on the left, disheveled and thin. One wore an old T-shirt, the other brown flannel. As I got closer, the man in the T-shirt looked up and sniffled.

Not a man. A kid, maybe sixteen. Scruffy brown hair, red-rimmed hazel eyes.

"Some protectors of the human race you are." I elbowed Rocky in the gut, but all it did was send painful tingles down my arm.

"We got fired." He stopped at the middle cell. "Stand back."

The pacing woman scampered to the rear wall and flattened herself against it. Ivy didn't look up, just hugged herself and swayed back and forth.

Rocky unlocked the cell and pushed me inside, keeping his Thing-like body between me and freedom. He needn't have bothered—trying to outrun them wasn't worth the effort.

He relocked the cell and left. The clang echoed in my ears, sapping what little energy I had for a parting quip.

"Who are you?" the pacing woman asked. She was about Dad's age, with graying chin-length dark hair and brown eyes. Her voice trembled, but a sad note of hope stood out.

"My name's Grace. Are you Anita?"

Her eyes lit up. "Yes."

"People are looking for you." I raised my voice a little. "They're looking for all of you. We're going to get out of here."

The man next door scoffed, but the kid just squeezed his eyes shut and nodded fast. Ivy lifted her head and stared at me.

"I know you," she whispered.

"We met the other day."

She cringed back and glared. "This is your fault! You sent those things to my house!"

I shook my head. "No, I *tracked* those things to your house. I was trying to stop them, but I was too late." Not that I could have done anything anyway.

"What about Jared? Did they hurt him?"

"Your son is safe."

Ivy blew out a breath and cried softly. Some inspirational rescuer I was. Maybe I'd been too hard on Rocky.

I looked at the others. With the exception of Ivy, they all had oily hair and rumpled clothes, and a sour odor that said no one had had a shower in a quite a while. The man had a pretty good beard going. "My father was here, do you remember him? Anthony?"

The kid sucked in a sob. "They killed him."

"Stop your whining," the man with him grumbled. Older as well, maybe mid-fifties, but solid through his core. "We don't know what happened."

"They took him and he didn't come back, and now *she's* here, just like the others." The kid pressed his hands against his head. "He's gone, man."

I walked over to the bars separating us and wrapped my hand around one. "What's your name?"

"Wil."

"Anthony's fine. I traded places with him, so that's why he didn't come back."

His face scrunched. "Why would you do that?"

"He's my father."

"The guy was dying! You could have been safe. That was stupid!" Wil turned and fled to the back, kicking the stone wall and cursing the world.

The man moved closer to me and the bars. "Nothing you say is gonna help that kid. He was screwy when he got here. I'm Jerry."

"Grace. How long have they had you all?"

"Few days to a coupla weeks far as I can tell. People come and go. Not all of 'em come back."

So much for Libby's stocking-the-pantry theory. "Did they take everyone's blood?"

He nodded. "First thing. The big guys take us out sometimes, can't say what for though." His brow furrowed, and he licked his lips. "They slip drugs in the food, knock somebody out. They go away, they come back with Band Aids or achy bits." He gestured near his crotch and glanced away.

Ew.

Movement behind me caught my eye and I turned. Anita had frozen mid-step, her eyes wide as if I'd scared her, but then she darted to us. "They're testing us," she said breathlessly. "Like the abductees you read about in the tabloids."

Jerry huffed and shot her a look. "They're crazy people, not aliens."

"I didn't *say* they were aliens, just that it was *like* that. I'm a nurse. I know what a medical procedure looks like."

"She's right about the tests," I said. Anita lifted her chin higher and gave Jerry a victorious huff. "I've been working with an investigator on this, and all our evidence points in that direction."

"Testing for what?" Jerry asked.

"I don't know yet." Libby's DNA theory made the most sense so far, especially if they were poking around the naughty bits. "What about the lab minions? Do they stay here?"

"Twelve-hour shifts near as I can figure. The scary bastards bring them down and take them away."

Anita tucked a loose strand of hair behind her ear. "I heard one mention dorms once. They have a lounge upstairs. Did you see it?"

"I did." It made sense that the scientists lived and worked there, practically prisoners themselves, but with much nicer accommodations. "What about guards?"

"Nothing obvious," Jerry said, "but there's nothing out there but nothing for a whole lotta miles."

Anita held up a finger. "In the desert. Even if they didn't catch us, we'd die of exposure before we reached help."

I sighed and rubbed my eyes. Unless Daniel had stayed close with the tracker, I was well outside its range. Being underground sure wouldn't help either.

Daniel...

I snapped my head up. "Was anyone else brought in last night? Tall guy, spiky blond hair?"

"You mean him?" Anita pointed to the cell on the right side. Someone lay huddled in the far corner beside the cot, curled into a tight ball.

I walked over and stuck my arm between the bars, but couldn't reach him.

"Zack? Are you okay?" We hadn't officially met, but if he worked with Daniel he had to be a decent-enough guy. Eddie had said as much, though he wasn't much of a character reference.

"All he does is moan," Ivy said. "Did you put him here, too?"

Technically, yes, but I was feeling less guilty about her every time she opened her mouth. "Zack, are you hurt?"

He had to be, or he would have broken these people out of here by now.

"Zack!"

The pile moved and a spiky-blond head appeared. His dusky skin looked sallow and sickly, his eyes glazed and hurting. "You?" he rasped.

"We have to get out of here."

He chuckled slowly, sadly, and dragged himself around to face me. He let the blanket fall away. "Can't."

They'd chained him in silver. Thick manacles encircled both his wrists and ankles, chains attached to both. One chain ran from his hands up to a choke collar around his neck. The skin under the silver was raw and blistered.

"Silver," I said softly. "That's just mean."

"Hurts."

I pressed against the bars, inching my hand as close as possible. "Grab my hand."

"Your comfort is appreciated, but—"

"Daniel can stand on church property when he's holding my hand. It might help. Do it."

Zack's eyes flickered. He gritted his teeth and dragged himself closer, hissing with every inch. Cold, shaking fingers slid into mine.

Relief washed over his face and he took a trembling breath. "Not... possible," he whispered.

"So I've been told." I glanced at the shelves of file boxes between us and the lab. Not bad cover, and the lab rats had seemed intent on their work. "Are there locks on those cuffs?"

Zack took another breath and dragged himself the last few feet to the bars. He squeezed my hand, looked me in the eyes, and the desperation in *his* eyes sent a chill down my back.

"You can't let him take you. Kill yourself. Kill yourself now."

Chapter Twenty-Three

I pulled my hand away, but he wouldn't let go, getting stronger the longer we touched.

"I think you've been in that silver too long." I aimed for flippant, but the crack in my voice betrayed me. Maybe unlocking his cuffs wasn't such a good idea.

"This miracle proves Kokabiel is right."

"Stop talking." He was making the other captives nervous.

"End of Days," he whispered.

"That's crazy talk." Sure, some days it *felt* like I was living in a Joss Whedon world, but there was no end of everything, no impending apocalypse.

Just like there are no vampires? No angels?

"What's wrong with him?" Anita asked. She'd moved closer, but no one came within grabbing distance of the bars.

"Allergy to silver."

"That doesn't make you—"

"It's a *severe* allergy."

"I can do it for you," he whispered. "It would be quick." He looked at my neck and the pop of vertebrae echoed in my mind.

—a green field stretches before me, hundreds of beings scattered across it. I swoop from on high and my blades slice flesh, take lives, protect those who have faith. The grass is soft under my feet as I land. A being larger than the others charges, knocks my blade away, and I seize it by the throat. Twist. Throw it away and move to the next—

I leaned back as far as his hold on me would allow. "We'll stop Kokabiel. The world will keep on turning, and we'll all go home."

Whimpering, Zack hung his head and flashes of glass towers and shining streets cut through my brain. "Not possible. Daniel was wrong. God will never forgive us."

"Even if that's true, I'm still getting us out of here."

Anita crouched down, but kept her distance. "What's he talking about?"

"He's in a lot of pain. People say crazy things when they're being tortured."

Zack slumped and pressed his forehead against the bars. "He will never let you leave. He spent two thousand years looking for you."

"Hate to break it to you, pal, but I haven't been around that long."

"Your family has. The line of the Mother. He's obsessed with her descendants."

"That bastard killed my mother, so I don't think—"

He chuckled slowly, helplessly. "*His* mother, not yours."

"Kokabiel's?"

"The Son of God's," he murmured.

Jesus Christ! I jerked back and smacked my elbow against the bars, but he still wouldn't let go of my damn hand. "You're telling me I have—"

"No, His blood is divine. Her other son."

No way. No freaking way. Everything in me wanted to let go and run screaming from the room. Hell, from the whole damn state of Arizona. I didn't care what Rabbi Cohen had said over and over as he'd struggled to teach me the *Torah*—none of those stories were real. They were just *stories*. I could believe vampires. I could even accept fallen angels, but not this. Not the *divine*.

"That's not *possible*. I'm *Jewish*."

"So was she. So was His brother."

"What brother? You think I'm...?" The great-great-great-*a lot*-niece of— *don't say Uncle Jesus, just don't do it*—of all the insane things that had entered my life, this tipped the lunacy meter deep into the red.

He patted my hand. "I *know* you are. Why do you think we protect you and those of your line?"

That son of a...I closed my eyes and took a breath. Daniel lied to me. He *knew*. I'd sat there and asked him point blank why Kokabiel wanted the blood and he'd *lied*.

Angel my ass.

That lying sack of muscles could bite me.

Anita cleared her throat. "Grace?" she whispered hurriedly.

I wasn't explaining this to the group. I couldn't even explain it to myself. My throat caught on a laugh as it hit me—everyone here shared my blood. My family. These people and I were all *distantly* related.

The sense of spiders ran across my skin and the hair on my arms stood up. Incoming.

"You are indeed everything I've hoped for," Kokabiel said, walking up to the bars. Stealthy little sucker.

I scoffed. "You're not my type."

"Oh, but you're mine. The preliminary tests prove it." He grinned and his sheer beauty almost overwhelmed me. I fought to maintain my scowl against his smile. "I've searched for you for millennia."

"Should have started earlier. Gone right to the source."

"Not, as they say, an option at the time."

I shifted on the floor of the cell and leaned back against the wall. Forcing my gaze away, I stuck my legs out straight and crossed them at the ankles. Inside, I shook like a paint mixer.

"I take it my blood is full of tiny organisms that give me magic powers?"

"It's full of promise." He smiled wider. "It's full of hope."

"Yeah? Well, you're full of shit. I don't care who or what you think I am, but you're wrong."

He chuckled softly as if I were a stubborn child. "Not this time."

"What do you want?"

"At this moment? Nothing. I simply wanted to see you."

I posed, head turned sideways, one arm up like a spokesmodel displaying a product. "Take a good look, then."

He laughed again. "You are a delight."

I glared. Hard to taunt someone when they found you funny. The least he could do was show a little respect.

He watched me a bit longer, making every inch of my skin crawl. Finally, he nodded slowly. "Thank you. Now, if you'll excuse me, I have much to prepare."

No one spoke to me after Kokabiel left. Anita and Ivy kept on the far end of the cell, huddled together and watching me as if I was one of the Pretty Boys. Jerry studied me like hunters studied prey that might go on the attack at any moment. Wil sobbed in the corner.

Zack wouldn't shut up about killing me.

"It's the only way to stop him," he muttered through the bars. At least he was staying quiet about it and only freaking *me* out.

"If you say that one more time I swear I'll drive a stake right through your heart." The cots were wood. I could do it. I'd sidelined my "get Zack free so he can help us escape" plan. A weak Zack made for a healthier Grace.

"The fate of the world is in your hands."

"Tell it to take a number." Kokabiel hadn't done much more than test my blood and get excited. I didn't want to think about his "preparations," but clearly, he wasn't afraid of anyone barging in to stop his nefarious plan. Chalking it up to his arrogance kept most of my hopelessness at bay.

The fact that I hadn't been rescued yet meant nothing. I glanced at my watch. It was barely past two. If Daniel *had* managed to follow me, he'd probably just be getting back to town for reinforcements around now. He wasn't dumb enough to take on Kokabiel's stronghold by himself.

Libby's face flashed in my mind and a dull ache spread through my chest. I'd tried so hard not to think about her bleeding out in Cavanaugh's office, but with nothing but impending doom, the lives of six people, and a potentially divine family tree to distract me, she kept popping into my head.

Dad will take care of her. Or Cavanaugh. Or even Dandridge. She'll be okay.

Didn't mean I wasn't going to kick the ass of the woman who'd shot her. I'd even hold her down while Libby got in a few licks.

Keep dreaming, Grace-face. You are so screwed and you know it.

"What time do the scientists leave?" I asked Anita. She was the only other person wearing a watch. She twitched and squeaked like a startled mouse.

"Six."

"Thank you." Not too much longer. "Is that the only door in and out of here?"

Anita squeaked again.

"Oh for the love of Pete, I am *not* the scariest thing down here."

Jerry grunted. "But *you* know what is. Bothers me you're not sharing."

"What do you want me to say?"

"The truth."

An urge to bark back hit me, but only I'd see the humor in it. But I could skirt the truth. "That blond guy who was here before? He's a deranged religious nut who thinks some blood ritual will get him and his followers into Heaven. Somehow he got it into his head that our blood has supernatural mojo."

"Some kinda cult?"

Good a word as any. "Yes."

Anita hesitated, rubbing the back of her neck. "What kind of cult members?"

"Extremely dedicated ones."

Jerry didn't look like he was buying any of this. "That blond one's a charismatic bastard."

"You have no idea."

"You one of them deprogrammers?" He lifted his chin at me. "I read about them when those comet folks were in the news."

"No, I was just trying to find my father and screwed up royally."

He pursed his lips and nodded slowly. "Does seem that way."

"What about him?" Anita asked, her finger shaking as she pointed it at Zack.

"He escaped the cult, but they pulled him back in. He's having a tough time separating reality and fantasy."

She made a sympathetic sound. "Poor man."

"He's been through Hell."

"Not quite."

I jumped at an unfamiliar voice. Guess it was time for our hourly check-in.

A Pretty Boy I hadn't seen before stood outside the cell in tailored silk and a haircut that must have cost more than my car. Darkly handsome where the others were beautiful, but tastefully so.

"Will you people stop sneaking up on us!" No one else was with him. "Where's your boss?" I asked.

GQ Fangel frowned. "I'm no one's dominion."

I'd expected words dripping with fangel arrogance, but he stated it as a fact, plain and simple. He could have said, "The sky is blue," with the same inflection. Kokabiel's ally? Anger boiled under my skin. This had to be Suriel, Kokabiel's partner. One of *his* minions killed my mother. When I got my hands on him I'd do the same thing I'd done to his buddy in Lauderdale.

"What do *you* want?"

He stuck a key into the lock of my cell and swung open the door. "Come."

"I'm good here, but thanks."

"Come or I'll break one of the others." The same matter-of-fact tone and all the scarier for it.

The air grew tense behind me, but everyone stayed silent as stones. Zack let go of my hand and I walked forward. "You're a dick."

Suriel stepped aside and I left the cell, nerves tight as he relocked it. I wasn't restrained. He had no hold on me, but there was nowhere to run to and no way I'd escape his reflexes or speed.

"Does Kokabiel know you're here?" My skin crawled, a maddening itch warning *danger danger* as loud as it could.

I was in serious shit.

Over Suriel's shoulder, I spotted Kokabiel, a frown on his chiseled face. "The others have been delayed," he said, a weariness to his voice. "Put her back."

Suriel rumbled, almost a growl. "I'm tired of delays. The tests confirmed this is the one."

"Patience, Suriel. We'll perform the rite traditionally this time. It's the ritual *with* the blood that creates the miracle."

Suriel barked something in the angel language and they snapped at each other, their shoulders back, heads high, standing their ground—total power struggle at play here. Kokabiel must have an ace up his sleeve. Maybe Suriel didn't know how to do the ritual?

Kokabiel smiled at him, again the parent who's trying hard not to yell. Tolerant, tight, with a "don't make me tell you again" craziness in his freakishly beautiful eyes. Darker now, with more orange fire than gold luminescence.

"Waiting is good," I said. "I can wait."

Suriel stepped into Kokabiel's personal space. It was weird, so much anger on such beautiful faces.

"Better listen to him, Surry," I said, putting a little attitude into it. "It's not a good idea to mouth off to your superiors."

Suriel's scowl shifted to me, and Kokabiel gave a tiny, self-satisfied grunt. He said something to Suriel I didn't need a translator for. Smug, condescending, the words of someone who'd won that round. Be nice if he gave me credit for the assist.

Suriel stepped back. Giving up that ground had clearly cost him. Anger churned under his perfect skin and his eyes flashed.

"Like I told junior there," I said, "if it's blood you need, we can work something out."

Kokabiel looked at me almost in reverence. He wasn't seeing me, but the DNA swimming in my veins. Not a person, a golden ticket home.

"I can help you."

He smiled bright as day. "You will, and we thank you for that."

CHAPTER TWENTY-FOUR

"Well that was a mite odd," Jerry said after Kokabiel and Suriel had gone. Everyone else had huddled together and stared at me as if I were just as weird as Kokabiel. I guess to them, I was.

"These cult fanatics really go all out, don't they?" I tried to laugh it off, but it sounded weak.

Zack was still whimpering in the corner. I returned to his side and took his hand. "We need to get out of here."

"No kidding," Ivy scoffed. She'd been picking at the lace on her shirt, unraveling it inch by inch.

Jerry nodded. "No way to escape far as I can tell."

"Do they feed us dinner?"

"Comes in right before the lab shuts down."

I didn't see any dirty plates lying around. "They come back for the dishes?"

"We get a half hour to eat. Sometimes less."

If the lab rats left at six, that gave us a few hours to prep. "Zack, what's your recovery time if I get those cuffs off you?"

"I...don't know."

"Can you be mobile in four hours?"

"I can't fight them all."

"I'm not asking you to. I just need to know if you can walk."

"Walking, yes. I don't know about anything else."

"We'll keep our fingers crossed. Anita," I called softly, "could you please give us some cover?"

She hesitated, but got up and stood in front of me, blocking any unexpected visits from the lab rats. "What are you doing?"

I knelt and pulled my lock picks out of my sock. Rocky had found all my weapons, but lucky for us, his crispy and smoking arm had distracted him from a more thorough search. "Getting us out of here."

The cuffs unlocked with little trouble and I carefully slid them off Zack's wrists. The collar came next, then his ankle cuffs. He shuddered, taking deep breaths.

"Thank you."

"Repay me by *not* snapping my neck, okay? Hide those under the blanket, and act hurt." I rose as he huddled back into his ball, then I gestured at the others to meet on the other side of the cell by Jerry and Wil.

"You're making me a tad nervous," Jerry said. "You've got a doing-something-stupid look about you."

"Nice to know your instincts are on target." I tucked the picks back into their sheath in my sock.

Anita tipped her chin at me. "Can you use those picks on the cells?"

"Yes. We'll wait until after they take the dinner plates away, unlock the cells, and make our way out."

"We have to go past the lounge," Anita said.

"Zack can get us past them."

"How?"

"He has a few tricks up his sleeve." As long as anyone in the lounge was human. "Listen everybody. I know this has all been weird, and it's going to get weirder, but if we keep our wits about us and accept whatever freaky things happen, we'll be fine."

"What kind of freaky—"

Jerry huffed. "Give it a rest, Anita. If we get out of here with our hides intact I'm sure Grace'll explain everything." He gave me a pointed stare. "Won'tcha?"

"Absolutely." Not that they'd believe a word of it. "Does anyone know how to destroy those computers without making a lot of noise?"

No one said anything.

"Won't do you any good," Wil muttered from the floor in his corner of the cell. "They'll have backups."

"Can we destroy those, too?"

"Not if they're offsite."

"What does it matter?" asked Jerry.

In the grand scheme, it probably didn't. Kokabiel had blood banks and hospitals all over the country collecting data. The master list of potential victims might not even be here.

"It doesn't," I said, sighing. "We can't risk the time for something that can be recovered by pushing a few buttons."

"That's not how it works," said Wil.

I also didn't have time to argue with a kid over the proper procedure for restoring fangel data. "I don't know what will happen once we get outside. There was a van before, but it might not be there now. It's possible we'll have to escape on foot."

"We won't make it without water," Anita said.

"We'll get water on the way."

"How—?"

"I don't know yet. There's a kitchen. They have to bring in supplies and store them for the hu—cult members. We'll just have to improvise."

"What do we do if we can't find anything?"

"Then you'll just have to decide where you want to die. Here in some creepy ritual or out in the fresh air fighting for your life."

DINNER CAME AND we ate in silence, consuming every calorie we could manage. Jerry licked his plate clean, and I followed his example. It might be the last food we would have for a few days.

It might also be our last meal.

No one mentioned this, though at least Jerry and Anita were thinking it. Both carried themselves like condemned prisoners who had one last Hail Mary pass in the air. Maybe we'd survive, but no one expected it.

Rude Dude from the plaza attack showed up at six and took the lab rats away. Fifteen minutes later, the two minions I'd seen in the lounge took the plates. Neither had spilled sauce on themselves at lunch, which for some reason annoyed me.

I waited another ten minutes just to be safe, and went to work on the locks. Ivy looked ready to bolt, but Anita was holding her steady. My cell opened with a quiet *snick* and I slipped out and over to Jerry and Wil's.

"You got the kid?" I said under my breath.

Jerry nodded. "He's skinny enough to carry if it comes to that."

The lock opened.

The door to the lab creaked.

Jerry's eyes went wide and he motioned me back to my cell. I was already moving, pulling the door shut. It wouldn't relock unless I slammed it, giving us away.

Anita leaned close behind me. "You didn't get—"

"I know." I tucked my lock picks away out of sight.

Kokabiel arrived with Rocky at his heels. Damn.

I caught Zack's eye and gave the other captives a pointed glance. If I didn't come back, it was up to him to get them out.

"It's time."

Anita and Ivy stayed back, huddling together like before. Jerry stood at the door, one hand on the bars and a slim finger keeping the bolt from relocking the door. Zack moaned.

"Could you come back later?" I said, exaggerating a stretch. "I was about to take a post-dinner nap."

Rocky and I would never have a future together if he kept ignoring me. Without even a glance, he put the key into the lock. *Don't notice it's open. Focus on me.*

"Ten minutes is all I need. Come on, big guy, do a gal a solid."

Snarling low, he yanked open the door. "Out."

"Fine, but if I fall sleep and mess things up, it's on you."

I left the cell and he slammed the door closed.

The hopeful look in Anita's eyes went out as they hauled me away.

"Holy cathedral," I whispered.

Kokabiel had carved a church out of a mountain. From the way he'd pushed open those lovely double doors I'd seen on the way in, he was proud of it, too.

Twice the size of my entire apartment, with walls smooth as the best drywall work I'd ever seen Dad do. Four pillars lined each side of an aisle down the middle, left in place when they'd cut the rest of the rock away. Gleaming redwood pews angled between the pillars, also four to a side. An altar rose out of the stone at the far end in one seamless piece of red and gray striated rock, and stained glass in an excavated half circle completed the illusion. No sunlight shone through the glass, but something lit it just enough to suggest the sun.

Dad would love this room.

I jerked to a stop. The Pretty Boys should hate this room. They should be sparking and flaming and experiencing all sorts of painful reminders of their naughty behavior.

Kokabiel walked across the polished stone floor toward the altar without smoldering.

"Why aren't you on fire?"

"This is *our* holy ground."

I gave the cathedral a closer look. As perfect as the craftsmanship was, it wasn't a *true* church. No crosses anywhere, no holy books or scrolls. Even the arched windows depicted angels in battle instead of saints, their wings sharp as the swords they wielded.

Holy to them, but not consecrated.

"How long did it take you to build this? It has that new-cathedral smell."

"Bring her."

Rocky followed him down the aisle and I stopped being quite so awed at the construction marvel. Candles burned in sconces along the wall, and more ringed the half-circle dais in the rear. White silk draped a Grace-sized altar with gold bondage rings at the corners, sitting under the fake stained glass. Two robed fangels stood behind it, Rude Dude and one I hadn't seen before. Fabio's replacement or one of Suriel's minions? Another robed figure stood in the corner by a door made from the same redwood as the pews. A woman, so not a fangel.

"Let's talk about this!" I yanked back, but Rocky had been waiting for it. He caught me easily and held me down with both hands, one on each of my upper arms.

"We should have drugged it," Suriel called, leaning against the wall with his arms crossed.

"Drugged *her*," I quipped. "You've been here how many millennia and you still don't know pronouns?"

Tough talk, but I shook like a wet puppy, on the verge of tears and doing something thoroughly embarrassing like begging for my life to creatures who didn't value it.

"I'll not risk the purity of her blood." Kokabiel gestured and Rocky pushed me toward the altar.

"You can't do this!" I twisted, kicked, bucked, but Rocky had me tight.

"Secure her."

Rude Dude and his buddy came forward as Rocky lifted me over the altar's steps.

"Let me go!"

Rude Dude grabbed my legs. The other tied me down with white silk to the gold rings embedded in the altar. Rocky held me with one hand on my throat while the other two bound my arms above my head.

Strapped down like a sacrifice. I'd had a lot of nightmares about this day, but none had ever included this.

A breeze ruffled my hair and Suriel appeared at my shoulder, carrying a worn gold cup the size of my fist, with a curved spout on one side, and two prongs on the other, spaced about an inch apart.

I gulped, bile hot and bitter in my throat.

He was going to tap me like a keg.

"You don't want to do this," I said, licking my dry lips. "You read the fine print? This ritual of yours could cause the end of the world."

He pressed his fingers against my chin and pushed my head to the side. I pushed back, my neck muscles straining, but even his fingers were stronger than I was.

"Look, if it's blood you want we can work out a deal. I'll donate a few pints every month like I'm the Red Cross. Your own private blood bank."

Fingers pulled the skin above my carotid artery taut.

"Wait, Suriel," Kokabiel said. "You must learn patience."

Suriel rumbled low in his throat, but stepped away from me as muffled shouts drifted in from another room. Zack and the others?

Please be a rescue, please oh please.

It didn't sound like fighting, though it did sound angry, maybe righteous. A minion with a gun entered the cathedral, a man in tow. My hopes sank.

"Cavanaugh?"

He stumbled, his eyes wide, his face bruised, with a nasty cut on his cheek. He clearly hadn't come willingly, but he shouldn't have been here at all. He was supposed to be with Libby at the hospital. They were both supposed to be safe.

"Grace! Oh no, I'm sorry, I'm *so* sorry."

The minion brought him to the altar. Kokabiel snapped his fingers and another minion brought over a flat, museum-quality wooden box inset with jewels and gold filigree. He lifted the lid and presented the box to Cavanaugh.

Cavanaugh stared into it, his brow wrinkled, his expression confused.

"Priest," said Kokabiel, a hint of respect in his voice. "You will perform for us this service."

I twitched. They thought they had Dandridge.

"Prepare the offering for the Sacrament of Sacraments."

I did not like the sound of "offering." I didn't even like the word "priest" right now.

Cavanaugh paled and shook his head. "No."

I waited for the "I'm not a priest, idiot," but none came. Maybe he was playing it smart. They'd probably kill him if they knew they'd grabbed the wrong guy.

"You will bless the blood."

"*No.*"

Suriel appeared beside him and pressed a long, thin knife to his throat. My breath caught and Cavanaugh stiffened, his head held high, defiant. If we survived, I owed him a bunch of apologies.

"Hear me," Suriel said, the same indifference in his voice. "I don't share his belief. I don't believe a human prayer will have any effect on the validity of its blood. Do *not* refuse his command again."

Cavanaugh's jaw tightened, resolve burning in his eyes that warned he was going to refuse and then some. He didn't realize Suriel cared more for his shirts than he did us.

"Hang on a minute," I said, straining against the silk. "He'll do it! Just let me talk to him."

Suriel hesitated, but he shifted his scowl to me. I was tired of that sidelong sneer.

"Put the blade away, Suriel," Kokabiel scolded. "This should be a joyous occasion."

The knife withdrew.

Cavanaugh sucked in a ragged breath, and grabbed his neck with one hand. "This isn't going to work. You can't command miracles," he said.

Kokabiel smiled. "*You* can. You've been blessed with such power and you will manifest it for us, in her most precious blood. Take the sacred book of your people. Perform the ritual on our altar. Bring about the miracle so we may return home."

"If I don't?"

Kokabiel said nothing, but Suriel's eyes gleamed and he ran a finger along the edge of the knife. "We'll find another priest who will."

"Hey," I said, my voice trembling almost as badly as he was. All he had to do was fake it. "It's only a little blood. No one has to die."

"You don't understand." He looked at me, his eyes wide, scared. "He wants me to perform the Eucharist. He wants me to offer communion with *your* blood."

I pictured people lined up to get a thin wafer and a sip of wine. I was nobody's buffet. Wait...that was awfully specific—

Holy crap, he is *a priest?* How could he be a priest? I'd never seen him in a collar, or with a cross or anything.

Suriel stepped forward with his knife, but Kokabiel stopped him with a gaze. Then he looked at me.

"Your priests perform this miracle every day. You, holy daughter, can grant us a soul so we may enter Heaven."

"Like hell I will. I'll make you choke on it."

"I won't do it," Cavanaugh said.

Suriel tapped the knife tip against Cavanaugh's cheek. "Then it dies."

"Bet I get to Heaven before you do," he said.

Suriel flicked the knife across Cavanaugh's cheek. He grunted and blood welled. Kokabiel shook his head and pulled Suriel's blade away. "Have you learned nothing?"

"Only that we were fools to lie with these creatures."

"Let's correct that mistake." Kokabiel took Cavanaugh's face in his hands. "You *will* do this for us."

My skin tingled. I knew that look. He'd used it on me outside the plaza. Suriel had even tried it, but it hadn't done more than annoy me. Cavanaugh had almost succumbed from across a parking lot. He didn't stand a chance this close.

Cavanaugh's eyes glazed and he trembled.

"You will perform the sacrament and send us home."

Cavanaugh's shoulders dropped and the tension left his body. He reached into the box and pulled out the ancient Bible.

"Stop it!" I twisted sideways, useless, but Kokabiel took my hand and squeezed it gently, then patted my head.

"Shh, be still, child."

His skin was cool against mine. *Two can play mind games, Bucko.* If they could shove crap into my head, maybe I could shove it into theirs.

I pictured the flash of Daniel's curved blade ripping through Kokabiel's throat, as graphic and violent and bloody as the goriest slasher movie I'd ever seen. I imagined his perfectly muscular body breaking into a million pieces and shattering all over the room. I pressed the images into his mind like I'd press that knife into his throat.

He gasped and stepped away, and the barest hint of fear flickered across his features. Cavanaugh staggered back, pale and sweaty.

Kokabiel looked at his hand, then at me, and grinned bright as the sun. "Such power through a mere touch," he whispered. A rock formed in the pit of my stomach. "I *told* you she was special."

Suriel hesitated, looking from me to Kokabiel as if debating if my blood did indeed do a body good. If he decided they didn't need Cavanaugh...

"Will you two wait one freaking minute," I said. "If he does your communion, will you let him go?"

Kokabiel rubbed one finger along his jawline in a creepy all-too-human gesture. "We'll have no use for him after we've returned."

Such insane certainty of that, no matter how many times he must have done this before and failed. But never with *my* blood *and* a priest to do the ritual. Crap, maybe it *would* work.

"Here's the deal," I said, giving Cavanaugh a quick *play-along* look. "He'll bless me and my grade-A blood, you let him go. But we do it *right*. No half-assing the ritual sacrifice."

He pondered it. "Agreed."

"I get last words."

Kokabiel looked confused, and so did Cavanaugh. "Last rites?" Cavanaugh asked.

"No, the other one." Dammit, the term was right there, I just couldn't remember— "Confession! I get confession first."

Cavanaugh's eyes brightened and he nodded fast. "Yes, I have to hear her confession and absolve her of her sins or her soul won't be clean." He wiped his upper lip and looked Kokabiel right in the eyes. "You want to manifest a clean soul, don't you?"

He nodded once. "I do."

Suriel scoffed and looked like he wanted to gut all three of us. "It's stalling."

"Perhaps. We've waited millennia. I won't indulge your impatience and risk her lineage." Kokabiel turned to Cavanaugh. "Proceed."

"Um, confession is a private matter."

"Her sins are irrelevant to me."

"Not to God." Cavanaugh crossed his arms and held his head high, though the tips of his fingers trembled. "She gets to confess in private, without judgment. That's how it works if you want this done right."

Suriel stalked off, muttering in his angel language that seemed *really* suited to swearing. I bet even sweet nothings sounded like curses.

Kokabiel hesitated, but nodded. "Very well. We'll wait until it's complete." He turned and walked away, gesturing to the others to follow. They trailed him to the far end of the cathedral and gathered by the doors like they were waiting for a store to open.

I sighed. "Bless me Father, for I have been a stupid, stupid person."

He frowned. "You know I'm not really hearing your—"

"Oh for crying out loud, of *course* not!"

"All right. But yes, you have."

After we got out of here, he could lecture me all he wanted and I'd take it without complaint.

"What are you doing here?"

"One of those things grabbed me out of my car when I tried to follow you."

"You left Libby!"

He winced. "No, Aaron and the paramedics were with her."

"She's alive?"

"I think so."

A bit of weight lifted off my chest. At least something good happened today. I took a breath and looked at Cavanaugh. He faced me on the altar, his back to Kokabiel and the others. Not the best cover, but it would do.

"Listen, act all priestly, but see if you can get me loose." I glanced up toward my wrists, hidden from the fangels by his body.

"Technically, I always act priestly."

"We are so having a conversation about that later, *Father Sneakypants.* You should have told me."

"It was easier not to." He spoke Latin and waved his hand over me, his other hand working at the knot on my wrists.

And then what?

Where would we go? If we tried to leave this room there were at least five fangels who'd be on us in a heartbeat. If we got out of the lair, Zack and the others were still trapped inside. If we somehow managed to get them *and* us outside, how would we get away? Hope the minions left the van running out front, gassed up with the keys in the ignition and Red in the bushes taking a leak?

"We're not getting out of this," I said, more realization than confession. "Not unless Daniel followed you here."

"Who's Daniel?"

Oh boy. "A friend I'd hoped could help. I'm so sorry, Cavanaugh."

"It's not your fault. I chose to look for these things, and I chose to come after you. I'm a Catholic priest. Fighting evil is what we do, remember?"

The silk pulled loose and he squeezed my hand. From him, the gesture *was* comforting.

I smiled despite how hopeless this was. "It would be a lot easier if they *were* demon vamps. At least then we'd have ideas on how to fight them."

Cavanaugh froze, and his fingers tightened on mine. "Great idea." He turned his back to me and opened the Bible. "She's ready for the blessing," he called.

The what? No, I wasn't.

Kokabiel swooshed to my side, eager anticipation shining in his eyes. Suriel walked back, the pair of matching fangels trailing him. No humans in the bunch but us.

Kokabiel set the blood tap and an old gold pitcher on a small table next to Cavanaugh. "Proceed."

Cavanaugh opened the Bible, flipping the beautifully illuminated pages like he knew what he was looking for. He stopped and read, his voice deep and powerful, resonating in the harsh room as if *he* were the one in charge. Neither Kokabiel or Suriel had caught on yet that to bless little old me, he ought to be facing *me*, not *them*.

"I cast you out, unclean spirit, you and your foul companions."

That didn't sound like a blessing.

Kokabiel's eager grin turned worrisome, and Suriel growled deep in his throat.

"Begone and stay far from this child of God," Cavanaugh cried, flinging the words like weapons. "In His name I command you!"

A faint golden-green glow emanated from the robed fangels' skin. They looked at each other, worry wrinkling their perfect faces. Rude Dude grunted, but the other whimpered and backed away, arms raised.

"In His name I cast you out, as He flung you from the Heavens," Cavanaugh sang, and even Suriel took a step back. Kokabiel's face twisted in clear pain and sparks of lightning rippled off of him, but he didn't move away. Gasping, Rude Dude and the other fangel took off.

Cavanaugh's shirt stuck to his skin, drenched in sweat. He kept reading, kept fighting, pushing them back, but Kokabiel was too strong, and any second now he'd break whatever hold Cavanaugh had containing them and rip out his throat.

We needed more than words. We needed holy water or garlic or—I cursed myself. *Idiot.* A cross was a cross and you couldn't banish evil without one. I yanked my wrists free and reached under my shirt.

"Cavanaugh!" I shoved Dad's pendant into his hand, covering it with my own. *Please work. Please, please work.*

He jumped, glancing at me, but kept reading.

"Be gone, in the name of the Father, and of the Son, and of the Holy Spirit!" he shouted.

Brilliant white light blazed from between our fingers. The darkness at the edges of the room curled away, and the room looked two-dimensional, as if everything had been painted on a white canvas.

Suriel shrieked, one arm covering his eyes. He shrank back and disappeared. Kokabiel cried out and backed away, one hand up as if he was struggling against the wind.

Light that bright should hurt, but I wasn't even squinting. It was warm as a bath, soothing and invigorating at the same time.

"Begone!"

Kokabiel broke, gasping and nearly falling. With a hateful glare, he blurred and vanished.

I dropped my hand and the light ceased, though flickers of it still danced across the altar and pews. Cavanaugh opened his fist and gaped at the pendant. The amethyst glowed softly, growing lighter with every heartbeat. "How...?"

I patted him on the shoulder. "You are one freaking badass cleric, that's how."

Chapter Twenty-Five

Cavanaugh staggered and placed his other hand on the altar, steadying himself. "Will you still think I'm badass if I collapse?"

"Absolutely. What did you *do*?"

He grinned sheepishly, sweat beading at his hairline. "Exorcised our personal demons. I don't know how long it will last, though."

"Lock the door." If I remembered the layout of this place right, the door in the back corner most likely opened into the hall right outside the lab—and across from the room Suriel tried to drain me dry in. "We can't leave until we get Anita Rosenberg and the others."

"They're still alive?"

"He's got them locked in his evil testing lab." I flicked a hand at the double doors. "Go!"

He stumbled his way to the doors and pulled them shut. "There's no lock."

Naturally, everything else he locked up tight, but *this* room Kokabiel left open for business. "Can we barricade them?"

"If we can lift those." He gestured at the pews. We each grabbed an end and wrangled it against the door.

"Put another one on top."

"At least one."

We dragged over a second pew, then for good measure shoved a third up against them both. It would stop a human no problem, but Kokabiel or Suriel could probably bust through it without stopping. "Think they're weaker after the light show?"

"No idea," he said, then gave the barricade a funny look. "Isn't this our only way out?"

I jerked a thumb over my shoulder. "Another door in the back. I think it leads to the lab."

"Does *it* have a back door?"

I hesitated. "No."

"I think we need a new escape plan," Cavanaugh muttered, swaying slightly.

"I think you need to take it easy for a few minutes while I figure one out." I led him back to the altar and sat him on the steps.

He took deep, ragged breaths, his face damp and pale. "I'll be fine. Just running on fumes."

I wasn't so sure of that. His skin felt clammy more than sweaty. Whatever he'd done had taken a serious toll, and we'd need more of it to get out of here.

"Well," he said with a soft laugh, "we're lucky to have survived this long, so maybe someone up there likes us."

"Are you telling me to have a little faith?"

"Try a lot. A lot is better."

I'd do my best. "We need to hold this room until I get the others out."

He spread his hands and laughed wryly. "With what?"

"Holy ground?" I said. A longshot, but that and holy water were the only things I'd seen that kept the Pretty Boys at bay. "It's a church. Can you consecrate it?"

"Maybe, but the normal people can still walk right in."

"They're easier to deal with than the fangels."

He took a deep breath and rose shakily to his feet. "Go get the others. I'll do what I can here. Just hurry. I'm running out of miracles."

The rear doorknob turned smoothly. Sighing, I cracked the door and peeked into the hall. It wasn't the same hall I'd seen outside the lab, and another door sat at the far end, about forty feet away. That *could* be the right way, or it could dump me directly into a Pretty Boy rec room.

Not like I had a lot of options.

I ran down the hall as quietly as possible, fingers crossed that nothing interested in eating me would pop out the other side. Pausing at the door, I pressed my ear against the wood.

Shouting. A woman's quick scream. Ivy? A heavy thud, followed by another.

Not good. I backed away, heart pounding. Kokabiel must have had guards posted, or his minions had run for the lab as soon as Cavanaugh exorcised them. He'd probably kill Zack this time.

The door opened.

I sucked in a breath and turned back toward the cathedral. *Please be holy ground by the time I get there.*

"Grace!" Zack called.

Somebody up there *did* like us. "Is everyone safe?"

He stepped aside and Anita came through the door, followed by Ivy, then Jerry and the kid. Zack was the last one in, shutting the door behind him. "Where's Kokabiel?"

"Shaking off an exorcism with his pals, but he'll be back. This way."

Cavanaugh was walking around the edges of the cathedral when I returned. He paused only to check that we were us and not the bad guys, then continued on. "This is Father Cavanaugh," I said, still finding that hard to believe. "He's with me."

"Does that mean we're getting out of here?" Anita asked.

"Working on that." I waved a hand at the pews. "Zack, a little help with the rear guard please?"

He nodded, then picked up the pews like they were made of cardboard and piled them by the back door. I frowned. Yeah, those things wouldn't stop a healthy fangel one bit. At least they made Anita and the others feel better.

"How we doing, Cavanaugh?"

Still walking the perimeter, he held up one finger, his lips moving fast. "Done."

"Did it—"

Zack shrieked. Blue sparks raced along his skin. *Oh crap!* I dashed over and grabbed his hand. "Sorry about that!"

Cavanaugh sank onto the altar's steps, his eyes wide as he stared at Zack. "Is he a—"

"He's on our side. I guess it worked."

More shrieks erupted from beyond the double doors, a mix of anger and pain. Ivy yelped and buried her head in Jerry's shoulder.

"Hold it together, ma'am," Jerry said, disentangling himself. He scooted away and came over to me. "We're out. What you got in mind now?"

"Not dying." My head spun, and the rest of me shook; I had far too much adrenaline racing through my system.

"After that?"

I had no idea. We were safe for a while from Kokabiel and crew, but the minions would be hammering on the doors before long. Zack could take them out if they got past the barricades, but if any of them had guns—I pictured Libby and my chest tightened even further—fangels were fast, but not Superman fast.

"I..."

Jerry nodded slowly and patted my shoulder. "That's what I was afraid of."

CAVANAUGH'S CONSECRATION WON us seventeen minutes of peace. After that, a full-on assault began on the cathedral. Kokabiel was a jerk, but he knew how to build himself some angel-proof doors. They held tight despite the banging and crashing against them.

I sat between Zack and Cavanaugh, flinching with every strike on the door.

"Think you can perform another holy light show?" I asked Cavanaugh.

"No. It's a miracle I'm still conscious as it is." He kept the cross tight in his fist anyway.

A much *bigger* bang shook the doors and cracks appeared in the frame.

"That last one sounded a bit like a battering ram," Jerry said.

"They have a battering ram?"

He pursed his lips and nodded. "Could be a tree."

Wil whimpered and pulled his knees tighter against his chest. "Should've stayed in the cage."

"No," I said. "Even if they break those doors down, they can't send in more than we can handle." I glanced at Zack and he shrugged. How very reassuring.

Anita licked her lips. "But how—"

"Just trust me, okay?" She flinched away and I sighed. Great. Scare the kidnap victim.

Another bash against the doors and they shook yet again. With a deep breath, Jerry got to his feet. "Next one ought to do it."

"Stay behind the altar," I told the others. Anita pulled Wil over and they huddled together with Ivy. "You too," I said to Jerry.

"Nah. I'm a mite curious about what's on the other side."

On the next smash, the wood tore and the stone cracked open. Minions or fangels pushed on the doors and the pews scraped against the floor, but only left enough room for maybe one person to step through at a time. We could handle it if they came at us one at a time.

Someone barked orders, and synchronized hits knocked the doors wider. Wood creaked and fangels groaned. Rocky and Rude Dude each grabbed a door and shoved, pushing them wide enough to walk through with ease. So much for our tiny advantage. Blue sparks and pale smoke danced across their arms.

No humans. That was good, right?

The others stepped back and Kokabiel appeared out of the dusty air, blue-white lightning sparking across his shoulders and down his arms. He looked very, very pissed.

"Come here," he said to me.

"Make me."

A breath of air that smelled like flowers left too long in the vase hit me an instant before he did. Zack flew sideways as Kokabiel whisked me to the altar, slamming my back against the stone. I cried out, pain shooting through me. Zack echoed my cries. Everyone else dived out of the way.

Except Cavanaugh.

Shouting, he lunged at Kokabiel, Dad's cross thrust forward. Kokabiel spun and backhanded him, sending him soaring across the room and into a stone pillar. His body slumped to the floor, smearing blood along the rock.

I clawed at Kokabiel's hand on my throat, skin against my skin. He scowled, but there were no sparks, no smoke as long as he had a hold on me. I pictured shredding him with my bare hands, pouring holy water into the wounds, crushing him under the biggest cross I could think of, but he shrugged it all off.

"Such imagination, Hannah Grace."

He dragged me closer to the table that held the golden tap and pitcher. My back spasmed, everything hurt, but none of it mattered. His eyes swirled in red fire and I doubted he gave a damn anymore about the proper way to drink me.

"Wait! I wasn't blessed! You'll screw up the ritual!" I fought him, but it was like wrestling with one of those pillars.

"I'll risk it."

Grabbing my hair, he shoved me to me knees and yanked my head to the side. All-too-familiar images of women running, drowning, dying, filled me, the pain of betrayal, the ache of loss and longing of home, so much worse than anything I'd seen or felt before. I gasped, overwhelmed, crumbling under the weight of so much heartache.

"Please—"

He jabbed the tap into my neck.

I screamed.

Pain lanced through me, the prongs burning deep in my flesh where my shoulder curved into my neck. It hurt, holy hell did it ever. I twitched and trembled like a caught fish, resisting every instinct to jerk away and tear myself open. He might have missed the artery, but just barely.

"Hold still, child," he said, tightening his grip on me. He grabbed the gold pitcher and held it under the spout of the blood tap.

"Go to Hell."

"Not anymore."

"You're a lousy angel."

He didn't answer, but his fingers dug into my shoulder. I willed myself to bleed slowly.

Shouts rose outside the cathedral, muffled, but growing louder. Kokabiel cocked his head and looked warily at the door while my blood *tap-tap-tapped* into the pitcher.

Still sparking, Zack slammed into Kokabiel, ripping him and the tap from my neck. I screamed as both fangels rolled down the steps of the altar. The cathedral spun and I fell forward, one hand pressed against my ragged skin.

Don't pass out, don't pass out...

Fangels shrieked high and loud. Anita and Ivy screamed. Wil sobbed and Jerry swore a litany that was almost a prayer itself.

I'm not dying this way.

Lightning crackled and hissed. I fought against the darkness swarming around me, damp and cold.

"Grace!"

I blinked. Libby?

Kokabiel raged, screaming in pain and anger, but hope stopped my fall. I forced my eyes open. Libby stood in the shattered doorway, a giant Super Soaker in her arms.

Chapter Twenty-Six

Libby swung the Super Soaker toward an already smoking Kokabiel and opened fire. Holy water shot out, drenching him *and* his damn button-down shirt. Sparking, smoldering, and screaming in a way that gave me warm fuzzies, the fangel blurred out the door.

Libby ran to my side. Someone else took her spot guarding the shattered double doors—big man, bigger gun. Roberto.

"You brought the Marines," I said, voice shaking. My shoulder throbbed like a 2 a.m. rave.

"Shh, stay still. You're losing a lot of blood." She put the water gun down and pulled gauze from a medical pouch on her belt. Roberto covered us both.

"You're not dead."

She tapped her chest. "All hail the mighty Kevlar."

"Look at you, soldier girl."

"Don't get all delirious on me."

Hard not to. Lights danced between the pillars, shapes in the rock dust floating on wind currents. People, maybe, or memories of the fangels Cavanaugh had somehow managed to shake loose during his exorcism.

"Cavanaugh," I whispered.

"Hang in there." She pressed a bandage against my neck and I sucked in a breath, fresh pain brightening an already too-bright room.

"He's hurt."

"So are you. Stay put, I'll go get him." She picked up the Super Soaker and rose, but three fangels appeared in the doorway.

"Incoming!" Roberto yelled.

Libby turned, sliding the water gun back up and taking aim in one smooth motion. She fired, and holy water arced across the room. The fangels retreated. Roberto switched to an actual gun and bullets flew.

"I'll get Cavanaugh." I struggled to stand. "Go kick ass."

"Hang on, you can barely walk." She rooted in the med pouch and pulled out a tube. "Brace yourself."

Pressure and a sting in my leg. The adrenaline hit my blood and the world became brighter, faster, more *there.*

"Whoa, better than espresso," I said, my head clearing.

Libby helped me up. "You good?"

"Yes."

She hesitated, her gaze shifting over my shoulder. "Those the pantry folk?"

I nodded. "Jerry'll probably fight if you give him a gun."

"Works for me." She headed for the altar while I stumbled toward Cavanaugh. "You Jerry?" she asked. "Take this. Soak anything that tries to get through those doors."

"Grace said it was gonna get weird."

"You have no idea." They both joined Roberto on the front lines.

I dropped to Cavanaugh's side and felt for a pulse. Thready and weak. Blood pooled on the floor under his head. Either would have been bad, but together? "Come on, Padre, we need you mobile."

Still unresponsive.

"I had such a good chewing out planned for you, Father Sneakypants. You owe me that." I ran my hands over his face and head, hoping I wouldn't find—

My throat caught. A bit of clean fluid dripped from his nose. *No, please, no.* I lifted one eyelid, then the other. The left pupil was dilated, the other not.

Nothing in Libby's first aid kit treated this level of brain trauma. He was dying, and there was nothing I could do about it.

I bit my lip and swallowed the frustrated scream building in my throat. It wasn't fair. All he'd wanted was to help people, even when they were too stubborn to accept his help. He wouldn't have even been here if it wasn't for me.

None of them would be. Libby and Roberto held the fangels at bay for now, but they'd run out of holy water eventually. Jerry was standing strong beside them, and even Anita had joined the fight, backing up Roberto's real bullets with the other Super Soaker.

Zack was nowhere to be seen, but the rear door was open and the barricades pushed aside. Two had cracked and the third lay in pieces along the wall. He must have been in quite the hurry to get out of here. I'd no idea where Daniel was, and I'd probably never see my father again.

We were all going to die under this stupid red rock.

"It's going to be okay, Nate," I lied softly, taking Cavanaugh's hand. Smooth wood and warm metal pressed against my palm. Dad's cross. A single swipe of blood marred the amethyst at the center.

I folded his fingers around it and held tight with both of mine. I'd never been one for prayers—all I knew was the Shema—but maybe the actual words didn't matter.

Help him, please. He's a good man. He deserves a second chance.

Something stirred in my chest, a ripple of sensation I couldn't name. It ran down my arms and pooled in my hands. They tingled on the edge of painful. Light blossomed, bursting from between our fingers bright and warm. It washed over him like sunlight across a smooth lake, motes of gold swirling and flickering along his skin—no, *under* his skin. He glowed from within, warm and peaceful.

And then it vanished.

He snorted awake, eyes bleary and unfocused, but his pupils were once again normal. "Urf?"

Impossible.

Just like everything else in my life. Relief burst from me, half sob, half laugh, and I kissed him full on the lips, clergy be damned. "You're... you're..." Alive? Back from certain death? I didn't even know where to begin.

"What?"

Fangels screamed and raged in the other room and some of his confusion faded. Fear took its place. He tried to sit up, but none of his limbs worked.

"Take it easy," I said, steadying him before he hurt himself again. "Give yourself time to, um, adjust."

A *little* time. The stream from Libby's Super Soaker looked thin, and I hadn't heard a gunshot in at least thirty or forty seconds.

Wait...time. It hadn't stopped once, and if ever there was a good time to hit the pause button, it was now. Was it the consecrated ground? The holy water? Something was interfering with the fangels' special skills.

It we survived this, I'd have a long talk with Daniel about that later.

"Can you stand?" I asked Cavanaugh.

He shrugged, but managed to get his arms working and pulled himself up to a sitting position. I helped him to his unsteady feet and put an arm around his waist. He stayed standing. Staccato taps of gunfire rose above the angry snarls of the Pretty Boys' and Kokabiel's fury.

"I'm pretty sure all Hell's broken loose out there," I said, forcing a grin.

"Not...funny," he rasped. He gave me a weird look, like he wasn't sure where he was or what was going on.

Libby and Roberto had the Pretty Boys at bay, but she looked worried.

Kokabiel bled green goo from multiple bullet holes. He stood in the hall, as close as he could get without getting in range of Libby's holy water.

"Zack?" I yelled. No answer. Damn. "Everyone, gather up. Time to go."

Ivy gaped at me from behind the altar for a few seconds, but she reached behind and grabbed Wil's hand. They darted over and met us behind Libby and Roberto.

Fingers encircled my wrist. "I'm here," said Zack, his voice sounding strained. "I can steady him if you take my hand."

"Deal."

He took it, and then grabbed Cavanaugh in one arm.

"What's the plan?" I asked Libby. Hopefully they had a way to get nine people past four pissed off fangels. Five if Suriel came back to play.

"Get in, save you, get out again." She shrugged. "I wasn't planning on that tunnel entrance, so we had to improvise. Backup's waiting if we can get outside."

Daniel? That would make it two Pretty Boys against four. Still lousy odds, but Libby and Roberto had put a serious dent in their advantage. We'd held them off this long, so maybe we could push them back enough to get outside.

I tightened my grip on Dad's cross and aimed it at Kokabiel. "Be gone, demon!"

He glared at me.

"Shoo!"

He snarled and took a step closer, pushing the border of Cavanaugh's holy ground. Kokabiel was more beast than angel, and he didn't seem as interested in drinking my blood now as he was in shedding it.

"Abracadabra!" I screamed, shoving the cross at him. "You pathetic babysitters, get the hell away from my friends!"

The cross flared, not as bright as what Cavanaugh had summoned, but from Kokabiel's cries, still painful. The fangels dived for cover and their boss staggered a few steps back.

"Advance!" Roberto yelled, taking the water gun from Anita. He stayed at my side and we moved forward as a team, Zack and Cavanaugh an arm-length behind, Libby behind them, and the rest behind her.

Rocky, Rude Dude, and the unnamed fangel had fled all the way to the door on the far end of the hall. Kokabiel stood at the halfway point, one hand raised, the promise of a slow, painful death on his perfect face. Suriel was nowhere in sight.

"Move, move, move!" Roberto laid down suppressing water fire and we moved toward the entrance tunnel. If minions with guns were in there, we'd be trapped. If Suriel was in there, we'd be toast.

I released Zack's hand once past the threshold of the cathedral, and reached for Cavanaugh's arm.

He held up a hand and shook his head. "I'm good. I can walk."

He shouldn't have even been breathing. I tightened my grip on the cross. Dad had a lot of explaining to do when we got home.

"Stay close and keep moving," Libby said, dropping back to the rear. She covered us, leaving puddles of holy water in our wake. Zack grimaced, but he barely sizzled.

We rounded the S-bend and twilight shadows cut across the wall. Roberto paused and I froze with him, the cross in front. He signaled and we stepped out into the open.

What the?

Dad stood in the back of an old pickup truck, holding the wand of an industrial-sized pressure cleaner. The engine drummed with a rhythmic *tick-tick-tick*, ready to fire. Daniel stood on the driver's side, the door open, the truck engine also running.

"Y'all get into the truck," Dad called.

Zack moved to the opposite side of the cave entrance. Cavanaugh and the others filed out and ran toward the truck, piling into the bed and dropping down.

A snarl echoed from the cave.

"Incoming!" Libby yelled, backing out at a jerky run. Her Super Soaker gave a final squirt, then died. "Light 'em up!" She dodged out of the way and Dad opened fire with the pressure cleaner. Rocky took a hit right to the face and screeched before he dived back inside.

"Clear the cave," Daniel shouted, running forward.

"The phrase is, "Fire in the hole," Libby said.

Daniel yanked the pins out of two grenades and lobbed them into the tunnel entrance. The explosion wasn't nearly as loud as I'd expected, but the pissed-off shouts of the Pretty Boys made up for it. Rock crumbled and fell. Dust poofed in mini-mushroom clouds. It was a beautiful thing.

Zack and I dived into the truck, while Libby raced for the driver's side, tossing the spent water gun into the bed and nearly beaning Wil on the head. Daniel jumped into the truck bed and watched the tunnel collapse with a worried expression on his face. His gaze caught mine and he smiled.

"You're alive."

"For now. How long will that hold them?" I had no illusions a tunnel of rubble would trap Kokabiel. He'd built *into* the rock, not under it, and there wasn't enough rock here to bury him for good.

"An hour at most."

Libby floored it, the tires spitting out gravel as she fled down the trail, but running wasn't going to save any of us, not now. Kokabiel wasn't going to stop just because his pet humans got out of the yard.

But for the next hour, maybe, we were safe.

"I'm pleased as punch to see you, Butternut." Dad hugged me with one arm and held on tight with the other. I hugged him back, barely believing the strength he had. Last hospital visit, he'd hadn't had the strength to lift his arms for more than a faint squeeze. "That was a dumb thing to do," he said over the wind.

"I know."

"Daniel and I were worried."

I glared, though it was just for show. "You two have a lot of explaining to do, young man."

Dad grinned. "I know." His gaze shifted and I turned. Wil was looking at him like he'd come across Santa by the tree. "Hey kid. You doing okay?"

Wil gaped, then nodded. "Thought you were dead."

"So did I."

The kid lurched up and threw his arms around Dad, knocking me out of the way. I staggered back and Jerry caught my arm and set me right again.

"They kinda bonded," he said.

"So I see."

Libby was navigating the topsy-turvy elk-path of a road, but it was already sunset and night was coming fast. No sign of pursuit yet, but they'd be after us soon as they got out of the lair.

I looked at Roberto. "Not that I'm complaining, but what are you doing here?"

"You missed your eight a.m. sitrep."

"So you grabbed grenades and drove on out here?"

He nodded. "More or less."

"He was en route when I called him," Libby added. "Daniel reconned where you were and we got creative with a holy assault vehicle."

Seriously? "How did she convince you of *that*?" I didn't know what Libby had told him, but he was taking this all in remarkable stride.

Roberto tipped his head at Daniel. "He picked up a car. I've seen my share of strange and I trust my Liberty."

Me, too, and I'd never thought I'd trust anyone other than Dad. "Where *are* we?"

"Somewhere between Sedona and I-40. Too many twisty dirt roads and trails to know for sure. I'd never have found you if Daniel hadn't followed."

"Thank you," I told Daniel.

He smiled again and reached for my hand. I hesitated, but he deserved it. His gaze zipped up over my shoulder to the rear window. It didn't stay long. Not enough light for a reflection I guessed, but he didn't let go of my hand. He looked at my neck and frowned. "You're hurt."

"It's fine. Doesn't even sting anymore. Any ideas on how we can get Kokabiel off our backs?"

"Heavy ordinance?" Roberto offered.

Daniel shook his head. "Not strong enough."

"All we can do is run, my radish," Dad said. He looked at the shell-shocked group huddled in the truck bed and sighed. I knew what he was thinking—all those families, all those lives disrupted like ours had been.

Ivy was crying, pressing ruined lace trim against her eyes. Anita was comforting her, but she looked ready to crumble as well. Wil *wasn't* in his usual ball of denial but still clinging to Dad, and Jerry looked like he was just trying to keep from freaking out. These people didn't deserve to have their lives ruined.

"I'm not running anymore." I watched rocks and juniper flash by, trying my damnedest to ignore Daniel, who kept petting my fingers like I was some kind of cat.

"Will you please stop doing that."

"Sorry. Touching you is…compelling."

"I've got a squirt gun full of holy water if you don't keep your hands to yourself, Bucko."

He bowed his head and pouted, but I didn't think he was sorry at all. Dad raised his eyebrows and gave me a protective look.

I sighed. It was fine, really. Sweet, in a weird way. I'd had a lot worse guys paw at me, and he did risk his life to save us. Besides, he was easy on the eyes. *Stop having those thoughts!* I cleared my throat. "Uh, what about that knife of yours? Can we use that?"

"It wasn't the knife. It was you."

"No, it—" I was tired of this debate. "Barky died when I stabbed him, right?"

He nodded. "Baraqijal, but yes."

"Then we can kill Kokabiel and the others."

"No. There are too many."

I rubbed my eyes, burning from the dust and dirt of the road. We had a reprieve of insanity, nothing more. Kokabiel had a network of minions to find us again, and if he gave up on us, he'd just grab the next likely subjects on his list. That would be on me.

Fingers brushed my hand again.

"If we can't kill him and his beastie boys," I said, "how can we trap them for, oh, say decades or more? Keep them from messing with humanity until we can permanently contain them."

"You can't."

"Yes we can," Cavanaugh called. He'd been stealing weird glances at me since his…*don't say resurrection*…remarkable recovery, but had so far stayed quiet about it. He duck-walked to the front of the truck bed, but didn't get too close to me. "Remember what Aaron said? The Watchers were bound in the earth and covered with darkness. They were imprisoned underground."

"I thought fallen angels went to Hell."

Daniel shook his head. "There's only one angel in Hell. *We* were bound in the earth."

"Well, if we're stuffing them underground we'll need something with serious mass they can't dig through to bury them with, like a canyon, or a cave or..." I grinned. "Thank you Ms. Karmichael."

"Who?"

"One of my fifth-grade teachers. Woman was obsessed with reports and dioramas, and she was equally obsessed with the wild frontier of the Southwest." I'd gone to a lot of schools in my life, but she had been my favorite teacher and I'd loved that diorama. I'd copied one of Dad's favorite engineering marvels, and he'd gotten me real sand for it.

"Daniel," I said, "will Kokabiel follow us?"

"Definitely. He still wants your blood, and I suspect I've gone well past irksome to him now." He grinned at that, just a little. "If he fails this time, Suriel will use it to humiliate him and claim his dominions as his own. Kokabiel will lessen in the eyes of the others. He'll do whatever he can to maintain his status."

"Good." I made my way to the open window behind the cab and crunched down. "Lib, on the way in, did you pass any mines?" If Ms. Karmichael knew her stuff, this whole area had been active back in the gold rush days, and had kept on mining up through the fifties.

"I don't know. I wasn't looking for any. There were a few overgrown turnoffs and some old junk piles about twenty minutes from here. Might be something." Libby glanced at me, her eyes weary in the bouncing rear-view mirror. "How much blood did you lose again?"

"I have a plan."

"The four scariest words in the English language."

I rubbed my hands together. "We're going to put those blood puppies back underground."

Chapter Twenty-Seven

Daniel frowned. "They're too strong, and you're not God."

Cavanaugh twitched and looked away as if that wasn't so far from the truth. I added him to the list of people I needed a long sit-down with, but not now.

I looked at Daniel. "Doesn't mean I can't borrow from his greatest hits. Roberto, you have enough explosives to take out a mine shaft or two?"

"I'm a Marine."

"I could kiss you right now." I turned to the group. We didn't have much light—or time—left. "Everyone keep your eyes peeled for anything that looks like a mine or campground. Even an old road might lead to something we can use."

Standing in the truck bed offered a pretty good view of the area, though it was hard to spot anything until we were practically on top of it. This part of Arizona went up as much as it went out, and judging distance and altitude was rough.

There wasn't much for a while, until Libby called out and pointed. "That's the road I saw coming in." She slowed down and stopped.

It was old, but wider than the trail we were on. A pile of old boards and what looked like a half-buried ore cart on its side marked the entrance to somewhere.

"Zack, Daniel, you guys see anything that looks like a mine down there?"

They both looked, peering into the lengthening shadows. "Some wooden buildings," Daniel said. "Mostly frames now. Old machinery. There's a few deep shadows in the rocks that could be tunnels."

Good enough for me. "Libby, hang a left."

"Eureka, folks!" I cried. "We've struck silver."

The old road led to a long-abandoned silver mine. The camp itself was out front, the scattered buildings in various stages of decay. The interior walls were peeling and many of them had crumbled to the floor. Metal frames of bunk beds peeked out from inside the skeletal remains of one of the larger buildings on the left, with an old Coleman heater in the center that probably hadn't been made since the 40s or 50s.

At some point in the last sixty years, an outbuilding on the slope of the hill had collapsed into a pile of dark-brown wood and corrugated metal, with old mattresses and furniture poking through the broken beams and fallen walls. A pot-bellied stove had tipped over on its side and its iron stovepipe poked out at an angle parallel to the hill.

I hopped out of the truck. "Let's see what we've got."

Dad pointed to some rails running around the side of one of the buildings. "Those ore cart rails'll lead to the entrance."

"Lead the way."

We walked single file down the middle of the rails, sliding a bit down the hill's slope. A second set of rails joined us and both ran directly into the mine, the two rails barely sticking out of the dirt leading into a boarded up entry maybe twenty feet across. Heavy timbers framed the entrance, like the facades of old Western buildings. It looked old, authentic. Some mines had gone all touristy after they'd dried up, but not this old gal. She wasn't a sellout.

She'd clearly been mined out long ago, but I'd bet enough trace silver still lived in her rocks to make a fallen angel uncomfortable.

The warning signs screaming, "Abandoned Mines Will Kill You" and "Keep Out—Danger" were enough to make *me* uncomfortable.

"Will this work?" I asked, though we didn't have any other choice. We were short on time as it was.

Dad paused, hands on his hips, and surveyed the site. "Depends how big the mine is, but those double tracks into the incline shaft are a good sign. It ought to be a good-sized mine, so there are probably tunnels on other levels. We ought to scout around that hill there. Look for the tailings pile—a lot of rocks and gravel—odds are you'll find another tunnel near there."

"Zack?" I called.

"On it." He blurred and zipped around the hill, gravel clattering down the slope as he moved.

"Daniel," I asked next, "could you rip off those boards, please?"

He hesitated. "Must we go down there?"

Oh. Right. Kokabiel and his dominions weren't the only ones who'd been trapped beneath the earth for millennia.

"You okay with this? We can't do it without you."

He swallowed, jaw tight. "I'll manage."

"That's all I ask."

Anita seemed uncertain. "They know who we are and where we live," she said. "What's to stop them from kidnapping us again?"

"This plan succeeding."

The group exchanged uneasy looks. I didn't blame them. If someone suggested a better idea, I'd take it in a heartbeat.

Nails screamed as Daniel ripped the boards off and tossed them away. I winced. Worse than fingernails on a chalkboard.

I ignored it best I could and stayed focused on the group. "I promise I'll do everything I can to keep you all safe."

I left them by the truck and returned to the varsity team. Daniel caught up to me, dusting his hands off as he approached. "We'll need to scout out the mine first," I said. "Find the right spot to lure them in."

Dad frowned. "Lotta mine down there."

"I know." I glanced at Daniel. He wasn't going to like this. "Daniel, I'm sorry, but you're the only one who can safely scout down there fast enough to see if this plan will even work." If too many wood beams had rotted, or there'd been heavy cave-ins, the mine might not be safe enough for us to use as a trap.

Roberto pulled out a small leather notebook. "Take this. A rough map is better than no map."

Strong as he was, Daniel shifted from foot to foot, eying the dark entrance to the mine. "How deep?"

"How much mountain will it take to bury Kokabiel?" More than what he was hiding under in his lair for sure.

Daniel cringed and closed his eyes for a moment. I didn't need physical contact to know what memories haunted him this time. "We'd need to go deep. Hundreds of feet at least."

Silver mines ran deep. And the silver would weaken them. "It's our only option. Kokabiel is probably already through the tunnel, and we left a clear trail here."

"What if it's not safe?"

"Then we fight and hope we can kill them."

Daniel sighed, then took Roberto's notebook. "All right." He walked stiffly to the mine, pausing at the now-exposed entrance as if he expected to die down there. I gave him a thumbs up and a smile, and he flashed a tight grin back and vanished into the darkness.

We prepped the gear while Daniel scouted, refilling the Super Soakers and water pistols with whatever was left in the pressure cleaner's tank Dad had brought. I handed out the pistols to Anita and Jerry, but kept the bigger guns for us. Libby took a sawed-off shotgun out of a duffel bag and slid it into the coolest holster ever on her back. She dug out four flashlights from the same bag and hung a cool mini-lantern that looked like a giant Christmas tree light on her belt. She grinned ruefully.

"If I'd known we were going spelunking, I would have stocked up."

"We'll make do."

"There's a penlight on the truck's key chain." She shrugged. "Not much, but maybe it's enough for Daniel and his super-vision."

"Hope so." One flashlight per two people in a mine wasn't just dangerous, it was outright stupid.

"Tony," Roberto said to Dad. "You got the civilians?"

"I'll keep them calm." Dad gathered the others in a tight group, speaking in low tones. I couldn't hear what he was saying, but I'd been on the receiving end of his "it's all going to be fine" pep talks enough to guess the gist of it.

I watched the mine entrance. "Think he's okay?" I whispered. Sure, he was a bit handsy, but a good guy overall.

Libby nodded. "He's tough."

Zack returned first. "Two exit tunnels," he said. "I didn't go into them, but I heard Daniel in one and he followed my voice out. He's checking the last of the tunnels now."

A ball of worry in my chest uncoiled. "That's good." Better than good.

A few minutes later, Daniel popped back out of the mine like a groundhog who'd been under too long. "It's dangerous, but it should suffice." He showed the notebook to Dad. "The main tunnel goes down five levels, with multiple branches and a few excavated areas. One tunnel on the third level leads outside to where Zack was, and one on the fourth level might. I smelled fresh air, but didn't follow it too far. Level five is small, no exits, one shaft down."

Dad ran a finger along the quickly drawn lines on Daniel's map. "Any lower tunnels with a lot of timbering? Wooden beams bracing the walls and ceiling?"

"Several here, here, and here."

"Good. Those are the weakest areas. We blow those tunnels, gravity'll do the rest. Which areas are closest to the exit?"

"This one on level three, this one on level four. This one on three is the farthest away, but it had multiple shafts around it, and one bigger area that might have had a bridge across it at one point. I didn't follow it all the way, but it looked like it went down to level four or deeper."

Dad looked at me and I sighed. "That's the spot, right?" I said.

"Sounds like it." He looked at Daniel. "How deep?"

"Seven, eight hundred feet. I estimate the mine bottoms out around a thousand." He twitched, and Zack blanched.

I didn't blame them. Even I didn't want to go down there. "Is it safe?"

"No." Dad chuckled. "It's a mine."

"Right." I rubbed my eyes. Dad and I had visited a lot of mines in my childhood. They had so many ways to kill us, Kokabiel would have to get in line. "It's go or no go time. We doing this?"

Roberto and Libby nodded. So did Dad. Cavanaugh took a breath before agreeing. Daniel glanced back at the incline shaft and swallowed, but nodded. Zack stared, eyes wide and shook his head.

"I can't," he whispered. "I can feel it. The darkness. The *pressure.*"

Daniel said something softly in the angel language, but Zack shook his head again.

"It's fine," I said. "We'll need someone to protect the others anyway, and they know Zack."

Cavanaugh's brow furrowed. "We're not all going in?"

"Not if I can help it." I called over Anita and the others who'd been in the cells with me. "I know you've all been through a lot. The rest of us have to go into that mine, but you four don't. Zack will take you around back and hide you inside one of the exit tunnels. If we succeed, we'll pick you up on the way out. If we fail, there's enough water in the truck to hold you til morning. You'll be able to make it back to Sedona on your own then." If Kokabiel left them alone and didn't go after them after he'd killed us.

Zack nodded, his shoulders slumping. "I'll protect them."

That was it, then.

"It's a go, people."

"Stay frosty," Roberto said as we moved into the entrance shaft, one flashlight for each of us. Daniel took the penlight, but he used the lantern to guide us down.

Twin rails entered, then sloped sharply downward about forty-five degrees. Heavy timbers braced the walls and ceiling, dusty and pale. Misty cobwebs draped the tunnel from beam to beam. Outside, the rocks had been red and brown, but in here, they faded to gray and white. Nothing was flat except the wood.

"Hope no one's claustrophobic," I kidded, though the ceiling wasn't more than a foot above our heads. Nobody laughed.

Daniel headed down, picking his way carefully over the rocks to the left side. A manway—like a mine sidewalk if I remembered Dad's lesson correctly—ran parallel to the rails. Wooden boards lay atop the gravel, with two-feet wide two-by-fours nailed into them like a long, flat ladder, giving us purchase on the way down. A rusty red water pipe followed the wall. It was too thin to be used for ventilation, and not sturdy enough to keep someone from falling. Old electric cables hung above it, a few bulbs still intact. Debris cluttered the manway; bits of old metal, tubing, even a faded pack of cigarettes no one made anymore.

"You want us to walk down *that*?" Cavanaugh said, voice trembling. "There's not even a handrail."

"Take it a step at a time," Dad said.

We moved slowly toward the first drift level, one of many horizontal tunnels, and my nerves tensed with every minute. If Kokabiel got out before we made it down, or if he found us before we were ready...I shuddered from more than the chill wafting up the shaft.

Up ahead, the rails and cables for the switching station appeared, antique contraptions that once raised and lowered the tracks and shifted the ore carts between mine levels. They were bent and broken after decades of neglect. On the right-hand wall, "Bill Rogers, 1931" was scrawled in black paint, and next to it, a cartoon drawing of a man in an old-time miner's hat.

Dusty shadows wrapped around us, stinging eyes and filling noses. Tunnels branched outward from the main shaft, the tracks curving through rough rock and broken lumber. Our flashlights barely made a dent in the darkness. Rock pressed in on every side, held back by beams thick as I was. Stone ought to last forever, but decades of drilling had turned this giant chunk of rock into Swiss cheese. What looked like solid ground might be thin as paper.

At the second drift level station, a tunnel led off to the right into a Y-junction. One of the tracks veered right, and a second tunnel veered left, vanishing into the pitch black just beyond a cobwebby ore chute. We kept following the main shaft.

"It's blocked ahead," Daniel said. "I made room, but we'll have to squeeze through. I didn't want to disturb it too much in case..." He waved a hand, and no one really wanted him to finish that sentence. We all knew what could happen if the wrong thing got shifted down here.

My flashlight caught the worn yellow paint of an ore cart lying upside down across the rails. Ribbed pipes big enough to hold a person were piled up beside and on top of it.

"Ventilation tubing," Dad said.

Between the tubing and the cart was just enough room to get by. Daniel showed us how to wriggle through and we followed.

Such blackness beyond. Roberto followed Daniel, but Dad took my hand and held me back. "Grace, I never wanted you to have to deal with... all this."

"We can talk about *all this* later."

He started to say something, but I stopped him. An abandoned mineshaft was hardly the place for a heart to heart, especially when we might all be dead before long. I loved him, I was pissed at him, I wanted to hug him and scream at him and then curl up on his lap as if I were six, and none of that would help us survive long enough to actually do it.

I couldn't even count on having enough time to set the trap.

As far as I could tell, we'd escaped Kokabiel's lair about forty minutes ago, tops. I hadn't exactly checked my watch when we'd peeled out of there. Daniel had estimated an hour to dig free, but what if Rocky had lived up to his name and just chewed through the stone? They could be on us any second.

This was crazy. They could have had a back door we didn't know about, and the grenade we'd thrown might have delayed them only minutes.

If so, they'd be here now.

Unless they missed the obvious turn off the road. Or they were waiting for us to come back out. Maybe they'd all feel like Zack and refuse to come down after us.

Stupid plan. Such a stupid plan.

"Ladies first," Dad said, gesturing at the tiny gap. I turned sideways and slid through, the edge of the cart pressing on my already sore back.

On the other side, a pile of spare rail tracks and a stack of wood blocked the manway.

Daniel shifted right. "Use the rail side to get past that."

More tubing, piled knee high, narrowed the tunnel further. Another ore cart—this time right-side up—waited empty but sturdy on the rails.

We passed through drift level two and headed for the station at drift level three, deeper and deeper into the mine. I sensed a hint of moisture in the cold air, and faint drips echoed in the dark. The darkness settled around us, heavier than it had been closer to the surface. Even the ceiling was lower.

More ventilation tubing crowded the incline shaft. Tubing also ran along the ceiling, parts of it crushed and dented, others torn between the metal ribs. The floor was rougher here, with more chipped stone and chunks of missing rock.

"The weakened tunnel is this way," Daniel said softly, heading into the station tunnel. It branched in three directions. In the center, massive timbers were stacked like Jenga blocks from floor to ceiling, shoved tight against the ceiling beams.

"What is that?" Libby asked.

"Cribbing," said Dad. "It's bracing the tunnel."

"That can't be good."

"For our plan it is. Plant a charge there and it'll come down easy as pie."

One set of tracks turned into the far right tunnel while the other continued down toward level four. Only one track down, now, as the main shaft was half as wide as it had been farther up.

Daniel shined the lamp down the right-hand tunnel with the tracks. "That way leads to the exit tunnel."

He took the middle tunnel. Timbers and wooden retaining walls lined both sides. The ceiling beams bowed from the pressure, most with wide enough cracks in the wood to make my skin crawl. Rocks and decent-sized boulders peeked through the space between the boards of the retaining wall.

"Does it feel damp to anyone else?" Libby asked.

"Yes," Dad said. "We must be near the aquifer."

The tunnel grew even narrower, with bowed and cracked timbers every few feet. I passed an oil barrel with an unfamiliar logo against the wall, a shallow puddle of water on its lid. White mold or some kind of fungus grew on the timbers overhead like they were dusted with snow.

Daniel stopped and turned around. "This is it."

The tunnel took a strong right turn, and just beyond it, a jagged hole plunged who-knew-how-far down. Moist air wafted up, and the scent of decay. Libby pulled a rope from her backpack and tied it off on one of the beams, then tossed it down into the hole. We'd be crazy to put our weight on it, let alone go down there, but between the rope, the displaced cobwebs and the footprints in the dust on the ground, we'd made a huge trail. If Kokabiel followed it and assumed we were hiding down here, he'd fall right into the trap. *Right, 'cause he's stupid.* I sighed.

Daniel was ghostly pale in the beam of the flashlight. I reached out and covered his dirt-smudged hand with mine. His trembled, and for a heartbeat, I felt his fear overpower my own. A terrified angel didn't bode well for our survival, but we were all scared. Why should he be any different?

"Thank you for this," I said, meaning every word. "If we live through this, you're the reason why."

His mouth twitched. More than a brief smile was apparently beyond him at the moment, but the steel in his eyes shimmered, and he once again looked like an angel with shit to prove. "We *will* survive this."

Libby and Roberto were already setting up.

"Tony," he said, "suggestions on the weakest parts to set the charges?"

Dad nodded and pointed out beams and walls. Roberto followed him and rolled out a long cord attached to rectangular boxes I assumed were the explosives. He started burying them behind the rubble and close to the walls, right up against the beams. While he worked, Libby kicked dirt over the cord, hiding it from view.

I wiped the sweat off my brow. "We can blow them up from a safe distance?"

"Affirmative."

Excellent. "The blast will seal them off from the exit tunnels as well?" No point in going through this if Kokabiel could escape the same way we did.

"If we do it right," Roberto said.

I held up both hands and crossed my fingers. He chuckled.

"Anything I can do to help?" I asked.

"Grab Cavanaugh and see if you can find something to cover our tracks to the exit tunnel."

"Roger that."

I picked up one of the thin pipes lying about and tied my jacket to the end. Not the best broom, but it worked well enough to swish around the dirt and grime. Nothing I could do about the broken cobwebs, but they weren't as noticeable in the dark up against the pale rock.

"I wonder if Kokabiel will use a flashlight," I said as I swept. He probably wouldn't even think to bring one, though there could be something in the van. A pang pinched my chest and I stopped. Damn. My knuckledusters were in that van along with my backpack and whatever of Roberto's gear Rocky had pulled off me. I loved my dusters.

"Grace?" Cavanaugh said softly. I tensed at the hesitancy in his tone, pretty sure I knew where this was going. "What did you do to me?"

"What do you mean?"

"In the lair."

"You missed a spot there, by the pipe."

He tossed a handful of dirt over the print. "You healed me."

"Oh. That." I shrugged, faking a calm I wished I felt. "Wasn't me. It was that fancy estate jewelry."

"I don't think so."

"Losing your faith, Padre?"

"No, the opposite. I was dying, and now I'm not."

"No you weren't." But he was. Uneven pupils, the fluid from his nose and ears, the blood under his head—all signs of brain trauma and someone who was never going to wake up again.

"Grace."

"Cavanaugh."

"It was a miracle."

I shoved my hair back off my sweaty face, grateful for the faint light. "We've been living with miracles for days now. Maybe the universe decided it didn't want to bench you for the rest of the game."

"You brought me back."

I rolled my eyes and pulled the cross from my pocket, shaking it in his face. "This thing's *obviously* loaded with powers beyond our comprehension."

"This isn't a joke."

I handed it to him. "No, it's our lives at stake. You take it. You're the one with the big theology guns."

He looked at me as if he didn't believe that and never would, but took the cross. "You might not like it, but you have to accept what you did."

Like hell I did. "Keep moving. We're running out of time."

I swept, he shook handfuls of gravel over the path, neither of us spoke about miracles or divine intervention. I tried hard not to think about them either, but every time I bumped into him I felt...something...like a tug toward the pocket he'd slipped the cross into. Like it was calling to me to pick it back up and do something with it.

This shouldn't be happening. All my life I knew I was weird—it wasn't normal to have monsters chasing you—but I'd thought whatever was wrong had to do with them, not me. Or they'd been after Dad and I was collateral damage.

Every kid grew up wanting to be special, but special sucked. I wanted to be normal.

Daniel appeared in my light beam. "They're here."

Damn. "Already? You sure?"

"I can hear them at the top of the shaft, but they haven't started down yet."

Bonus points for us. "Too scared?"

"Let's hope it slows them down."

We were close to finished, but Libby, Dad, and Roberto were still in the kill zone. I hurried back, staying to the sides of the tunnel and stepping on rocks when I could.

"Time's up," I whispered. This had better work. For the first time in my life, I actually had things and people I didn't want to lose.

"Last charge." Libby covered the last bit of cord, then nodded. "Done. Leave the lamp."

Roberto hung the lantern on a nail near the hole and followed us to the exit tunnel. We traced my path back, staying close to the wall without touching it or disturbing the dirt and webs.

I brought up the rear, washing away any last traces with my makeshift broom. We headed into the escape tunnel and ducked behind an ore cart.

Rock clanged against metal, bouncing down the incline shaft and into the belly of the mine. They hadn't taken long to build up their courage, and they weren't taking their time. A heartbeat later a loud clang echoed and rattled, metal against stone. The upside-down ore cart? Crap, they were moving fast.

"Lights off," I said.

Blackness descended.

And the angels fell.

Chapter Twenty-Eight

No one moved. I barely breathed, watching the blackness ahead and praying for a clue that Kokabiel and his lackeys had taken the bait.

The longest minutes of my life passed before sounds of feet on rock crawled through the inky blackness and reached us. Nothing human about those noises, more akin to giant bugs skittering along the wall in the middle of the night. Gooseflesh rippled my skin and I bit my lip, holding back an undignified whimper.

A hand gently took mine. Strong, male. I gripped it tight.

Moments later, a light thud sounded close by—feet landing on dirt? A second followed, then a third. Rocks skittered and clicked, followed by the scratch of displaced gravel. A pale flash of light broke through and danced across the rock for an instant, reflected from somewhere above.

So they *had* brought flashlights. Not many, though, or it would be brighter. They could see far distances, but could they see in the dark? Maybe they had low-light vision, or something along a different spectrum like night-vision goggles. Maybe they'd adapted after so long underground. They could be mere feet from us and we'd never know.

No, Daniel would know. If they could see, he could see, and he'd needed *some* light.

The lantern we'd left as bait glowed pale at the edge of the trapped tunnel. Another thud echoed, larger and heavier than the others. Kokabiel? Maybe Rocky. He was large enough. The hand in mine slipped away and coolness brushed my skin.

I forced myself to breathe slowly, calmly and blanked my mind from the fear. *Just think about the trap.* I pictured us descending into the hole, gripping the rope in fear. Projected us scrambling over rocks and trying to hide in the deep shadows. It probably wouldn't do any good, I'd always needed skin-to-skin contact before—but any edge we could get could make the difference.

Flashlight beams grew brighter, and a second beam joined the first. Footsteps crunched through gravel at a steady pace. Shadows flickered across the pale lantern light as they followed our trail and entered the tunnel.

I held my breath.

Kokabiel spoke in the angel language, sounding so close, but exactly where we needed him to be. A fangel replied, soft, yet sharp.

BOOM!

The world shook as the blast reverberated in the darkness. The lamp's light vanished, but the flashlight beams danced. More blasts echoed in a short string—*bang—bang—bang*. Fangels cried out, Kokabiel roared, and the mine shuddered. It groaned, broke. Wood cracked and rock crumbled. The shockwave hit, blowing rock and gravel over us.

Ears ringing, I huddled with the others as sand and bits of wood settled around us. No one moved. I'm not sure we even breathed. The mine kept shaking, louder and louder, and there was no way to tell if we'd gotten them.

A light snicked on behind me, casting its beam toward the entrance of our exit tunnel.

"Everyone okay?" Cavanaugh whispered.

Something stepped into the light. Taller than any Pretty Boy I'd ever seen, wider, its pale skin glistening hard as real marble. Muscular arms hung lower almost to its knees, its hands ending in sharp talons. It barely fit within the tunnel, yet it moved with deadly grace.

"What the hell is *that*?" I forced the words out, fighting against the fear. Screw what Dandridge believed—*this* was a demon. A nightmare come to life. More lights clicked on.

"Kokabiel!" Daniel gasped and took a step back.

"No way," I said.

"He's taken the primal form." Daniel held his arms out, shielding us. "It's his battle form."

Fear held me still. "Can you—?"

"No. Run, fast as you can. Don't wait for me. Get to Zack. Go!"

Kokabiel snarled and Daniel lunged, slamming into him at waist height. Kokabiel never budged an inch. He twisted and knocked Daniel away with ease. Wood cracked and chunks of dirt dropped from the roof, but the rumble beyond the fight was growing louder. The mine was still caving, still falling. I was still shaking, too scared to move.

Daniel dragged himself up, but Kokabiel grabbed him by the leg and threw him into the wall on the other side of the tunnel. A chunk of rock broke free and flying shards sliced my cheek.

"Shoot 'em?" Libby shouted.

The fear in her voice pulled me out of my own terror. "Not yet!" I grabbed a chunk of wood and hefted it like a bat. I wasn't leaving Daniel alone to fight *this*. All I needed was an opening.

Cavanaugh stepped forward, chanting in Latin, Dad's cross in his outstretched hand. No light this time, no glow. Maybe we'd used up all its mojo. Maybe it didn't work on actual demons. Or maybe it just needed both of us to do any good.

"Silence, priest." Kokabiel snatched up Daniel and flung him at Cavanaugh, knocking him off his feet. Both tumbled back into the shadows of the tunnel.

"Now," I yelled.

Soakers rose and holy water gushed. The streams caught Kokabiel from multiple angles and he shrieked, sparking blue as a gas flame in the shadows. He blurred past me and knocked those armed with Super Soakers to the ground. The water guns skittered off into the tunnel.

"Pray you're worth this trouble," he said to me, low and threatening. He glared, his beautiful face now made of sharp angles and planes, his marble skin smoking and sparking as the holy water dripped off him. "If your blood fails me, I will soak the ground with it."

Daniel staggered to my side, pale yellow-gold smudges on his face and neck. He favored his left leg, but his knife glinted in his hand. "I told you to run."

I swallowed, shoving my terror away. "When has that *ever* worked?"

"You're too weak to protect her," Kokabiel taunted, extending impossibly long and deadly arms.

I inched closer. "Give me the knife," I whispered.

"You're deluded," Daniel spat back. For a second I thought he'd meant me, but his gaze never left Kokabiel. "A brief manifestation of a soul won't fool Him, no matter what ritual it comes from."

Daniel lunged at Kokabiel's heart. He dodged under his strike and slashed him across the chest. Kokabiel grunted and turned, seizing Daniel's arm and twisting it. Bone snapped and he screamed, dropping the blade. Kokabiel tossed him against the wall yet again, turning his back to me.

I swung the makeshift bat. It shattered across Kokabiel's shoulders like it was clay. For a moment, he stood alone and clear in the angled beams of the flashlights, and terrifyingly beautiful.

"Down!" Roberto yelled.

I hit the dirt as deafening gunshots filled the tunnel, followed by flashes streaking through the darkness. Kokabiel barely staggered back, shrugging the bullets off as if they were pebbles thrown by a child. He snatched what was left of a beam and threw it at Roberto. Roberto dodged and the light shifted, coating me in shadows. I had no clue where my flashlight had fallen.

In a heartbeat, Kokabiel's fingers gripped my throat, the tips of his claws sharp against my skin. He bent me backward until I hung from his hand. I pulled at his fingers, but it was pointless.

I was going to die here. We'd all die here, all except the one who deserved it.

Kokabiel ripped the bandage off my neck. He smiled, and a set of fangs glistened in the dim light. "It lacks the elegance of the ritual, but this is how your legends do it, yes?" He sank his fangs into my neck and I screamed.

Visions swirled in my mind; the village, the running women, a city of light and beauty. Kokabiel lifted his head and gasped, a wondrous ecstasy shining on his face.

I bit back the pain as his skin shimmered, his face growing brighter with every breath. Luminescent.

"I feel it," he gasped. "My *soul*."

My fingers raked over the shattered wood around my feet. *He wants to play vampire? Let's see if he dies like one.*

I found a shaft of wood, sharp on one end. Kokabiel's shirt hung in tatters, exposing the gash across his chest like a crack in stone. Legends or not, the stories had to come from somewhere, and he was *not* going to cheat his way into Heaven.

White light shimmered under his skin and radiated from him, brighter than our flashlights, but not quite as bright as Dad's cross had been. Kokabiel gazed down at me, smiling. "Thank you, Hannah Grace."

"You don't deserve Heaven." I dragged myself to my knees. He deserved every horrible option available. "Go to Hell." I plunged the stake into his heart—*this is for my mother.*

Gold light burst from him, illuminating the wood from within. He screamed and staggered back, but the light grew brighter, purer...

"No!" He did *not* get to use *my* blood to get *his* way. I reached for another stake and—

The light darkened, shifting to a deep and ugly red. Gold sparks flickered across his skin and dropped like molten metal to the ground. The floor cracked where the sparks fell, gravel sliding into the earth, widening the crevices beneath him.

A *much* deeper rumbling shook the mine.

Uh oh.

"Knock him into the incline shaft!" I shouted. I rolled to my back and kicked Kokabiel with both feet, shoving him a few steps closer to the mouth of the tunnel. Pain vibrated down my legs.

Metal cocked and Libby surged forward with the shotgun in her hands. She fired and Kokabiel stumbled back another step. The red light bled into the green as cracks formed in his skin.

The rock around him bubbled and a wave of heat washed outward, racing down the tunnel. Sulfur burned my nose and eyes, and I *really* wanted to believe it was just bad air released in the blast.

Something that wasn't Kokabiel growled and I chilled despite the sudden heat. He looked wildly about, kicking below him in the shadows. The fissures in the shaft's floor widened and dark shapes crested the surface like long-limbed, lethal dolphins.

"Libby! He's still too close!"

She fired again. Kokabiel stumbled out of the tunnel and fell to one knee next to an ore cart, as far as he was going to go. Tons of rock and earth blocked the tunnel where we'd laid our trap. The fissures raced after him, sucking down more stone and turning the rock into a pool of molten sludge.

Kokabiel thrashed and screamed. A fiery orange glow turned his beautiful features into a nightmare. Charred claws burst from the sludge and seized his arms. More scaly black hands raked the ground, widening the hole further.

Okay, now *those* were definitely demons.

Daniel stumbled to my side and braced himself on the wall. He gaped at the demons dragging Kokabiel down. "What did you do?"

"Told him to go to Hell. I didn't think he'd *do* it."

He stared at me, fear and awe rippling across his face like the lights across the rock walls. "You *punished* him," he whispered, and fear won control of his expression. "That's not possible."

"I just stabbed him with a stick. I didn't do anything else." I did *not* have superpowers. Especially not ones that frightened fallen angels.

Daniel stared at me, looking dazed. This was not a good place for this conversation. *There will never be a good place for this conversation.* I backed away and waved at Roberto, holding several grenades in one hand. "Plan B!" I shouted.

He lobbed the grenades. The blasts drowned out the shrieks and snarls, but the rock groaned louder, then shifted. Red light illuminated tiny stones as they whizzed down the tunnel like missiles, cutting skin and bruising bone.

Kokabiel roared, other voices laughed, but he—and they—vanished under the rumble of stone, the snapping of timber, and the whine of metal. The shaft collapsed. Heat rolled out, thick with the smell of sulfur and a disturbing hint of honeysuckle.

Roberto yelled something I couldn't make out, but his face told the story I couldn't hear. The mine was coming down and it didn't care if we were in it or not.

I caught a stronger whiff of sulfur and shivered. Or whatever had opened for Kokabiel was pulling the mine under. *What you opened, you mean?*

Not thinking that. It wasn't me.

Libby kept her light on the rubble filling the incline shaft, watching molten sludge seep through the rocks. Cavanaugh stood beside her, staring at me with that same horrible awed expression he'd had before.

"We gotta move, now!" I said.

Libby wiped a hand across her mouth. "What the hell was that?"

"Come on."

Daniel twitched, but didn't move. I grabbed his arm and dragged him away from the collapsing shaft, running with the others down the exit tunnel. We fled the hissing and scratching and indescribable noises coming from inside the rocks.

"Did you see those...things?" Libby asked.

I'd see them every time I closed my eyes for the rest of my life. "You know what they say—when Fate closes a door she opens a window."

"Did you see that freaking window?"

"Pretty sure it led into the basement."

I stopped thinking, kept moving, while the tunnel grew hotter and hotter. Sweat dripped down my face and back, but my feet were freezing and sluggish, every step an effort.

That wasn't right...

I looked down.

Water swirled past my ankles. Crap. "Guys, don't panic or anything, but I think we cracked into the aquifer. The mine is flooding."

Roberto grunted. "Double time, people."

The gurgling grew louder as we hurried down the tunnel. Debris-filled water flowed past us, cold and dark, almost to my knees now and rising up the walls at an alarming pace. Sparks of gold and green flared in the light as they whooshed past.

I kept moving. Wood creaked from above and I tried not to picture the braces giving way and dumping tons of rock on our heads. *Refused* to think about demons and portals and where Kokabiel had gone. What he had become.

"How much farther?" I asked.

"I see the winze," Dad said, shining his flashlight over the connecting tunnel between drift levels. A hand-built ladder stretched upward, and the narrow passage was barely wide enough for Roberto's shoulders. Dust and bits of gravel rained down through the hole.

"It goes up about thirty feet," Daniel said. "There's another tunnel that leads to the outside."

We sloshed through the water and climbed the ladder, Daniel zipping up first. He held the light down for us and we climbed after him. Roberto came last, pushing through with a grunt.

"This way." Daniel led us down the dark tunnel. The dust in the air made it difficult to see and just as hard to breathe. I pulled my shirt over my nose and mouth, but it didn't help much. No water yet, but the creak of wood and scrape of settling rock echoed all around us.

"Is that light?" Cavanaugh asked.

My night vision was screwed up, but the tunnel ahead looked more gray than black, and small silvery pieces glinted in the shadows. Then a bright flash nearly blinded me. I held up my hand and blocked the beam from the flashlight.

"Grace?" Anita called.

"It's us!"

"Thank the stars."

Pale light brushed the edges of the tunnel, growing brighter the closer we got to the exit. The sun had set, but night hadn't quite fallen. We reached the others, standing close together a few dozen feet in from the exit.

"We got them," I said, and five relieved breaths exhaled as one. "But we need to get out of here before—" The mine shook, staggering us. Everyone reached out to grab whatever was closest.

"We can talk later," Jerry agreed.

We ran to the exit. The others kept going over the edge and down the slope. I stopped and grabbed Roberto's arm. "Do we have any grenades left to seal this tunnel?"

Roberto held up two. "Was saving these for just such an occasion."

"Blow it."

We moved away from the entrance and he tossed in the grenades. A few seconds later double explosions shook the trail and the mouth of the cave collapsed. Roberto and I half fell, half slid down the rim of a basin that had probably been filled with water at some point, maybe the old slurry pond. Small spouts of water squirted out from a few spots lower down the slope, gathering at the bottom.

Libby held up both hands, her fingers crossed.

The dust cloud cleared. Cavanaugh sighed, but I waited for something horrific to seep through. "Think we trapped them?" he said softly.

Still nothing. I exhaled, daring to hope. "We might not know for—"

The ground below us rose and a deep thud echoed through the rock, more felt than heard. The slope dropped away and we tumbled farther into the basin.

Rocks bit into my skin as I bounced between Libby and Cavanaugh. Roberto and Daniel fell below us. The rest above us. We all hit a muddy pool in a tangle of arms and legs and a whole lot of swearing.

Above us, the mine...burped...jerking into the air, then collapsing in on itself and a good five feet lower than it was a few minutes ago. Dirt poofed into the twilight and glittered as it floated on the air and settled around us.

Libby sat up first and pushed her muddy hair off her face. She gazed up at the now-closed shaft. "I think you killed it."

Maybe, maybe not, but as long as we'd trapped everything inside for the next hundred years, I could live with that.

CHAPTER TWENTY-NINE

I pulled myself up. "Everyone okay?"

Roberto gave me a jaunty salute. Cavanaugh hesitated, then nodded. Jerry stuck a thumb in the air.

"You guys good?" I asked the others. Wil was staring at the mud like he had no idea where he was. Dad was helping Anita to her feet. "I'll let you know," she said.

"You did it." Daniel glanced at the mud-covered people around us. "This was…impressive."

"No, that rescue plan was impressive. Libby, Roberto, MVP status, absolutely."

Roberto chuckled, but Libby rolled her eyes. "I think she's delirious."

Just happy to be alive.

I crawled up the side of the basin and followed the now-uneven path to the mine entrance. The mine wasn't so pretty anymore, poor old gal. The facade had cracked down one side and collapsed, leaving a shallow pit where the incline shaft used to be. No one was getting in or out of there any time soon—a good thing considering where the back door led.

We followed the bent and twisted tracks around to the front. Several of the buildings had given up and fallen down, and one had joined its sibling in a tangled pile on the side of the hill. A few pipes jutted out of the ground that hadn't been there before.

The truck sat where we'd left it, although at a sharper angle than before. If Libby had parked it ten feet closer to the mine entrance, we'd have been walking back to Sedona.

I turned to Daniel, scanning the area. "See anything?"

"No. I heard everyone but Suriel in the mine, and he's not up here."

"What about—"

Daniel raised a hand and spoke to Zack in the angel language. From the tone and the way they both kept glancing over, they were talking about me behind my back right to my face.

I crossed my arms. "That's rude, you know."

Daniel chuckled, but his expression was grim. "He thinks Suriel went back to the mountain to collect his data and scientists."

"We can't leave that place open for business," Libby said. She whistled sharp and loud and everyone turned to her. "One more stop before we head home, folks. This isn't over yet."

Groans all around, even from me.

"She's right, Grace," Dad said, frowning. Clearly, he didn't want to go back any more than I did.

Daniel nodded. "It must be destroyed."

"Back to the evil lair we go, then."

SURIEL WASN'T THERE. Neither were any scientists.

The tunnel had been cleared enough for one person at a time to crawl through, but everything else was pretty much as we'd left it. Daniel and Zack had done a lengthy recon to make sure it was safe, and now it was our turn to explore.

"Computers are missing," Dad said as soon as we walked into the lab. "I'll check the files, but even money says they're gone too."

He was right.

Everything else was still here—the lab gear, the chairs, the beds, even the fancy TVs. Suriel must have had the scientists grab what they could carry and skedaddle.

"We can blow this up when we're done collecting evidence, right?" I asked.

Dad nodded, Roberto smiled, Libby shook her head. "No more explosives," she said.

"I'll check the shed," Dad said. "They had to blast this out somehow. Could be some dynamite left."

He and Roberto headed out, Zack behind them as security—just in case.

"Okay people, let's see what we can find."

After an exhaustive search, we'd found little more than a few papers with hospital names and numbers, a coffee cup from a local shop, and the fancy Bible Kokabiel had given Cavanaugh to use for the communion ritual. It was a little damp around the edges, but it had escaped most of the holy water.

Even though he'd seen it before, Cavanaugh held it like it contained all the knowledge of the universe. Who knew, maybe it did. It looked old enough.

"This is priceless," he called back to me, standing on the steps of the altar. The silk they'd used to tie me down was still there, stuck to the stone after the holy water attack. "Just look at the craftsmanship."

I stayed in the hall outside with Daniel while Cavanaugh and Libby went through the cathedral. Cavanaugh paused at the now-dried smear of his blood on the pillar and looked at me. I shrugged. He could think what he wanted about his recovery. I had no better answer for him.

"You ready?" Daniel asked.

"Yes." I had one room I wanted to search personally, and he insisted on coming with me.

I headed to the far end of the lair, which Libby had dubbed the fangel dorms. Five rooms of various styles, from Spartan-bare to Vegas-casino-opulence. Three of them had been setup for roomies, but the last two had been home to the big boys.

"Which one do you think was Suriel's?"

Daniel peeked in both rooms and pointed to the one on the right. "That one."

It took three seconds to realize telling the rooms apart was easy. Just like his clothes, everything about Suriel's room was subdued style. Well-made furniture, tasteful art, rich carpet. No computer or any personal items. Nothing to tell me which of his minions killed my mother.

"Do you guys sleep?" A full-sized bed sat tight against the wall. I'd have figured Suriel for a king size.

"We rest. It's not the same."

It irked me, Suriel having this nice room while the people he'd kidnapped shivered in the cells. He deserved to be back in a cold, dark, hole deep in the ground.

"You'll find him for me?"

He cringed, cocking his head a little to the side like a cute little puppy. "I'd prefer you let him be."

"Not after what he did." He'd clearly been working with Kokabiel for years, tracking down people with the right DNA. Mom must have been one of them. Dad, too. Two thousand years was a long time for genetic material to scatter throughout the world.

Daniel smiled gently. "Avenge not yourselves, but rather give place unto wrath: for it is written, Vengeance is mine; I will repay, saith the Lord."

"Preach all you want, I'm still staking that bastard."

"It won't be easy. He won't stop trying to find a way home. None of us will." A dark flicker rippled across his face. "Most of us, at least."

"All the more reason to find and stop him. If he took the lab equipment he's going to start this all over again." I poked him in the chest with one finger. "That means looking *me* up again."

"Not if he has other options. He knows you're more trouble than your worth."

Not if he ever found out my blood *had* worked. Granted, not the way Kokabiel had wanted, but maybe if Cavanaugh had blessed me and done the communion it would have.

Still, it was small comfort. I was safe, but not the next person in my "family" who had the right DNA. "Listen, is all that Mary stuff Zack told me true?"

Daniel cringed again. It really *was* cute. Annoyed as I was about his holding that little tidbit back, I could almost forgive him when he did that. *Man, I must be tired.*

"Yes," he whispered. "But...there's more to you than just her blood."

"Well, sure, considering how diluted it must be by now."

"No, it's what you've done. You should never have been able to kill Kokabiel. Even banishing a seraph is impossible."

I almost blamed the knife again. Or the cross. But I'd killed him with nothing more than a stake of old wood and a lot of unresolved anger.

"Suriel is the same level angel as Kokabiel, right?"

"He is."

"So he'll have minions of his own working for him."

"Yes. Seraphim don't usually work together, but pairing with Suriel was smart of Kokabiel. He'd know what to look for in the blood."

"He's got a genetics degree from Johns Hopkins?"

"Suriel is an angel of death."

There were some things a girl really didn't need to know. "He's the *Angel of Death*?"

"Not *the*, *a*. Suriel is merely one such angel." He smiled and leaned closer, near my ear, and whispered, "Still want me to find him for you?"

He was getting *way* too comfortable with me. I cleared my throat. "I'd like him gift wrapped, please."

"If I find him, I'll let you know."

He seemed sincere, but angels were excellent liars. "Thank you. We should, uh, probably check Kokabiel's room now."

Kokabiel had liked his luxury. Here was the king-sized bed, the thick carpet, the fancy and gold-plated everything. The room could have come straight from the palace at Versailles.

"I bet he and Louis the Fourteenth would have gotten along great."

"They did."

I sighed. Either Daniel needed to learn to recognize sarcasm or I had to keep my quips to myself.

"Aside from gaudy, it looks normal in here." Still no laptop or earth-shattering evidence of an evil plan, but he had left behind his e-reader. I picked it up and flipped through it. "There's nothing but religious texts on here."

"What did you expect?"

"I don't know. Erotica? Westerns? Something unbecoming of an angel."

"He's a single-minded individual." He paused and shook his head, brow furrowed, avoiding looking at me. "*Was*. It doesn't seem possible that he's dead."

Considering what dragged him down underground, he might not be. Another thing to add to my long list of what not to dwell on. "Um, what did you mean before when you said I'd punished him?"

Daniel faltered, needing a second try to shut the drawer he was looking into. "I misspoke."

"Stop lying to me."

He sighed. "Only the divine can punish us. You cast Kokabiel into Hell, which requires judgment that deems one unworthy to enter Heaven. You're human. You shouldn't have been able to do that, even if you are of Her blood."

"Does this mean I'm a superhero?"

"Must you *always* joke?"

"I thought you knew me."

He smiled and stroked my hand. "Not well enough."

Oh boy.

"Um, I don't see anything valuable in here either." I kept the e-reader in case Cavanaugh could find something useful on it. The interests of a fallen angel might give him some insights to what Suriel might do.

Daniel glanced about the room. "No."

I doubted we'd find anything else, but it didn't hurt to be thorough. I helped search the rest of the angel dorm, then helped Cavanaugh with the last of the human quarters. They held even less than Kokabiel's room.

I walked with Daniel back to the entrance and ran into Dad leaning against the wall just outside the cathedral. He stood straight when he spotted me. "Got a minute?" he asked softly.

"I'll be, elsewhere," Cavanaugh said, then vanished fast as a fangel.

I stared at Dad, feeling weird. I wanted to talk, needed to, but I had no idea where to start or what to say. I knew one thing, though. I didn't want to do it in this damned lair.

"Why don't we go outside?"

He smiled. "Sounds good to me."

Outside seemed a good spot for a heart-to-heart. Quiet, dark so we could avoid looking at each other, but within sight of a strong reminder why we needed this conversation. We sat on the tailgate in the truck bed, swinging our legs in unison to keep warm in the midnight chill.

Dad chuckled softly. "I hadn't realized I'd raised a vampire slayer."

"You know they're not vampires." It came out harsher than I'd intended, but I was tired, and frustrated, and pissed at things I could do nothing about.

"I know." He sighed and rubbed his face with both hands, then sighed again. "I was never sure, you know. Daniel doesn't like to talk about himself."

"Not without bribery."

"I *did* think they were vampires until your friend told me otherwise."

I glanced at him, eyes narrowed. "For real?"

"For real. Maybe not like the movies made it out to be, but close enough. Names are just what we call things."

"A Pretty Boy by any other name is still a pain in the ass."

He laughed again, and some of the tension in my shoulder loosened. "I've missed you," he said.

"I've missed you, too." It would be so easy to just forgive him. It must have been hard, trying to keep us safe and not scare the crap out of me. I'd seen Mom die. I knew the truth, even if I'd been too young to understand it.

"I'm sorry, Grace," he said softly. "I never wanted this to affect your life more than it absolutely had to."

"You should have told me about Daniel."

He twitched as if I'd surprised him. "That's what you're upset about?"

"Well, not just that. But you were regularly talking to a Pretty Boy and didn't tell me. He could have answered so many questions."

"Sweet Potato, you've spoken to Daniel more than I have. He'd show up every few years, tell me we had to go, and I'd go. We weren't drinking buddies."

"No?"

"No. Every time I asked him a question he'd give me some cryptic bullshit answer."

I grinned. "I'm familiar with his bullshit."

Dad looked at me, his concern bright even in the dim light from the cave. "A little too familiar."

"Really? You're going to play the overprotective father card?" He'd been protective my whole life, but not like that. We'd never lived anywhere long enough where he'd needed to chase away interested boys.

"He's obsessed with you."

I shrugged. Fascinated was more likely. Intrigued maybe. "I defy his expectations. You know how men are."

"He's not a man."

"I can handle Daniel." How I wanted to handle him was another story.

He hesitated, lips pursed, then nodded slowly. "I suppose you can. Doesn't mean I won't worry about you."

We watched our feet a while, not saying a thing. I sorted through my questions, discarding the ones I knew he'd not be able to answer if he was telling the truth about Daniel. Setting aside the ones I wasn't ready to ask yet.

"Where'd you get that cross?" I said. "The one with the amethyst?"

"You have it?" He blew out a breath. "Good. I thought I'd lost it."

I shifted on the tailgate. "I, uh, gave it to Cavanaugh to study."

"You need to keep that. It'll protect you."

Apparently he hadn't noticed I could protect myself just fine without magic crosses. "He'll give it back. He's a good man."

"But this cross is special. Daniel gave it to me."

Of course. "Did he tell you anything about it?"

"Only that it was old and powerful." He huffed and shook his head. "You shouldn't have given it away. Can you get it back?"

"Yes, but we'll learn more about it if Cavanaugh studies it. He's a priest and a decent investigator. If anyone can figure out what it is and what it does, he can. He's seen it work first-hand."

Dad's head snapped up and he looked at me, eyes wide. "Work how?"

Oh crap. I'd forgotten he hadn't been there for that. "He used it against Kokabiel and Suriel. Exorcised the bastards and sent their angelly butts running. It puts on quite the light show in the right hands." My fingers tingled and I shoved both hands under my legs. Okay, fine, it was hypocritical of me to lie to him, but I didn't know what any of what happened meant. Until I did, anything I said would just worry him, and he'd had a hard enough life as it was.

"A priest, eh?" Dad cocked his head and reconsidered.

"Catholic and everything."

"All right, as long as you get it back, I guess that's okay."

I put my hand on his arm and squeezed. "He will." And hopefully when he did, he'd know what I'd done with it and how. *Speaking of miraculous healings...*

"How are you feeling?"

His legs stopped swinging and he tensed again. "Good. Clear, though I feel like I've forgotten things."

"You were pretty fuzzy the last six months. Mixing up what year it was."

More silence. "I'm sorry I put you through that."

"Wasn't your fault."

"Still. I'm supposed to take care of you, not the other way around."

At least he didn't have to worry about that anymore. I elbowed him. "Hey, I bet you can get on all the morning talk shows about your 'miracle cure.' You could be famous."

He chuckled. "The ladies do love a celebrity."

"Wait until your hair grows back."

"Are you kidding?" He ran a hand over his smooth head. "Bald is sexy."

I made a face. "Ew."

Still laughing, Dad pulled me into a hug and squeezed me tight. I hugged him back hard enough to make up for all the hugs I'd missed.

"It's all going to be okay, my Radish," he said. It probably wasn't, but for now, I'd believe him.

By the time the lair was looted and explored, it was almost dawn and I was close to collapse from exhaustion. Dad and Roberto had found some dynamite in the shed, and had the charges ready to blow this joint. We moved the party outside. The pale skies looked clear, promising a nice morning. Chilly, but not as cold as yesterday. Ivy had fallen asleep in the truck, and Anita kept triggering an avalanche of yawns in all but Zack and Daniel.

"Who wants the honors?" Libby asked, wiggling the end of the fuse. The truck was parked out of range, and everyone else huddled down behind some boulders for safety.

"Me," Wil said, his arms tight across his chest. Libby handed him a lighter and held the fuse out for him.

Wil lit it, glaring as the spark sizzled its way into the lair. A less impressive explosion this time around, but enough to shake the ground and put another dent in the Arizona landscape.

Wil sighed and let his arms drop. "Will they be back?"

"I don't know."

It was quiet until we turned onto an actual road, and everyone heaved a collective sigh of relief. Civilization didn't equal safety, but it felt better than being in the desert. I sat with my back against the cab, Daniel on one side, Libby on the other, cataloging the vast number of sore muscles I was going to have before day's end.

On the other side of the truck bed, Dad and Cavanaugh spoke in low tones. A serious conversation with serious expressions, much more intense than any conversation at this time of the morning had a right to be. Maybe Dad was trying to get his cross back.

I stretched my neck and rolled my shoulders. Sunlight had finally crested the mountains and chased away some of the chill I'd carried since the mine, and the warmth felt good.

I jerked straight. Sunlight. Zack was driving, but the truck's windows weren't tinted. He and Daniel were going to get mighty crispy awfully fast.

"Do we have a tarp or anything?" I asked.

Roberto shook his head. The others just stared at me. "What's wrong?"

"The *sun*."

Daniel sucked in a breath and flinched away, but he'd been sitting in direct sunlight, same as I had.

"Daniel?"

He laughed and held up a hand in the sunlight. "It doesn't burn."

I held up both hands. "It's not me. I'm not touching you. Zack? You doing okay up there in the sun?"

The truck jerked left and swerved a bit, but he got it right back under control. "I'm...unhurt," he said, awed.

Daniel kept staring, alternating between his hands and the sun. "A miracle." His gaze darted to me. "Some of us think redemption is possible, though I never believed it."

"But you helped us. Protected us."

He nodded. "That's what I was sent here to do. There's no reward for doing your job."

"You sure?" I thumbed at the sun. "Because you should be on fire."

His wonder and delight said he wasn't sure, but didn't care. "We have to tell the others. They think they've been abandoned, but they *haven't*."

"That's...good?" Daylight had been one of the few things restricting Kokabiel's actions. If Suriel now had free reign to plot against humanity...

"It's good if we *can* earn our way back into His favor." Daniel laughed again and slowly wiggled his fingers in the light. "Perhaps He *will* let us come home one day."

"The slow way home?"

"The *worthy* path home. This proves it's possible."

For his sake, I hoped so.

Chapter Thirty

The sun was officially out by the time we pulled up to St. Mary's, and neither Daniel nor Zack had burst into flames once.

"You sure you want to do this?" I asked them.

Daniel nodded. "We need to know." He hopped out of the truck bed and slowly approached the edge of holy ground. Zack stayed in the truck.

We must have looked like lunatics, the whole group of us leaning over, watching a grown man tiptoe up to a parking lot.

Daniel stepped off the sidewalk and onto church grounds. Sparks danced across his skin, though not as bright as the ones that sizzled off Kokabiel and the others.

Hissing, Daniel jumped back. Zack sighed, but Daniel smiled. "It's better," he said. "Still stings, but not as painful."

I grinned back. "So go save a few more humans and test your sparkability."

"Can we go home now?" Ivy grumbled. "Or should I run to the police?"

Anita shot her a disgusted look. "These people saved our lives. Be grateful."

"If you can't be grateful," Jerry added, "then think how you'll sound to the cops. You'll be under 'psychiatric observation' by lunch."

Ivy muttered, but settled down and went back to staring at her feet.

Cavanaugh cleared his throat. "I've been investigating most of your cases," he said, looking over Anita, Ivy, Jerry, and Wil, "so why don't you four come with me. Father Dandridge and I can help you with any questions you still have, and we can figure out how to explain all of this to the police and get you home."

Jerry huffed, but agreed. "I think we ought to stick to Grace's cult story."

"I second that," Anita said. Wil nodded. Ivy grunted.

"Okay, good, good." Cavanaugh looked at me and Libby. "You two want to sit in on this?"

Not particularly, but he'd need back up. "Lead the way, Padre."

Dad waved us on. "I'll take the boys out for breakfast and meet y'all back here," he said, then leaned in and whispered to me, "That Dandridge priest is a bit of a dick."

I held back my snort. "You've no idea."

ALTHOUGH SHOCKED TO his core, Dandridge handled it better than I'd expected. He seemed genuinely concerned about Kokabiel's victims now that they were in his office, and had even managed to find his compassion under all that ambition. Of course, now that he knew the truth, he was even more curious about me and my link to the Pretty Boys, but I'd deal with that when—and if—I had to.

"He's not going to stab us in the back or anything, will he?" I asked Cavanaugh as he walked us back out.

"No. Finally understanding what we're fighting helped reset his priorities."

I huffed. "You heard him. He thinks they're devils now instead of demons."

"Theologically speaking, he's not wrong."

"Lucifer does set precedence," Libby added.

I shivered. "Please tell me he's not running amok in the world, too."

"Probably not." Cavanaugh chuckled. "He wasn't one of the Watchers."

Whew. "I'm still not comfortable with Dandridge knowing about Daniel and Zack." We couldn't exactly tell our stories without mentioning them, but we'd left out the part about them tossing back breakfast sandwiches with Roberto and my dad instead of proving their divine powers to Dandridge. The less contact he had with them the better.

"I'll take care of it, Grace, don't worry. He's an excellent and knowledgeable researcher, and he can help us find Suriel and the others."

We reached the lobby. Dad and Roberto were on the far side, chatting next to the holy water basin. Roberto had a backpack slung over his shoulder. I guess Daniel and Zack had taken off, though they could have said goodbye.

"You sure about moving here?" I asked Cavanaugh as we walked over. During our meeting, he'd announced he was leaving his church in Florida and transferring to Sedona to work with Dandridge tracking down Suriel and the others who'd escaped.

"We'll need a base of operations, and Aaron *has* done a lot of the preliminary work. He tracked them here, remember? If he found them once, he can do it again."

True. Dandridge still hadn't told us exactly how, though, which bugged me.

"We also have a lot to read," he continued, patting the box containing Kokabiel's Bible and e-reader. "Plus all the hospital research to go over, and it's too much for one person to comb through quickly. Now that I know what to look for, it'll be easier to track any leftover minions of Kokabiel's."

"Let us know if you need help with that."

"He has help," Dad said. "I'm staying, too."

"What?" I said a tad too loudly.

Cavanaugh shifted uneasily and scooted a few steps back.

"Hear me out before you start yelling," Dad said, chuckling. "Nate and I discussed it at length on the drive back. Between the two of us, we have a stack of puzzle pieces to what the—what did you call them again?" he asked Libby.

"Fangels," she said.

"Right. What the fangels are doing. Grace, you said it yourself—Suriel isn't going to give up, and we're the best people to find him."

"You're supposed to come back with me."

"Retire to Florida?" He shook his head. "I'd be a bother down there, Sweet Potato, you know that. How often does someone get a second chance? I don't want to waste it. I've wasted enough years already."

"That's why you should come home."

"Florida hasn't been home in a long time."

Not since Pensacola, when Mom was still alive. It had been hard for me to move back, too. "This sucks."

He gave me a tight hug. "I know, but it's what I have to do."

"This isn't about you and that cross, is it?"

"No," he said, chuckling. "You were right, Nate is the man for the job. I want to help him."

I glared at Father Sneakypants over Dad's shoulder, then broke the hug. "Can't you come back for a little while?" I asked Dad.

"I'll make you a deal. Soon as I get settled, I'll come for a nice, long visit."

Not nearly good enough, but it'd be easier to bend rebar than change his mind when he looked that determined.

"Deal. But if you're not in Lauderdale in the next month, I'm coming back to get you."

"I can live with that." He ruffled my hair.

At least in Sedona he had Cavanaugh to look after him. Dad was probably safe. Traveling for a visit wasn't going to be an issue anymore. Suriel knew Dad's blood couldn't help him, though he might try to use him as leverage to get me again. Daniel didn't think so, since the ritual idea was really Kokabiel's evil plan.

But what was Suriel's? That part still bothered me.

Whatever it was, we'd figure it out. Libby and I weren't going anywhere just yet, so Dad and I had some time before I had to get back to work. We'd make the most of the next few days.

"Well, I guess that's it then." Cavanaugh hesitated and I tensed. He had that look again. No matter how many times he'd asked, I couldn't tell him what had happened in the fangel cathedral. I hadn't mentioned the whole Mary thing. I suspected he'd have more trouble dealing with that little tidbit than me bringing him back from the brink of death. Or maybe he was just worried what I'd do to him for stealing my father.

"You'd better take good care of him," I said, putting a little threat into it.

Cavanaugh grinned nervously and crossed his heart. "Promise."

We all gave Cavanaugh a hug and headed back to the truck, parked at the edge of holy ground. Daniel and Zack lounged in the back, their faces turned toward the sun.

"They're still here?" I said, a little disturbed at my relief. I was getting too used to them being around. *Them or him?*

Dad nodded, but he gave me a pointed, protective-dad look. "They wanted to make sure we *all* made it home safely."

"That is their job, you know." I glanced back at Daniel, grinning like he was on vacation. He lifted his head and met my stare, then smiled wider. And waved. I smiled and waved back. Crap. This was going to get complicated. "Remind me to buy them sunscreen."

"Do angels burn?" Libby said.

I scoffed. "Kokabiel did."

She groaned.

"Too soon?"

She held her fingers apart about an inch. "Just a little."

"YOU SUCK, GRACE-FACE," Daisy said through gritted teeth, but she held tight to the bars and shoved herself forward another step. I'd been back in Lauderdale for two weeks, and she'd shown up for every session. Libby had been quite impressed.

"That's Queen Grace-face to you," I said.

"This is child abuse."

I struck a soldier's pose. "This. Is. Therapy!"

She snorted and shook her head. "You are so weird."

Yes, but she was doing her exercises and she hadn't spit at anyone in days. I'd take that trade. I caught Libby watching us from the coffee stand and winked. She chuckled, which was good.

After we'd gotten back from Sedona, we'd driven down to her father's fishing cabin in Key Largo. She'd hidden it well, but being there had been hard for her, and she'd had to leave and sit by the water multiple times each day. I'd packed enough photos of her and her dad together to see how close they'd been. She'd gotten through it, though. My bestie was no wimp.

"Come on, peon," I said, returning to Daisy. "Three more steps and you can go harvest the fields before the sun sets."

"If I do four, will you promise not to be weird for the rest of the day?"

"I make no promises."

She did four anyway.

I canceled the funky chicken victory dance I had planned and patted her on the head instead. "Nice job."

She hesitated, eying me suspiciously from behind her hair. "Thanks."

"Now you get a prize." I handed her an electric orange hair scrunchy with purple zig-zag stripes and green metallic fringe. The corner of her mouth twitched.

"You'd better get that thing back into the ocean before it dies."

"Please, all the cool kids are wearing dead sea creatures in their hair." I pulled her blond locks back into a high ponytail with the scrunchy. "Beautiful."

"Fine, it obviously means a lot to you." She rolled her eyes, but checked herself out in the mirrored wall. Green fringe stuck out from her head like a dandelion. Wild, a little wacky, and daring you to notice it. No one would look at her legs with *that* thing in her hair.

Her parents arrived and waved from the waiting area near the elevators. Daisy groaned, but it didn't have the same level of annoyance that it had had last week. Baby steps, but progress was progress.

"They want to take me out for a special dinner tonight," she mumbled.

"Good deal, you must be hungry. You worked hard all afternoon."

She snorted. "Yeah, but I could do without the pity party."

"Then don't pity them."

A grin flickered across her mouth. "I'll tell them I want lobster."

"Do you like lobster?"

"Not really, but it's expensive."

I kneeled in front of her and bopped her on the nose with one finger. "Being seen with that scrunchy is punishment enough. You don't need to bankrupt them."

"You *gave* me this scrunchy like a minute and a half ago."

"Details, details." I hung her backpack on the back of her chair. "Okay, do your exercises at home, eat your vegetables, and finish your homework."

"I can't tell if you're being weird or not."

"What kind of school do you go to where homework is weird?"

She narrowed her eyes at me. "Still can't tell."

I rolled her toward her parents. "My weirdness is beyond your comprehension."

She laughed. "I *knew* you couldn't do it."

Maybe, but Dad was flying in tomorrow and I was happy. I tugged her ponytail and handed her off to her parents, who smiled at me with the same polite detachment they probably used on waiters and cashiers. They heaped praise on her, though. Daisy endured their support and waved as the elevator doors closed.

"You made her laugh," Libby said, handing me a steaming cup of coffee.

"It's all done with mirrors."

She toasted me with her cup. "Mighty fine illusion."

"Don't forget to tip your waitresses. We still on for tonight?"

"I'm game if you are. It's a big step. No turning back once you bring it home."

"It's a big-screen TV, not a Russian orphan."

She scoffed. "Spoken like someone who's never tried to return a large household appliance."

Maybe not, but I'd bought my share of them in the last two weeks. A bread maker, a vacuum, a new car to replace my clunker. Technically, that didn't qualify as a household appliance, but it was large and I *had* registered it in Florida. I had a Florida driver's license and everything.

Not with my real name, but with luck, Harper would be the last name I'd ever use.

First thing I'd done after getting home—checked to see if Andrews Medical was connected to the Ascendant Health Hospital Network in any way. Nothing so far, but I'd be reading those corporate newsletters a lot more closely from now on.

A faint shiver ran along my skin and I breathed deep. Woodfire smoke. I turned just as Daniel stepped off the elevator. He'd shown up outside my door two days after I'd gotten back, claiming even with Kokabiel dead, I still needed protection. Libby had agreed, otherwise I would have sent him packing.

Maybe.

More than one person paused to ogle him, and I didn't blame them. The angel was built for tank tops and shorts, and now that he could stand the sun, he was making the most of wearing the least.

"What's he doing here?" I asked Libby.

"Who do you think is carrying that big-ass TV?"

"He agreed to that?"

She snickered. "I promised him he could hold your hand through dinner."

"Libby!"

She elbowed me playfully in the side. "Come on angel-bait, let's go home."

Home. Yeah. That sounded good.

About the Author

J.T. Hardy is the writing team of Janice and Thomas Hardy. She's the word smith, he's the idea generator, and together they bring their worlds and stories to life. They frequently get caught up in weird conversations over lunch, and many of those conversations lead to more book ideas than they have time to write.

Janice is also the author of the teen fantasy trilogy The Healing Wars, including *The Shifter*, *Blue Fire*, and *Darkfall*, from Balzer+Bray/Harper Collins. When she's not working on novels, she writes books on the craft of writing.

Janice and Thomas live in Central Florida.

Visit www.janicehardy.com for more information about the novels, or www.fiction-university.com for more on writing.

Thanks for Reading!

Thank you for reading the first book in the Grace Harper series. I hope you enjoyed it!

- Reviews help other readers find books. I appreciate all reviews, whether positive or negative.

- I also write fantasy adventures for teens and tweens under the name Janice Hardy. Look for The Healing Wars trilogy: *The Shifter*, *Blue Fire*, and *Darkfall* from Balzer+Bray/HarperCollins, available in paperback, e-book, and audio book formats.

- Keep up-to-date on new releases, news, and events at my websites: www.janicehardy.com or www.fiction-university.com.

Are You a Writer?

I even write books on the craft of writing, as well as run a writing site dedicated to helping writers improve their craft.

- My in-depth Skill Builders series includes: *Understanding Conflict (And What It Really Means)*, and *Understanding Show, Don't Tell (And Really Getting It)*. For planning and developing a novel, try my Foundations of Fiction series, with *Plotting Your Novel: Ideas and Structure* and the *Plotting Your Novel Workbook*. If you're revising a manuscript, look for my Revising Your Novel series: *Fixing Your Character & Point-of-View Problems*, *Fixing Your Plot & Story Structure Problems*, and *Fixing Your Setting & Description Problems*. All are available in paperback and e-book formats.

- **Would you like more writing tips and advice?** Visit my writing site, Fiction University at Fiction-University.com, or follow me on Twitter at @Janice_Hardy.

- **Want to stay updated on future writing books, workshop, or events?** Subscribe to my newsletter. As a thank you, you'll receive my book, *25 Ways to Strengthen Your Writing Right Now*.